Praise for *Ashton Hall*

"Exquisite . . . The way the author has weaved several storylines together is brilliant."

—*Mystery and Suspense*

"[Lauren] Belfer's writing is gorgeous."

—Jewish Book Council

"Belfer explores timeless ideas of family, sacrifice, and female resistance. . . . The labyrinthian portrait she paints of [Ashton Hall] successfully conveys mystery and adventure. . . . For lovers of libraries and Tudor history."

—*Library Journal*

"[*Ashton Hall's*] strength comes from the archaeological details (did you know that the pigment that creates red hair is the slowest to break down?) as well as the grace and attention given to both Hannah and Isabella—two women separated by hundreds of years but bound by a common humanity. A touching story about the themes that resonate through centuries."

—*Kirkus Reviews*

ASHTON HALL

ASHTON HALL

A Novel

Lauren Belfer

BALLANTINE BOOKS
NEW YORK

2023 Ballantine Books Trade Paperback Edition

Copyright © 2022 by Lauren Belfer
Book club guide copyright © 2023 by Penguin Random House LLC

Published in the United States by Ballantine Books, an imprint of Random House, a division of Penguin Random House LLC, New York.

BALLANTINE is a registered trademark and the colophon is a trademark of Penguin Random House LLC.
RANDOM HOUSE BOOK CLUB and colophon are trademarks of Penguin Random House LLC.

Originally published in hardcover in the United States by Ballantine Books, an imprint of Random House, a division of Penguin Random House LLC, in 2022.

ISBN 978-0-593-35951-8
Ebook ISBN 978-0-593-35950-1

Printed in the United States of America on acid-free paper

randomhousebooks.com
randomhousebookclub.com

2 4 6 8 9 7 5 3 1

Book design by Susan Turner

For Michael

What seest thou else
In the dark backward and abysm of time?

— The Tempest, Act I, Scene 2

And some there be, which have no memorial;
who are perished, as though they had never been.

— Ecclesiasticus 44:9

ASHTON HALL

CHAPTER 1

O n a Sunday morning in late June, I waited with my son at the side entrance of a stately home near Cambridge, England. We stood on a stone bridge that spanned what was once a moat, the water drained, a grassy pathway beckoning at the bottom, the moat's walls overgrown with greenery.

"Seven fifty-four A.M.," Nicky said, reading from his phone. He was nine years old.

I rotated the lever that controlled the bell. The sound grated within. Metalwork vines covered the cracked wooden door. Above me, the panes of the broad mullioned windows were like multi-faceted mirrors, reflecting fragments of gray-bottomed clouds and blue sky.

The house, dating from the early 1600s, was a red-brick extrava-ganza of turrets, chimneys, and Flemish gables. Cream-colored lime-stone outlined the windows and doorways. Statues of cows, pigs, and sheep, whimsical barnyard gargoyles, stared down at me from the gutters. Ever since the eleventh century, a home had stood here.

This was my third try with the doorbell. I now had reason to worry that Christopher wasn't going to answer. He was old, he was ill, he was dead. Fallen to the bottom of the stairs in a heap. Collapsed on the kitchen floor. Peacefully slipping away while asleep in his bed—the option I wished for him, for his sake and my own, because I loved him and didn't want him to suffer.

"Seven fifty-five A.M.," Nicky said.

What next?

I turned away from the door. The garden spread before us, sparkling in the morning sun, saturated with color, the rising terraces culminating in a tempietto, a round, open colonnade covered by a dome, at the top of a hillock. At the perimeter of the garden, thickly planted trees created a wash of green dotted by the darker copper beeches. The breeze was a moist caress upon my skin. The air carried a scent of lavender. *I know a bank where the wild thyme blows*—the line from Shakespeare's *A Midsummer Night's Dream* came into my mind. A shower had passed through shortly before, and the paths were damp. The flowering fuchsia along the moat dripped with raindrops, glowing in the sunlight. Off to my left, behind the house and across the rain-drenched lawns, an incandescent mist rose from the ornamental lake.

"Seven fifty-six A.M."

Christopher had arranged for a car and driver to meet us at Heathrow after our flight from New York, to bring us here, and leave us here.

And here we remained, surrounded by luggage, on a bridge over a moat at the side entrance of a Jacobean mansion, with no one answering the door.

Nicky pressed his head against my shoulder. I wrapped my arms around him and pulled him close. He was growing so fast. How young and adorable he looked, at this moment of calm.

In front of the house, the estate's original farm buildings, also red brick with limestone trim and a series of Flemish gables, framed a ceremonial approach to the mansion's formal entrance. These accommodated a café, visitors' center, and secondhand bookshop. At ten o'clock, they would open to the public, along with the gardens. At noon, the mansion's historic rooms would open. Was that the aroma of fresh coffee, wafting on the air from the café? Of brownies baking? Definitely.

Go find help. I should have been striding to the visitors' center.

"Seven fifty-seven A.M."

I couldn't make myself move, jet lag triumphant.

"A dog is barking." Nicky disengaged himself from me. He frowned, listening.

Insects buzzed, birds sang, bringing the air to life. I didn't hear a dog.

Nicky studied the woods near the lake. I studied his hazel eyes, his dark brows, his straight brown hair, cut in a bowl style.

"It's coming closer. I bet it's Duncan." Duncan was Christopher's dog. "Do you hear him now?"

"I wish I did."

"What the fuck is *wrong* with you? Do you need fucking hearing aids?"

His words stunned me, even though I'd heard such language often enough from him before. No one spoke to Nicky this way—not me, not his father, not his teachers. Yet this was the way he spoke to us. I was worn down from the effort of keeping myself prepared to respond to his outbursts. "Watch your tone! Watch your language."

"Sorry."

He sounded contrite. As usual, I couldn't judge whether he truly was contrite or had said what he needed to say to avoid punishment.

"Look!" he said.

Bounding from the woods near the ornamental lake—Duncan, a cream-colored golden retriever, raced across the lawn.

Christopher emerged from a woodland path, too, bent over his cane, picking his way forward. Beside him, a well-muscled man kept a hand on Christopher's elbow. With a respect obvious from a distance, his T-shirt and jeans transformed into the most professional of uniforms, the man guided Christopher along the path.

"Duncan, Duncan!" Nicky was gone from my side.

As I walked toward the two men, dread slowed my steps. I didn't want to see what Christopher's illness had done to him. He was in his late eighties and suffering from a type of cancer whose details he refused to discuss. *The nasties,* he called it, in his way of brushing off matters of greatest concern.

"And a fine good morning to you," Christopher called as I approached. His voice was hoarse. Once, he'd stood straight, his bearing dignified and patrician. Now he was shrunken, his skin blotchy, his eyes hollow. Nonetheless, he was dressed for a better world, or his view of a better world: white flannel trousers, paisley ascot, blue linen jacket, straw boater. *Keeping up appearances—the only defense against the nasties, or anything else,* as he might say.

I hugged him. His bones were sharp, from his weight loss. His hand trembled as he patted my back. When we separated, he swayed. He clutched his aide's arm. He made an effort to breathe and to smile. "Allow me to introduce Rafe Connors, my assistant in life's daily rituals and travails. Rafe, this is Hannah Larson, my honorary niece."

"Good morning," Rafe said. We shook hands. He looked about thirty-five, his short-clipped hair receding. Tattooed images of angel wings encircled his arms. "Mr. Eckersley has spoken of you."

Rafe's brogue sounded Scottish, and his voice was surprisingly gentle for his tough-guy physique. I wanted to clutch Rafe's arm, too, to help me negotiate the gap between the Christopher I remembered and the man I faced today.

"I trust your journey has done you no lingering harm," Christopher said. "How marvelous to welcome you"—he gestured in the direction of the house—"to this, my humble abode."

CHAPTER 2

From his place at the head of a well-polished dining table that could have seated fourteen, Christopher said, "Porridge and yogurt, toast and jam. What the nasties prescribe."

Safely inside, revived by tea, he seemed stronger. He'd lost his hair from chemotherapy, but his spirit was unflagging. I remembered this dining table from his home in London, where he'd presided over festive evenings with friends.

"Nursery food. To prevent one from experiencing . . . how should one say, *gastric disturbance.*"

Christopher's ground-floor apartment wrapped around one corner of the house. From my seat, I had a panoramic view of the gardens, which were at the side of the house, and the ornamental lake set amid the wide lawns to the back. The apartment, with its high ceilings and expansive proportions, had a sleekness that felt spare and modern, despite its geometric moldings, white wainscoting, and antique furnishings. Because of the tall windows, light suffused the rooms and lent a clarity and grandeur to everyday endeavors. I pictured myself in a long taffeta dress, my son in breeches and a riding jacket.

"I like nursery food," Nicky said.

"Then you shall find every meal gratifying."

Refusing my offer of assistance, Rafe had prepared our breakfast in the kitchen across the hallway. Its windows faced an inner courtyard. Now he stood sentry-like, legs apart, hands clasped behind his back, at the threshold of the dining room.

"About our neighbors," Christopher was saying as he refilled my teacup and his own. "Mrs. Felicity Gardner is the briskly efficient administrator of the house and grounds, and she occupies a flat in the opposite wing. Closer to home, indeed *upstairs*"—he transformed it into a place of dazzling intrigue—"there lives a long-retired general. Ninety-three, up at dawn every morning to jog at a measured pace along the River Cam, regardless of the weather. This followed by calisthenics in the tempietto on the hilltop." Christopher shook his head in mock consternation. "If that's what a healthy dotage requires, count me out. Sir Jeremy Aubrey. He manages the secondhand bookshop in the barn."

Christopher had moved to Ashton Hall a few years before, after hearing about the apartment through a friend. The trust that held the property wanted people to live here so Ashton Hall would remain a home rather than turn into an ossified museum. The rental fees also helped to offset the tremendous expense of maintaining the house and garden, woods, and farmland. *I've always wanted to live out my personal fantasy of an English lord,* Christopher wrote in the email he'd sent me about the move.

Christopher St. John (pronounced *Sin Jin*) Eckersley. His name sounded aristocratic enough for the role of an English lord, but he'd grown up in Arkansas, the son of a mail carrier. Although he had a law degree, his primary career had been as an art dealer. His wife, Constance, who'd died several years ago, had also been an attorney, an expert in international maritime law. Her work had prompted them to settle in London decades earlier. In the photograph on Christopher's sideboard, she was the elegant woman I remembered, hair pulled back, pearls understated. Constance had been my mother's favorite cousin. Because Christopher was ill, and he and Constance had no children, Nicky and I had come to live with him for the summer, to give him a family.

"The general has kindly allowed us to take possession of two spare bedrooms at the end of his corridor, reachable via private stairway. Thankfully, one need not concern oneself about the possibility of a sleepwalking peer of the realm. A door that bolts on your side divides the hallway between the spare rooms and Sir Jeremy's flat. Your section of upstairs includes a rather nicely renovated bathroom. Renovated in 1910, truth be told, but still functional in the ways that matter most. For a bathroom. Water closet mercifully close by."

"What's a water closet?" Nicky asked.

"Excellent question. I'll let you discover the answer for yourself. Next, the estate possesses a veritable library of bicycles, waiting to be borrowed, in a structure referred to as *the lower greenhouse*. Every other week, a skilled professional attends to giving Duncan a bath, among other canine necessities. These ritual ablutions take place in *the new stable*. There is no old stable. I feel confident that you, Nicky, would like to assist in the maintenance of Duncan's personal grooming."

"I would!" Nicky said, filled with enthusiasm.

I was on edge, watchful, praying Nicky wouldn't begin swearing in front of Christopher.

"Good lad. Opposite the estate gates is our pub, the White Hart. All the locals frequent it, Rafe and I included. The pub is among England's great and peculiar inventions, working to counteract, whilst at the same time bolstering, the relentless hold of the class system. Five minutes' walk from the pub is a moderately picturesque village with what is called a high street, where you will find various small shops."

When I was younger, I'd been obsessed with English history and literature and with movies and TV shows set in Britain. Like Christopher, I was about to fulfill the dream of living in an English stately home. I should have been excited. But I'd mostly lost track of those old dreams. Now I was Nicky's mother, with little time left over for anything else.

"Along the high street is a rather fine bakery. Alas, the most delicious items sold there are baked in strictly inadequate quantities, creating an unseemly rivalry among would-be consumers. Ask for the chocolate–almond croissants, and you'll discern my meaning. Spoiling the already limited village charm is a Tesco Express, suitable solely for milk-and-egg emergencies. For true sustenance I'd advise you to ride your bike a mere stone's throw down the road to the divine Waitrose. Each week Rafe and I ring a taxi service and undertake a pilgrimage there, to wend our way along the dairy aisle and be transported to every cheese-producing shire of the nation."

I wished I could view the world as Christopher did, a place where the most mundane errands were part of an adventure story.

"Ah, Hannah," he said, turning wistful. "I'm so very glad you and Nicky are here with me. Especially because I'm leaving tomorrow."

"You're *what*?"

"I'm taking the eleven-fifteen flight from Heathrow to New York tomorrow morning."

"Nicky and I only just arrived."

"And very kind of you to visit, I must say."

"I don't understand. Is this a joke?"

"Life does tend toward surprise." He gave me a puckish grin. "I made the decision three days ago, when my doctor at Addenbrooke's, our renowned local hospital, reported she'd been in communication with physicians at Sloan Kettering in New York, and I'd been deemed eligible for an experimental targeted study. Nothing like the words *experimental targeted study* to make the blood rush in the veins of an otherwise hopeless case like me. Given that I'm an American citizen, everything fell into place with ease."

"We'll return with you." I pushed down my incredulity, my frustration that we'd undertaken an international flight for nothing.

"I'm moved by your offer, truly I am."

"Will Duncan come with us?" Nicky said. "Does Duncan like airplanes? Will Duncan like New York?"

The dog emerged from under the table and pushed against Nicky, who embraced him.

"Insightful questions, my boy."

"Thank you," Nicky said.

"I'm confident Duncan would revel in the hustle and bustle of New York City. I'm also confident he'd abhor air travel. A big dog like him, trapped in a crate in the cargo hold for seven or eight hours or more, depending on scheduling delays and wind velocities. The experience could very well endanger his health. Not to mention his life. Therefore, you and your dear mother must remain here and provide him a home."

"Don't be scared, Duncan." Nicky rubbed his nose against Duncan's. "I'll take care of you."

"Christopher, *stop*," I said.

"Rafe will accompany me. A friend has offered accommodation for those days when my presence isn't required at the hospital. I'll keep you informed of developments. We can speak on the phone every day if you like. By the way, you're the executrix of my will."

"We're not discussing your will right now!"

"As you wish. Did you follow my request and bring the draft and research notes for your dissertation?"

His question opened a door in my mind that I preferred to keep shut. Years before, I'd been working toward a PhD in ancient Greek art. I'd put it aside when Nicky's needs became clear, giving up my career and letting myself become financially dependent on my husband. After Christopher made his request, I'd followed the path of least resistance. There was always a chance that finishing the degree was still possible. "Yes, I brought everything."

"I've hired an exceptionally winsome young woman, recently out of school, to be Nicky's companion. Her name is Alice. She comes to us highly recommended. Indeed, she's the granddaughter of the aforementioned Mrs. Felicity Gardner, estate administrator, and she'll be living with her granny. Alice is eager to make a start in life, and she's counting on this job. We mustn't disappoint her."

"Thank you, but no. I should be with you in New York."

"But my dear Hannah," he said, exasperated, "I've arranged this summer for you as a gift."

"You've given me enough gifts already." When I was growing up, money had been tight for my mother and me. I'd never known my father. Christopher and Constance had been generous on my birthdays, and they'd paid the part of my college tuition not covered by financial aid. "I want to give *you* a gift, by helping when you need . . ." I wouldn't embarrass him by being blunt. "When you might appreciate company."

"But how would I feel if your great potential were reduced to hours in hospital rooms, waiting for me to die? If Nicky were cooped up inside rather than running free at Ashton Hall? Duncan in a kennel or farmed out to strangers. Alice without a job. Therefore, I must ask *you* to give *me* the gift of accepting my gift to you. And when your dissertation is published down the road, think how proud I'll feel, how absolutely smug, even after I'm dead, knowing I will have played a role in the creation of a book. That would be a first for me."

I had no ready reply to counter his vision of our lives here and his confidence in me.

"I'll take your silence for a yes." His eyes were bloodshot and moist. "Thank you."

CHAPTER 3

The next afternoon, amid trembling patterns of light and shadow, Nicky, Alice, and I sat on blankets beneath the embracing boughs of what Alice called the Big Old Tree, opposite the ornamental lake and near the perimeter of the woods. In the distance, down a verge thick with shrubbery, the River Cam flowed.

Alice had organized a ploughman's lunch for us from the café, and we ate in a contented, drowsy silence. The bread for the sandwiches was fresh, the crust crisp, the inside slightly sour. The extra-sharp cheddar was pungent, complementing the tangy relish and the tart green apple sliced on the side. She hadn't included onions, most likely because Nicky disliked them. The brownies for dessert were soft, warmed by the sun.

Christopher and Rafe had departed early, and I'd spent the morning unpacking and organizing while Alice took Nicky on a tour of the grounds. The two seemed to be getting along well.

And so I allowed myself to drift into a soothing bliss. Sunlight reflected off the lake. Tourists strolled here and there. Sheep grazed. Gardeners trimmed the shrubs, snipping with shears, as they would have done hundreds of years ago. The scent of freshly mown grass filled the air. Duncan sniffed along the underbrush at the edge of the woods.

"*Over thirty types of bugs live in the woodland park surrounding Ashton Hall. These include wood louse, harvestman, and slug. See how many you can find,*" Nicky read aloud from a brochure. "I'm going to do that. I'm going to see how many bugs I can find and write their names in my notebook."

"That's a good idea," I said. "What are you reading?"

"*The Children's Guide to Ashton Hall and Estate.* Alice bought it for me in the shop."

"Thank you, Alice. Please keep track of your expenses, so I can reimburse you."

"No worries. Mr. Eckersley gave me a credit in the shop and the café, plus money for incidentals."

How scrupulously Christopher had prepared.

Alice moved one of the blankets into the full sun. Delicate-boned, her skin flawless, she was an ideal English rose except for the multiple strands of pink running through her pale brown hair, four earrings in her right earlobe, three in her left, and a tattoo of green and red leaves, its design evocative of the Pre-Raphaelites, rising up her left leg from her ankle to her calf and continuing under her flowing skirt.

"I wanted to mention," Alice said. "I mean, I wanted you to know, I'm planning to begin a cookery course in the autumn. If I can earn enough this summer for the tuition. I'm happy to work as many hours as you need."

Her spirit reminded me of myself, in younger days. "Thank you for telling me."

"I like to cook," Nicky said. "I like measuring."

"Brilliant! We'll practice cookery together." Alice leaned back onto her elbows, her legs outstretched. She closed her eyes and basked in the sunlight. "I want every single ray of sun to seep into me."

"Alice is exaggerating for fun," Nicky said to me, in the confiding tone he used when ideas were abstract and hard for him to grasp and he wanted to reassure me, and himself, that he understood what was being said. "It's not scientifically possible for every single ray of sunlight to seep into someone."

"I'm imagining it's possible," Alice said. "You've brought us a perfect summer day."

"No, I didn't."

Duncan barked to gain our attention, then gripped in his teeth a stick about four feet long. He began shaking it back and forth.

"Silly Duncan!" Nicky ran to the dog, grabbing the end of the stick, and they made a game of pulling it away from each other.

"Alice . . ." I knew I had to warn her about Nicky's sometimes-erratic behavior. I searched for the right words to begin with. He didn't have a formal diagnosis. He was simply himself, in all his wonder and complexity. "Nicky can sometimes be . . . impulsive. You need to watch him carefully."

"Oh, I'm used to that. My younger brothers are regular little mischief-makers," she said with an affectionate smile. "Boys. They're all alike."

"Not exactly in this case." A few days before we left New York, he'd dropped my hairbrush out our twelfth-floor window, maneuvering it around the bars of the child-safety guard, just to study how it fell, which was straight to the sidewalk, he reported when he found me in the bedroom, folding laundry. I rushed to see if anyone had been injured; mercifully not. After locking the windows, I'd explained, not for the first time, why he mustn't throw things out of them. Then I'd complimented him for trying to test gravity, and we talked about finding a safer way to do it. Although I wanted Alice to have a chance to get to know Nicky without prejudging him, I needed to make her see how easily and inadvertently he could hurt himself, or someone else. "Nicky can be more extreme than the standard mischief-maker. He can also be aggressive. Especially when he's frustrated or tired. It's hard to imagine him like that when he's happy, the way he is today, but he—"

"Any lunch left for me?"

We were joined by a no-nonsense type of woman with short slate-gray hair styled in firm waves. A ring of keys was fastened with a carabiner to the belt of her lilac-colored shirtdress. She wore stylish red glasses. She was handsome, in the English way that made *handsome* a compliment for a woman. The clipboard she carried was thick with papers, and a pen on a string was attached.

"Hello, Granny," Alice said, sitting up.

"Hello, Granddaughter."

Alice introduced us: Mrs. Felicity Gardner, the estate administrator. We shook hands, her handshake firmer than I anticipated, as she used my grip to help her sit down.

"Bones a bit rickety. To be expected at my age."

"You're not old, Granny."

"Let me be the judge of that." She didn't seem the least bit rickety to me. "Welcome to Ashton Hall, Ms. Larson."

"Please, you must call me Hannah."

"Thank you. I will."

She did not invite me to reciprocate.

All at once Duncan was beside her, pushing his head against her shoulder. When he sat properly, she gave him a treat from her pocket. Nicky joined us.

"This is my son, Nicky," I said to Mrs. Gardner.

"Nicholas Larson Donovan; pleased to meet you." He primly reached out his hand as if he'd been taking etiquette lessons.

"How do you do, young man," she said as they shook hands.

Mrs. Gardner poured herself a glass of water from the bottle in the wicker picnic basket and reached for a sandwich. "First break I've had all day. And in this heat, too."

Sitting down on the blanket, Duncan curling next to him, Nicky checked his phone. "The current time in Cambridge, United Kingdom, is one twenty-six P.M. The current temperature in Cambridge, United Kingdom, is 71 degrees Fahrenheit, 21.6 degrees Celsius, which is the predicted high. The current time in Chicago, United

States, where my daddy is for a trial, is seven twenty-six A.M. The expected high temperature for today in Chicago is 83 degrees Fahrenheit, 28.3 degrees Celsius."

At the mention of Kevin, my insides congealed. Three weeks ago, I'd seen him with someone else—the old cliché, *it'll never happen to me,* until it does. I'd believed our twelve-year marriage was stable, trusting, passionate—and stronger than many, because we'd weathered the challenges of raising Nicky. I wanted to rage, scream, tear Kevin's hair out. But I couldn't. For Nicky's sake, I was pretending all was well.

Kevin was a partner at a Wall Street law firm, and he often traveled on business. Being away from his dad had become routine for Nicky. They spoke on the phone every evening around Nicky's dinnertime. Kevin would be arriving at the end of next week, visiting us for the July 4 holiday. I hadn't told him what I'd seen, but I'd pledged to myself that I would. I was trying to put the coming confrontation out of my mind so it didn't paralyze my thoughts. Nonetheless, I woke each morning at around four feeling as if I'd received an electric shock, my heart racing. Was our marriage over? And if it was, how would I manage without him?

"Today the temperature will be 12 degrees Fahrenheit, 6.7 degrees Celsius, hotter in Chicago than it is in Cambridge. That means it's not very hot here, compared to Chicago."

"Physical perception depends on what you're accustomed to," Mrs. Gardner said.

"Does it?" Nicky said.

"In my opinion. Something for you to consider."

"I will consider it."

"There's the general," Alice said.

The man identified as the general, wiry and overly thin, sedately jogged along the lakeshore and headed toward us.

Mrs. Gardner said, "Jogging in the afternoon heat. Whatever is he thinking?" As the general approached, she called to him, "Take care of yourself, with these temperatures. Keep yourself hydrated."

"No need to fret about me."

The general wore form-fitting running shorts, a T-shirt printed with an image of the Beatles in their Sergeant Pepper period, and a straw hat held in place by a string under his chin, a surprising outfit for an elderly titled general, at least to my way of thinking.

Mrs. Gardner introduced us.

"Thank you for giving up part of your apartment for Nicky and me."

"Delighted," he said, catching his breath. His face was lean and wrinkled. His tan accentuated his cornflower-blue eyes. "Never used those rooms. Furnishings belong to the hall."

"Am I not correct that you exercised early this morning?" Mrs. Gardner asked, more an accusation than a question.

"Second session of the day. Good of you to notice," he replied affably. "How about a game of croquet, young man?"

Nicky stood at military attention. "Yes, sir."

Alice rose with a sigh.

Duncan rolled upright and barked.

"Race you." The general took off, Nicky promptly outpacing him. Duncan came from behind and went into the lead, glancing over his shoulder at the others at regular intervals to confirm he was going in the correct direction. Alice walked. The croquet lawn was at the back of the house. Mrs. Gardner and I could see it from where we sat.

When they were too far away to overhear, Mrs. Gardner said, "We all become a bit eccentric with these hot temperatures."

Alice and Nicky went inside to fetch the croquet set, and afterward I could just make out the general showing them how to set up the wickets.

"Don't be fooled by Alice's pink hair and unfortunate tattoo," Mrs. Gardner continued as we watched them. "My granddaughter is a trustworthy girl, unlike some at her age."

"She and Nicky have already developed a bond." Trying to get to know Mrs. Gardner, I said, "This is such a beautiful place. How long have you worked here?"

Instead of responding, she looked away with a frown that seemed to indicate my question had been too personal. "Ah, well." Her face softened. She must have decided I was simply a harmless American, tending to do and say the wrong thing but with good intentions. "I grew up here on the estate. My father farmed the land. I left for some years to work at smaller houses, earning my spurs, as it were, before I was returned to where I began."

"You met your husband here?"

"No, no, we were thrown together elsewhere. He eventually became the chief handyman here, though. He could repair anything. He died far too young."

"I'm sorry for your loss."

"It was a long time ago," she said, shaking her head with regret but saying nothing more. She studied the group playing croquet. "I should think the dog ought not to be allowed on the croquet lawn," she said, an abrupt shift. "He might very well dig it up."

I roused myself. "I'll tell them."

"Oh, on second thought, leave him be. The dog of a dying man. We'll give Duncan some sympathy." Mrs. Gardner eyed me with some sympathy, too, as if she saw into me. "Have you toured the house? Have you claimed bicycles for yourself and the boy? Have you been to town?"

Her questions buffeted me into silence.

"I see the answer is no. Come along, then. You've plenty to do. Best make a start of it."

Holding her clipboard, Mrs. Gardner led me up the staircase, *the turret stairs*, she called it, in Christopher's vestibule. At the landing, she unlocked a door and motioned me ahead.

The house was a long rectangle, and I entered a magnificent room that stretched almost the entire side length of this wing. A series of Persian rugs in muted shades of red and blue created an illusion of a single enchanted carpet, leading me forward. On my left, bookcases alternated with tall windows that overlooked the gardens. On my right, an unbroken line of bookshelves rose from the floor almost to the ceiling. Ladders on runners allowed access to the higher shelves. The ceiling itself was a miracle of plasterwork—rabbits, squirrels, and foxes peering from behind foliage.

"This is the Long Gallery," Mrs. Gardner said after locking the door behind us. In tour-guide mode, she began to walk backward down the room. "It's over thirty-eight meters, or one hundred twenty-five feet, in length. The ceiling is amongst the treasures of the nation. Although this room is called the Long Gallery, it's actually part of the library. Our book collection constitutes the greatest country-house library in the United Kingdom. The library has existed continuously since the late Middle Ages. Many of our books are rarities. What you see here is only a portion of the collection. The majority resides, if you will, in what we call the Old Library, beyond the Long Gallery." She gestured toward the wall. "The Old Library is closed to the public," she added, as if responding to my immediate, unspoken desire to see it.

Midway down the room, a young woman sat at a table in a window embrasure. Stacks of books covered the table, along with a pile of index cards of the type used in old card catalogs. The woman, who appeared to be in her mid-twenties, was checking the cards against the books and periodically typing information into a laptop computer.

"Here is Martha Tinsley, PhD, bringing us into the twenty-first century at last," Mrs. Gardner explained, as if Martha Tinsley were part of the house tour. "She's creating an online catalog of our entire book collection and making important discoveries about our holdings in the process."

"Good afternoon, Mrs. Gardner," Dr. Tinsley said, standing to greet us. A pageboy haircut framed her face and accentuated her dark eyes. Despite the summer heat, she wore a buttoned-up white blouse, a red-plaid pleated skirt, black tights, and black patent-leather shoes.

"Dr. Tinsley is a highly skilled research librarian and scholar. She came to us from the university library, and we're proud to have her. I daresay she's older than she looks."

"I daresay you are correct," Dr. Tinsley said with a smile.

"This is Hannah Larson. An American. Staying with us for the summer. The ward of Mr. Eckersley."

Was I Christopher's ward? I'd never considered myself as such. Does anyone outgrow being a ward, or is it a lifetime condition?

"Lovely to meet you," Dr. Tinsley said. "I know you've only just arrived, but if ever you have a few hours, we always need book-loving volunteers to help with the collection. Mr. Eckersley mentioned that you're completing a PhD."

Her invitation was appealing. "Thank you, I'd—"

"I don't intend to be rude," Mrs. Gardner interjected, "but you two may become acquainted on your own time."

"We will," Dr. Tinsley said, amusement playing at the edges of her lips.

"At half past three, I've a meeting about drainage problems in the far swamp. That is to say, the problems are centered in the far swamp, but the meeting is in my office."

"You're handling everything these days, Mrs. Gardner."

"Glad to make the best of it." This sounded like an order, to herself and everyone around her. "The point being, Ms. Larson and I must rush, which is just as well, because you, Dr. Tinsley, are rather busy."

"Yes, I am rather busy." She regarded the books and index cards on the table with a warm indulgence.

"Remember to close the windows when you leave."

"Thank you for the reminder," Dr. Tinsley said.

Everyone I met seemed to be performing in a play. Each had a well-defined part. Even the way the two women addressed each other as *Dr. Tinsley* and *Mrs. Gardner* seemed to be an aspect of their performance. What was my part? Ward of Mr. Eckersley. Harmless American. I bristled at having my role determined for me, rather than creating it for myself—an example of how American I truly was.

Mrs. Gardner resumed the tour. "The Long Gallery takes us to the South Drawing Room."

The rooms flowed directly into one another, enfilade-style, without a hallway in between. The South Drawing Room was at the front corner of the house.

"Note the family portraits and the marble mantelpiece," she said.

Before I could register them, she turned to her right and went through the next doorway.

"Here we have the Chinese Bedroom."

The Chinese Bedroom faced the front lawn and had a second doorway on the opposite side from where we'd entered. Despite its name, most of the furnishings in the Chinese Bedroom were antique British. These included a heraldic banner featuring a unicorn, attached to the headboard of the heavily draped four-poster bed.

"This wallpaper is another of our treasures." Mrs. Gardner positioned herself by the wall, and I joined her. The paper showed a landscape with small figures painted flat against the picture plane instead of using Western perspective. "The paper was hand-painted in China, in watercolor and ink, in approximately 1760. It was restored several years ago, and the colors are as pure and bright as they must have been originally. Study, if you will, the detailing."

Women dressed in silk robes and holding parasols crossed a footbridge over a mountain stream. White birds with flowing feathers perched on the slender branches of fluffy trees. Beside a lake, four men played mah-jongg in a round summer house, its walls made of filigree screens. At the edge of a bamboo forest, a peacock emerged from the undergrowth.

"How many lives can you count, in the wallpaper kingdom?" Mrs. Gardner said, more to herself than to me. "I've always wondered, ever since I was a little girl. My father had us put on dress-up clothes and wash our hands when we visited the big house."

Visitors entered the room from the doorway on the opposite side. "Gather round, everyone," their guide said. "We've much to see here."

Mrs. Gardner lowered her voice. "How many lives can you imagine yourself living, amidst the bamboo forests and the mountain streams?" She glanced at me, her expression so vulnerable that I was taken aback. "I've known this house all my life."

She seemed to need comforting, and I reached to touch her shoulder, but she stepped away.

"Onward," she said tersely.

Eight rooms were open to the public. Others were used for trust offices and for a book-conservation center. Many rooms were closed off, abandoned, awaiting funds for restoration. We completed our tour downstairs in the kitchen and the servants' hall, where an exhibition presented the lives and the duties of the staff whose labors had made the house run smoothly.

For some reason, throughout the weeks to come, Mrs. Gardner's question, or a version of it, continued to haunt me: *How many lives can you imagine yourself living?*

CHAPTER 4

About a week later, I surprised myself by sleeping soundly, my fears concerning the future for once not preying on me in the middle of the night. I woke to the sun shining and a cool breeze flowing through the open window. My bed was a four-poster with a carved headboard that looked centuries old. The bureau and wardrobe were decorated with floral-patterned Art Nouveau marquetry. The ultramodern desk, by contrast, was an expanse of wood resting on four steel legs, accompanied by an ergonomically designed office chair. Christopher must have bought them for me.

On the desk were my laptop and the binder holding a printout of my dissertation. Today, I felt settled enough to begin work.

How many lives can you imagine yourself living? My alternate life spooled out before me like a film: The dissertation finished and published years ago. A professional position at the Metropolitan Museum, my goal as I worked my way up from the part-time internship I'd had before Nicky was born to research associate, assistant curator, and, eventually, curator. I saw myself organizing exhibitions, borrowing art from other institutions, preparing exhibition catalogs, writing journal articles and books. I was independent, able to support myself and my son, if ever I needed to.

"Mom." Nicky knocked on the door. "Wake up, Mom."

Duncan barked, heightening the urgency.

"I found Fred's girlfriend," he called.

What was he talking about?

"Come in, Nicky."

He opened the door and approached my bed. He was dressed in his customary cargo pants, with a hooded sweatshirt for the morning chill.

"The birds woke up Duncan and me with their singing, and we went exploring. That's how I found her."

"Exploring where?"

"In the castle," he said.

"What castle?"

"The other part of the house. The big part. The old part."

"You mean the public rooms?" I sat up.

"The public rooms and the other parts. The castle."

"You shouldn't have gone there by yourself." The idea that he might, or could, hadn't occurred to me. I'd assumed the entrances were locked.

"I wasn't by myself. Duncan was with me."

I struggled to control my voice, to stay reasonable. This was the best way to respond to him, or so his therapists told me. "Duncan isn't allowed in the public rooms, either."

"I couldn't stop him. He refused to let me go alone." Nicky regarded me with a panicked sincerity. "Also, I had my phone. I charged it overnight. It was one hundred percent when I started. I could call you if I needed you, and you could call me. That means you were with me, too."

Ah, Nicky.

"Don't you want to see her?" His face fell, and a look of hurt came over him. "She's Fred's girlfriend."

In my decaffeinated state, I slowly pieced together the reference. In the science classroom at Nicky's school in New York, a replica of a skeleton, inexplicably named Fred, was attached to a pole in the corner. The science teacher dressed Fred for various occasions. Bunny ears for Easter. A Santa Claus hat and beard for Christmas.

Suddenly I realized what Nicky was telling me.

With Duncan trotting alongside, we went down the back stairs to Christopher's apartment. Near his dining room, Nicky directed me through an unlocked door and into a long, straight corridor. He flipped on the switch for the ceiling lights, which were evenly spaced every fifteen feet or so. The walls were undecorated. This must be a passageway for use by servants or maintenance workers, I decided. Multiple doorways opened off it, on the left side only. On the right, several small windows, so high on the wall that we couldn't see out, most likely opened onto the house's inner courtyards.

At the end of the passageway, Nicky opened another door, and abruptly, effortlessly, we entered the public part of the house. We were in the monumental front entry hall, where giant paintings of family ancestors lined the walls, representing a way of life far removed from our own. The house was vast but interconnected, and I realized that Mrs. Gardner had shown me only a small part of it. Nicky led us up the grand double staircase, with its ornate balusters and newel posts. From the landing, we entered the Chinese Bedroom. Nicky went to the wall on the left side of the bed.

"Do you see the door?" he said.

"A door?"

"It's hidden by pictures of those big grasses in the wallpaper."

"That's called bamboo," I said.

"Bamboo," he repeated, committing the word to memory. He glanced over his shoulder at me. "The bamboo hides the door opening. Nobody would ever know, except Duncan and me. That's the kind of thing we notice."

In the wallpaper world, a boy carried water buckets suspended at each end of a stick that was slung across his shoulders. The boy's back was bent from the weight. A troupe of musicians played instruments that were distant cousins of the flute, the banjo, and the violin.

"Keep looking," he said.

And like a pattern coming into focus, once seen, never to be unseen, the outline of a door revealed itself amid the bamboo.

"This part that looks like a rock in the pond—it's really a latch for the door." Using his index finger, he opened the latch and pushed the door inward. He walked through, into the darkness beyond. He held the door, waiting for me. "It's safe. There's no lock on the latch."

I went through. Nicky turned on his cellphone flashlight, and so did I. Oddly, we seemed to be in a long-deserted corridor that followed the inner line of the rooms. The wallpaper here looked Victorian, a floral print, peeling at the top of each sheet. The air was stuffy. A string hung down from an electric light fixture on the ceiling. With our flashlights already on, I didn't pull the string. This must have been another passageway, like the one we'd walked through downstairs, for the domestic staff, or for the lord of the manor to visit his lover's bedroom during the night or escape from his enemies.

Duncan didn't follow us.

"You wait there, Duncan. I don't want your fur to get dirty. We'll be back soon."

The dog lay down on the carpet, chin on paws.

Nicky shut the door behind us. "Duncan doesn't like dark, cramped places," he whispered. "They make him scared. I didn't want him to feel bad about himself for being scared. So I told him the white lie that I didn't want his fur to get dirty."

"You're very kind to Duncan. You're a good friend to him."

"He's my dog. He always waits for me."

Always? How many times had Nicky passed through this door? Adventures through the hidden door in the Chinese Bedroom had never appeared in the *What We Did Today* report that Alice and Nicky presented at dinnertime.

"Let's start." Nicky turned right and walked along the passageway to its end. At the corner, a narrow circular staircase gave us a choice of up or down. Nicky chose to go up. At the next landing, two more corridors opened before us. Nicky turned right.

We entered a room filled with hard-backed chairs, dozens of them, placed haphazardly and draped with dust covers. The chairs evoked formal dinner parties, the crystal dazzling, thirty guests or more seated in Ashton Hall's majestic dining room downstairs, now open to the public.

Walking through this room to the exit on the other side, Nicky led me into a corridor where rolled-up carpets had been pushed against the walls. Exiting the carpet corridor on its opposite side, we proceeded around a bend, up two steps, along a short passageway, and down six steps. I became disoriented. I could no longer match where I was with my mental map of the house.

"This is kind of a tricky part," he said when we reached . . . what was it? It seemed to be a fake wall, crumbling. "You have to turn sideways, and make yourself skinny, and push through it. It's tricky like the door in the Chinese Bedroom."

Stepping through the tricky part, plaster dust sticking to our clothes, we were in an entirely different house. We'd slipped through time. Slipped *into* time, the house a palimpsest, each version of itself existing simultaneously, going back to the first house, in the eleventh century.

We turned left and left again. We climbed a spiral staircase made of stone, damp against my fingertips. Apart from our steps and our breathing, there was no sound. The air was still. The temperature shifted from warm to chilly to warm again.

"The castle isn't haunted," Nicky said, picking up on my thoughts. "It's just itself."

We turned down another long hallway, this one with alcoves opening off it. One alcove held a spinning wheel of a simple design. Another, a loom. These must have been the workrooms of servants who were centuries dead. Here was the everyday domestic routine of the house, grinding and mundane, hundreds of years of cold winters, wet springs, hot summers. The alcove windows had been bricked over from the outside. If anyone had explored these corridors in the recent past, surely the spinning wheel and loom would have been taken downstairs and put on display.

Nicky's flashlight bobbed ahead of me. "Not much farther. Don't worry, I know the way back." He didn't falter.

With a familiar jolt of helplessness, I understood that controlling him was impossible. I could put an audio monitor in his room, but he could be silent if he had reason to be. A video monitor? I needed to sleep sometimes; I couldn't watch him every second. I didn't want to lock his door at night, in case he had to use the bathroom or there was an emergency. I couldn't risk him dying because he was trapped in a locked room during a fire.

Another turn in the corridor. Another spiral staircase, steep and narrow, the steps worn from use.

"These steps are a little wet. You should put your phone in your pocket and keep your hands pressed against the wall. Wait—I'll run to the top and hold my flashlight facing down." He scampered up. With the curve of the stairwell, the flashlight provided only a glow. "Hands pressed against the walls. You can do it!" At his encouragement, giving back to me the words I often told him, I felt like weeping from my love for him.

Why shouldn't he explore? Once at a party in New York, I'd heard a British colleague of Kevin's say, *We're raising adults, not children,* to explain why she and her husband were sending their seven-year-old twin sons to boarding school in England. Their two older children, ages nine and eleven, were already there. How shocked I'd been by the idea that seven-year-olds were better off at boarding school than at home. I could imagine her adding, *You Americans, hovering over your children. Give him some freedom.*

Except if on one of his expeditions he fell down this flight of stairs and broke his leg or hit his head, and his phone ran out of power and I never found him again, no matter how many years I searched. If anything ever happened to him . . . Nothing must ever happen to him.

The damp walls were oily against my palms. I reached the landing.

"You did it!"

We were in a high-ceilinged vestibule. Here, too, the windows had been bricked over. We faced a wall where architectural logic called for open space. I made out the stones of an archway above us.

Nicky pointed with his flashlight to a misshapen opening in the wall about a foot off the floor. Approximately six inches wide and four or five inches high, this opening was part round, part rectangle, shaped by mice or by the disintegration of the wall or both. "I saw a mouse coming out of the hole, and I thought, a mouse must be coming out from somewhere. I'll look in first to see if Fred's girlfriend is still there." He leaned over and positioned the flashlight. "Yep, just the way she was before. Still asleep. She didn't move or get rearranged. Your turn."

Taking out my phone, I knelt. Leaning over, I peered into the opening, maneuvering my flashlight. A wave of terror swept through me. My hand trembled from anxiety. In the light's narrow beam, and from this low vantage point, I realized I was looking into a room, but I could see only parts of objects, which gradually took shape as I moved the light. A table, with a plate and cup. A chair beside the table. A musical instrument, and the word *virginal* came to me. A desk and its chair. Books on the desk. A cross, not a crucifix, untarnished, so made of gold. A candelabra with an interlacing of cobwebs between its branches, the webbing illuminated by the flashlight. In the corner was a prie-dieu, a piece of furniture with a low bench for kneeling to pray and a tilted tabletop or shelf on which to place one's elbows or a prayer book. No prayer book rested on it now. Behind the prie-dieu was a statue of Mary holding the baby Jesus. The paint used for their garments and their faces was still vivid. Mary smiled tenderly upon her child.

Someone could enjoy a comfortable life in this room. It was about
the size of my bedroom downstairs. It didn't appear to be a prison.
But there was no door. And these windows, too, had been bricked over
from the outside.

On the floor, where pieces of rotted wood formed the shape of a
pallet . . .

No, no, no. I ordered myself to look. I had to see what Nicky had
seen.

I had hoped I'd misunderstood him—but I hadn't. For there, on
the floor, was a skeleton. The skull was human yet not human, the
teeth huge, the eye sockets seeming to protrude, the skeletal face glow-
ering. The bones had collapsed, the clothing had mostly disintegrated,
but the shreds of a gown and of long reddish hair remained.

CHAPTER 5

A female skeleton imprisoned in an attic: A metaphor. A literary trope. A macabre tale for Halloween.

But this specific woman had once been as alive as me, Nicky, and Mrs. Gardner, who knelt and peered into the hidden room after Nicky and I had guided her here.

"I never dreamed." She sounded stricken.

Keeping a hand on the wall to support herself, she stood. We held large flashlights—*torches*, as the British called them—and the light bounced against the walls in crisscrossing beams as we moved. The air felt heavy and close.

"I've never been in this part of the house," Mrs. Gardner said. "I don't believe this area has ever been explored. Not in our day. One hears stories from other homes, about concealed corridors and hiding places and priest holes coming to light after centuries. A house begins to disintegrate, and all its secrets are revealed."

"There are always more things to learn," Nicky said cheerfully. "You have to keep an open mind."

She loomed over him in the shadows. "Pay attention, Nicholas Larson Donovan: Until I tell you otherwise, this discovery is a secret. And it isn't *your* secret. It's a secret of the house. You mustn't tell anyone until I give you permission. Until the experts determine what this is. I don't want rumors circulating."

"I can't tell Alice?"

"Telling Alice is fine, but not anyone else. It's a secret that doesn't belong to you. Do you understand?"

"What about my daddy? Can I tell him?"

"Yes, yes, your dad."

"How about Uncle Christopher?"

"And your uncle Christopher," she said, becoming impatient. "No one else. I want to hear you say it."

"It's not *my* secret. It's a secret of the house. I mustn't tell anyone until you give me permission." He spoke in an exact imitation of Mrs. Gardner's tone and accent. "Excepting Alice. And my dad. And my uncle Christopher."

Mrs. Gardner stared at him, appraising him anew. "You're a very specific boy," she said without emotion: a truth, stated.

"I know."

"Should we call the police?" I asked. The skeletal face had taken over my mind, impossible to dislodge.

"The police aren't quite right for this. Not from 999, that is."

Mrs. Gardner was referring to the British version of 911, and she was correct, this wasn't an emergency. If any crime had been committed, it had been done decades or even centuries before, or so I presumed.

"I need to consider this. Feeling a bit wobbly, though." She gripped my upper arm as she swayed. She took a few slow, deep breaths and recovered. "We ought to go downstairs, have a cup of tea, and collect ourselves. But I'm reluctant to leave her."

"I'll stand guard over her," Nicky said.

"You're a good boy, too. Despite disobeying the rules. A good, brave boy."

He looked aside, avoiding eye contact with her. "I can be."

"You not only can be, you are. You found her, didn't you?" Mrs. Gardner said. "It's because you're *you* that you found her. People have been studying this house for years, and no one found her. No one else *could* have found her. Only you."

It was true. Nicky's quirks and obsessions, his innocence, impulsiveness, and lack of fear—these characteristics could be positives. I felt my eyes smart with tears at the thought of it.

"You're an explorer," Mrs. Gardner said. "You're the Finder."

"Thank you," Nicky said, biting his lip.

"You can't be here on your own, however. We need to stay together. We'll go downstairs, have our tea, and I'll have a think about this. She'll be fine whilst we're gone," Mrs. Gardner said, seeming to reassure herself as well as us.

"Can we have crumpets from the café?" Nicky asked.

"What a good idea," she said.

"The food in the café is *ethically grown and sustainable*. I read about it on a sign. That means we have to eat it, it's good for us. Especially the crumpets. Alice told me."

"And she's right," Mrs. Gardner answered, then smoothed her skirt as if to say, *That's that, forward we go.* "You'll need to lead us back. I'd never find the way on my own. I'd be lost if not for you."

"I never get lost."

"Of course you don't."

Later that day, while Mrs. Gardner determined the next step, I unlatched one of my bedroom windows and swung it open, letting in the fragrance of hay, flowers, and farmland. Nicky, Duncan, and Alice came into view, kicking a soccer ball across the lawn. Duncan pushed the ball with his paws, which apparently wasn't a violation of soccer's no-hands rule.

A knife blade of guilt twisted in my chest. Nicky could have died on his explorations. *Died.* And where was the person who was supposed to protect him, who should have expected this and planned accordingly—where was *I* while he did his exploring?

Asleep.

Selfish mother, incompetent mother . . . the voice of judgment whispered inside me.

Forcing the voice away, I sat down at the desk. I had to use this precious time, while Nicky was with Alice, to do my own work. Anxieties about Kevin welled up, and I forced them aside. I studied the binder. The last time I'd looked at the dissertation, Nicky had been about eighteen months old, opening every cabinet, pulling out every drawer, tossing aside the shoes in every closet. I'd had to watch him each second he was awake.

Before Nicky was born, Kevin and I had made the choice that I'd stay home with him during his early years. We'd considered ourselves fortunate that Kevin's salary gave us the choice, and we'd thought raising a child would be an exhilarating experience. When I became pregnant, I was finishing the coursework for the PhD. Our plan was for me to leave my position at the Met and write the dissertation while caring for our baby, who'd nap in a basket beside my desk.

One day I was researching and writing, and the next day I wasn't—that was my recollection. From the exhaustion of days filled with chasing Nicky and coping with his tantrums and nights he rarely slept through, I'd lost the ability to register the words on the page. Being Nicky's mother eventually took a toll on my confidence. Second-guessing myself became my primary trait. Sometimes getting through another day felt like my greatest achievement.

I opened the binder. The dissertation was two hundred thirty-seven pages of text, with fifty-six additional pages of illustrations. As I read it, I was mystified: Who had written this? I didn't recognize the smooth flow of the analysis. The logic of the arguments.

The topic was children as portrayed in ancient Greek art, primarily of the Classical period, approximately two thousand five hundred years ago. My inspiration had been a heartrending stone carving at the Met of a girl with two doves. One dove was perched on her hand. The other, which she cradled to her chest, touched her lip with its beak. The image was from a child's funerary stele dating from circa 450 BCE.

In the ancient world, infant mortality rates were as high as one in three. Of the infants who did survive, only half were likely to reach adulthood. Children would have suffered the deaths of multiple siblings.

Scholars often claimed that because so many children in the past died, their parents couldn't risk loving them. As I paged through the illustrations I'd collected, of stone carvings and vase paintings, most commissioned by grieving parents, I knew this wasn't true. A young girl played with a doll while a small dog stretched up a paw to touch her hand. A boy stood in a child-sized chariot pulled by goats. Another boy tossed a yo-yo. A toddler offered cake to a pet bird. A baby reached his arms toward someone he trusted.

When I finally looked up from my reading, the light in my bedroom had shifted. It was midafternoon. Stunned, I realized the dissertation was almost finished. I had to write the conclusion from the outline I'd already prepared and do the abstract. I also needed to go on JSTOR to read any secondary literature that might have been published recently on this specialized topic. The rest was basically mechanical work, like creating the table of contents and double-checking the footnotes.

I was baffled. The finish line had been within sight when I dropped out of the race. How had I let myself become distracted, for years? What had I been doing instead?

Nicky, Nicky, Nicky.

Kevin and I had never told our friends, or anyone in our families, about how hard it was to raise him. The truth was too painful to talk about with others, beyond the multiple therapists we saw. Plus, we didn't want to worry our friends and relatives. My mother had died when Nicky was still within the normal range of the terrible twos, so

I hadn't had to face telling her. I'd never told Christopher. How do you tell those who care about you and your cherished son that on the few playdates he was invited to, he began cursing uncontrollably? I couldn't bring myself to say that sometimes he became so enraged he pounded his head against the handlebars of his bike, bruising his forehead before I could reach him. Or that he turned on me in his rage, kicking and beating me with his little-boy fists, hurting me. He could also be brilliant and marvelous, amazing me with his questions and insights.

Like many moms, I'd grown distant from many of my women friends who didn't have children, and as for the ones who did, with Nicky's unpredictable behavior, I couldn't take the chance of spending much time with their families. I was afraid of their judgments—judgments I heard in my mind anyway. I stayed off social media and internet groups, to avoid being mom-shamed. I was desperate for companionship. Desperate to say an honest word to someone other than my husband and the therapists. But I'd been raised to put on a strong, upbeat façade and move forward, no matter what I was feeling inside, and that's what I did.

I pushed the binder aside and logged in to the email for my part-time job. A half dozen inquiries awaited me. The first was from a jigsaw-puzzle designer and manufacturer in Sweden. He was looking for Hieronymus Bosch images appropriate for a series of Christmas holiday puzzles.

I worked at a small family-owned firm that handled licensing arrangements for museums. If a manufacturer wanted to find, say, a Cézanne landscape suitable for reproduction on a mouse pad, I'd research and recommend several options from the firm's database of thousands of images from museums around the world. The licensing fee, minus my firm's commission, went to the museums that owned the objects. I'd found art images for scarves and potholders. I'd helped to place Klimt's lovers onto silk robes. Botticelli's Venus onto the packaging for perfumed soap. The Unicorn Tapestries from the Met onto needlepoint pillows.

The paintings of Hieronymus Bosch were an odd choice for holiday puzzles. I reviewed the firm's online catalog. Dozens of gruesome Bosch images came up, nothing I'd want to look at while a Christmas tree twinkled nearby. Researching some alternatives, trying to strike a balance between the unconventional and the seasonally appropriate, I settled on several Bruegel images, which I included in my reply to the client.

I responded to the other requests. A company in Manchester, England, wanted posters extolling the Russian Revolution to put on a series of mugs. *These mugs are meant to be campy,* the company rep noted. Most mug-makers wanted paintings of cats, with nothing campy about them. This was a nice switch. Next, my refrigerator-magnet client was looking for Tiepolo images.

The job was fun, and absorbing, but it didn't lead anywhere. I couldn't support myself with it. My work required several hours a day, with no benefits, but I made my own schedule and never needed to go to an office: That was the trade-off. I earned what earlier generations of women would have called *pin money.* But I was always available for my son.

When Nicky was four, he outwitted the child lock on the utility drawer in the kitchen, grabbed a hammer, and threw it at his babysitter. The hammer hit her shoulder, bruising her. From then on, at the recommendation of therapists, Kevin and I rarely hired babysitters. I took Nicky to school, picked him up afterward, spent the rest of the day with him. He still attended the mainstream private school where he'd started in pre-K. The school had a noncompetitive, no-right-answer philosophy, and the teachers and administrators insisted they could help him, going out of their way to find special projects that might interest him.

Often these projects *did* interest him, inspiring him to seek out library books and ask me to take him to the American Museum of Natural History or the New-York Historical Society, so he could pursue a subject that intrigued him. I loved seeing the look on his face, wide-eyed, with a kind of hidden inner smile, when he made a discovery. In third grade, he'd become obsessed with manhole covers, and we'd spent hours wandering our Upper West Side neighborhood as he'd photographed the many varieties. I wished more people could see this side of him. We'd tried a variety of medications to help control his rage, but they'd all made Nicky dazed and silent, suppressing the affectionate, delightful, and curious side of his personality, which Kevin and I never wanted him to lose.

Another knife twist of guilt: I should have warned Alice about Nicky's behavior more clearly and directly, so she could be on her guard.

And yet . . . Nicky was older now, more able to moderate his actions. I had to give him a chance to behave well. I had to have some time off.

You have time off five days a week when your son's in school, the voice of judgment whispered, *and you never do much with it.*

With Kevin traveling so much on business, school mornings were the hardest for me. Often enough, Nicky would lie down in the front hall of our apartment and refuse to move. I'd have to pick him up as he kicked at me, screaming, and try to get him outside. After the morning struggle, I couldn't compartmentalize, my heartbreak playing through my mind as I tried to summon up energy to face my own day. During school vacations, I took care of him full-time, relegating my paying job to the early-morning hours before he woke or after he went to bed at night. Kevin was terrific with Nicky, but Kevin's schedule meant he was rarely around for the daily tasks. I knew how lucky I was, though. Many mothers faced much tougher situations than mine.

Who exactly do you think you are, to be entitled to more?

"Hi, Mom."

Nicky was at the door. This morning he'd become the Finder, and we had no idea where his tragic discovery would lead.

"Alice and I are going to ride our bikes to the market in the town square," he said, excited, looking forward to the next adventure. "We're going to buy vegetables and other things to make dinner. We'll decide what we're cooking when we see what the farmers are selling."

"That sounds like fun."

"Alice said, tell your *mum* so she won't wonder where we are. I could have sent a text, but I decided to come upstairs to tell you *IRL, in real life*."

I wanted to sweep him into a hug, but I held back. He didn't like surprises involving his body. "You're being thoughtful."

"Thoughtful." He pondered the word. "I *think*. Does that mean I'm *thoughtful*?"

"Being thoughtful means you think about what's good for others, not just yourself, and about what will make other people happy."

"I always think about what's good for Duncan and about what will make him happy."

"And now me."

"Thoughtful," he repeated. "I'm thinking about *thoughtful*."

My love for him filled me to the brim and overflowed.

CHAPTER 6

Holding her clipboard, Mrs. Gardner swept into Christopher's dining room the next morning.

"Sorry for the delay." She explained she'd been detained by a consultation with the plumber, who was repairing a water leakage in the central line of the sprinkling system that served the garden.

She'd called us together so that the police could interview Nicky. With Mrs. Gardner busy, I'd organized the introductions: Detective Chief Inspector Reginald Layton, who happened to be Mrs. Gardner's second cousin, dressed in a suit and tie, his hair white and wavy, his skin ruddy; his assistant, Constable Valerie Perridge, a stolid-looking woman who stood by the windows with pad and pencil at the ready; and Professor Matthew Varet, an archaeologist from the university, his family name pronounced *VAR-et*, as in *claret*, he'd explained. Dressed in a collared shirt and tweed jacket, Varet had brown hair and a Vandyke beard.

"Let me introduce everyone," Mrs. Gardner said.

"Ms. Larson did the honors," DCI Layton said.

"Did she indeed." Mrs. Gardner sounded mildly surprised.

I sensed I'd done something wrong—I didn't know what. I was nervous on Nicky's behalf.

"Let's sit down, then, and begin," she said.

Mrs. Gardner, Alice, Nicky, and I sat on one side of the table, DCI Layton and Professor Varet on the other. Constable Perridge continued to stand. The chair at the head of the table, Christopher's chair, was empty. He and I had been speaking on the phone every day, and he sounded strong and optimistic. Last night I'd briefed him on Nicky's bleak discovery. I ached for his presence and imagined him with us now, in his customary place, sharing his impressions.

"Good to see you, Professor," Mrs. Gardner said. "I didn't expect you here today. I'm glad of it."

"DCI Layton contacted me, in view of the . . . situation," Professor Varet said.

"You two have met before?" DCI Layton asked with a touch of suspicion.

"Professor Varet is a longtime friend of Ashton Hall. He's esteemed in his field," she added, a motherly pride in her voice, as if she couldn't stop herself despite her other, more pressing concerns. "He's received extensive recognition for someone of such relative youth, including a professorship at the university."

"You're very kind, Mrs. Gardner," Professor Varet replied with a nod of gratitude, "but I must point out that my field of study is rather narrow, so there's little competition." Whether this was British understatement or the truth, I didn't know. "Let me note that I'm here today in an observational role only. The individual in question might appear, superficially, to have died centuries ago but in fact may have been murdered relatively recently. The hidden room could have been arranged as an elaborate and depraved ruse. None of us should jump to conclusions."

"This couldn't possibly be a recent event," Mrs. Gardner said, rushing through the words, her voice strained, "given the obstacles to reaching the location, through a formerly blocked passageway, in one of the oldest parts of the house, dating from the Tudor era or earlier."

"We have to maintain our objectivity. Examine the evidence," Professor Varet said. "Are there any legends about such an individual in the history of the house?"

"None that I've ever heard. But you'd need another Master Nicky to find that room, let alone to drag someone there, dead or alive."

Clearly she didn't want this to be a recent crime, committed within her lifetime, during her girlhood on the estate or when she was in charge of the hall. "Judging from discoveries I've heard about at other historic homes, young boys disregarding the rules often find what their elders have long missed." She looked at Nicky as if he could confirm this.

"We'll know soon enough," DCI Layton said. He turned to Nicky. "First, young man, let me say you're not in any trouble. I do need to ask you some questions, though. Mrs. Gardner gave me a general overview, but I want to hear the details from you."

"I'm ready."

"First, for the record: What's your full name?"

"Nicholas Larson Donovan, called Nicky."

Valerie Perridge wrote this down.

"And your age?"

Nicky checked his phone. "Nine years, ten months, five days, sixteen hours, and twenty-three minutes. Seconds unknown."

The detective paused, seeming to mull over the best way to deal with Nicky. "And this is your mother, sitting next to you?"

"Yes. Her name is Hannah Larson. Sometimes she says Hannah Donovan, for grocery deliveries and when she has to call the superintendent or the doorman in our apartment building in New York City, but that's just to make things easier, so my friends who work in the building don't have to remember so many names."

While Nicky spoke, Professor Varet watched him with an amusement that I didn't appreciate.

"My daddy's name is Kevin Donovan. He's going to arrive in England to visit us in less than twenty-four hours. In exactly . . ."

As Nicky reached for his phone, my dread of Kevin's arrival came zinging into my consciousness, stopping my breath. I pushed myself back into this moment, this room, this conversation, and Nicky's discovery, horrifying no matter what era the murder had taken place in.

"Moving along," DCI Layton said, interrupting Nicky's recitation of Kevin's travel plans, "how did you happen to go through the jib door in the Chinese Bedroom?"

"It's called a *jib* door?"

"I believe so."

"Why?"

"I don't know." DCI Layton sighed, seeming to be flummoxed by the twists and turns of Nicky's thought patterns.

"I'll ask Siri," Nicky said.

"Put it on your list for later, sweetheart," I said.

"Okay." Nicky retrieved the small notebook and pencil from his cargo pants pocket and made a note.

Mrs. Gardner said to Nicky, "A jib door is meant to blend into a wall and not call attention to itself with moldings or special details. Like many houses of its type, Ashton Hall is lined with inner corridors and passageways, designed primarily for use by the staff. Years ago, when the family lived here, the jib doors allowed servants to enter rooms discreetly. Most of the family's former bedrooms, as well as the Long Gallery, the various drawing rooms, and of course the dining room, have jib doors in addition to the regular ones."

"I've used them!" Nicky said. "I go everywhere," he offered to DCI Layton. "I'm an explorer. Mrs. Gardner told me."

"Then we know it's true," DCI Layton said, glancing at Mrs. Gardner with a hint of a smile. "Now then, tell me what happened, from the beginning."

"When was the beginning?"

"Give me whatever you think it was."

Nicky considered this. "I was born in New York City at—"

"Start more recently, Nicky," I interrupted gently. "From when we were already here at Ashton Hall."

"Okay." Again he pondered. "I wake up early in England. Duncan wakes up early, too. The birds wake us first. Then the light. Yesterday morning, the day I found her, Wednesday, July first, the sunrise was at four forty-two A.M. In New York City yesterday, the sunrise was at five twenty-eight A.M. That's a difference of forty-six minutes. What are Duncan and I supposed to do with ourselves when we wake up early? Uncle Christopher doesn't have a TV. We have to do something."

"You could read a book," DCI Layton said, apparently deciding to meet Nicky on his own terms. "You, that is. Not Duncan. You could read aloud to Duncan. Just an idea."

"Bedtime is for reading a book. Morning is for exploring. I've explored the walled garden, and the topiary garden, and the round temple, the icehouse, and the orangery."

All this while I slept, or when my middle-of-the-night torments were still consuming me.

"Had you ever gone through the jib door in the Chinese Bedroom before yesterday?"

"Yes. I entered that door three times total, and I exited it three times total, for a supertotal of six times, before the times I went in and out yesterday."

"Did you find anything noteworthy during those other visits?"

"I found a room with wooden horses that rock back and forth. Those are called rocking horses. I didn't have time to ride them."

"And?"

"A room full of big books lying sideways on shelves, and drawers filled with papers, and a big trunk that was locked."

Mrs. Gardner said, "You didn't tell me about that room yesterday." She spoke quite harshly. "Why didn't you tell me?"

"You didn't ask me." Nicky turned away from her and began pulling on his hands, which he did when he was upset. "I would have told you. If you'd asked me."

"You're right. I didn't ask you. Not to worry." She made herself sound cheerful. "You'll show me today."

After a moment, Nicky folded his hands on his lap. "Okay." He bit his upper lip.

"Those documents might provide some context for this discovery," Professor Varet said.

"True enough," DCI Layton said. "Did you find anything else, lad?"

"A spinning wheel. A loom. A room with four cradles. I looked, but I didn't find any babies in the cradles."

"That's a relief," DCI Layton said.

"Is it?" Nicky asked.

"The last thing I need is a collection of baby—" Mrs. Gardner coughed, and DCI Layton shifted. "Weren't you afraid, when you looked into the opening and saw a skeleton?"

"Should I have been afraid?" he asked. I'd been terrified, sickened, but Nicky, it seemed, had felt only curiosity. "Would that have been good for me, to be afraid?"

"I'm not saying it would've been good or bad. I just want to understand. I'm a curious fellow," DCI Layton said.

"I'm a curious fellow, too," Nicky said.

"I can see that." For the first time, DCI Layton regarded Nicky with warmth. "You'd make a fine detective."

Nicky smiled. "I read Sherlock Holmes stories. At bedtime."

"So you're halfway there."

"Halfway where?"

"To being a detective. You're just like Sherlock Holmes."

"That's right." Nicky glanced at me, meeting my eyes, his happiness like a huge embrace between us.

"Felicity," DCI Layton said, "I tend to forget the local aristocrats. What was the family here?"

"The Cresham family," she said. "With the title *Southbrooke*. Lord Southbrooke. The title became extinct—"

"A bit like the dinosaurs, eh?" DCI Layton said.

Mrs. Gardner was unfazed. "—during the Great War."

I knew what this meant. On the bureau in Nicky's bedroom was a photograph of three young men standing at the front entryway of the house. They wore the military uniforms of World War I, and they were smiling, confident. I felt a passing shiver. *The title became extinct* represented a multitude of young men killed in battle. An ocean of sorrow.

"Right." DCI Layton rose. "Let's proceed. I've a forensics team outside, including a forensic anthropologist."

"And I have a student with me," Professor Varet said.

"I know about those people," Nicky said.

"How do you know?" DCI Layton asked.

"I looked out the window."

"Excellent sleuthing on your part."

Going outside, we crossed the bridge over the moat. Sunlight flared on the trees. A breeze mussed Nicky's hair, and he didn't object when I smoothed it into place.

Four people awaited us. They wore white jumpsuits over their clothes as well as cinched hoods and face masks, which were pulled down below their chins. One of them was a woman with a regal bearing who looked to be in her fifties or sixties, although it was hard to tell because of her cinched hood. From the way she stood apart from the others, her distance a measure of her authority, I guessed this was the forensic anthropologist. All of them had flashlights, either handheld or strapped to their foreheads. Metal boxes and large duffel bags rested on the grass beside them.

Mrs. Gardner checked her wristwatch. She must have been anxious to get the group inside before the grounds opened to the public.

DCI Layton motioned Nicky and me forward. "This is Nicholas Larson Donovan, who made the discovery, and his mother."

"Call me Nicky," he announced. "I want a flashlight to wear on my forehead." Before I could correct him for his demand, he said, "May I please have a flashlight for my forehead?"

"Anyone have an extra headlamp?" DCI Layton asked.

A young man in a jumpsuit, one blond curl emerging from his hood, searched his duffel bag, pulled out a headlamp, and adjusted it around Nicky's forehead. Nicky wore it proudly, his chin high.

Alice said she'd stay behind with Duncan and held his collar. The rest of us went into the house. We climbed the turret stairs in Christopher's vestibule. At the landing, Mrs. Gardner unlocked the door, and we entered the Long Gallery. As we walked through the room, the group spread out in a line. Professor Varet stepped beside me. He was taller than me, and he leaned down toward me, speaking in a low voice, confidentially.

"Your son is rather unusual," he said.

"So I've been told," I replied, trying to discourage him. Nicky was up ahead, in the lead, talking to DCI Layton with animation. I wouldn't discuss my son with a prying stranger.

"I've a daughter who's somewhat similar. It was all I could do not to laugh during the interview, imagining Janet offering the same responses."

"Why would you laugh?" I asked angrily.

We passed Dr. Tinsley, the librarian, who stared at our group with surprise. I raised my hand to her in greeting.

"Sorry. I'm not being clear. I enjoyed watching how his mind works."

I looked at him afresh. "Thank you for your understanding. I don't find it very often for Nicky."

"And vice versa, with Janet."

The young man who'd found the headlamp for Nicky overtook us. "Excuse me, Professor, I'm afraid I've forgotten to bring . . ."

I moved ahead of them.

When we reached the Chinese Bedroom, DCI Layton attached police tape to one of the bedposts.

"Must the tape be there?" Mrs. Gardner asked, glaring.

Without comment, he retied it, to the foot of the bed. He gave the roll to Constable Perridge to unravel as we went.

Nicky said, "There are different ways to get to the room, with different things to see. I promised Mrs. Gardner to show her the room full of papers. That's one of the quickest ways, too."

"Then take us that way," DCI Layton said.

Nicky didn't wait for stragglers. Again, I walked through the room full of chairs and the corridor of rolled-up carpets. When we reached the *tricky part*, Constable Perridge began to bash in the sides to make the opening wide enough for the equipment. Grimacing, Mrs. Gardner reached out a hand to stop her, as if to protect the house, but then she withdrew, acceding to the inevitable.

"Here's the cradle room," Nicky called over his shoulder as we passed it. "Then the rocking-horse room."

Another corridor, and up a flight of stairs, a left turn at the top. The team had difficulty hauling the equipment up the spiral stairways. The dense silence was filled with the screech of metal against stone and muffled swearing.

Nicky stopped, bringing us up short. "Here it is. The paper room."

Mrs. Gardner and Professor Varet scanned the room with their flashlights, revealing shelves filled with ledgers and manuscripts, placed sideways; a substantial wooden trunk with multiple iron locks; and a section of numbered drawers. DCI Layton opened several of the drawers, which were filled with rolled documents.

"Astonishing," Professor Varet said.

A thick layer of dust covered all. The table and chair in the middle of the room were connected by a diaphanous spiderweb that swayed in the air currents created by our presence. The table held a quill pen, an inkwell, and an open ledger, along with a pitcher and a cup, as if one day the ledger-writer had stood up, left the room, and never come back.

"I knew there had to be such a room," Mrs. Gardner said.

"How did you know?" Nicky asked, his voice echoing, breaking the mood of reverence that had come upon us.

"This is a muniment room, sometimes called an evidence room," she explained. "A place for the storage of important papers. Title deeds, accounts, leases, land surveys, anything financial or legal relating to the household and the estate. Old houses like ours always have such a room, and in fact there's another muniment room, in the newer, seventeenth-century part of the house. This room and these documents were lost to us."

"Until Nicky found them," Professor Varet said.

"Precisely," Mrs. Gardner said. "Well done, you."

"Thank you." Nicky turned to me. The look on his face . . . He was transformed by their praise.

"I wish you hours of spellbound reading," DCI Layton said. "But let's move along."

"Okay, I'm moving along." Nicky hurried ahead, the rest of us trying to keep him in sight. "She's waiting for us. This is the last stairway. It's kind of slippery, and everybody has to watch out."

The shifting beams of the headlamps and flashlights played along the damp steps. When I reached the top of the stairs, the vestibule looked larger than I remembered, the ceiling higher, as the multiple lights revealed the full dimensions of the space.

DCI Layton knelt and peered through the opening into the hidden room, maneuvering his flashlight. He changed places with Professor Varet, who examined the room briefly. "Dr. Evans?" DCI Layton said.

The older woman also knelt down and peered into the opening. Afterward she went to the far wall, out of everyone's way. This was her profession, and she, like Layton and Varet, must be accustomed to it. But I felt a creeping along my skin. Last night, the skeleton had filled my sleep with fear, the empty, glaring skull seeming to slip between life and death.

We stepped aside as the team spread tarps on the floor of the vestibule and set up battery-operated high-intensity lights on tripod stands. Photographs were taken of the wall while one of the team passed around latex gloves and pairs of cloth booties for the crew to put over their shoes. Professor Varet and DCI Layton took face masks and white jumpsuits for themselves, although they didn't yet put them on. Professor Varet's student assisted DCI Layton's team.

"Look." Nicky pointed to the area near the middle of the wall, at roughly his height. "There's something different in that part of the wall. I didn't see it when I was here before." He took the cloth tape measure out of his pocket and measured. "Sixteen inches across, eleven inches high."

Professor Varet's student held a flashlight sideways against the wall, and the beam raked across the surface. With the light at this angle, I, too, saw the rectangular indentation in the middle of the wall. Photographs were taken of it.

"Splendid, Nicholas Larson Donovan," Professor Varet said. "If you don't become a detective, you'd make an excellent archaeologist. Actually, they're rather similar professions."

"What caused it to happen?" Nicky asked.

"I'm speculating," Professor Varet said, "but possibly the indentation marks an opening created when the wall was built, to pass through water, food, and other supplies and to take out waste. The height of it is appropriate for such a use. Then the opening was filled in at a later date, in a somewhat makeshift manner. You can see how different it is from the haphazard shape of the hole near the floor."

"Right," DCI Layton said, indicating that speculation was at an end. "Everything ready?"

"Yes, sir," said one of the figures dressed in white. The team raised their face masks.

"Excellent. The time has come for the civilians to depart. And I don't mean the professor and his student."

"The reason for our departure?" Mrs. Gardner said.

"To prevent extraneous DNA from entering the room, amongst other factors."

"I'll expect a comprehensive report."

"When it's available," he said.

As Nicky, Mrs. Gardner, and I moved toward the stairway, one of the white-clad figures took out a chisel and began to enlarge the mousehole near the bottom of the wall. One of the others took a similar tool and scraped at the central indentation Nicky had noticed.

Observing them, Mrs. Gardner halted.

The scraping sounds were loud in the confined space. A third person snapped open a plastic bag and took out a small broom, preparing to sweep the detritus into the plastic bag.

"Stop!" Mrs. Gardner ordered. "Stop where you are."

Everyone did stop and look at her.

She appeared uncharacteristically flustered by the team's immediate reaction, and she clutched at the fabric of her dress. "We're moving ahead too quickly. This is a grave. A burial site." Regaining her composure, she continued with greater formality, "I do regret the delay and the inconvenience, but we'll need to wait until a vicar or priest can officiate. We need to show proper respect before we disturb her."

DCI Layton exchanged a glance with Dr. Evans, who shook her head sharply *no*. She raised her chin and appeared even more regal than before, as if she was, in fact, the one in charge here. DCI Layton turned to Mrs. Gardner and said, "I understand the impulse, but we don't have time."

"She's my responsibility, and the decision is mine. I don't care how she came to be here, or when, whether yesterday or five hundred years ago. This isn't a treasure hunt."

"No one views this as a treasure hunt," DCI Layton said quietly.

"We'll give her the respect she was denied when she was left here to die." Mrs. Gardner took out her phone. "No signal." She shook it, as if that would make a difference. "These thick walls. I'll go downstairs, and I'll call the rectory."

Nicky squeezed my hand. Arguing between adults scared him.

"Felicity," DCI Layton said, even more quietly and gently, "the answer is still no. The forensics team is here. We're moving forward."

With the high-intensity lights and all of us crowding the space, the vestibule was becoming oppressively hot, my hair clinging to my neck.

"As the representative of the trust that—"

"Recite the Lord's Prayer," Professor Varet said, interrupting her. "That will show her respect. We all know that prayer."

He assumed a common culture among us. I did know the Lord's

Prayer. I'd recited it each morning, in the King James Bible version, in chapel at the high school I'd attended.

"There are different versions of the Lord's Prayer," Mrs. Gardner said.

"The small variations don't matter," Professor Varet said. "God will understand your intentions."

Whether Professor Varet sincerely believed this or had landed on it as an expedient solution to the impasse, I couldn't tell.

"Very well, then." She brought her hands together, one over the other, fisted. She closed her eyes, as if to focus her thoughts. She began:

"Our Father,
Who art in heaven,
hallowed be thy name."

In the deep silence that surrounded us, her words reverberated off the walls.

"Thy kingdom come,
thy will be done,
on earth as it is in heaven."

At school, I'd rushed through the prayer, mumbling, my thoughts on a geometry test later that day or on an upcoming rehearsal of the latest school play, my lines circling through my mind as I tried to memorize them. Morning after morning, I'd rendered the words meaningless. This was the first time I'd actually listened to them. Mrs. Gardner made the words profound.

"Give us this day
our daily bread.
And forgive us our trespasses,
as we forgive those who trespass against us."

A woman, walled into a room and abandoned . . . Who was it who'd trespassed against her?

"And lead us not into temptation,
but deliver us from evil."

I stood where the woman had stood. Where those who'd imprisoned her had stood. I closed my eyes, and I heard her screams. Felt her terror.

"For thine is the kingdom,
and the power,
and the glory,
for ever and ever."

Tears constricted Mrs. Gardner's voice. I heard the unknown woman weeping.

"Amen."

"Amen," we repeated.
Work resumed.
Nicky guided Mrs. Gardner and me back to the public areas of the house.

CHAPTER 7

That evening, after Nicky was asleep, I took Duncan for a walk across the back lawn. It was past nine, but the sky was bright. We were about a week and a half past the summer solstice. The long, pale twilight of northern Europe hinted that the day could drift into eternity.

I checked Nicky's windows. His nightlight was a soft glow. No shadows, no silhouettes to indicate he'd woken up and was getting dressed, preparing to head out to explore, despite my warnings.

When I tucked him in, he'd told me how many hours, minutes, and seconds remained until Kevin's arrival in the morning. I wished I could look my husband in the eye and talk about our past and future dispassionately, as equals—his affair, staying together, or separating, as equals.

But I couldn't. My dependency gnawed into me. If we divorced, I'd be worried each month about whether he'd actually pay whatever child and spousal support I was awarded. Where would Nicky and I live? What work would I do to support the two of us? Who would pay Nicky's school fees and therapists if Kevin refused to? Years before, in my misguided confidence and romanticism, I'd taken what I'd thought would simply be a break from my job, and I'd never even considered the possibility that someday I'd need to demand money from the person I loved.

I took stock. If in fact I was able to publish the dissertation with a university press, it would be an honor that would bring little money. The credential of the PhD might allow me to find a teaching job, but the competition was fierce. To return to my old dream of a museum career, most likely I'd have to begin again at the bottom, earning almost nothing, if I could find a position at all. Others were waiting, dozens of women and men, younger than me, a new generation.

Things weren't supposed to be this way. Once I'd been a girl who was considered feisty and fun by her many friends. A young woman who was curious, striving, passionate in pursuing her interests, and on a path toward a viable career and financial independence. As I walked across the lawn, I could picture that young woman clearly in my mind.

Once upon a time, when I was in my early twenties, I'd spent my working days with naked men. Sadly or luckily, depending on your point of view, they weren't real. More precisely, they weren't alive. Some of them were painted onto vases. Most of them were made of stone. They were statues. They lived—I thought of them as possessed with a spiritual, or at least metaphoric, vitality—in the Greek and Roman galleries of the Metropolitan Museum. I knew them well. I enjoyed imagining plausible lives for them outside the confines of the Met. The Archaic statues, forthright and bold, holding their briefcases and striding to their offices. The Classical athletes, lithe and languorous, waiting for the subway. The gods Apollo and Dionysus, graceful and alluring, gazing at me from the glades of Central Park.

I was acutely attuned to the physicality of the ancient statues—the male statues, that is. The female statues didn't interest me, not in the same way. The marvel of these aestheticized male bodies: The curves of their shoulders and upper arms. Their taut leg muscles. The energy that charged through them. The Greeks considered nudity a reflection of the highest moral purity.

Because I was fluent in ancient Greek and Latin, my professor of classical art at Barnard College, who was also a curator at the Met, had hired me to translate inscriptions. I would have thought that all the Greek and Latin inscriptions ever written had been translated decades before, but evidently not. Boxes of stone fragments awaited their turn in the Met's basement. Many of these fragments had only a few letters carved into the stone, others a word or two, some a brief phrase.

I loved the hours I spent in my cubicle on the lower level, numbering and translating each fragment. I was riveted by the possibility that I might find, amid the boxes of single letters, parts of words and truncated phrases, a few lines from a lost play by Aeschylus, or an unknown poem by Sappho, or perhaps just an ancient accounting of the purchase of grain, evoking images of the seller and the buyer.

My linguistic expertise was the result of an experiment my mother had performed on me. My mother, Margot Larson, had dreamed of becoming a professional chemist, but her college professors told her that such jobs belonged to men and refused to write recommendations for her. Although she'd tried to find a way around this stricture, she was stymied. She'd found fulfillment, though, teaching biology, chemistry, and Latin at the Macaulay School, a day and boarding secondary school for girls in Buffalo, New York, and we lived in a Victorian mansion that had been converted into a residence hall. Free tuition being a perk of her job, I entered Macaulay in ninth grade after attending the local public school.

Margot was a dedicated teacher and mentor for the students at the school. During the term, our apartment door was always ajar. When she couldn't become a scientist, teaching became what Margot described as her *calling*. Finding a calling and pursuing it, she'd taught me, was the most important goal anyone could have. Raising children was a calling, too, she said.

My mother had been born in Germany before World War II. When she was four years old, she was part of the Kindertransport, and with other children, she traveled from her home in Hamburg to England, where she lived outside London with an older childless couple who doted on her. After the war, she was sent to distant relatives in Cincinnati, and this family included Christopher's future wife, Constance. Like my mother and me, Constance and her family were secular Jews, knowing their identity, not practicing their faith.

Decades later, Margot was able to confirm that her parents had gone into hiding when the war began, sheltering behind a false wall in the home of friends. In January 1945, they were betrayed by a neighbor and shot on the street outside the house. Shot next to the couple who'd hidden them. Hamburg was liberated by the Allies in May 1945, so they'd survived almost to the end of the war. Survived the bombing raids, the fires and food shortages. But they didn't survive long enough—that's what always hit me the hardest, that they'd almost made it through, only to be murdered near the end. Margot could never determine if the neighbors had been paid by the authorities to betray Jews or if they'd been committed Nazis. I didn't know which was worse, to be killed for money or by fanatical believers. Margot had tried to find these neighbors, but everyone she spoke to on the street claimed not to know who they were. She also did research and tried to locate other relatives—her aunts, uncles, and cousins—but found no one still alive.

Although her students called her *Mrs. Larson*, Margot had never married. Teaching had always been the center of her adult life, she'd explained to me, and she'd never met a man who didn't ask her to compromise. When she reached forty and worried she was becoming too old to have children even if she found a partner, she opted for the scientific solution: artificial insemination. *After three tries over eight months, I was pregnant with you,* she'd said, sharing a bit of insider information I'd have been happier to live without. Remarkably for that era, the school had supported her decision. Nonconformist that she was, she wanted me to call her by her first name once I was no longer a toddler, but I never did, not to her face, at least, and certainly not at school.

How much one must want to have a child, to go the scientific route. I hoped Margot never regretted her choice. Fortunately, my temperament was suited to hers and to the school residence where we lived. I'd been happiest when I could sit on the window seat of my bedroom and read English history and literature, as well as mystery novels. When my assigned homework wasn't enough to fill the evening, I made up extra projects. I began to write short stories and poetry. As I grew older and was encouraged by my teachers, I contributed to the literary journal in high school and, later, in college. Pursuing creative writing as a career, though, had never seemed like a practical choice for me.

Friends were shocked that I'd never tried to find my biological father. I'd researched the question enough to know that the process was time-consuming, and I never felt strongly motivated to pursue it.

In her reading of British history, Margot learned that many scientifically minded English gentlemen of the eighteenth and nineteenth centuries had been taught Latin and ancient Greek when they were young and achieved impressive fluency by the ages of five or six. The sexism grated on her, and she wanted to try this sort of education on a girl: on me. She knew Latin from her own school days, and she hired a graduate student from the university's classics department to teach me ancient Greek. Her experiment was successful, if success can be measured by my ability as a college student to impress a museum curator enough to be offered a low-paying job translating inscriptions in a basement.

Each morning at the museum, I took a circuitous route to my cubicle, wandering through the exhibition galleries before they opened to the public. I experienced an electrifying sense of my good fortune. Here were the greatest expressions of humanity, from across cultures, gathered in one place and waiting for me: Gods and demons. Rulers and ruled. Mothers, fathers, children. Priests, warriors, and farmers. I basked in the peace of a summer's day at the beach, as captured in a painting by William Merritt Chase. I lost myself in the Zen-like tranquility of a celadon-glazed porcelain bowl from Japan. I'd found my calling.

When Kevin and I met, at a party hosted by mutual friends, I was about to enter the PhD program in classical studies at Columbia, while keeping my part-time job at the Met. My graduate school tuition was covered by fellowships. Kevin was attending law school at Columbia. He was from Albany. He'd been raised Protestant, but he no longer went to church. His father taught math in a public high school, and his mother taught fourth grade. Scholarships had financed his education.

We found pleasure in our daily lives together, taking long walks, reading in cafés . . . in simply being alive, together. Kevin supported my ambitions. I regarded him as possessing what the ancient Greeks called *sophrosyne:* self-knowledge, excellence of character, moderation, and more. In my idealism and happiness, I decided that he and I, united as a couple, epitomized *homophrosyne:* one mind. These erudite concepts had seemed real to me then. And were foolish and naïve in retrospect.

Don't cry. *Don't cry.* Margot hadn't tolerated emotional outbursts, and I'd learned early not to have any. To keep my feelings to myself. I'd been raised by a woman who'd escaped the war but whose parents and other family members had been murdered. She'd survived by maintaining a façade of self-control, of tranquility and contentment, first with the adults who'd raised her in London and Cincinnati, and then with the world.

When Duncan and I, now well into our evening walk, reached the end of the lake, I caught sight of a figure in white emerging from the bluish-gray shadows on the far side of the house. In the dusk, the figure moved in and out of focus, corporeal one moment, a blurred glow the next. Abruptly, the skeleton in the hidden room pushed into my sight, superimposed upon and merged with the figure in white. A terrible chill rushed through me. Keeping the spectral figure in my peripheral vision, acting as if I didn't see it, I continued on. It came closer, walking rapidly. I didn't believe in the supernatural. The figure approached ever closer.

No. No. My heart was racing, adrenaline spreading through me, preparing me to fight.

Duncan stopped his explorations, lifted his head to sniff the breeze, and in ecstasy ran toward the figure. When he reached it, he rose on his back legs, and they embraced.

All at once I felt foolish. Ghosts don't hug dogs. Not that I had any previous experience with ghosts, but this seemed a logical assumption. Nicky's discovery must be upsetting me more than I'd realized, especially now, when I was already feeling vulnerable because of Kevin's arrival.

Breathing deeply to calm myself, I walked toward the hazy figure and saw it was Mrs. Gardner, wearing a white cable-knit sweater over her shirtdress. She pushed Duncan down and scratched behind his ears. Gave him a treat.

"Ah, Hannah. Last walk of the day?" she called as she leaned over to rub Duncan's chest. "What a fine and noble creature he is."

Spotting a rabbit on the grass, Duncan raced away.

"Such a lovely evening," she said. "Shall we walk together?"

"I don't want to impose."

"Not at all."

We headed toward the path along the river.

"Have you heard from DCI Layton?" I needed facts to counter my fears—even though I realized the facts might turn out to be far more horrifying than anything I could imagine.

"I spoke with him just now," she said.

"Did he have any news?"

"He confirmed the deceased is—was—female, as your son intuited. Apparently, sex is somewhat easy to determine, based on the shape of the pelvis and so on. She was an adult, based on teeth and bone growth."

"Does he know yet if this is"—I reached for the right description—"a contemporary crime or if it's something for the archaeologists?"

"I asked him how far in the past an unexplained death has to be in order to be considered archaeology." I heard the stress in her voice, the attempt to restrain her feelings. "Roughly a hundred years, he said."

"A hundred years? That seems like a long time ago, for a contemporary crime."

"I thought so, too. Then I began thinking about my mother-in-law, thriving at ninety-six, Lord bless her, living alone and sharp as a tack, and a hundred years became an instant."

The light was fading, and birds began singing, a chorus all around us.

"The coroner will be informed," she said. "I don't know if there'll be an inquest."

"I don't want Nicky involved in an inquest. He's already given a police statement."

"We'll hope that's enough. Nicky certainly explained the situation with care," she said, mildly teasing, despite the stress she was experiencing.

I accepted this as an overture of friendship instead of a criticism of my son. "He did. He always does."

We reached the river, more like a slow-moving canal than a rushing torrent. Here and there mist rose from the water, obscuring the reflections of the shrubs and trees along the bank.

"A hawk," she said, pointing above us.

We watched the wide-winged bird, magnificent as it soared. As we walked on, I sensed Mrs. Gardner's preoccupation.

"What's going to happen next?" I asked.

"The other evaluations will take time. DCI Layton warned me again that I mustn't jump to conclusions about the time frame. Of course, the story is appalling no matter the time frame"—nervously she pulled at her sweater—"but I do pray the unfortunate woman wasn't kidnapped, locked up, and left to die within the past hundred years."

The scents of the coming night rose around us.

"I hate even to think about it," she went on. "A local woman whose family is still in the neighborhood, and they claim her body and speak with the press about their memories of their beloved great-aunt who disappeared without a trace decades ago, but they remember her, and, look, here's a photograph of her on the day she finished school. Her family rightly demanding justice. And who put her there? Are *his* descendants still in the neighborhood? Was he a member of the household? Of the Cresham family itself?"

"It wasn't necessarily a man," I said. "Or one person alone."

"You're right. But no matter the details, her story transforms the history of the house. I don't want Ashton Hall to become known as a place of horror. I'm sorry to speak this way, in light of her suffering. A woman not yet buried, lying forsaken in a forensics lab somewhere in town. It's incomprehensible. Although I can almost hear the vicar say, *'Tis not for us to understand the mysteries of the Lord.*"

Mrs. Gardner paused and seemed to be whispering a prayer.

"Ashton Hall seems like such a happy place now," I said after a moment. "It's so beautiful. It's breathtaking, in fact."

"Thank you." Sounding more her usual self, she added, "I like to think I've helped to make it that way. Our finances are a bit threadbare these days. I've had to furlough some of my staff, which I regret. But we're making do."

I remembered the reference Martha Tinsley had made to Mrs. Gardner handling most everything.

"No one would ever think of Ashton Hall as a place of horror," I said.

"That's because Ashton Hall is basically a museum now, existing outside time," she said. "Far from the passions of the past. Some of these old homes have terrible histories. Many were built from the profits of the slave trade or money made from the labors of enslaved people in the Caribbean, facts that I believe have to be recognized and discussed. Luckily, Ashton Hall was built before those dreadful days. Our house has had its share of family tragedy. All three Cresham sons were killed in battle during the First World War."

I remembered the photograph on Nicky's bureau.

"A period of neglect followed," she continued, "and the house and estate were in a shambles when the trust took over."

"Then it's all the more impressive, what you and your predecessors have built here over the years," I said.

"You're very kind." She gave me a quick glance of gratitude. "I must admit, well, for my own . . . mental health, I suppose I have to call it, I'd like the skeleton to be several hundred years old at least. The passage of centuries would render her story less threatening—for me as well as our visitors. The fact of her having been found by a young boy could be made into a charming counterpoint to an otherwise disturbing tale."

We walked for a time without speaking. Duncan raced ahead of us, stopping here and there to nose around in the underbrush.

"The world gives your son some challenges, am I right?" she asked.

Despite the prickling on my skin as she questioned me, I appreciated her formulation: The world, not Nicky, was out of joint. "Yes."

"I thought so. I know how hard that can be. My younger son was different to the ordinary, as well. He manages well now, but he could be a holy terror when he was young. Unable to sit still. Walking out of school in the middle of the day, disappearing for hours. Constantly talking back, challenging every rule, with me and his teachers both. Once he even found the matches . . ."

As she told the story, a memory assaulted me: I was in the kitchen preparing dinner, and Nicky was in his bedroom, supposedly doing his homework. This was about a year ago. I smelled smoke, first faint, then stronger, then close by, and I raced to him, to flee the building with him. But when I reached him: *Mom*, he said, *paper burns so fast! I wonder how fast my socks will burn. And my pillow.* These items were laid out on his desk, ready for testing. Flames were shooting up from his white plastic wastebasket. The basket was beginning to melt, becoming brown and misshapen.

I'd pulled a lighter from his hand, and in a panicked rush, I covered the basket with his quilt and, not caring if my fingers were singed, ran with the wastebasket to the bathroom and tossed it into the tub. I turned on the shower and put out the fire.

Then I sat beside Nicky on his bed and explained what he'd done wrong until he cried and begged me to believe how sorry he was, because he didn't know until this very second, he said, what would happen if he tried to find out how fast different things burned. He'd found the lighter, he told me, in Central Park during gym class.

Afterward, his therapist warned me that a time might come when Nicky would need to be hospitalized in a psychiatric ward for kids, or sent away to an institution, which the therapist called a *residential care facility* to cushion it. *You need to get used to the possibility,* he said. But Kevin and I were in agreement: We'd never send Nicky away.

"Enough of that," Mrs. Gardner said, a command that felt intended for both of us. "The point is, my lad's all grown up, safe and sound, and the rest of us survived it. So did he." Her voice softened from her love for him. "He owns a popular garden center, not too far from here. He's always adored plants, from the time he was five or six. No matter how defiant he became towards adults when he was young, he stayed wonderful with plants. Sometimes I think the plants are what saved him. His own garden is a marvel. He makes even the daisies look exotic. He and his wife have three children, all perfectly behaved, wouldn't you know."

"He's Alice's father?"

"No, no. Alice is the eldest child of my eldest son. He became a primary school teacher. I never would have predicted that. They always surprise you as they become themselves."

Nicky . . . growing up, becoming ever more himself. The thought was bittersweet.

"He also has three children," she said.

"You have a lot of grandchildren!"

"Indeed, I do," she said, pleased that I'd noticed. "I've been blessed. Well, listen to me—I'm becoming positively American, with all this confession. What about you? Alice mentioned that your husband arrives tomorrow. You must be looking forward to seeing him."

"Absolutely."

The *absolutely* slipped out without conscious thought, and it was a giveaway. A *tell*, as Kevin often said. Something he listened for in his legal work. *Of course. Absolutely. Naturally.* Defensive words, indicative of inner doubts and concealed truths. How many hours, minutes, and seconds now remained until his arrival?

"And Nicky will enjoy seeing his dad," Mrs. Gardner added.

"He will."

The moon rose, full and brilliant against the darkening sky. I glanced back at Ashton Hall. Moonlight touched the turrets, and Nicky's nightlight glowed.

CHAPTER 8

On a Sunday several weeks before we left New York and traveled to England, Nicky punched a classmate at a birthday party. The party was being held at a children's gym, and one of the boys tripped Nicky during a basketball game, making Nicky drop the ball. The referee didn't see this, and the other team scored. Overcome by anger, screaming, *Fuck you, fuck you,* Nicky punched the boy in the stomach so hard he fell backward onto the floor. Fortunately, the boy wasn't hurt. The other parents looked at Nicky as if he were a monster.

Nicky and I left the party. This was our rule: If you hit someone, if you swear, you go home. Sometimes his classmates baited and taunted Nicky, or even shoved him, until he retaliated. Then they turned away in laughter while Nicky was punished for his reaction. Despite the possibility of these things happening, Nicky wanted to attend all the class parties, and I couldn't protect him at every moment.

The gym was near 86th and First, across town from where we

lived, at Riverside and 83rd. Nicky and I went to the bus stop and waited. When it arrived, the 86th Street crosstown was crowded and airless. We couldn't get seats. The traffic inched along. Because of a parade on Fifth Avenue, the bus was diverted up Madison. As the stench of exhaust fumes filled the bus, I began to feel light-headed and ill. When the bus stopped unexpectedly at Madison and 96th Street, I took Nicky's hand and led him off. I needed fresh air. We would walk across Central Park.

As we passed through the park's stone gateway and walked up the rising path, we entered a protective tunnel of trees. Here, the breeze was cool as it washed across my skin, cleansing me. The boughs of the giant elms arched down to touch the grass. Despite the conversations among the many people around us and the shouts of kids in the nearby playground, every sound seemed muffled amid the trees, sunlight, and shifting shadows.

"One fifty-eight P.M.," Nicky said. "Can we go to the playground?"

Even though going to the playground would at least fill the hours we would have spent at the party, hours that gaped before us, I couldn't allow it.

He accepted my answer without the battle I'd anticipated. He seemed to have no regrets about leaving the party. He'd already moved on. I was the one stuck behind. I would have appreciated an afternoon without a crisis. I would have enjoyed chatting over coffee with the other parents, who accepted me politely enough despite Nicky's behavior, although they didn't invite me to their book groups or their organizational meetings for school causes. Sometimes I wondered if Nicky would do better at a special-needs school, but when I toured these schools, exploring our options, I saw so many overmedicated kids asleep on the floors of their classrooms that I knew I could never send him there. The mainstream public schools often had thirty or more kids in a class, and that setting didn't seem appropriate for him, either.

We crossed the East Drive and walked through a break in the foliage, onto the Bridle Path, which curved around the reservoir. The water itself was concealed from us by an incline overgrown with shrubs and trees. Nicky walked ahead a bit. I didn't have the energy to make him stay next to me, holding my hand. He approached a boy about his age, skinny, wearing a blue polo shirt and carrying a foam football. Nicky introduced himself, and the other boy said his name was Peter.

"You want to toss?" Peter asked, holding up the football.

Nicky looked at me for permission, and I nodded yes. He was good at meeting other kids. One side of his ever-shifting temperament was open and friendly, happy to greet whatever the day presented to him.

The boys threw the football back and forth, jogging ahead at a steady pace while Peter's mom and I followed. I loved watching Nicky play, the way he reached for the ball and threw it in a perfect arc. He was graceful and athletic, like his father.

The Bridle Path came level with the reservoir, and the view to the south opened into a vista of the city, the skyscrapers radiant in the sunlight. White wavelets patterned the surface of the water.

Peter's mom had straight, shoulder-length blond hair and wore a floral shift dress. Her shoes were taupe-colored ballet flats. She carried a straw picnic basket with leather straps to latch it shut. She was a traditional upper-class, Upper East Side mom, and I was an Upper West Side mom, also traditional in my T-shirt, flowing skirt, and comfortable walking sandals. My hair was a frizzy mess. I felt unkempt and ever so slightly inferior as I walked beside her.

"Beautiful day," I offered.

"When we came out of the house, everything was sparkling, and I told Peter we were walking across the park, no objections allowed. We're meeting friends for a picnic at the Safari Playground, by Central Park West."

"That's a lovely spot."

We settled into a conversation about schools, neighborhoods, and favorite playgrounds. Peter attended an Upper East Side school, prestigious; I didn't know anyone at his school, and Peter's mother didn't know anyone at Nicky's. Protected by this anonymity, I could pretend Nicky was just another boy. A *normal* boy, attending a school for *normal* kids. Experts condemned the term. But sometimes—when, for example, I was walking across the park and trying to progress through the day with minimal turmoil—*normal* seemed like the most worthy goal possible.

The Central Park Tennis Center came into view down the grassy hill on our right. The courts, more than two dozen of them, stretched into the distance. When Nicky and I left home for the birthday party, Kevin was coming here to play tennis with Tim, a law school buddy. They played many weekends, weather and schedules permitting.

"I love tennis," Peter's mother said. "I'm not able to play as often as I'd like. I have three more kids at home."

"Four kids! You must be busy."

"Busy is an understatement."

Her happiness was palpable and somehow told me that none of her children had challenges like Nicky's, or if any did, she'd found a better way to cope. I felt a pang of jealousy.

"I forgot about these courts," she said.

"My husband plays here. You can reserve online." I looked down the hillside. Maybe I'd text Kevin, see if his match was done. A tall chain-link fence surrounded the courts, and a path followed the outside of the fence, benches positioned along it.

And on one of the benches, framed by the boughs of an oak tree, Kevin sat with Tim. I knew Tim. He'd attended our wedding with his then-girlfriend, now-wife. They had two children, younger than Nicky.

Seeing Kevin as he lounged on the bench in his tennis clothes, I felt a quick stirring. Kevin still looked to me like a classical Greek statue of an athlete; the Hermes of Andros, from the workshop of Praxiteles, was a close comparison. Often at the playground, I heard women make rueful jokes about how children had ruined their sex lives. I felt lucky that despite the daily exhaustion, raising a child hadn't ruined mine.

As we drew closer, I saw Kevin lean close to Tim, whispering something to him. He shifted his hand onto the inner part of Tim's leg, behind Tim's knee. He caressed the back of Tim's leg.

I knew that gesture. I could almost feel it, feel Kevin caressing the soft skin behind *my* knee. A hundred times. A thousand times, he'd done it to me. A half-hidden caress of love. A touch that said, *Until later*. Or, *Do you remember before?* Tim leaned closer to Kevin in response.

My sight turned speckled, as if a veil had been drawn across my face, separating me from the world. Peter's mom said something— I couldn't grasp what, because of a screeching in my ears. Part of my brain must have registered her words, though, and I must have responded, because she responded, and I again responded . . . pretending everything was fine.

Nicky continued to toss the football with Peter. The trees, the reservoir, the orange daylilies, the city where I'd made my home for years—everything remained the same. My sight blackened around the periphery, my perceptions narrowing. Closing.

We approached a fanciful footbridge that spanned the Bridle Path.

Nicky gripped the ball and stopped jogging. "Why does the sign say *Bridge Number Twenty-Eight*?"

I didn't understand what he meant. The image of Kevin and Tim was seared into my perceptions and kept replacing the scene before me.

"What makes this into Bridge Number Twenty-Eight?"

I forced myself to examine the bridge. With its sweeping arches and inventive grillwork, it must have been built in the park's early days, when horseback riders frequented the Bridle Path. It was a seemingly weightless Gothic Revival span. It might have led to a cathedral. Instead, it led to a sight fully as remarkable: the reservoir and the soaring skyline beyond. A sign nearby identified it as BRIDGE NO. 28.

"Where are the bridges with numbers one through twenty-seven?" Nicky wasn't asking me, or anyone. He might have been questioning the universe. He clenched the football so tightly his little-boy arm muscles bulged.

A rush of foreboding came over me.

"Come on, let's keep playing," said Peter.

"And twenty-nine through— How many? How many bridges are there?" His hands began shaking. "How many? How many?" he shrieked. "Infinity? Do the numbers go to infinity?"

Taking measured steps, I moved toward him. "It's okay, Nicky." I tried quietly to defuse him, using the approach his current therapist thought best.

"Throw the ball," Peter said.

"Here's your fucking football." Nicky slammed the ball into the path, rather than into Peter's face, as he might have done, a small mercy. The ball veered off at an angle, and Peter ran to retrieve it, with a dismissive shrug of *What's wrong with him?*

"We'll continue on our way," Peter's mom said, and she gave me a look of such understanding—

Stay with me. Help me. Please, don't leave me, I begged her in silence. *I'm drowning.*

But she did leave. She and her son continued along the Bridle Path, toward their picnic. Nicky howled, "*Why Bridge Number Twenty-Eight?*" He stamped his foot onto the Bridle Path over and over, as if he could force the earth itself to answer. Or to open and consume him. "*Why Bridge Number Twenty-Eight?*" Passersby edged away from us.

"Ask your phone." I struggled to keep tears from welling in my eyes. I had to will myself into absolute calm, in order to maneuver Nicky into regaining self-control. This was the only remedy the therapist could give for Nicky's outbursts: Show no emotion, regardless of your anger, grief, and helplessness, as you see your beloved child transformed into a raving stranger. "Find out."

Ask your phone. Find out. I repeated this like a mantra. Like an incantation or a prayer.

It brought him around. He took the phone out of his pocket and dictated his question. He read the results. He examined the underside of the bridge.

Usually I'd ask him to explain what he was reading, to share it and create a positive interaction between us. Our therapists, Nicky's and mine, valued *positive interactions.* I was supposed to make a list to give the therapists each week, so I wouldn't lose track of them amid the barrage of negative interactions.

This time I didn't care.

Kevin returned home later than I'd anticipated. On a typical day, I wouldn't have noticed.

I had to tell him about the birthday party and about Bridge No. 28. We had to help Nicky finish his weekend homework so he'd be ready for school in the morning. Then prepare dinner. Clean up. Nicky needed to take a bath. We entered our evening ordeal, Nicky balking at every step because he hated school, he hated homework. Often he seemed to hate being alive.

By the time Nicky was asleep, I was exhausted, and I couldn't bring myself to ask Kevin about what I'd seen. After Kevin packed (he was leaving early the next morning for Houston), we read in bed. Yes, I had to lie down beside him and pretend I was fine. I consoled myself with the possibility that many, if not most, married people did exactly that, night after night, month after month, one way or another. Like them, I had to keep going. I must have done this well, because Kevin didn't ask me if anything was wrong.

The work week and the school week began, the unending struggle to help Nicky through another day continued, and I never did confront Kevin.

CHAPTER 9

On Friday, July 3, the sun rose before five, shining through the mullioned windows of my bedroom, waking me. What sounded like a hundred thousand songbirds greeted the day with rapture.

Nicky was up at six, consulting a flight-tracker app. Kevin's plane from Chicago landed early, at 6:54 instead of the scheduled 7:20 A.M., causing Nicky much excitement. Passport control was surprisingly fast. We monitored another app so Nicky could follow the exact course of his father's journey, with traffic updates texted from Kevin.

When the car became visible along the estate's entry drive, Nicky, Duncan, and I were waiting outside. Sunlight glinted on the car's hood. Because of the darkened windows, I couldn't see Kevin, only a shape, a shadow within the darkness. The car stopped. Kevin opened the passenger door and stepped out.

I took in the details of him. The side of his tortoiseshell glasses. The angle of his head. His dark hair disarrayed from travel. His long legs. His blazer outlining his torso. He wore chinos and an oxford shirt. He'd never wear jeans and a T-shirt on a flight. He was from a family that considered air travel a treat and a privilege and worth dressing up for.

"Daddy, you arrived at Ashton Hall sixteen minutes earlier than Google Maps predicted at the start of your trip."

"Thanks for keeping track." After giving Nicky a quick hug, Kevin went to retrieve his suitcase, reaching into the trunk before the driver had a chance to do it. Kevin didn't like people waiting on him. He paid the driver and said a few words of gratitude to him.

So much of what I loved about Kevin was encapsulated in these small gestures. The generosity. The respect for others. The way he moved, with low-key assurance. The lithe ease of his body.

I met his eyes. He regarded me with humor, exhaustion, desire, love.

The driver turned the car around. "Daddy, you had a Panther car," Nicky said, spotting the company insignia on the car door. "A giant cat carried you on his back from the airport."

Sometimes he surprised us with these flights of fancy.

"You're right," Kevin said.

He was beside me. I reached for him, holding him as he held me. He was over six feet tall, and I fit perfectly beneath his chin. I loved him, ached for him. My love for him wasn't a switch I could turn on and off, and at this moment, it swept away anger, fear, confusion, betrayal.

Nicky joined our embrace, and Kevin spread his arms around both of us.

Stepping away, Nicky took the handle of Kevin's bag and pulled it toward the house. Kevin and I followed, hand in hand. We went inside and sat down to breakfast.

"Nicky's doing so well. It's great to see," Kevin said.

We walked along a woodland path in Ashton Hall's park, amid the oaks, sycamores, and chestnut trees.

"He *is* doing well," I said. "I can't explain why, but the change is astonishing."

"We had a terrific time on our bikes this morning. He showed me all around the neighborhood. The supermarket, the bakery, the hairdresser where Alice once went to have her hair dyed purple except it came out a color Nicky called *sick green*."

"I haven't been there."

"For about the tenth time, he told me every detail of how he found the skeleton."

"For him, it's just something intriguing and fun. But it's far from that."

"I know. But the point is, I've never seen him so relaxed and happy."

We could easily spend this entire walk discussing our son. During the past days, for Nicky's sake, I'd gone through the motions of being a contented spouse. As a family, we'd visited the tourist sites. We'd dined at the White Hart. Kevin and I had even made love. Tomorrow he was leaving. I had to stop pretending and confront him *now*. I felt my anger building, at him and also at myself, because confrontation was so hard for me.

"What's wrong, Hannah?"

I couldn't say it. Maybe I'd be better off not saying it, not ever, focusing on Nicky, helping him to grow up, putting the rest of my life aside.

"I know something's wrong," Kevin said.

In former days, the gentleness of his voice would make me feel as if he'd taken me in his arms. Fear constricted my throat. By confronting him, I could lose our love. Our lives together. The stability Nicky needed.

But I couldn't go on pretending.

"Kevin, do you remember the Sunday a few weeks before Nicky and I came here, when I took him to a birthday party and he punched a classmate? You were playing tennis in the park that day."

He seemed to think back, then said, "Those birthday parties all blend together."

"Nicky and I walked home across the park that day, and I saw you and Tim sitting on a bench after your tennis match."

"You should have stopped to say hi," he said. No hesitation or self-consciousness. No hint that he was hiding something. Could I have imagined it? "We must have been waiting for a doubles match," he added.

"I saw you . . ."

He pushed back my hair. Put his hand on my shoulder.

I made myself meet his eyes. "I saw you caress the back of his leg, just the way you do to me."

His expression didn't change. He let go of me. Turned away.

So I hadn't imagined it.

"I'm sorry you found out that way," he said.

"For how long?" I managed to ask.

A pause. He seemed to be calculating the best response. The best degree of truth to share with me.

"A long time," he said.

"What does that mean, *a long time*?"

"From before I met you. We—"

"*We*, as in you and Tim? Are you saying you've had a relationship with him for *years*? A sexual relationship? Running parallel to our relationship?"

"I guess you could put it that way. More or less."

"How can that even be?" A kind of film of all the years of our lives together began to run in my mind, and I tried to find the occasions when they'd met and the false explanations Kevin must have given me about where he'd been. "It doesn't make sense. Why stay with me if you want to be with someone else?"

He didn't respond.

"Do you love him?"

He didn't answer.

"Answer!"

He didn't.

I hurried ahead. I couldn't scream at him or cry. I kept my cries and screams inside, fighting to get out. I made myself study the ferns that lined the shaded path. Oh, yes, the ferns were lovely here in the woods, raindrops still held within the fronds from a passing shower this morning. The scents of the soil were dense, warm.

The path led around a stand of trees, and the towers of Ashton Hall came into view. Somewhere in that beautiful house, a woman had been imprisoned. I was in a shaded bower, and the towers and the lawn were in sunlight. The sounds of laughter and of barking drifted toward me. Nicky, Alice, and Duncan were in the distance, playing croquet. Nicky had become captivated by croquet, with its exacting rules and scoring. I stopped to watch them, to catch my breath, as pain pressed within my chest and suppressed tears burned my eyes.

Kevin joined me. "Don't we all love different people in different ways?" he asked, his voice so gentle. "Even that dog is loved, in a different way from the way I love you, which is different from the way I love Nicky."

"Betrayal isn't love."

"I'd never pursue an affair with a woman."

"I suppose that's a relief." The cruelty in my voice shocked me. Cruelty wasn't part of who we'd ever been together. Above us, sunlight shifted through the canopy of leaves. I walked on, and he was beside me. The path curved away from our son.

"This must be confusing. You must have a lot of questions."

"Don't give me those platitudes." Several years before, Kevin's law firm had offered a mandatory class in sensitivity training. The section on empathy had provided these stock phrases. We'd both laughed when he'd shared them with me. "Do you consider yourself gay?"

"Desire is a continuum, flowing from women to men and men to women." He said this like a lecture, yet tenderly, trying to help me understand, and he went on for a while, explaining the intricacies of sexual orientation to me as if I'd lived in a nunnery for the past twenty years. He sounded as if he'd prepared this conversation in advance, like a legal brief, or an obituary, to have at the ready if he needed it.

"Haven't you ever felt attracted to women?" he asked.

Irrelevant. But because he was my husband and I loved him, I thought about his question . . . about the young women in my college dorm. I'd never fantasized about being close to them. I considered the classical statues of women in the galleries at the Met, naked or with drapery clinging to their bodies like a wet film. The drapery was a feat of artistry. But alluring? Not to me. Nothing flickered in me when I went into the women's locker room at the gym, and I felt only anger when I saw the exploitative repetition of naked female bodies presented in movies and television shows.

"No, I don't feel that. I've never felt it."

"You're at the far side of the continuum, then."

"And you?"

"Toward the middle. I've always been this way. Our marriage isn't a sham. I'm not pretending that I love you, that I desire you."

Hadn't I learned anything from studying classical art? I knew about the sexual fluidity of classical culture, although I'd never applied it to my own life: upper-class married men in that era going to the baths, attending dinners, being intimate with other men, often younger men.

"We've shared a life for years, and slept next to each other, and had a child together, and meanwhile you were leading a whole other life?" I asked in disbelief.

"This type of arrangement is more common than you think. Men married to women and involved in other ways. Women married to men, the same. In public, people try to paint life as gay or straight. In public, people don't like to recognize the shades in between. Some arrangements work because that's who the people truly are." He was professionally trained to create a logical, convincing argument, and he never raised his voice. A raised voice was also a *tell*, another attempt to cover the truth. "I haven't betrayed *our* life together."

"You haven't? Then why did you hide it?"

"Years ago, things were different. I've met older men who were disbarred after they were caught up in police raids on gay bars. Lives destroyed, and why? What harm was being done?"

It *was* tragic, and yet he'd put me into a corner. How could I criticize him if he was part of the fight for justice? Part of the struggle for basic human rights that I myself believed in? Nonetheless . . . "You assumed *I* would condemn you, too? That's a terrible way to view the person who's supposed to be closest to you. It's patronizing. Judgmental, against me. Assuming I wouldn't understand or accept you."

"I never saw it that way."

"What about health dangers?"

I couldn't make myself ask him directly if they were using protection when they had sex. Christopher retreated into the *nasties* because real words could attack you, make you double over in anguish. "You've made me risk my health, and for years."

"We both have a lot to lose, Tim and I. We're careful."

"*Careful?* You put your family's well-being in his hands. You trust him that much?"

"He puts the same trust in me, to safeguard his family. We're close friends, in addition to . . . the other. I realize it's exceptional, the level of trust we have."

"The level of trust you *believe* you have. He could betray your trust anytime."

"This is an issue we've discussed. We're not young anymore. Family life is demanding, combined with work. For us both."

Sometimes at museums, restaurants, or bookshops, we ran into women Kevin had dated before we married, just as we ran into former boyfriends of mine, greeted with quick hellos and introductions. Now I faced the fact that we might also have run into former boyfriends of Kevin's, individuals to whom I wasn't introduced, and that acknowledgments were exchanged with them when my back was turned.

"The world has changed," I said. "You could come to a realization that you're . . . on the furthest side of the continuum, and leave me for Tim or another man, and create a new life for yourself, without worrying about your job or society's judgments."

"You could do that, too. With a man or a woman."

"That's ridiculous. I'm a woman in my late thirties with no career and a demanding child. You know finding a new partner would be much harder for me than for you."

"Are we actually talking about separating?" he asked with a tinge of panic in his voice.

I was jolted again by my dependence on him. Before we got married, I'd done something stupid: I'd neglected to hire an attorney of my own to review the prenup drawn up by his attorney. I couldn't afford an attorney, and I also couldn't conceive that Kevin and I would ever divorce. Although I didn't remember every detail, I knew the agreement would limit whatever settlement I received.

Kevin didn't wait for me to answer his question. "Being with Tim is part of who I am, not the sum total. If a person were, say, a prism, my time with Tim would be one facet. A facet that has nothing to do with you. My relationship with Tim"—he struggled to find the words—"has a different kind of tenderness. An entirely different closeness."

He said this as if he thought it would make me feel better, but instead it was like a blow in the gut. "Are you willing to give him up?"

"No." He didn't need to think about it. "I'm not going to make promises I won't keep. I've known plenty of men who make promises like that, then continue as before, while trying to be even more discreet."

"Monogamy is impossible for you, then?"

"I know our culture teaches that monogamy is the way things should be. But what if the truth is that in actual, lived life, over decades, monogamy is the exception? What if there's a gap between the rule and reality?"

"Monogamy has always been easy for me. It's never felt like a rule." I choked over these words, words I'd never thought I'd have to say. "I love *you*. I don't want anyone else."

"This is my wiring," he said with finality.

His *wiring*. From the therapists Nicky had seen over the years, I had the impression that wiring couldn't be contradicted. They made *wiring* sound irreversible, not subject to compromise or even discussion; it became a word requiring solely acceptance or capitulation. I knew that sexual orientation could be called *wired*, but did the term even apply to what Kevin was demanding: simultaneous long-term relationships with two people?

"Maybe from here on out," he said, convinced of it, "we can create a new kind of life together. A life where we don't have to hide who we really are."

"You mean you want an open marriage? To me, that phrase means a man doing whatever he pleases while a woman stays home raising children."

"Of course I don't want that. What I want is just the same as we had before, but now you know. Nothing else has changed."

"Everything's changed." Again I saw how powerless I was. My dependence made me captive to Kevin's decisions on how we'd live our lives together. The idea of separating from him felt like an abyss, emotional and financial. And yet I couldn't simply give in; everything inside me rebelled against giving in. "I need time to figure out if I can live with the . . . arrangement you've set up for yourself. We're away from each other for the summer anyway. I'll think things through. In the meantime, I don't want Nicky to sense any change between us. I don't want to upset him."

"Okay." Kevin's voice was strangled; this was hard for him, too. "If that's what you want."

The path meandered toward another opening in the trees. No doubt sniffing us on the breeze, Duncan ran toward us. Nicky chased Duncan, and soon we were together, united, a family: Kevin and Nicky, the two loves of my life.

"Daddy, play croquet with us."

"I don't know how to play croquet," he said. I heard the tears behind his words.

"I'll teach you. You'll like it. There's lots of exercise in croquet. Mental exercise. From a distance, croquet looks like an easy game, but it isn't. You can do it, though. You just have to try. Learning something new can be scary, but after you learn it, it's easy." He parroted the lines that Kevin and I often put to him.

"You've convinced me." He suppressed his emotions and managed to smile his agreement, putting on the façade of supportive good humor we both tried to maintain in front of Nicky.

We walked to the croquet court. Glowing in the sunlight, the house rose behind us, concealing its secrets. Under Nicky's direction, Alice demonstrated for Kevin how to use the mallet to hit the ball. Nicky explained the rules involved in progressing through the wickets, with Alice illustrating his points. Kevin asked questions and listened carefully to Nicky's replies. As ever, he was wonderful with Nicky. Seeing them together filled me with thankfulness.

Duncan stayed beside me, a big, adorable dog, rubbing his furry head against my bare legs, licking my calf. He was probably just enjoying the taste of salt on my skin, but his touch felt loving all the same.

Later, in the dark. Nicky was asleep across the hall. The windows were open to the sound of rain tapping upon leaves. The scents of the night, the fragrance of the woods and the garden, wafted around us. Should I have refused when Kevin turned to me? I couldn't refuse, because I'd already turned to him, my husband, lover, friend, the same man I'd known before.

His legs and his chest were warm against mine. He ran his hands from my shoulders to my thighs. I wanted him. Craved him. Not just anyone. *Him.* Tomorrow he was leaving. Already I missed him, our closeness made even more compelling by the wrench of parting. Years together, and still I felt this way about him.

I couldn't bring myself to ask him to use a condom, if he even had one. He was my husband. Desire led me forward. Not simply for a body in the dark. For *his* body, for his entire being, spirit, soul, mind.

For years, I'd trusted him. Trusted him with my life, and his tenderness had surrounded me and still did.

The tautness of his shoulders, my hands across and down his back, his legs, the curve where his hip and back met. He was everywhere around me. I felt a desperation for him, mixed with anguish. A voice in my mind said, *You may have to leave him. You* will *have to leave him.* My response was to grip him tighter, pulling him closer as he slipped inside me.

How I loved him, in a constellation of love. Giving and receiving. Longing. All this I felt for him, and from him. Him, me, us, we, entwined.

CHAPTER 10

The next afternoon, as I approached the Big Old Tree, Nicky called, "Mom, this morning we started working in her room!"

Nicky, Alice, and Duncan sat on blankets with Professor Varet and the young man with blond curls—Iain Clarkson was his name, I learned when Alice introduced us. Nicky had texted me to join them. Alice had already spread out a formal tea service, complete with small sandwiches and the irresistible shortbread cookies from the café.

"What's going on?" I asked. As I sat down, I heard a crinkling sound; Alice must have put a waterproof tarpaulin beneath the blankets, to protect them, and us, from the damp ground. After a night of rain, the skies had cleared, and the morning had been shining when Kevin departed. I'd spent the day working on my dissertation and my part-time job. Now the sunny weather was beginning to turn again, and the gathering gray clouds contrasted with the dense blue behind them.

"Detective Chief Inspector Layton said the lady and the hidden room belong to us!" Nicky said, rising to his knees in excitement.

"A few days ago," Professor Varet explained calmly, his composure a contrast to Nicky's enthusiasm, "I received word from DCI Layton that Dr. Evans had approved the archaeological unit at the university to take possession of the skeleton for further study." He sat on the blanket with an absolute ease, despite the awkwardness he might have felt from his lanky frame and long legs. "I'm pleased to report that I was able to exploit my influence to move her to the front of the queue for radiocarbon dating, from which we've learned—"

"She died between 1545 and 1610!" Nicky said.

"The dating isn't as precise as we'd like; radiocarbon dating seldom is. But in conjunction with other evidence in the room, we'll develop a context that—"

"—will tell us every single thing about her!" Nicky said.

Professor Varet regarded Nicky with good humor, seeming to enjoy his fervor.

"Iain and Professor Varet arrived at ten thirteen this morning, and they brought lots of equipment and a white zip-up jumpsuit for me, so I could help," Nicky said.

"I blessed Iain and Professor Varet for *not* bringing a white zip-up jumpsuit for me," Alice said.

Possibly due to the warm temperature and rising humidity, Iain's cheeks reddened.

"Then we went to work," Nicky said. "Alice came with us. She sat on a folding chair in the first room and reorganized her recipe file on her tablet. That means she was doing something important, too, and didn't feel left out. She said so."

"I'm glad. Have you told all this to Mrs. Gardner?"

"Yesterday on the phone," Professor Varet said. "Asked her if my graduate students could take on the project as a case study."

"She must have been pleased," I said.

"She was rather brusque, actually. Said, *Fine, fine,* and rang off."

"Granny's almost always brusque when things are important to her," Alice said. "That's how I can tell."

"After we went into the hidden room," Nicky interjected, "we set up more lights. Operated by batteries. We took pictures of everything, including the spiderwebs and the dust. We didn't clean or rearrange anything. Iain has to do a drawing first, on graph paper he calls a *grid*. We're going to measure every single thing. And make an inventory. That means a list. Look: Professor Varet brought me some *tools of archaeology:* a red-and-white meter stick and a directional arrow." He showed me. "You put these in the photographs to show the scale and the direction of everything in relation to north."

Gesturing toward Nicky as if presenting him on a stage, the professor said, "Tell your mother what you found."

"A sewing needle. On the floor. Under the desk." His entire body seemed bursting with this news.

"Nicky is an excellent volunteer," Professor Varet said with a generous smile. "He's able to slip into every corner."

"The needle must have rolled there, and she couldn't find it. But I could. It's not smooth and slick like our needles. It's rough-shaped, from being old. It's *corroded*." Nicky said the word boldly. "Iain put it into a plastic bag. We're going to study it later. And we found a string of beads called a *rosary*. A rosary is important to Catholic people. *Catholic* is a religion. Professor Varet told me. He told me about the priedieu and the statue. So probably she was Catholic."

"If she died during the reign of Queen Mary," Professor Varet said to me, "being Catholic wouldn't have created problems for her. Thus far nothing proves she was in the room *because* she was Catholic. Right now we've no idea why she was there."

"We're going to find out," Nicky said. "Professor Varet explained to me exactly how we're going to do it."

"I gave a basic introduction," Professor Varet demurred.

"I learned already that the technology for archaeology is so excellent you can tell what a person ate for dinner hundreds of years ago. You can figure out if they could afford to eat meat and if they liked it and ate a lot of it."

"Really?" I asked.

"Basically, yes," the professor said, almost shyly, beginning to look a bit overcome by Nicky's barrage.

"I had no idea," I said.

"You can figure out where they grew up," Nicky said. "Their teeth show what kind of water they drank, not just their cavities. Their bones show stuff, too."

"The science is complex," Professor Varet said, "but the purpose of archaeology—or, rather, one purpose—is to discover how individuals in the past lived from day to day. To learn, if we can, their motivations and how they viewed their world, without projecting our own worldview onto them." I could see he had a gift for teaching, for bringing erudite concepts to life in a way that I, and even a nine-year-old, could understand.

"We'll find out who *she* was," Nicky said. "Not someone else. *Her.*"

I felt an ache. My compassion grew for the unknown woman, alone in her prison. I studied the house. The clouds made moving patterns of shadows across the façade. Although I knew my reaction was more emotional than rational, I began to feel an uncanny link to the woman, a compulsion to determine who she was. To understand the life she'd led and why she had died where she did.

"Alice is telling me about the kings and queens of England. Only her favorites. Ethelred the *Un*ready. Whenever the Vikings invaded, he wasn't ready. Richard the Lionheart. He didn't really have a heart from a lion; that was his nickname. I wonder why *nickname* has *nick* in it. Do people ever say *nicky-name*?"

Nicky was speeding now. The familiar nervousness crept into me. I caught myself gripping the blanket, preparing myself for him to lose control.

"King Arthur and Queen Guinevere. The king named Arthur

had a big round table to sit at with his knights. He named it the Round Table. Really, he did."

Glancing up, I saw that Matthew Varet was watching me with concern. I looked away, embarrassed.

"We'd better be going," Varet said.

Inwardly, I thanked him.

Nicky jumped up. "Can we walk to the car park with them? Mom, *car park* is *English* English for *parking lot*. The name turns the cars into trees."

Another flight of fancy.

The car park was located at some distance, on the far side of the house in an area concealed by woods. Nicky and Duncan ran ahead, Iain stayed close to Alice, and I walked beside Professor Varet.

"Thank you for including Nicky in the project," I said. "I'm afraid he does make it into something of a treasure hunt. It's affected me in a . . . the truth is, I can't stop seeing her face in my mind in the middle of the night."

"My feelings run along the same track as yours. But Nicky's able to meet the situation in his own way, and I'm glad to encourage him." He hesitated. "I've been pondering a possibility. Sorry in advance if it's unwelcome or if I'm speaking out of turn." Again, the hesitation. "My daughters are with me at the weekend. Janet is twelve, and Rosie is eight. Their mother and I are divorced."

Nicky led us to a shortcut, through a latched, unmarked door in an otherwise plain brick wall. Judging from his sure steps, he might have lived at Ashton Hall all his life.

The door led into the walled garden. White roses covered the trellises. Hollyhocks—red, pink, and a purple so dark it looked like black velvet—rose on slender stalks to almost my height. Two lines of pear trees created an allée down the center. One section was devoted to the needs of the café kitchen, with beds of lettuce, spinach, rhubarb, and more. A variety of herbs grew in another section. I caught the scent of basil and of still-ripening cherry tomatoes warmed by the sun. Strawberry plants, low to the ground, covered another section. We passed an area called *Medicinal,* where the plants were labeled with their uses. Bees went about their work, paying us no notice. We reached a bed of lavender. Another of ornamental grasses. Rain would begin soon; the air itself was darkening as moisture filled it and accentuated the garden's colors and fertile abundance.

"Perhaps you and Nicky would like to visit us for lunch on Sunday. Rosie never worries me, but I must tell you that making friends is hard for Janet."

I felt a deepening sympathy toward him. "I understand."

"She and Nicky might find they have a lot in common. And if not, they can torment each other for the afternoon," he added wryly, "while Rosie gardens—her favorite weekend pursuit—and possibly you and I can even relax with a bottle of wine."

This made me smile. "Sounds like fun. For all of us."

"Indeed. Our house is in Chesterton, on the north side of Cambridge, about a half hour from here by bike on the scenic route, which I'd insist you take. Faster via car service, if you prefer. I can send you a map."

I felt the usual pang of anxiety as I contemplated taking Nicky to a social gathering. He might start swearing the moment we sat down to eat. But if he did act out, I'd find support, not condemnation, from Matthew Varet.

"Sunday would be good for us."

"Thank you," he said.

"No, thank *you.* You're the one inviting us."

"It's an invitation you may live to regret, so don't thank me yet."

CHAPTER 11

In the hidden room, Nicky pointed to the woman's storage chest: "The blankets and clothing in the chest are in better condition than anticipated, because it was closed for centuries." Nicky spoke like an expert, his gift for mimicry and memorization allowing him to take on a new vocabulary. "Professor Varet told me the fabrics are covered with dog fur. That means she had her own Duncan. Her dog wasn't here with her, though. We didn't find a dog skeleton." He glanced at me with sadness. Today his mood was circumspect, melancholy. "I'm going to tell Uncle Christopher about her dog when we talk on the phone tonight. He'll want to know about that."

"I'm certain he will."

I'd asked Nicky to bring me here, and we were alone. Via text, Professor Varet had given us permission and asked only that we not touch anything. In the coming weeks, the contents of the room would be dismantled, Professor Varet's graduate students taking the items to

Ashton Hall's conservation center for further study. Under the supervision of Dr. Tinsley, the librarian, they were already boxing the documents in the muniment room.

"She has two candelabras, one on the eating table and one on her desk, but the candles are burned all the way down, and she doesn't have any more."

The battery-operated lights attached to tripod stands created a precision far different from the wavering candlelight she would have known . . . until the candles burned down and went out. From then on, apart from whatever moonlight reached the room, she would have spent the nights in darkness.

"We're trying to figure out the building campaigns for the house." *We.* Nicky was part of the team. "We want to know if the windows were bricked over when she was here or if that happened later."

Please, let it have been later. So at least she had natural light during the day, and sometimes moonlight at night, and could stand on a chair and study the world outside.

"Look at her shoes."

They were under the chair by the table. How fine the leather appeared.

"The soft leather proves she was from a rich family."

Was she part of the family that lived at Ashton Hall? A maiden aunt, or a daughter-in-law shunned by the rest of the family? Except for the lack of candles and the absence of her dog, she had everything she needed here. Almost as if she'd chosen everything herself. Had she?

Next to the chair was a disintegrating basket with needles and thread at the bottom. Her embroidery basket. Beside it, a wooden stand for needlework. The cloth that had been stretched across the stand had fallen away in the middle. Nearby was the keyboard instrument, with a music manuscript propped on it, tiny holes eaten into the paper by insects. In the corner was the prie-dieu and, behind it, the statue, about five feet tall, of the Virgin Mary holding the baby Jesus.

I imagined the woman doing needlework. Practicing music. Kneeling in prayer. Venerating the statue before her.

On the desk were four books of varying sizes, the titles on the bindings faded or absent. I visualized the pages disintegrating in my hands if I touched them.

Next to the books was a large stack of volumes, well over twenty, all measuring roughly nine by twelve inches, with similar leather covers.

"Professor Varet wonders if those might be her commonplace books," Nicky said, following my gaze. "Commonplace books were common in the old days. It wasn't a diary. You wrote down quotes from books you read, poetry you liked, and random thoughts you had."

Unless she used the commonplace books differently. Maybe she *did* keep a diary. Or she might have been a mystic, like Julian of Norwich or St. Teresa of Avila, and the commonplace books were filled with her visions, and that was why the family brought her here—because she was beyond their understanding. Because she frightened them.

Also on the desk, the golden cross. An inkpot made of red pottery, with a stopper to keep the ink from spilling or drying out. A quill pen. A knife with an ornate tarnished-silver handle, a *pen knife*, which she would have used to sharpen the quill. A bowl with pieces of what looked like charcoal. Another with sticks of what appeared to be multicolored chalk. A type of pencil, miraculously still wrapped in string.

I imagined her sitting at her desk, writing. Waiting for the minutes to pass.

At the corner of the desk was a wooden box, about eight inches by ten, and four inches high. Oak leaves were carved into it, the workmanship skillful and refined. The top was attached with hinges, and the metalwork of the hinges and the front latch was incised with decorations. Gingerly, Nicky raised the lid. "When I was here yesterday, Iain told me I can open it," Nicky said, looking up, assuring me, "but to not touch anything."

It seemed to be a keepsake box. It held . . . folded letters tied with a frayed red ribbon, the color preserved because of the protection provided by the closed box. Were these love letters? Was this the solution to her mystery? She'd tried to run away with a man, or woman, whom her parents disapproved of, and as a result they'd locked her away?

Alongside the letters lay two baby-sized mittens, embroidered with tiny pink flowers. Mittens for *her* baby? In one corner was a wooden carving of a dog, possibly a spaniel, a few inches tall, standing on its feet. *Her* dog? Propped upright against the inside of the box were two silver coins.

Her treasure.

When I was a girl, I'd kept my most treasured possessions in a cardboard cigar box covered with Art Nouveau images of angels. My mother didn't approve of the box, because it smelled of cigars, but I refused to give it up.

In my cigar box, I kept: A penny from 1921 that I was convinced would one day be worth a fortune. A small plastic magnifier, for studying the penny. A deck of cards with an image of a Paolo Uccello painting of a man on a white horse, from the National Gallery in London. This was a gift from Christopher and too precious to use to play a card game. A postcard from Tuscany, sent by Christopher and Constance when they traveled there one summer. Inside a yellowed envelope, a photograph of my grandparents with my mother, when she was four years old, before she was sent to England. My grandmother had stashed this photo in Margot's suitcase. It was just a family snapshot, taken outdoors in what appeared to be a park. This was the only photo Margot had of her parents. All three wore hats, which shadowed their faces. I'd never seen my grandparents' eyes.

Gently, I closed the keepsake box. I felt I was invading the woman's privacy, as if I were searching through her underwear drawer. I wouldn't want someone violating me that way. I needed to protect her, even from myself. And yet . . . this was what she'd left behind. The proofs of her existence.

What evidence would be left behind from *my* existence? The contents of the apartment in New York: the mid-century modern furniture; my clothes and shoes; the blankets, sheets, towels, dishes, silverware, pots and pans that Kevin and I shared. As I visualized my possessions, every item seemed generic. It was just stuff, and it could belong to any woman of my age and economic bracket. Only the books would provide clues to who I truly was, shelf after shelf of books about art history, Greek and Roman drama and poetry, English history, literature, mysteries . . . and, on the highest shelves, the spines turned inward so Nicky couldn't read the titles, the books I'd studied to try to understand my son.

Imagine, I told myself, the unknown woman's childhood, the future limitless before her—no, not limitless, because she was a daughter, not a son. A daughter who would grow to be a woman, and who would be expected to be bound in marriage to create an alliance. *Limitless future* was an American myth.

Nonetheless, imagine her as a girl, running across the estate's verdant lawns with her dog. Learning how to embroider, under her mother's tutelage. Taking music lessons. Walking in the walled garden. Reading. Growing up.

Imagine the tone of her voice. The sound of her laughter. The turn of her head. The fall of her hair. The gestures that announced, even from a distance, *this* individual, and no other.

When her body was found, she wore no wedding ring, so she wasn't married. Unless she'd taken the ring off when she became a widow, or she'd been cast aside when her husband wanted a different woman. Maybe the ring was at the bottom of the keepsake box and would be found when everything else was removed. Or the person who'd locked her in this room had stolen the ring.

"That's her chamber pot," Nicky said, breaking into my reverie. He pointed at a corroded charcoal-gray basin with a handle. The object was covered with plastic wrap. "It's made of pewter. It looks empty, but special scientists at the university are going to study it.

That's why we covered it, in case it might have DNA or other evidence."

"That's awful to think about."

"No, it's not. You have to examine the poo and wee—it's scientific. We can learn a lot about her from studying it. I learned a new word about it." He reached for his pocket notebook. This morning, Mrs. Gardner had given him a new one as a gift, because he'd filled the last one. The cover of this notebook had a photo of Ashton Hall taken from across the lake, the house reflected in the water. He found the page he needed. "Really, really old poo is called *cop-ro-lite*." He enunciated each syllable, frowning, listening to himself, to be certain he pronounced the word correctly.

"I never knew that."

"A person should always be learning new things," he said.

"You're right."

The unknown woman would be humiliated by this discussion. Or was I projecting my own feelings onto her, humiliated on her behalf? She might be fascinated. Or she'd simply shrug, having suffered many more indignities than this. She might also have rags hidden somewhere, for her period. Menstruation was rarely if ever discussed in examinations of the past, because most histories were written by men, who would have deemed it irrelevant or distasteful. Women historians, too, seemed uncomfortable discussing this most persistent aspect of female life. Knowing whether she menstruated would help to determine her exact age. I couldn't bring myself to ask Nicky about any bloodstained rags he and his . . . *colleagues* seemed at this point to be the correct word, might have found.

"A person can live . . ." Nicky found the passage in his notebook. "*On average for three weeks without food, but no more than four to seven days without water.*" He looked at me. "Professor Varet thinks for sure she lived here for a while with someone bringing her food and water through the opening in the middle of the wall. Then the someone got sick, maybe from the plague, and died, or decided to go away on a trip, and didn't take care of her anymore."

Imagine the moment she realized no one would be returning to help her. When she knew she'd been left to die . . . the desperation spinning out before her.

"I'll tell you a secret. Iain picked up the coins and looked at them. When Professor Varet wasn't here. But I was here, and Iain showed me. He told me they have a picture of Queen Elizabeth on them—the first Queen Elizabeth—and a date: 1582." He turned to the next page in his notebook and read aloud: "*Two silver threepence coins minted in 1582.* Iain said the coins prove the woman died *after* 1582. Though they don't tell us how old she was when she died." A glimmer came into Nicky's eyes. "I want to turn over the letters in the box. Then we'll know her name and address. Iain said they didn't use envelopes in those days."

"Professor Varet told you not to touch anything," I said firmly.

"But Iain already did, with the coins. And I really want to know. I'm going to look."

Before I could react, he reopened the box, took out the packet of letters, and turned it over. My helplessness and anger fanned out in response to his disobedience.

"What the fuck. The words are squiggly. I can't fucking read this." He thrust the packet toward me. "Read it."

The usual conundrum: *No, I'm not going to read the words for you, because you shouldn't have touched the packet. And you shouldn't use swear words. Put the packet back; I refuse to look at it.*

But he was already holding it. And I wanted to know the answer, too. "Watch your tone. And your language."

"Sorry. Could you read the words to me, please?"

I experienced an eerie disquiet as I took the packet. The old paper had a different feel from what I was used to, more textured, less smooth. I held the packet up to the light. The centuries-old lettering was as lovely as lace.

A name has power. It possesses a force like magic. A name conjures an object, or an individual, into existence. Christopher, Alice, Kevin, Mrs. Gardner—to hear their names is to see them in your mind. Names define the world: tree, flower, book, shoe. I'd taught Nicky those words, among many others, pointing at the objects, showing him pictures, practicing with him.

As I stared at the lettering, trying to decipher it, gradually the words became clear, and with this clarity the unknown woman took on a weight, an identity, a physical presence in the room. Nicky and I stood within the life she'd led, and she was everywhere around us.

Her name was Isabella Cresham.

CHAPTER 12

I parked my bike outside the estate's secondhand bookshop, and a bell jingled as I opened the door. The shop was cavernous and resembled the barn it used to be. Rows of freestanding shelves, stuffed with books, were crammed into the space. More volumes were stacked on the floor at the end of each row.

The general sat on a stool behind the counter, wire-rimmed reading glasses propped on his nose. Piles of books rose to his left and right, framing him. Under a navy-blue blazer, he wore a T-shirt imprinted with the cover of the *Rubber Soul* album by the Beatles. The song "Norwegian Wood" played on the sound system.

After the general examined each book on his left, making a few markings on the inside cover, he added it to the pile on his right, which was becoming precariously high.

"Ah, Ms. Larson." He took off his glasses. "Welcome to my hideaway."

"Thank you. Please call me Hannah."

"Very good then, Hannah."

"What a wonderful shop."

"This establishment is more a service to the community than an actual shop. Mrs. Gardner doesn't charge me rent. Anything in particular I might help you with today?"

"I'm interested in learning more about, well, something my son—"

"I must confess," he lowered his voice to a whisper, even though we were alone, "I'm amongst those happy few who are in on the secret. Mrs. Gardner and I partake of tea on a regular basis, and she briefs me on developments. *Isabella Cresham.* I do wonder what her sad story will prove to be."

I'd told Mrs. Gardner about the letters and coins immediately. Despite her extensive knowledge of Ashton Hall's history, she hadn't recognized the first name and so didn't know where to place Isabella within the time range provided by the coins and the radiocarbon dating. Sixty-five years: 1545 to 1610. Five rulers: Henry VIII, Edward VI, Mary, Elizabeth I, and James I. Four Tudor monarchs, and the first of the Stuart kings. I knew the basics, but I needed more than just the history of kings and queens. I needed to know about individuals living their daily lives on estates like this one.

"Now that we have a date range, I want to learn more about the era, so I can begin to understand Isabella Cresham's life, not just her death."

"Ah, yes, 1545 to 1610. Years of traumatic religious upheaval, played out against crop failures, famine, smallpox, sweating sickness, plague. Also, a flowering of culture, of poetry, music, and drama."

"I'd like to focus on everyday life, away from the royal court."

"Precisely what I'd expect from a broad-minded young person completing a PhD." At my surprise that he knew this about me, he gave a Cheshire cat smile. "Eckersley told me the details over a pint at the pub, and extremely proud of you he was, too."

"Thank you for saying so, but the degree has been a long journey."

"As worthwhile journeys tend to be. Any word on how my friend is faring across the sea?"

"We talk on the phone just about every day. The treatment's going smoothly, although it's tiring. He's optimistic." This was no longer exactly true; the treatment was more than tiring, it was exhausting, and Christopher often sounded weak. However, I wasn't going to share my anxieties about his condition with the general; Christopher wouldn't want him to worry.

"Do give him my regards. I miss him. His ever-intriguing observations. Look forward to his return. In any event, the truth is, most people never go beyond the kings and queens. They're fascinated and often amused to learn about the six wives of Henry the Eighth, and they embrace the Golden Age under Elizabeth the First, but religious persecution? Epidemics and mass graves? Crop failures and starvation? Those are most definitely *not* fun."

He slammed shut the book he'd been examining.

"No thought at all," he said fervently, "to what the Dissolution of the Monasteries meant to the thousands of monks and nuns thrown out of religious houses, often into lives of poverty. Or the monastic schools and hospitals shut down, leaving the common people with even harder lives than before."

He shook his head at the injustice of it.

"I find that Americans in particular have their own ideas of what we British once were and should be now." He shook his head again. "Ah, well. Why disillusion them, why wake them from their dream of us? *Don't ask, don't tell,* to repeat one of your military rules from some years ago."

I couldn't protest; he was right. "I read a lot of English history when I was younger, but I'm afraid my eyes glazed over whenever anything about religion came up. I never registered what the religious conflicts must have meant for regular people, away from the centers of power."

"Please, my critique isn't meant personally. Having rather a quiet day here, and my thoughts do wander. I'd be glad to locate a few tomes to fill you in." He left his perch. "Won't be but a moment."

I stayed near the counter, riffling through a rack of tourist guides to Cambridge, as he disappeared behind the shelves, muttering as he went. He returned with four hardback books that looked swollen from a flood.

"Here we are. Three social histories and a you-are-there guide to everyday life in Tudor England."

"Thank you. How much do I owe you?"

"Goodness me, nothing."

"Please, I can't take them for free."

"We'll call them a loan. When people in the village have books they no longer need, this shop provides a refuge whilst the volumes are in transition to new homes. That's the point of books, isn't it? To be passed from hand to hand, until they fall apart. Part of the great river of life."

"What a touching image."

Putting on his glasses, he paged through one of the volumes. "Catholic, Protestant, Catholic, Protestant, shifting with the monarch. Under Catholic Queen Mary, two hundred eighty Protestants were burned at the stake. Fifty of them were women. When the Protestants were in charge, Catholic priests hid in sewers and beneath floorboards and were tortured and executed if they were caught."

Peering above his glasses, he studied me. "Even our local church, by the estate gates, where the family worshipped, shifted back and forth between the two religions, the same priests adjusting services to suit the law of the day. Put yourself in the shoes of someone living then. The recurring outbreaks of plague led to mass death. In Norwich, about sixty miles from here and a major city in those days, a third of the population died of plague in one year alone. The terror of it could destroy all sense of community and family. Do you take care of the town's ill and risk becoming ill yourself, or do you leave them to die? Do you risk your own life to tend to your parents, or do you run away with your children, because you don't want your little ones to become orphans? Let's hope we never face such choices."

Listening to his words, I thought about how certain I was that I would have fled with my son, keeping him safe above all, while I deserted the others I loved—Christopher, my mother, when she was still alive, even though I would never have forgiven myself for leaving them behind.

"All these questions made the religious controversies more fierce. If God controlled the world and everything in it, what message was He sending through the plague? That you should be Protestant, or Catholic? Both churches taught that one's fate in eternity depended on being in their camp." He paused. "I do assume Isabella Cresham was imprisoned for religious reasons. Mrs. Gardner isn't sure."

"I'm not sure, either. But I have to say . . ." I tried to articulate the uneasiness he'd made me feel. I couldn't shake a sense that in a different era, in a different place, I, too, could be imprisoned in such a room. My grandparents had chosen to go into hiding, but when the choice is to hide or be killed, the word *choice* isn't really meaningful. "The story touches on my family, too. Not directly or specifically—"

"But in the sweep of history," he finished the sentence for me. "How well I understand. I'm ninety-three, did you know?"

"Christopher told me."

"You live this long, you see the world repeating itself. I was a bit of a pup during the Second World War. Learning as I went along. Malaya was my war. Nowadays only a precious few have heard of the British action in Malaya. It went on for years. From the late 1940s into the 1950s. I had friends who fought and died there, friends who live still in my thoughts and heart. All basically forgotten now. Willfully forgotten, like so much unpleasantness. I've been conducting a poll. You say you've read a lot of British history. Have you ever heard of our war in Malaya?"

"I'm sorry, I haven't."

I felt a sense of awe in his presence. He'd lived through the Great

Depression. He was in his teens when World War II began in Europe. He'd seen almost ten decades unspool.

"It's simply an informal poll. An attempt to learn the full extent of the forgetting."

Behind me, the bell sounded as the door opened.

"Customers," the general said, *sotto voce*. Returning to the performance art of being British, he called to them, "Anything in particular I might help you with today?"

They were a middle-aged couple, American, I deduced from their turquoise polo shirts, khaki shorts, white socks, and sneakers, man and woman dressed in similar styles.

"Just lookin' around," the man said.

The Americans did a circuit of the rows of bookshelves. "Nothing interesting here," the wife said. "Let's see what's in the gift shop." Without a word to us, they left.

The general and I regarded each other in silence. The forgotten war in Malaya: I'd research it later.

"I have to get going," I said, rousing myself and gathering the books. "I have an errand to do in the village. Thanks for your help."

"Anytime." As I turned away, he added, "Rather deeply shaken, Mrs. Gardner was, by what your son found. She's doing better now. Funny, though, isn't it: Isabella Cresham has never been a ghost, haunting us. Tells you something about ghosts. If you don't fear their presence, they leave you alone. We'll see if she starts haunting us now."

As far as I was concerned, she already had.

CHAPTER 13

Books secured in the bike basket, I sped along the drive. An avenue of mature lime trees—called linden trees in America—formed an arch overhead. Sunlight dappled and flashed around me. The lime trees gave off a sweet scent, and I breathed deeply, willing myself to remember the fragrance, nostalgic for this moment even as I lived it.

Just inside the estate gates was the church, a plain gray stone structure with a squat tower. Parts of it dated from the twelfth century. A graveyard surrounded it on three sides, the burial markers covered with green lichen. Wild grasses and bracken filled the spaces in between. A giant yew tree, many hundreds of years old, embraced all. According to legend, yew trees warded off evil spirits.

The church was open to the public a few days a week, staffed by volunteers. Nicky, Kevin, and I had taken a tour. The crypt was kept locked because the vicar didn't want to disturb the peace of the departed, our guide told us—absolutely *not*, she'd added with a wink, because of the precarious condition of the steps.

Stopping, I studied the church. I visualized myself on a Sunday morning, sitting in a pew while plague raged outside. Catholic, Protestant—was the difference worth being put to death? No. Who would take care of Nicky if I decided to become a martyr? I would have ignored the controversies and got on with things, trying to protect my family. Daily life back then was brutal enough.

But for some individuals, the difference *was* worth risking their lives. They couldn't simply go along, because heaven and hell were as real for them as their lives on earth. Was Isabella Cresham among them?

I rode on, cautioning myself against quick conclusions. Even during eras of religious upheaval, people were murdered by random strangers, and also by those closest to them, for reasons that had nothing to do with faith.

At the main thoroughfare, full-leafed London plane trees lined the roadway and made a tunnel of shade. I dismounted and pushed my bike along the sidewalk, toward the village high street. British schools were still in session, and black SUVs created a traffic jam as their drivers headed to and from school pickup, kids in their uniforms staring out the open windows.

The village was no picture-postcard scene, but nonetheless it was historic. The two-story buildings were brick, utilitarian, built for the laborers of centuries past rather than for the parade of the prosperous filling the roadway today. I locked my bike beside the half dozen others at the rack by the shops.

At lunchtime I'd received a text from Rafe reporting that Christopher was having an especially exhausting few days and needed a boost. I was hoping to find an amusing anecdote to relate, or the inspiration for making one up. As I opened the door of the bakery, the aroma of warm gingerbread enveloped me. I loved that smell. It reminded me of my childhood. At the beginning of every semester, my mother hosted a gingerbread party for the students in our dormitory, and she and I would spend the day baking together.

A counter and display case lined one wall of the shop. Voices and laughter came from the back, where the kitchen must be. The woman presiding over the cash register at the counter wore a blue apron over a flower-print dress. Her white hair was pulled into a bun. Her skin was youthful and unwrinkled, a striking combination with her hair. FIONA, read her nameplate.

"If you wish to buy chocolate–almond croissants," Fiona was saying to a customer, "you must be here early in the day." Fiona's accent was recognizably British but different from the accent of those at the hall.

"You're baking the croissants anyway. How about baking a few dozen more, to meet the demand?" The customer spoke with a firmly American accent. She was a woman of about my age and height, who had the angular edges to her face and figure that come from being extremely fit. Her blond hair was pulled into a ponytail. She was dressed for riding a bicycle for exercise rather than errands, and her helmet, chinstrap buckled, hung from her elbow. I could only dream of being so skinny and athletic. She wore a waist pack with an image of water lilies painted by Monet at Giverny. I recognized this waist pack, because two years before, I'd arranged the licensing for the image.

"Our dedicated customers know to arrive in the morning."

How pleased Christopher would be: I'd stumbled upon an argument of the type he had predicted. Surreptitiously, I made my way closer to the two, while examining the cakes, cookies, and scones in the display case. Several types of whole-grain bread were stacked on racks attached to the back wall.

"I *am* a dedicated customer."

"Since we're always running short, we may well just have to stop offering our special croissants altogether."

"Don't you *want* to make a profit?"

I couldn't believe how rude this woman was.

Fiona sighed, clearly working to keep her temper in check. "Why don't you try the Waitrose up the road, madam. Waitrose sells many varieties of croissants."

"I have no intention of going to a chain store. I believe in support-ing local, family-owned businesses."

"Would you be needing anything else today?" Fiona asked with exaggerated patience.

"No." Turning away sharply, the American left. Her bike helmet banged against the glass door as she went.

I approached the counter. "Sorry about that."

Fiona sighed once more. "You're American, as well?"

"Afraid so. May I have a gingerbread loaf, please?"

I waited for her to say that Americans were overrunning the neighborhood, but instead she chose one of the larger gingerbread loaves, placed it into a box, and tied the box with blue and white rib-bon, creating a lovely bow. She pulled the ends of the ribbon with scissors to make them curl.

"Thank you, that's very pretty."

She told me the price. I searched to find the right coins from what had become a weighty collection in my handbag, feeling exasperated because I still needed help with British money. Two-pound coins, one-pound, fifty pence . . . I held out my palm, and Fiona picked the cor-rect amount.

"Thanks again."

"Good day to you." Fiona busied herself rearranging the breads.

My fellow American was still outside, standing next to my bike, blocking my departure. Her own bike was propped against her hip as she spoke on the phone.

"Excuse me," I mouthed, trying to make my point without dis-turbing her call. I motioned toward my bike.

"I have to hang up, darling." From her tone, she was speaking with a child, not a lover. "I'll be home soon."

"Sorry to interrupt," I said, although I wasn't.

"You're American?"

Twice in five minutes. "Guilty as charged."

She studied me. "You're not by chance the American woman who's living at Ashton Hall?"

"I'm staying there for the summer," I said, trying to put her off.

"Does this mean you're the mother of the boy who found something so shocking that speculation is running wild? Police *and* archaeologists called in?"

So the news was already common knowledge, despite Mrs. Gardner's warnings about gossip. Again the image of the skeleton thrust itself at me, making me squint with a pain behind my eyes. A skeleton, a person, once as alive and filled with love and hope, anger and passion, as this American woman and me. Isabella Cresham. I made my voice smooth. "That was my son, yes."

"No one who knows the exact nature of the discovery is willing to divulge it."

She spoke as if she expected me to fill her in, but I wasn't going to, despite our shared nationality. "We're sworn to secrecy while the professionals determine the facts. How did you hear about it?"

"My husband and I were at the White Hart for dinner, and everyone was talking about it, even though no one knew the details. This is a small community, and generally nothing exciting happens. Your son was the toast of the pub. I'm Lizzie Moran." She pushed her hand at me, and I shook it. "My daughter's ill at home, an excuse for me to play hooky from my job. Although I can never truly play hooky." Grimacing with a smile, she held up her phone as if tempted to drop it into the trash. It was a much more technologically advanced model than mine.

"What's your job?" I asked.

"Such bliss, to be asked that question."

I'd asked without thinking.

"The British never ask, and you're not supposed to ask them, either," she said. "Haven't you noticed?"

"No. But I haven't been here very long."

"In addition to jobs, you're never supposed to ask them about their families, their friends, where they live, where they went to school, or anything relating in any way whatsoever to their lives before the instant they met you. And you must never, ever, introduce yourself to

British persons the way I just introduced myself to you. Instead, you must wait to be introduced by someone who knows you both."

No wonder Mrs. Gardner sometimes glanced away from me in dismay. Since my arrival, I'd probably violated dozens of unwritten rules.

"The single exception to these limitations is that you may ask them, after you've been introduced, about the scenery where they grew up. You must remember, however, to formulate this as a strictly geographical question, not a personal one, so that the answer becomes an opening into a discussion of the alluring landscape and riveting nonpersonal history of that particular place. They find discussions of landscape to be deeply compelling. Almost intimate."

She took a swig of water from the plastic bottle attached to the handlebars of her bike and resumed with even more zeal: "From all this stems their main gripe about Americans: So *friendly.* Always asking intrusive questions, such as, *What's your name?* So earnest about everything. So enthusiastic. They call us *enthusiasts.* And they don't mean it in a good way. But I embrace my American heritage, and I adore questions of a personal nature. So I'll tell you: I work in tech. In Silicon Fen."

I'd never heard of Silicon Fen and didn't want to expose my ignorance by inquiring. I was to learn later, after a quick internet search, that tech companies from around the world had decided to make Cambridge their European headquarters, resulting in the influx of thousands of workers. Cambridge was at the border of the Fens, a marshy, low-lying area that had been drained in the seventeenth century and transformed into the fertile farmland of today. Ergo, *Silicon Fen.*

"What type of work?" She didn't seem like the stereotypical IT geek.

"I found the exactly right job, interfering nag that I am. I'm the mother hen, big sister, and supportive auntie-you-can-confide-in for my company throughout the UK. I guarantee that everything is functioning well from day to day, that staff have proper visas and comfortable homes, schools for their children, office buildings with adequate air-conditioning in the summer *and* sufficient heat in the winter— a more difficult task than you might think, in this country—plus a snack room full of healthy or pretending-to-be-healthy treats. Baked, not fried, potato chips, and all savory snacks must be low-salt. I supervise HR, among other divisions."

"You must be a very powerful person," I said, half-jokingly.

"I do believe I am. Thank you for noticing," she said, grinning. Regarding me with a surprising openness, she added in a tone of self-mockery, "I'm so powerful I never hesitate to give advice, whether people want it or not."

"Someone has to."

"My thought exactly."

Despite the way she'd treated Fiona in the shop, I found myself liking her.

"How about you?" she asked. "What do you do?"

I knew many mothers caring for their children who answered *nothing* to this question. Even they didn't recognize their contribution to society. They were simultaneously told that raising children was the most important job they would ever do and that it wasn't a job at all. I didn't have to answer *nothing* to Lizzie Moran's question, because I had this: "I work for a company that licenses art images. The waist pack you're wearing, that's one I arranged."

She examined it. "My children gave it to me for Christmas last year. I've always liked it. I'm pleased to meet you. Another American in the village. Someone who means what she says and says what she means. Along with everything I've already outlined, most English people never say what they mean. At least not to acquaintances. Have you noticed? *There goes the crazy American* beneath the surface of every *good morning*? And they'll almost never invite you into their homes. We bring them our adoration, and they give us an ironic glance of dismissal."

Possibly Lizzie's personality elicited this reaction. "No, I haven't noticed."

"You will. Well, I should return to Josie. That's short for Josephine. Born during a brief posting in Paris. She's sixteen, old enough to be on her own recognizance, but she has a touch of the flu and a low-grade fever, and I can't let her slip into a television stupor. Or maybe I should let her slip into a television stupor. At any rate, I'll be a good mother and go home to her, since I've been out for an hour riding my bike. I'd planned to be an *extra*-good mother and bring her a treat."

"Would you like to take her a gingerbread loaf?" I held up the beribboned box.

"Was your son counting on it?"

"He has the entire café staff at the hall wrapped around his thumb, offering him crumpets, biscuits, miniature cakes, and four types of scones." I placed the box into the basket of Lizzie's bike.

"Thank you." She eyed me shrewdly. "You're very generous. I'll accept the gingerbread if you'll allow me to host you for afternoon tea sometime soon."

A possible friend. A fellow mother. An American, even if occasionally rude. "Thank you. I'd like that."

We exchanged phone numbers via text.

CHAPTER 14

On Sunday, July 12, the rain clouds broke at midday, turning the air sparkling as Nicky and I set off on our bikes for Chesterton. When we reached Midsummer Common, I rechecked the hand-drawn map Matthew Varet had made and left for me with Mrs. Gardner. Instead of a simple listing of directions, it was a detailed portrait of a specific place, with small drawings of the colleges, churches, cafés, and noteworthy trees we would pass.

The Midsummer Common was a green meadow stretching into the distance, and the sky above it seemed vast. Church steeples rose on the far sides. Brown cows grazed in the corners. Bicyclists crowded the paths, swerving around people on foot. Many of the cyclists had grocery bags strapped to their backs.

When the meadow came to an end, we followed the roadway along the Cam. On our side of the river, a multitude of roses bloomed in the front gardens of the terraced homes. On the opposite side, the college rowing clubs were arrayed along the water, their garage-like doors closed; the university wasn't in session. Nonetheless, the river was busy with scullers, the boats holding singles or two, four, or eight rowers, some boats with coxswains calling out instructions, others with terrified beginners struggling to keep their balance in their wobbling sculls. The river was also busy with swans, parents surrounded by gray cygnets. The swan families retreated to the reed-filled edges of the waterway as the scullers glided past. Lining our side of the river were grimy houseboats, long, low barges with household goods and garbage stored on their roofs, the opposite of romantic.

We reached Stourbridge Common, another enclosed meadow, and we entered it through a gate across a cattle grid. On the opposite side of the river, the ample gardens of large homes fronted the water.

Stourbridge Common was a place of legend. From the Middle Ages to the 1930s, trade fairs took place here, drawing vendors from across Europe. Traces remained in the names of surrounding streets, such as Garlic Row and Oyster Row. Nicky led the way, following the path along the river. I tried to project myself beyond today's meadow grass and trees into the past, to Isabella Cresham's era—the merchant stalls arranged in rows bustling with shoppers, who came here to buy everything from china and cloth to jewelry, glassware, books, spices, horses. Some visitors came simply for the entertainment, for the jugglers and musicians, the storytellers and traveling players, the dancing and food, and the excitement of new sights and sounds.

That is, I *would* have projected myself into Isabella's era. I wanted to. But cows required my immediate attention. These cows weren't drawn on the map, and they were different from the proper, polite, and most crucially faraway creatures of Midsummer Common. Here the cows were immense tan-and-white beasts, and they lounged on the paths. They regarded passersby with lazy curiosity. The odor of cow patties dominated the breeze. I wore open sandals. Given that cow patties were . . . everywhere, I prayed to the universe: *Don't let me lose my balance; don't let me fall from my bike. Please, not before lunch.*

Pedaling onward . . . I'd never known that cows were enormous, like ships on land. I'd never known that flies covered them. In fact, I'd never known anything at all about cows, not as individuals, like the one directly ahead of us, spread horizontally across the path. It lifted its colossal head to stare at me. Cautiously I rode my bike onto the grass, following Nicky's lead and giving the cow a wide berth. Did cows bite?

Stourbridge Common was crowded on this summer Sunday, everyone from infants in strollers pushed by their parents to the elderly with canes (*walking sticks*, as the British called them), out enjoying the day, taking the cows in stride.

Tonight on the phone, I'd tell Christopher about this trip. He might dub it the *cow crossing*, following up on the *croissant confrontation* of a few days earlier.

The map showed a footbridge across the river. At last, there it was. Most people continued along the river path.

A metal grid prevented the cows from crossing the footbridge. Nicky and I dismounted and pushed our bikes. At the middle of the bridge, I stopped to look at the view. Sunlight suffused the weeping willow trees that lined the riverbank. The water glistened. The rowers became part of the golden scene.

"That must be the pub that's on the map," Nicky said, pointing ahead. We walked on. The pub was decorated with pots of red-blooming geraniums hanging from pegs across the front. It was called the Roaring Dragon, and a drawing of exactly that was on the map.

Following the instructions, I turned left and spotted, about a block away, a tall, solid wood gate with a deer head positioned above it. This was the entry to *the big house*, as the map labeled it. The roofline of a large home was visible above the closed gate. Built beside the gate, its front door opening onto the street, was a plain, simple cottage, painted pale green. The cottage wasn't a traditional gatehouse, but from its position, I guessed it might originally have been a watchman's house or some type of staff housing for the big house.

We made our way up the street and knocked on the cottage door. A girl answered. She was taller than Nicky, with strawberry-blond curls that fell around her face. She would have been a vision of Victorian childhood virtue, if not for her frowning, disagreeable expression.

"May I help you?" she asked.

"We're here to eat lunch," Nicky said.

"You're the Americans?"

"We're Americans. Are we *the* Americans?" he asked me.

"Are you?" the girl demanded of me.

"I suppose we are," I said.

"In that case, I will take the liberty of introducing myself. How do you do?" She held out her hand in a parody of courteous behavior. "I'm Viola Varet."

The professor hadn't mentioned a girl named Viola. She pronounced it *VI-o-la*, and her last name *var-A*, as in *beret*. Nicky and I shook hands with her.

"You do realize you're twelve minutes and thirty-nine seconds late, according to the clock on the hob, which is always correct?"

I wasn't about to quibble with her, even though we'd been told to arrive between one and one fifteen, and we weren't late. From her concern with the time, so very familiar to me, I deduced that this must be Janet.

"We stopped to look at swans and at rowers." Nicky didn't inquire as to what a *hob* was; who knew where that might take us.

"When you had somewhere to be. When people were waiting for you and delaying their own lunches until you arrived."

"Sorry," Nicky said.

"You may not enter here with your bicycles. Kindly proceed to your right, to the entry to the side garden, and I shall open that gate." She shut the door on us.

Nicky and I made our way to the other side of the cottage, to a smaller wooden gate, this one without a deer head attached to it. Janet ushered us in. The so-called side garden was a roughly ten-foot-wide stone-paved alleyway between the cottage and a high boundary wall. Trees growing on the other side of the wall provided shade. On our left, a door led into the cottage. A wrought-iron table and three chairs had been arranged near the door. Farther down, several bicycles had been placed against the wall, and four formidable garbage bins were positioned beyond these.

As we walked our bikes along the alleyway to stash them, I noticed a length of firm green rubber tubing emerging from the wall of the cottage, about three feet off the ground. This tube extended outward to a point directly above a round hole in the paving. Water filled the hole. What appeared to be oatmeal floated in the water. Also what looked like pale-green toothpaste and soap suds. Sticks were propped against the cottage wall near the hole.

At the end of the alleyway was a sizable greenhouse.

We placed our bikes with the others.

"This way," Janet said. "Through the glasshouse. The others are in the garden."

We walked through the greenhouse, or glasshouse, which was now used for the storage of gardening supplies and lawn furniture.

"Here we are," Janet said when we emerged at the other side.

And *here* turned out to be a multi-acre paradise. Full-blooming white hydrangea bushes, five feet high, dominated all. A partially enclosed, flamboyantly designed gazebo stood near the Cam. An ancient-looking weeping willow grew on the riverbank, its leaves brushing the surface of the water. The garden shimmered from the sunlight reflecting off the river.

Facing onto this paradise, within shouting distance of where we stood, was the big house, its design box-like. Although it was much smaller than Ashton Hall, it was nonetheless a substantial residence.

"Hannah, Nicky—welcome!" I was pleased Matthew dispensed with formality and used my first name. Taking off his gardening gloves, he rose from beside a lavish flower bed where he and a child younger than Nicky had been working. "Thank you, Janet, for show-ing our guests the way."

Janet said, "May I introduce my sister, Rosamund, commonly called Rosie."

With her broad face and dusting of freckles, Rosie was a softer version of her sister.

"Let us walk around the garden, Master Nicholas. You, too, Rosamund."

"I'm busy," Rosie said.

"We must be polite to our guest. He longs to tour the garden."

"Do I?" Nicky said.

"If you don't, you should. We're waiting for you, Rosamund."

"Oh, all right." Rosie threw down her gardening gloves.

The children went off together, Nicky looking a bit overcome, Janet pointing out the flora and fauna.

"I hope your journey was easy," Matthew said.

"Easy enough. I wasn't expecting the cows."

"The Cambridge herd. Grazing rights dating back centuries." He paused. "Possibly I should have warned you. Drawn them on the map."

The sincerity and concern with which he said this made me laugh. "Possibly."

He seemed to relax, joining my laughter. "If it's any consolation, you can dine on them in the autumn, when they're butchered and the meat is sold at the market in the town square. Free-range beef: a delicacy."

"I'll give that a pass, now that I know the cows personally. And no harm done. I was able to keep my feet on the bike pedals through the worst of it."

"Glad to hear it." For a long moment, he studied Janet, Rosie, and Nicky as they made their tour of the flower beds. He turned to me, his eyes strained, and he seemed about to speak about the kids, but instead he said, "Shall we have lunch?" Without waiting for me to respond, he called the children back.

After some tumult of handwashing and platter-carrying, we arranged ourselves around the table in the gazebo beside the river. Matthew poured white wine for us both.

The kids were silent through the first course, chilled gazpacho. As often happened in my experience of meals with children, the adults used the silence as a moment to regain their strength, and Matthew and I said nothing. Kevin's British colleague, she of the *raising adults, not children* quip, would have had no patience with this lunch, even though the wine was a pleasurable midday treat.

The soup was delicious, and after a time I was refreshed enough to try the conversational gambit of expressing this.

"The soup is delicious."

"You could buy it, too. It's from Waitrose," Rosie said. "Not Tesco," she added with great seriousness. I caught the sparkle in Matthew's eyes as Rosie spoke.

"Thank you for telling me," I said.

The second course was a salad of curried chicken with apples and currants, also delicious, as I reported to the table.

"It's from Waitrose, too," Rosie said. "Daddy and Janet and I went shopping yesterday. We only go to Waitrose. We never go to Tesco."

"Tesco is fine, though," Matthew assured us. "Rather similar. In most respects."

I'd never been to Waitrose or Tesco. Alice organized the grocery shopping.

"Our mother says Tesco is too crowded," Rosie said.

Matthew didn't respond to this information about his former wife.

"I go to Waitrose with my babysitter," Nicky said, "and it's almost always crowded."

"Not the way Tesco is crowded," Rosie warned.

"Perhaps we'll go to Tesco next time," Matthew said. "There's one not far from here."

"I've never been to Tesco, either," Janet said, taking a break from her Viola persona to add her reflections. "All my friends say it's too crowded."

The Tesco–Waitrose distinction was clearly important. Possibly the entire class structure of Britain was represented by who went to Tesco and who went to Waitrose.

"What about the chocolate cake?" I asked. The cake was resting in glory upon a crystal stand on a side table.

"I baked the cake this morning," Rosie said with pride. "It has buttercream frosting."

"Daddy and I helped," Janet protested.

"We all pitched in," Matthew said, mollifying them.

A return to silence. After a suitable interval, Matthew said, "Has everyone finished? Yes? Rosie, why don't you, as the prime baker, slice the cake."

This required the reorganization of dishes and lengthy consideration as to proper cutting methods and slice sizes. Soon we each had a piece of cake before us. Nicky, Janet, and Rosie picked up their cake forks and began to eat with gusto. I tasted the frosting first. It was luscious.

When he finished his cake, Nicky asked Janet, "How do you spell your name?"

"*V-I-O-L-A.*"

"Her name is Janet," Rosie said. She licked frosting off her fork.

"That spells *vee-O-la*," Nicky said. "A viola is a musical instrument. Part of the violin family. My school gives music lessons, so I know."

"My name is not a type of violin. My name is a name and it's pronounced *VI-o-la.*"

"Her name is Janet," Rosie repeated.

"The name *VI-o-la* is from *Twelfth Night.*"

"What's *Twelfth Night*?" Nicky said.

"It's a play by William Shakespeare," Janet said, looking aghast. "Don't you know anything?"

"Nicky is younger than you are," Matthew said reasonably. "He's probably not read Shakespeare in school yet."

"I've read Shakespeare in school," Rosie said, "and I'm younger than he is."

"In America they do things differently," Matthew said.

"*Vee-O-la*," Nicky repeated.

"Nicky," I said. "Don't make fun of Janet's name."

"Her pretend name," Rosie said.

"*Vee-O-la*," Nicky said, baiting Janet. "*Vee-O-la.*"

"Nicky—" Was I going to have to find a place for him to have a time-out? Or take him home, another outing turned to disaster?

"You are such a rude boy," Janet said. "A naughty, horrible, rude boy."

"Thank you"—a gleam came into Nicky's eyes—"*Vee-O-la.*"

"Okay, time-out," I said, getting up.

"You're going to be sorry." Janet stood, and holding her chocolate-frosting-covered fork in her hand like a weapon, she rushed around the table toward him. I felt an explosion of fear.

Matthew was there in an instant, just as Janet reached out, intent on grabbing Nicky's shirt or hair, Nicky putting his hands over his head to protect himself—but before Matthew could intervene, Rosie said, "You're so predictable, Janet."

Janet froze, the fork grasped in her fist. "I am *not* predictable."

"Predictable and boring."

"I am *not* boring."

"You're not?" Rosie gestured as if to say, *Hasn't this happened before?*

Janet sniffled. She returned to her chair and began to cry, with an absence of drama that made me feel sorry for her.

Matthew and I sat down. I decided not to take Nicky for a time-out. The chocolate-frosting-covered fork had made its point, and apparently Matthew had decided that Rosie's put-down of her sister was more effective than any discipline he could give. The fear I'd felt when Janet was rushing toward Nicky: For the first time, I understood the perspective of other parents as they saw Nicky lose control and go after their children.

"Would you like coffee?" Matthew said to me. I heard the weariness in his voice.

"Thank you, I would."

He stood and announced to the table, "We're going into the cottage to make coffee. You can stay outside, but don't go near the river."

"We'll be practicing our lines," Janet said, her tears forgotten. "I've prepared a scene from *Macbeth* to perform for you."

"Wonderful," I said, trying to sound sincere. "I look forward to it."

"I'm the best student in my form," Janet said.

"Don't brag," Rosie snapped.

Sighing, Matthew picked up a tray of leftovers, and so did I. We walked across the garden and toward the cottage. I looked over my shoulder. The kids were sitting in the gazebo, declaiming their lines. Was I taking a risk, leaving Nicky alone with Janet?

Matthew must have sensed my concern because he said, "Sorry. Rosie may think otherwise, but Janet is in fact rarely physically aggressive."

I was relieved. "Well, Nicky was taunting her," I said.

"That doesn't excuse it. But I'd be shocked if it happened again." He stopped walking and faced me. "You don't think Janet's spoilt, do you?"

Given Lizzie Moran's evaluation of the British as being reluctant to share personal information, his candor surprised me. "People express that opinion about Nicky. I don't think he is."

"My dad advises a good smacking. Although she's too old for that now. My dad regrets the good smackings not given to her in the past." I could sense his pain.

"I don't know about here in Cambridge," I said, "but in New York City, giving a child a good or any other type of *smacking* could get you arrested."

"Here, too, most likely. I don't want to test it." He looked anguished. "The sad fact is, my dad refuses to accept Janet for who she is. If she'd been born with a physical challenge, he'd be one hundred percent supportive and helping in any way he could. He'd be indignant if anyone criticized her. But because her differences are neurological, psychological, he condemns her *and* her parents. This goes for many, if not most, of my friends."

"I know. The same for me." I could let myself say this to him; I could let myself confess. "Sometimes I just feel, well, brokenhearted, for Nicky, and for myself. I try so hard . . ."

"And everyone has an opinion about what you're doing wrong. Janet has good and generous sides to her, too, not that many people recognize them. This past term, she helped her fellow students memorize their lines for *As You Like It*, the school play. Apparently she was a strict taskmaster, drilling them each for hours, and with an attitude I'm told didn't earn her any friends, but on the night of the performance, no lines were mangled or dropped, no one stared into space for long, painful moments waiting for someone to shout the next words . . . quite a switch from typical student Shakespeare productions, in my experience. Rather a fair bit of pride in our household over this. She gave up the opportunity to take a role herself, to help her classmates."

He sounded choked up, and abruptly he turned and walked on, ahead of me. After a moment, he called over his shoulder, "Coffee will help." He'd already retreated into his more customary detached and ironic British manner.

We entered the kitchen, a room that looked familiar from countless television shows and films—an English country kitchen, with a beamed ceiling and a plank floor shiny from centuries of use. A vase of white hydrangeas was on the verge of toppling from the mantelpiece. A hutch displayed blue-and-white patterned china, which appeared to be extensively chipped. Two windows brought light into the room. The floor tilted downward toward the far side, such that the second window was about five inches lower than the first, giving a skewed view of the garden wall on the opposite side of the street.

Sooner than I would have thought possible, as Matthew was searching for a serving tray for the coffeepot and cups, Janet was at the kitchen door.

"The actors are ready. Audience members, please take your seats. The performance will begin in three minutes in the side garden."

We went outside. Matthew put the tray onto the wrought-iron

table, and we sat down. He poured our coffee. It was strong, a good balance to the chocolate cake.

Coffee grounds now floated in the round hole, along with the oatmeal and toothpaste. Matthew had rinsed the container after grinding the beans. What could the hole be? A cesspool? A sewer? I couldn't help wondering. Thankfully, I didn't see any evidence of the toilet emptying into it.

The children had put sweaters over their shoulders, as costumes. Each picked up a stick from the pile next to the hole. Surely the toilet couldn't empty into it, if the children were using the hole as a prop in their playacting. But this was England, where anything could happen.

Janet announced, "We're performing Act Four, Scene One, of *Macbeth*, the opening section. Here are two production notes for your consideration: First, I removed every negative reference to people who are different from us, because at our school it's a rule that we don't say bad things about people who are different from us."

"At your school is it okay to say bad things about people who are the same as us?" Nicky asked hopefully, as if he'd enjoy attending such a school.

"Quiet. Second, in the original version of the play, the characters in this scene discuss committing acts of cruelty against animals. Because I love animals, including toads and lizards, and I believe in not being cruel to animals, ever—although I'm not a vegetarian, because that's not the same—I've taken the liberty of deleting some lines and rewriting others."

I had to admire her self-confidence.

"Curtain up. The setting is a cavern. In the middle of the cavern is a boiling cauldron." They began stirring the pool with the sticks.

JANET/VIOLA:
　　"Thrice the brinded cat hath mew'd.
　　Thrice and once the hedge-pig whined.
　　Harpier cries 'Tis time, 'tis time."

"What does that mean?" Nicky said. "It's nonsense words."

"It's Shakespeare. When you're British, it makes sense. To resume:"

JANET/VIOLA:
   "Round about the cauldron go;
   In the coffee grounds we throw.
   Tomatoes coming on to rot,
   Boil thou first in the charm-ed pot."

JANET/VIOLA, ROSAMUND, NICKY:
   "Double, double toil and trouble;
   Fire burn, and cauldron bubble."

JANET/VIOLA:
   "Fillet of dinner steak,
   In the cauldron boil and bake;
   Add shampoo to make a soapy stew,
   And so create a brothy brew."

I bit my lip, trying to stop myself from laughing. Her rewrites were brilliant.

JANET/VIOLA, ROSAMUND, NICKY:
   "Double, double toil and trouble;
   Fire burn and cauldron bubble."

JANET/VIOLA:
   "Crumbs of crumpets, dollops of jam,
   Many a biscuit, but never a ham."

"Why not ham?" Nicky asked.

"Shut up."

"Janet, watch your language," Matthew said.

"Sorry," she said.

"I like ham," Nicky said.

With a tremendous sigh, Janet said, "Rhymes with *jam*, can't you hear it?"

Nicky's eyes widened as if he'd experienced a revelation. "I do hear it: *jam* and *ham*."

"And the phrase matches the cadence and rhyme scheme of the previous line," Janet said. "It's called poetry. To continue:"

JANET/VIOLA:
 "Soon we'll go to Saffron Walden,
 And collect more ingredients for our cauldron."

JANET/VIOLA, ROSAMUND, NICKY:
 "Double, double toil and trouble;
 Fire burn and cauldron bubble."

"Time for our bows," Janet said.

Leaving their sticks in the pool, they bowed.

Matthew and I clapped. "Well done," he said. "Very well done, indeed. Brava, Janet. Marvelously clever."

Giving her father a broad grin, Janet bowed once more.

"What's Saffron Walden?" Nicky asked.

"It's a place. A town. Nearby. They used to grow saffron there. As you probably don't know," Janet said, "saffron is a spice. And a dye to make things yellow. And a medicine."

"It's where our mother lives," Rosie said, without any indication of distress about her parents' divorce.

"I like Shakespeare," Nicky said. "Now that I understand him better. I like the things Shakespeare is thinking about and the way he thinks them. I want to rhyme *ham* with *jam*. I want to learn more Shakespeare."

"I'll teach you," said Janet, world-weary, faced with a chore she felt duty-bound to take on. "You may enter the downstairs sitting room, also called the drawing room, and I will teach you Shakespeare."

"Let's all stay outside," Matthew said. "Before you do anything else, though, remove the sticks and place them where they belong against the wall. We also need to bring in the rest of the dishes from the gazebo."

"Then I'll finish the weeding," Rosie said. "I promised Mrs. Chatfield. She said she'd give me my tea afterwards. With lemon cake. You know how delicious her lemon cake is."

"Two cakes in one day for you, then?"

She gave him a beatific smile.

In due course, we'd rearranged ourselves, Rosie gardening, Nicky and Janet in the gazebo reciting Shakespeare from Janet's school editions, Matthew and I sitting in lawn chairs we'd dragged under a London plane tree that, judging from the circumference of the trunk, must have been several hundred years old.

This was normal. Children amusing themselves. Giving their elders a moment to breathe.

After I'd caught my breath, I was ready to engage Matthew Varet in conversation and to break through the humorous detachment that had been in effect ever since our discussion of the kids. But how? He seemed content to stretch his legs before him and enjoy the dappled sunlight. If Lizzie Moran was correct, he wasn't going to ask me about myself, and I wasn't supposed to ask him about himself, either.

Yet he'd been frank and forthcoming about Janet and about his father. I didn't want to keep talking about the kids, though. There must be a middle ground for the British, between silence and unfiltered disclosure. I already knew his profession, so presumably asking about it was within the boundaries of courtesy.

"Do you often receive calls to examine skeletons?"

"I daresay not often enough," he said.

His drollness sounded, to my earnest American ears, inappropriate, given that we were discussing a dead body, unless he simply meant that the call to examine a skeleton had led to our acquaintance.

"I have a confession," I said. "When Nicky showed me the hidden room, he disobeyed the rules and took the letters out of the keepsake box. We learned that the woman's name was Isabella Cresham."

He sat up, completely serious now. "The Cresham family owned the estate for generations."

"I remember Mrs. Gardner telling us. I'm sorry, I know we weren't supposed to touch anything. We put the letters back carefully."

"What's done is done." He waved it off. "So . . . Isabella Cresham."

"Just between the two of us, off the record, what's your opinion on how she ended up there?"

"Honestly, I don't know. We've much more to learn. Every case is different. *This* individual, *this* setting."

"I keep wondering . . ." I didn't know where to begin.

"Tell me what you wonder," he said, sitting at the end of his chair, leaning toward me. "No matter how far-fetched. I say to my students, let your speculation go everywhere. Afterwards you can narrow your ideas down to what's plausible. In the process, you might stumble upon a truth you'd never considered."

His words gave me confidence. I tried to shape the confusion of images pulsing through my mind. "First . . . I wonder how she got there. She might have been dragged to the room screaming, with three men pulling her up the stairs. Or she might have walked resolutely, chin high, accepting what she considered her fate or God's will. I wonder *why* she was there. Maybe because of revenge, or spite. Or to punish her. She'd been judged uncontrollable by her family. She'd had an affair, or she'd been attracted to women or dressed as a man."

"All possibilities," he said. "What else?"

"Her husband might have placed her there because he'd fallen in love with someone else. Or if she couldn't have children, he might have cast her aside because she was barren."

"And?"

"If she had an infectious disease—plague, leprosy—she might have been quarantined there. A servant might have been well paid to take care of her from a distance and keep her condition secret."

"The more-advanced scientific tests will tell us about infectious diseases, to some extent. I expect the results to begin coming in next week."

"I wish we had some way to gain access to her inner life," I said. "Her thoughts and feelings. Maybe she was a mystic, and the commonplace books will prove it."

"There is another possibility," he said, his tone somber, "one that none of us wants to be true, but we do have to include it: She might very well have been mentally unstable. What we would call schizophrenic or psychotic. Today we have medications to help, but in past centuries, caring humanely for the unstable was almost impossible. In that room, she could be sheltered."

No, I thought. I didn't want her to be unstable, another version of the madwoman in the attic in *Jane Eyre*. "It didn't seem like the room of someone who was psychotic or schizophrenic. It was neat and well ordered," I said, trying to convince him.

"Those characteristics might actually have been part of her instability," he said, making his point quietly, without trying to dominate or assert his greater authority and knowledge. "Above all else, though, we need to reach a more precise time frame so we can determine the official religion in the year she died."

"I have to tell you: Someone looked at the coins. Saw the date."

He laughed. "True confessions. Out it all pours."

"I don't want to get anyone into trouble. I wouldn't have mentioned it, except you brought up the time frame."

"While the cat's away, et cetera," he said, with a resigned yet playful shake of his head.

"Exactly."

"All right, then. Tell me."

"The coins are dated 1582."

"During the reign of Elizabeth. The Protestants triumphant. That makes the Catholic artifacts—the rosary, and the statue of the Virgin and Child—into stronger evidence. The coins are one proof amongst many, however," he added quickly. "I'm not ready to conclude she was a Catholic martyr."

"I wasn't raised with faith. I have trouble comprehending that kind of passion—sacrificing your life, unwilling to compromise."

"I can understand some of that fervor. I was raised in the Catholic church, but I lapsed from it years ago." He glanced away. "When my sisters were roughly the same age as our kids, teenagers threw rocks at them as they walked to school."

"What do you mean? Why?"

"This was in the mid-1980s, during the Troubles, a time of bombings and vicious attacks. We grew up near Leicester. My sisters had stones thrown at them because our family was Catholic. The kids who did it no doubt associated Catholics with the IRA, but we're not Irish; we can trace the family lineage back centuries in England—not that that's an excuse."

"How did they know your sisters were Catholic?"

"Because of the school uniforms."

"Did that happen to you?"

"No, I was the son of the family, so I was sent away for school. I'm also younger, and gradually the hostilities calmed."

I was shocked. I'd never heard about such things happening in England.

"Stoning," he reflected. "A biblical punishment. How do you mean, you weren't raised with faith?" he suddenly demanded. "That's unusual. Especially unusual in America, I should think."

I told him about my mother escaping to England with other Jewish children as part of the Kindertransport and about my grandparents being murdered near the end of the war. "My mother had a productive life, but I suspect some part of her never recovered from what happened to her family."

"That's a terrible story. I'm sorry."

"I always knew I had Jewish heritage, but we never went to synagogue or observed the Jewish holidays. Maybe my mother thought God had betrayed her. She never said."

"There remains the question of how to go on, without faith," he said. "How to raise children, and exist from day to day."

"How have you solved that problem?" I asked.

"By not thinking about it," he said. I expected he would laugh, that his words were meant ironically, but he was dead serious. "And you? How have you solved it?"

"It's never been a problem for me, I suppose because I wasn't raised with a mental framework of religious faith. I never had to reject it. I never find myself longing for the answers faith is expected to provide. The world has always been this way for me."

"So you just get on with things, finding connection where you can."

"What other choice do we have?"

He studied me. I felt as if we'd leapt over months of conversation in a few minutes, sharing too much for people—British or American—who'd only just become acquainted. The breeze picked up, churning in the dense leaves above us.

I needed to change the subject. But I found I couldn't steer clear of the personal. "How did you come to live here?" I asked.

He waited before replying—making up his mind about whether to move on from our discussion of faith, I thought. Finally he said, "This is the neighborhood's cottage for estranged husbands." Leaning back, stretching out his legs, he resumed what seemed a more comfortable demeanor for him, too. "A furnished way station before either a return to domestic bliss or the beginning of a new life. When my turn came to occupy the cottage for what I presumed would be the typically brief duration, I found I liked it. Mr. and Mrs. Chatfield, in the big house, are getting on in years. They've given me permission to use the garden—in fact they encourage me to—and I enjoy pottering about. With their children living in London, they're pleased to have someone steady and close by to look in on them. The cottage is comfortable enough, depending on one's definition of comfort. I keep my books and work paraphernalia at my office at the college, so I don't mind the meager furnishings. You've seen most of the downstairs already. I'll give you a full tour later if you like."

That was an unexpected invitation. Kevin once told me that men can't help it, they're sexually evaluating women (or other men, or men and women both—possibilities that Kevin didn't go to the trouble of mentioning) constantly. It was their biological nature. Their *wiring*. Kevin had always been my expert in men: He knew a lot about them. More than I'd ever imagined possible.

Had Matthew Varet already evaluated me? The possibility seemed . . . outside the realm of possibility. I hadn't thought of him beyond his profession and as a fellow parent. I hadn't done online research about him before coming here. I'd never truly looked at him— looked at him to actually *see* him.

Now I did look at him. Sharp-edged features. Dark eyes. Brown hair that was combed back and graying at the temples. His Vandyke-style beard was touched by gray, too. He had a way of relaxing in absolute, confident self-possession. Unlike Kevin, Matthew wasn't precisely the Hermes of Andros—he'd undoubtedly made a few more visits to the Roaring Dragon pub than Hermes had—but his quickness and wit made me feel fully awake in the moment.

Not that I was going to act on the fact that I found Matthew Varet attractive. I simply recognized it. But I'd assumed that if I was without Kevin, I'd never find anyone else. Now I realized the world might, just might, offer me other chances.

"Are you enjoying your sojourn on *this scepter'd isle?*" he asked.

"Shakespeare's *Richard the Second*."

"I knew you'd recognize the quotation," he said, making me smile at his certainty that Americans did, in fact, know Shakespeare.

"Originally I came here to help care for an ill relative who lives in one of the apartments at Ashton Hall. But he returned to America for medical treatment. My husband is away from home anyway, working on a legal case"—I skirted the truth about my marriage—"so being here turned out to be for the best. Ashton Hall is very beautiful."

"Yes, it is. Where did you grow up?"

"A city in New York State called Buffalo."

"I've heard of it. What's the scenery like there?"

Lizzie had mentioned the British predilection for discussing scenery. "It's on the shores of Lake Erie, which is like an inland sea. Much of the city was designed by Frederick Law Olmsted, who visualized it as a city inside a park. It has important historic architecture, too."

His question about the scenery somehow reminded me to ask a question I'd been pondering ever since Janet opened the gate to the cottage's side garden:

"I don't mean to pry, but what on earth is that hole filled with water in the alleyway?"

"I was wondering if you'd ask about it." He regarded me with an openhearted amusement that made me feel immensely fortunate to be sitting beside him. "It's a not-uncommon arrangement for houses built before indoor plumbing. This cottage was constructed in the 1640s. The toilet has its own line, connected to the sewer system, in case you were wondering," he acknowledged with a roguish grin, "but the other water leaving the house flows out of the tube into the open drain. Because of my work, I'm only too familiar with such makeshift plumbing. Nowadays many people in the UK have never seen such an arrangement and might insist no such drain exists, given that they've never seen it."

"How lucky I am, to be among those who know better."

"Yes, you are lucky in that way," he said. "This arrangement is called a *French drain*."

"What a remarkable expression. At one stroke it manages to both denigrate the French *and* elevate the drain."

"An exquisitely British linguistic feat. The drain requires stirring every day. If one cooks red meat, stirring the drain twice a day is advisable."

"What happens in the winter, when the temperature falls below freezing?" I asked. "Does the water in the pool freeze?"

"You've identified an important issue. Indeed, you've gone right to the heart of the matter. We have methods for dealing with French drains in such circumstances."

"Which are?"

"I'll let you see for yourself, when it's winter."

CHAPTER 15

In Ashton Hall's book-conservation center, I sat at a workstation with the volumes from Isabella Cresham's desk arrayed before me. Martha Tinsley had been encouraging me to volunteer, and today I did. I would try, step by step, to learn who Isabella Cresham was in life, not simply in death.

I reached for the largest, showiest volume. The binding was white and embossed with decorative patterns. With a jolt, I realized: Isabella must have touched this, held it in her hands. I felt a tingling in my fingertips. My heart beat faster. We were linked, two women, across the centuries.

The spine showed no title. The volume was about thirteen inches high, eight inches wide, and three inches thick. With care, I placed it in the book cradle, a kind of wedged pillow used to support the spines of rare books when they're opened. Finding the volume's title page, I read: *Thesaurus Ciceronianus, by Marius Nizolius*. It was a guide to the

Latin of Cicero, essentially a dictionary, and it was more than a thousand pages long. I wrote a basic catalog entry for it on my laptop, following Dr. Tinsley's instructions.

Turn every page was the research mantra I'd been taught, and I began doing so. Gloves weren't used in Ashton Hall's conservation center. This was an area of debate, and I agreed with Dr. Tinsley's opinion: Clean, dry hands were less hazardous to fragile materials than were gloved ones. I began to search for underlinings and annotations, anything Isabella might have left behind, any proof that she'd actually read the book. After all, I often left remnants of myself throughout my books. Exclamation points for passages I loved. Squiggly lines when I disagreed with what the author wrote. Three-by-five cards with notes, in books I used for research. In novels, postcards or other impromptu bookmarks, which I often forgot about, rediscovering them years later when I happened to take the book off the shelf and they dropped out, bringing with them memories of cozy Sunday afternoons on the sofa reading with Kevin, before Nicky was born.

Annotations filled the *Thesaurus Ciceronianus*, in the handwriting of several different readers. I didn't know Isabella's script and had no way of determining if any of the markings were hers. The edition dated from 1548, and presumably many in the household would have had access to it.

The volume was a clue in the mystery story that was her life, if only I could figure out how to interpret it. Was she obsessed with the writings of Cicero? Had she read Latin dictionaries for fun? I still didn't want to think Matthew Varet was correct and she'd been psychotic or schizophrenic.

Dr. Tinsley sat nearby, making her way through a stack of unbound yellowed documents from the so-called parish chest. This was the large wooden trunk, covered with iron braces and locks, that had been found in the newly discovered muniment room, thanks to Nicky. He had told me the history: Beginning in 1538, during the reign of Henry VIII, local parishes were required to register marriages, baptisms, and burials. Often the priest would also keep a record of the church's financial expenditures. These documents were placed in the parish chest, which was kept in the church—except our church's parish chest for the Tudor and early Stuart periods had been presumed lost. Now we knew that for reasons unknown, possibly after a fire in the church or during a time of political upheaval, it had been brought to the muniment room of Ashton Hall.

By law, the records in a parish chest belonged to the county, and Mrs. Gardner had reported our discovery. At some point, the county archivists would come to retrieve them, keeping the documents out of circulation for months until they could be processed and bound. In the meantime, Dr. Tinsley was reviewing them as quickly as possible, searching for evidence.

Despite the murmur of conversation among the several graduate students working on the far side of the room, the conservation center was quiet. No joking or teasing. No coffee cups on the tables. The center possessed high-tech digital microscopes, along with large-format computer screens. Venting tubes hung suspended from the ceiling. Stainless-steel sinks, broad and shallow, reflected the soft light from two incongruous chandeliers. Labeled containers of chemicals filled glass cabinets. In one area, there were large wooden frames and other equipment for bookbinding.

All this was held within a stately room decorated with ornate moldings and bearing a Georgian-era magnificence. The technological sophistication of the center was surprising, both because of the setting and the ample funds that would have been necessary to set it up—and because we were the only people there. The furloughs must have been more extensive than Mrs. Gardner had let on that evening when we walked across the grounds.

I reached for the next book. *De Imitatione Christi*, by Thomas à Kempis, in Latin, a printed edition from 1489, so already quite old when Isabella Cresham read it. This was a volume of Catholic devotion, treasured through centuries. She might have read it as part of her daily religious practice, taking solace from it as she knelt at the prie-dieu, propping the book on the tilted top shelf. The printing of this edition was lovely, with lines of red decorating the capital letters. The book was well used, the margins of the paper softened and discolored from the many hands that had held it, but the pages contained no annotations or underlinings.

The next volume was an abecedarium, a hand-illuminated presentation of the alphabet. Each letter was shaped with and surrounded by multicolored designs—geometric vines, extravagant flowers, dragons, and lions. I'd studied medieval books as part of my distribution requirements in graduate school. Basically, an abecedarium was intended to teach the alphabet, but it could also be a pattern book that artists copied. This volume repeated each letter in several different styles. Most likely, then, it was a pattern book. Why did this interest her?

Mrs. Gardner came in to the center. She held a black binder. "Ah, Ms. Larson," she said when she spotted me, apparently viewing the center as a public setting that called for the use of formal names. "I'm pleased to see you here."

"Dr. Tinsley invited me to volunteer, so here I am."

"Exactly where you belong. You're Mr. Eckersley's ward. Your son is the Finder. Ashton Hall is your home, and your presence is, I would go so far as to say, required."

I was moved as Mrs. Gardner said this, accepting me and giving me her trust, although I wasn't here for the house, or for Nicky, but for myself.

Mrs. Gardner established herself in the middle of the room, taking on the role of commander. "Dr. Tinsley, where do we stand?"

Dr. Tinsley pulled out a pad from the materials on her workstation and checked her notes. "With help from Professor Varet's graduate students, I've finished transferring all the documents from the muniment room. The materials are somewhat disorganized, and I've asked the students to create a detailed inventory, which will be a time-consuming project. As for myself, I'm reading the documents from the parish chest, as you requested."

"What of Isabella Cresham's letters and the commonplace books and other items on her desk?"

"Ms. Larson and I can handle the letters and books, but the commonplace volumes are in fragile condition." Dr. Tinsley motioned to several gray acid-free boxes lying flat on the counter along the wall, boxes that now protected the commonplace books. "I'll need to engage a specialist to reinforce and repair them. The volumes are actually sketchbooks."

This caught my interest. "Sketchbooks? What did she draw?"

"Family pets—primarily dogs but also the occasional cat. Horses. Birds. Informal family portraits. The flowers in the garden."

So much for my speculation that Isabella Cresham was a mystic, or that the commonplace books would somehow reveal her inner life through diary entries or other reflections, but at least this explained why she had an abecedarium: She was interested in art, a piece of evidence to place on my list.

"Quality of her work?" Mrs. Gardner said.

"Because of their fragile condition, I gave the volumes only a cursory review, but over time she developed into a competent amateur."

"Did she, then. I enjoyed a bit of sketching when I was young. Right. I received a surprise this morning." Mrs. Gardner held up the binder. "A preliminary analysis, prepared by the university archaeology department, of Isabella Cresham's body. Professor Varet has provided a translation for the less scientifically fluent amongst us." Unexpectedly, Mrs. Gardner's shoulders sagged, as if the wind had gone out of her sails. "Some of it is rather difficult reading."

I felt a nervousness creeping through me, for what might be revealed. I grabbed my pen to make notes.

Mrs. Gardner opened the report. "First off, we've been given an age range of thirty-five to forty-five years. By today's standards, she was in the prime of life."

Isabella Cresham was roughly my age when she died. The disturbing bond I felt with her became closer. As I jotted down the details, I listened carefully, trying to bring her image into focus.

"Her dental health would be considered better than average for that era. She suffered no skeletal damage from vitamin or iron

deficiencies. No signs of physical trauma, of fractures, healed or un-
healed. That is to say, no broken bones at any time during her life."

So she hadn't been beaten to death or tortured. At least not tortured in any way that left a mark on her body. Being imprisoned in the
hidden room was, of course, a kind of torture.

"Via the study of a chemical called oxygen-18—which, if I'm understanding this correctly, is absorbed by teeth and hair from drinking
water—the scientists have determined that she lived in this general geographic area all her life. From the level of nitrogen-15 in her bones, they
conclude that she consumed a good deal of animal protein, which includes meat, dairy, and also freshwater fish, and more specifically, in her
case, venison and pork. This is termed a *high-status diet*."

"Can they tell if she was on a more restrictive diet toward the end
of her life?" I asked.

"The professor explains that teeth and leg bones are slow-growing
and provide a long-term view of diet over decades, but ribs are continually regenerating, and one can make conclusions about recent diet
from analyzing the ribs. Isabella Cresham enjoyed a high-status diet
through to her death."

"Infectious diseases?" I asked.

"I seem to recall a section . . ." She searched for it. "A test called a
microbial detection array can determine if an individual died of certain
infectious diseases, by searching for traces of DNA from the infectious
microbes. Isabella Cresham did not have bubonic plague, cholera, tu-
berculosis, or leprosy. Other tests are listed as well, and"—she tapped
her fingers against the report—"I'm afraid I'm unable to follow all of
this, but there seems to be no evidence of smallpox. Or syphilis. The
next detail I must share is somewhat distasteful"—her brows came
together in a frown—"although it's merciful, too: The chamber pot
did *not* contain any evidence of . . . precisely what, I prefer not to think
about."

"I hope this never happens to me," Dr. Tinsley broke in, her voice
solemn. "Someone examining me like this. Sifting through the inner-
most aspects of my body."

I felt a complicated set of emotions—needing to know these intimate details in order to understand who she was, yet despising myself once again for violating her privacy.

"Here's a section about her hair: Scientifically speaking, we mustn't read too much into the fact that she appeared to have reddish hair. The hair pigment pheomelanin, which many people have to some extent, and which does create red hair when it's present in high amounts, is more stable than other pigments. As other pigments break down over time, pheomelanin could create a red-haired effect in the skeletons of people who didn't actually have red hair when they were alive. Nonetheless"—Mrs. Gardner glanced at us with a touch of mischief—"I prefer to think of her with red hair in life. The Isabella Cresham of my imagination possesses all the spunk redheads tend to have, and I shall not be persuaded to think otherwise."

"In the Middle Ages, red hair was considered the mark of the devil," Dr. Tinsley said matter-of-factly, pulling out the information automatically from her storehouse of knowledge and inadvertently spoiling Mrs. Gardner's vision of Isabella Cresham. And yet . . . the old superstition might have contributed to what happened to Isabella. It might have caused her persecutors to assume the worst about her.

"So it was," Mrs. Gardner acknowledged. "I must admit I'm somewhat . . . troubled by the conclusion that she lived her entire life on this estate. I'd assumed she would have spent several of her adolescent years in another household, training to be a lady. This was typical in the education of *high-status* girls during that era. I hope there was no . . . difficulty preventing her from following along in the usual way of her peers."

Mrs. Gardner must be wondering, as I was, whether Isabella had been a child like her younger son or like Nicky.

"Perhaps she went to live at a noble house nearby," Dr. Tinsley said hopefully, as if to console Mrs. Gardner, "a place where the mineral content of the water was similar."

"I suppose that's possible," she said. "Perhaps we'll find some indication of it in the various documents."

"This report," I said, frustrated. "It tells us about her body, but it doesn't tell us anything about her personality and character. We don't know if she loved to dance. If she had lots of friends or was a loner. Introvert or extrovert. Thoughtful or impetuous. Whether she enjoyed the music she played on the virginal, and the sketches she made, or practiced those skills only because they were required of a woman of her station. From this report, we know almost nothing about her at all."

I was surprised by my own vehemence, and I realized I'd possibly been rude. "I'm sorry, I'm just trying to understand . . ." I let my words drift off, as my feelings got the better of me.

"As are we all," Mrs. Gardner said. "Trying to understand. No need for apologies."

"And you're right, Hannah," Dr. Tinsley said. "There's still so much we don't know. We don't know if she ever loved someone. Man or woman. Or if she was raped in that room, before the wall was completed." Her voice caught.

Mrs. Gardner, inscrutable, studied us both for a moment and then moved on. "Here's one final piece of evidence. It says that if a woman gives birth, the inside of her pubic bone will show what are termed *parturition pits*. These are the result of the tearing of ligaments during the birth trauma. I never knew this."

I'd never known it, either.

"Isabella Cresham's skeleton shows no parturition pits. The conclusion is that she did not give birth."

Mrs. Gardner left us.

Martha Tinsley returned to her documents. I reached for the final volume from the stack of books that had been on Isabella's desk. This volume was roughly six by four inches, small enough to rest comfortably in my hand. The binding was brown leather, scuffed at the edges. I opened it. Inside: Acrobats performed, and jugglers. Fanciful creatures played musical instruments. A falcon frolicked in a birdbath.

These pictures, and dozens more, surrounded a central text written in Latin. Illustrations also filled the capital letters of each section of text. A unicorn nestled against a maiden, both held safe within the oval of the letter *O*. A cat stretched on the crossbar of the letter *A*.

It was a medieval psalter, a type of prayer book. This one, with its small size, must have been designed for private devotions rather than use in church. As with the abecedarium, I was familiar with these books from my studies. This volume was astonishing, the pictures executed in still-vibrant colors, through multiple shades of red, blue, green. Details painted with gold glittered across the pages. Nowadays such books might be geared toward children, but in the Middle Ages such whimsically illustrated prayer books were highly valued by the wealthy patrons who commissioned them.

Suddenly I was far from the stainless-steel sinks and large-format computer screens, gazing over Isabella Cresham's shoulder as she read the book in the candlelight while kneeling at the prie-dieu. She adjusted the pages to make the gold leaf shine. A red-robed woman played the harp. Rabbits nibbled in gardens. This book was a masterpiece of its type, possibly worth tens of thousands of dollars today. Isabella, or her family, must have paid a fortune for it.

"Dr. Tinsley," I said. "This is something we should look at together."

She joined me. Turning the pages one by one, I showed her. Around the prayers, knights in armor jousted. Boys flew kites.

"This reminds me of the Luttrell Psalter, one of the very greatest works of medieval illumination," she said. I heard the admiration and awe in her voice. She touched a fingertip against the edge of the pages. "The Luttrell Psalter was made in the first half of the fourteenth century, in Lincolnshire, the county to the north of us. This volume looks as if it was created by the same scribe and some of the same artists. The images are similar."

A mouse with wings took flight.

"I'm also reminded of the Macclesfield Psalter. It sold at Sotheby's some years ago for over 1.7 million pounds!"

So this volume, once read by Isabella Cresham, might be of similar value.

Sheep snuggled together for warmth in the snow.

We reached the end. I turned the final page.

And there, pushed into the hinge between the pastedown and the end paper, was a drawing, about four by five inches. It was a skillfully done portrait of a girl around five years old. Dark, straight hair. Wide cheekbones. Round eyes. The artist hadn't paid much attention to her clothes, just enough to indicate a high-necked dress. In one hand, the girl held a rough-hewn doll, cradling it against her chest. In the other hand, she held a quill pen. She sat in a child-sized chair beside a child-sized table. On the table were an inkwell and a sheet of paper on which she'd been practicing simple words. *Dog. Cow. Cat.* She stared up at the artist with an intense, questioning gaze.

Written at the bottom of the sheet, in the large, wide printing of a child just learning to write, were the words *This is me. Blanche.*

CHAPTER 16

At the famed Orchard Tea Garden in Grantchester, just across the river from Ashton Hall, I found a table in the shade of the apple trees. Brushing crumbs and brown curled-up leaves onto the grass, I waited for Lizzie Moran to bring our order. The chairs were canvas recliners, *deck chairs,* the name evocative of transatlantic voyages on luxurious steamships. It was a type of chair I hated, designed to force you to relax whether you wanted to or not. The type used at the Orchard Tea Garden didn't even have armrests for, say, placing a cup of tea. Bird droppings lined the tops of the chairs, but I did find two that were at least marginally acceptable.

On the plus side, the temperature was in the high sixties, the sky preternaturally clear on this mid-July day. The abundant still-green apples weighed down the branches of the trees. Lizzie had taken the afternoon off from work so that we could be here on a weekday, when the tea garden would be a bit less crowded, she'd said.

Theoretically, I was supposed to recline in one of these deck chairs and think about Virginia Woolf. She'd visited the orchard many times when she was in her twenties, if the legends were to be believed. I'd read the novels of Virginia Woolf, and despite the bird droppings, I was happy to reflect on her work and her life and legacy. At the tea garden, I could let myself be consumed by the dream of England in its glory: Virginia Woolf, and also the poet Rupert Brooke, philosopher and mathematician Bertrand Russell, novelist E. M. Forster, economist John Maynard Keynes, and more. They'd gathered here in their younger days, the men all associated with the university. This was in the early 1900s, before World War I. Woolf's brothers, Adrian and Thoby, attended Cambridge, and their aunt lived in the town. Woolf dubbed the group "neo-paganists." Rumor held that she'd gone skinny-dipping with Rupert Brooke in the Cam.

This was before Brooke died of sepsis, from a mosquito bite, while on his way to fight in the Battle of Gallipoli during World War I. Before Virginia Woolf put stones in her coat pockets and walked into a river and drowned, during World War II. Sitting under the apple trees, I could imagine myself among them all, when they were young, the world was at peace, and the future was filled with promise.

On an unoccupied table nearby, a covey of shockingly large bees—wasps?—gathered upon a blob of jam.

Lowering a heavy tray, Lizzie Moran said, "Excellent table. Well done."

"Thank you. And well done to you, for managing that tray." We'd ordered a large pot of tea and two currant scones with clotted cream and jam.

"My reward for years of arm exercises at the gym."

"Your arms are an inspiration."

After we'd arranged our order and stashed the tray against a tree trunk, Lizzie pulled her deck chair closer to mine, so we could talk without raising our voices. "As you see, I'm using my Monet waist pack again." She held it up. "Every time I look at my Toulouse-Lautrec cats coffee mug or my Van Gogh mouse pad, I think, *Hannah created that.*"

"Hardly created."

"Brought into being, then. All these everyday items I used to take for granted. Turns out I have a lot of them. Your work makes them special."

I was touched. "Thank you for saying so."

Leaning forward awkwardly in her deck chair to reach the table, Lizzie poured our tea. It was weak.

"They're a little skimpy on the tea bags here," she said. "They could do better with the upkeep of the place, too. But don't worry, I'm not going to complain. My children would kill me. I can already hear them: *Mummy, please, no.* My children are very British. The accents, the lingo, the standards of behavior. I don't know what we thought would happen, raising them here, but Max and I find ourselves constantly confused: Two English people are living with us."

"Josie and . . . ?"

"Ben. He's fourteen. Teenagers with English accents. Everything they say sounds terribly correct. They can be intimidating even asking about breakfast. What about you, just the one?"

"Only Nicky." Before Nicky was born, I'd imagined myself with three or four, to make up for the isolation of my own childhood, but after Nicky, I didn't know how I'd manage another.

Maneuvering to the edge of the chair, Lizzie ripped open the plastic container of clotted cream. As she broke off a piece of scone, she said, "A debate rages in this country between those who put the clotted cream onto the scone before the jam and those who put the jam on first, with the cream on top."

"Which group do you belong to?"

"I'm in the clotted-cream-first group, but you should try both." Plate in hand, she leaned back in the chair.

I, too, maneuvered to the edge of the chair. I broke off a small piece of scone and put the cream on first, then added the jam. The scone was dry—it was like eating plaster—and the clotted cream was tasteless except for a plasticky residue, and the jam was like sugar syrup. She was hosting me, however. "Delicious."

She nodded.

I took another piece of scone and put the jam on first, with the cream on top. "Also delicious."

"The difference is subtle. Maybe nonexistent. But the locals are obsessed with the issue. Are you able to discuss your son's discovery yet?"

This is me. Blanche. I felt a pull, back to the conservation center—to Isabella and this little girl who must have been important to her, and I had to figure out why. "I promise to tell you everything, when I can."

"Thank you. You won't regret getting my opinion. Next question—" Her almost extravagant directness made me smile. "Do you miss your husband, being away from him for the summer?"

Kevin, I miss you. I wish I could sit with you at the kitchen table after Nicky goes to bed and discuss the details of the day. I wish I could sleep entwined with you. I wish I'd never seen what I saw in the park that day.

"I know I'd miss Max." She sipped her tea, not appearing to notice my pause.

Nicky continued to speak with Kevin on the phone every day around dinnertime, and I facilitated these calls, but otherwise I spoke to him only to exchange required information.

Could I risk revealing the truth to one person? To this woman, successful and clear-sighted? I needed a new perspective, and Lizzie and I were from different worlds. We were like strangers on a train, except we were in a tea garden with wasps colonizing the next table. Working in HR, she must be accustomed to hearing personal stories and remaining unfazed.

"I'd like your opinion on something," I said, and I dived ahead. When I reached the end, she looked into the distance, at the rows of apple trees. She might have been trained to react this way, but even so, she certainly gave me the sense that she was considering my words with care.

"With all due respect," she said, turning to me, "and I don't mean to downplay your experiences, but for myself, I don't think these issues are as serious as they seem at first."

"You don't? What's serious to you?"

"First, illness. My sister Jocelyn suffered from pernicious anemia—very frightening until the doctors figured out what it was. My father died of pancreatic cancer when I was fifteen."

"I'm so sorry."

"I'm not exceptional. Everybody suffers and has their losses. You, too, I'm sure."

"Yes."

"I was in full-scale teenage rebellion when my father died." Her confident demeanor had dropped away, and her vulnerable inner self was exposed, her face haggard. "I never had a chance to make it up to him."

I squeezed her hand, and she reciprocated. Promptly, though, she let go and returned to her raconteur style. "On the global side: Mass murder. Starvation. War. What's a little well-concealed sexual infidelity in comparison?"

"Well, that's one point of view." I disagreed with her completely. Bringing starvation and war into this discussion was like saying it was okay to cheat on an exam because the exam was insignificant compared to the atomic bomb. Individuals as well as societies needed moral standards. But I didn't feel like spoiling our afternoon by arguing with her.

"I know it's an unconventional view," she said. "But hypocrisy rules. People set up an impossible standard and are satisfied with pretend adherence to it. There's a question of degree, I realize. I'm not talking about addictive philandering. I'm talking about the ins and outs of everyday life between two people through decades of marriage or partnership."

A large ant was moving methodically across the table and approaching my plate. Should I squash it and destroy an innocent life? Should I flick it away, which could bring unintended injury? I lifted my plate. The ant moved across the table and continued on its way, first toward Lizzie, then onto the edge of the table and over the side.

"If we were English or French, we'd have a different view of this.

Remember that president of France, François Mitterrand, and at his funeral, his wife stood with their sons, and his mistress stood nearby with their daughter? And in the English upper classes, the stories about husbands graciously raising other men's children? I remember reading about the marriage of Vita Sackville-West and Harold Nicolson—close, loving, even though, or maybe because, they had other lovers, men and women both."

"But didn't the husbands and wives you mention agree to these arrangements? And anyway, Kevin and I aren't French, and we aren't English."

She laughed. "Only too true." Continuing more seriously, she said, "I used to travel a lot on business. I've done some things. On occasion."

So that explained her perspective. "Does Max know?"

"I'm not certain. I've never told him, and he's never asked me."

"Do you ever think you should confess?"

"No. It didn't mean anything," she said. "It's not relevant to my love for him."

Hearing her justification hew so closely to Kevin's made me uneasy. "Wouldn't Max be upset if he found out? Aren't you worried about that?"

"I'm not sure he'd be upset. He might be fascinated." She warmed to this idea. "Why do people have to respond in the stereotypical ways laid out for them? Max is his own unique person. He'd respond in his own way. I've always been emotionally faithful. I've never loved anyone but him."

"How would you react if Max . . ."

"That's a good question. But I have trouble visualizing it. His interests don't tend to go in that direction."

How could she possibly know? Under her scheme, the entire point was that spouses kept part of themselves concealed. "Where do his interests lie?"

"Word games. Number games. Sudoku. An entire room in our house is devoted to his collection of jigsaw puzzles. He works in the fields of speech and language processing and computational linguistics."

I laughed. "I have no idea what that means."

She joined my laughter. "Sometimes I have trouble understanding his work myself. But he's passionate about it, and that's good enough for me. His specialty is *applied* computational linguistics, which basically means—I believe I'm right about this—developing and improving machine translation. It's connected to artificial intelligence. I like to think that in the pre-tech era, he would have been a professional creator of crossword puzzles. During World War II, he would have been a cryptologist hero, creating and breaking secret codes."

Her face lit up from the thought of it.

"I love him, also in fact *because* of his eccentricities, not in spite of them. In addition, he needs me to take care of him, and taking care of people is one of my specialties. We've been together since college, and our bond has never wavered."

Her voice caught. Obviously she'd never want to lose him. Lizzie looked at her plate, studying the remaining portion of her scone. She opened the second container of clotted cream. In a dramatic change of subject, she said, "This isn't the best scone I've ever had." She'd resigned herself to eating it nonetheless.

"Where did you have the best scone?"

"That prize goes to the bakery in the village, sorry to say, since I can never show my face there again."

"I can go on your behalf," I said.

"Would you? That's a great idea. And good for the shop, too." She took another bite. "People can surprise you, though. Maybe Max does have a secret life I know nothing about. I love him enough to grant him a secret life, if that's what he needs, as long as he isn't doing harm to others or breaking the law. I don't want him to end up in jail. I have to say"—she regarded me intently—"some women decide that if their husband's infidelity is with another man, it doesn't count."

"Doesn't *count*?"

"Like it's not competition. I'm just saying I've heard women explain their agreement that way. The husbands of bisexual women say that, too. Like it's a different category of relationship. But for myself, I believe some things between a couple don't have to be said or known. Individuals are entitled to a degree of privacy. There are many ways to fashion a marriage."

I recoiled from this, but if I was going to stay with Kevin, I'd have to accept it as my guiding principle. In our future life together, I would be faithful, and he wouldn't be—that was the standard he was setting up, trying to use his rational, lawyerly arguments to convince me to go along with something I didn't believe in. I had to find the confidence to resist him, while simultaneously protecting Nicky. Always, Nicky.

CHAPTER 17

Matthew Varet found me in the estate's gift shop and said, strangely impatient, "I've been looking for you."

I'd just purchased two large homemade dog biscuits. Christopher was organizing a party to celebrate Duncan's upcoming second birthday. Nicky and Alice would bake a cake for Duncan's British-based humans, Rafe would secure a cake in New York, and we'd celebrate together via video conference. We'd have a transatlantic birthday party for a dog, to bring Christopher an hour of happiness.

"If you didn't turn up today, I was going to send you a text. How have you been?" I thought he looked both dazed and acutely alert, wide-eyed, as if he'd missed a night's sleep and the five cups of coffee he'd had to make up for it had put him into some other dimension. He'd forgotten to comb his hair.

"I'm well. The scientific report you sent over was . . . informative." I wouldn't discuss it here.

"I thought so, too," he said. "What have you been doing?"

"Among other things, assisting Dr. Tinsley in the book-conservation center." I heard myself sounding stiff and formal, even though I didn't intend to. Part of me still wanted to keep him at arm's length, while another part . . .

"I'm glad you've joined the research team," he said, encouraging as ever.

In addition, this morning I'd finished writing the conclusion and started the abstract of my dissertation. But I wasn't about to tell this to Mathew Varet, either. I'd now read about him online. He'd published several books while raising, or helping to raise, two children, one of whom, I well knew, needed extra attention. His specialty was Roman Britain, so we shared an interest in the classical world, but I didn't want to set up a teacher–student dynamic, inherently unequal, by mentioning my dissertation. Trying to be helpful, he might ask to read the draft to offer advice, and I wouldn't feel able to refuse, in the process drawing attention to how much more he'd accomplished than I had in roughly the same number of years.

I took refuge in a new assignment for my paying job: "I've also been researching images from medieval tapestries and manuscripts that would look good on athletic shoes." Even illustrations from the magnificent Luttrell Psalter were available for licensing; I'd checked after Dr. Tinsley mentioned it.

"Why?" he asked, sounding taken aback.

"I realize you're properly polite and haven't asked me about my job"—this brought a sheepish acknowledgment from him—"but there it is, my job."

"Designing trainers?" *Trainers* must be, as Nicky would say, *English* English for *sneakers.*

"Not exactly. Finding art images for manufactured goods."

"Why doesn't the manufacturer hire an artist to create fake medieval images? Wouldn't that be easier?"

"I'm sure it would. But the head of this company is set on authenticity. She studied the Middle Ages in college, loved the art, and, from a marketing perspective, likes to sell the real thing. It's an original idea but poses a variety of technical issues." Again I heard my stiffness, felt my self-consciousness with him. "I've seen a mock-up of the shoes: no laces, and they come up around the ankle."

He pondered this. "It's hard to imagine. I've never thought about art images on everyday objects."

"Most people haven't thought about it." I needed to shift the conversation away from me. "And you?"

"Sorry?"

"How have *you* been?"

"Not especially well, actually." He pushed back his hair, once, then again, which somewhat made up for not having combed it. "My ex-wife has sprung something on me. Cecilia."

"Who?" I asked.

"Cecilia, my former spouse. I should put this more charitably. Cecilia has asked me for a favor."

We went outside. A soft rain was falling, the sound of it a murmur against the leaves of the nearby trees. We walked along the arched passageway, open on both sides, that led from the shop to the garden. The passageway was surrounded by full-blooming multicolored roses, part of Ashton Hall's collection of heritage varieties, wildly variegated, densely petaled. My favorite was a deep yellow with red outer petals. In the rain, their scent was heavy on the air. Raindrops rested on the rose petals, and the blossoms bowed from the weight.

"She and her new husband, Simon—and I must admit he's proven himself surprisingly tolerant of children who aren't his—Cecilia, Simon, and the girls, including the daughter from *his* previous marriage, have been invited to a wedding. A wedding taking place at a castle in Scotland. Before you're impressed, let me say there are many castles in Scotland, most of them dreary."

"Even a dreary castle in Scotland sounds impressive to me."

"I'll assume because you've never been to one. The point is, Janet did something rather troubling at school yesterday. She's on the verge of being dismissed." He sounded despondent as he continued, "She's made it this far solely because of the commitment of her extraordinary and long-suffering teachers."

The same was true for Nicky. His teachers constantly went the extra mile—the extra hundred miles—to try to help him. I empathized with Matthew. Such a confession couldn't be easy for him, and I was glad he felt he could unburden himself to me.

"After what happened, Cecilia rightly feels Janet shouldn't be rewarded with a weekend at a Scottish castle. Instead, she should be punished. Even more to the point, I'm sure, is Cecilia's fear that Janet will do something equally troubling at the wedding and humiliate herself and also, by connection, her mother. The wedding is on Simon's side of the family, posh, and Cecilia is sensitive in this regard. She'd prefer to leave Janet behind and find some innocuous excuse to give the gathered guests. Cecilia has asked if I'd take Janet this weekend, and how could I say no."

"Being with you is considered a punishment?"

"What's the alternative? We do need to take a stand: If you behave atrociously, all pending invitations to Scottish castles are rescinded. Rosie will have a wonderful experience, and Janet will miss out. Janet often misses out. It's terribly sad, really."

"Nicky misses out a lot, too."

"Janet claims that she doesn't care, this is what she wanted all along."

"She may be telling the truth," I said. "She may find Scottish castles unbearably cold and drafty."

He paused, a kind of reset, then glanced at me with the usual spark about him. "The English don't object to cold and drafty. In fact, we prefer cold and drafty—not the discomfort, per se, but the opportunity to be smug about not minding."

That smile of his, stirring to me.

"Nicky often acts out in order to receive the supposed punishment of doing exactly what he wanted to do in the first place, so we're left with the probability that Janet might truly enjoy being with you."

"I suppose I should take that as a compliment, but I'd been planning to spend the weekend finishing an academic paper that's woefully overdue."

"So you feel as if you're also being punished as a result of her punishment. I'm familiar with this." I thought of all the social gatherings I'd had to leave or refuse because of Nicky's behavior. All the friends I wasn't able to spend time with, for fear of his unpredictability.

"I'm formulating a redemption for myself. And for Janet. After I've enforced her isolation at home on Saturday—which, granted, she may view as a blessing—perhaps you and Nicky would like to join us for an excursion on Sunday."

This was an unexpected and welcome surprise. He was regarding me with worry, as if he thought I might refuse.

"I'd like to show you a house with a similar history to Ashton Hall's," he continued quickly. "Or, rather, a possibly similar history, since we don't yet know every detail about Isabella Cresham. But there might be connections between the two houses that no one has noticed before. I don't want to say more until we've actually gone there. Don't want to prejudice you one way or the other. It's called Oxburgh Hall. It's about an hour's drive from here, depending on traffic."

I felt a wave of pleasure at the idea. "I believe I speak for Nicky, too, when I say we'd enjoy an excursion."

"Excellent. I'll text you the details."

"Notice I haven't asked about the nature of Janet's troubling misdeed," I said.

"I appreciate your discretion, but I'm happy to tell you: She went on a verbal tirade against the headmistress because of an announcement that next year, the school will mount a contemporary play instead of the usual Shakespeare. Something more relevant to the students' lives. Supposedly."

"So Janet was standing up for tradition."

"She was."

"She's a remarkable person, fighting for what she believes in, at her age. Defending Shakespeare, no less."

"Indeed. But she might have gone about it in a somewhat different manner. Without calling the headmistress names I shall not repeat."

As we reached the end of the covered passageway and opened our umbrellas, he smiled fleetingly, and we said our goodbyes.

CHAPTER 18

Oxburgh Hall appeared to float on the water, the reddish bricks aglow in the sunlight, the house doubled by an exact reflection of itself in the moat.

To take in the view, we stopped on the path that led from the car park to the house. We were only a few miles off the main road, but the estate seemed eerily isolated, hidden as it was at the end of narrow lanes that meandered through the fertile farmland of the Fens. I felt as if we were hundreds of miles from Cambridge, let alone London. Beyond the house, fields of hay spread into the distance, and a spicy scent filled the air. The house would have seemed even more isolated when it was built, during the late Middle Ages. The roads would have been unpaved, uncared for, thieves lying in wait for travelers.

Janet said, "I don't care about a stupid castle."

Today, instead of being a Shakespearean actress, she was a sulky adolescent. At twelve, she was almost a teenager.

"You don't know yet if it's a stupid castle," Nicky said with his bright optimism. "It might be a smart castle. You have to give new things a chance. You have to have an open mind. Sometimes people and things can surprise you."

"Sod off, you tosser," she screamed, stamping her foot.

"Janet!" Matthew said.

"Sorry," she said nastily, not sorry at all.

Nicky regarded her with a placid smile, as if he hadn't even noticed her words or tone.

"Before we go in," Matthew said with forbearance, "I want to tell you some history. This house has always been owned by Catholics."

"Were they part of the Gunpowder Plot?" Janet broke in. She began to chant:

> "Remember, remember
> The Fifth of November
> The Gunpowder Treason and Plot.
> I know of no reason
> Why the Gunpowder Treason
> Should ever be forgot!

"Were they that kind of Catholic? Traitors? Hanged, drawn, and quartered?" she said, relishing the words.

Thrown off track, Matthew hesitated before responding, and into the silence Nicky said, "I don't like hearing about that. It's not nice to think about. Race you to the towers."

They took off.

Matthew watched them go.

"What did you want to tell us?" I asked.

"It's rather futile now," he said, sounding dejected.

"They're just kids," I said, trying to reassure him.

"But I'm a teacher. I'm compelled to teach people, whether they want to learn or not." He shrugged. "My job is to make them want to learn."

"I'm listening."

"And I'm grateful. But—well, we'd best catch up with them."

We continued down the path. A breeze rippled along the surface of the moat, turning the reflections of the house abstract. The sun warmed my skin.

"Tell me what you were going to say."

"I'll skip the rest of the Catholic history and just say this: The water for the moat is diverted from a nearby river, and the moat must never be drained. The foundation bricks depend upon the moisture. The structure will collapse if the moat is drained."

"Why didn't Ashton Hall collapse when its moat was drained?"

"The Ashton Hall moat is—actually, I know absolutely nothing about the moat at Ashton Hall. I must also explain that although the Oxburgh Hall moat is beautiful to look at, one must bear in mind that originally the latrines emptied into it. The stench would have been impressive. And there you have it: the sum total of my preparatory lecture, minus the Catholic bits."

"Thank you. I do feel better prepared."

"My goal fulfilled," he said, sounding more like himself.

When we reached the children, Nicky was counting the bricks of the left tower, Janet the right.

"Inside," Matthew called to them. Nicky ran through the gate-house. Janet hesitated, then followed.

I wish I could say the interiors were captivating. But as we strolled from one overstuffed room to the next, the guides explaining each detail, the furnishings became too much: too much historic wallpaper, too much carved wooden furniture, too much bric-a-brac covering every available surface. Many visitors were intrigued, though, study-ing and photographing every item.

"This isn't the part I brought you to see," Matthew said, and I was relieved to hear it. I wouldn't need to feign interest for the sake of politeness.

The kids found counting opportunities in every room, and some-how this put Janet into a better mood. They counted the panels in the coffered ceilings. The chairs upon which sitting was forbidden. Marble busts. Decorative plates in the dining room. Paintings of ancestors.

Going upstairs, we reached the room of the Marian Hangings, the so-named panels of needlework embroidered by Mary, Queen of Scots, and Bess of Hardwick.

"My two sisters, when young, worshipped at the altar of Mary, Queen of Scots," Matthew said.

"I've never been interested in her. I know she's romanticized, but she's always sounded like a tiresome, self-involved woman to me."

"Lack of interest in Mary, Queen of Scots, is amongst the many ways in which you do *not* resemble my sisters."

I tried to parse out the meaning of this—flirtatious, condemnatory, complimentary, or purely factual—but I couldn't decide and said nothing.

We proceeded into the King's Room. Here the décor was austere, with a massive fireplace and brick walls adorned with battle spears. The room had been named in honor of King Henry VII, who'd visited Oxburgh Hall, although he'd never actually slept in this room.

A guide stood at the entrance to the next room. She looked about thirty. Her hair was long and dark, and she wore straight, form-fitting trousers that accentuated her height. She reminded me of Nicky's first-grade teacher, an unflappable young woman driven by a sense of fun. The guide called to Nicky and Janet, "Would you two like to see the priest hole?"

"Yes," they said in unison.

"I knew you would," she said as they ran to her. "I'm Mrs. Parker."

She wasn't interested in Matthew and me, as if priest holes were meant only for children, but I was curious, and I joined them. Matthew stayed in the King's Room, studying the manuscripts and artifacts arranged in several display cabinets.

Mrs. Parker led us into the adjoining room, in one of the octagonal towers above the gatehouse. "Our priest hole was built about four hundred years ago, to hide priests in case enemies came searching for them, to arrest them. Four hundred years is a long time, and no enemies are coming to search now, so you don't have to worry. Many different types of priest holes were built during that era, some with fake walls, or constructed underneath the floors, or behind fireplaces. Our priest hole was built beneath what they called the *garderobe*, which is what we call the lavatory or toilet."

"Ugh," the kids said, glancing at each other and giggling.

"In those days, people kept their clothes in the lavatory. They believed the bad smell kept moths away. And their lavatories were much smellier than ours."

"That's icky," Nicky said.

"I agree!" Mrs. Parker said.

She led us up a few steps and into a narrow space that did look like a combination of walk-in closet and lavatory.

"Originally, the toilet seat would have been here"—she pointed—"and the opening beneath would have led into the moat. The hiding place for priests was constructed beside the passage to the moat, and rather clever it was, too. If you were a soldier, searching for priests, you'd never discover the secret; you'd think you were looking only at clothes and at the toilet. The toilet seat isn't here anymore, and the passage to the moat is closed. Nowadays the opening that leads into the priest hole is shielded from view by a trapdoor."

She swung open a heavy, bricked square in the floor and revealed the opening.

"Are you ready to climb down into the hiding place?"

"Yes!"

One after the other, they lowered themselves.

"There's an electric light now, but in those days the space would have been in total darkness," she called to them. "You'd have to feel your way. You wouldn't want to light a candle, because the glow could give the game away to the enemies searching for you."

"I'm a priest in a priest hole," Janet called, her voice reverberating. She and Nicky alternated, *I'm a priest in a priest hole*, testing the echo.

After the kids clambered out, Mrs. Parker led them back to the octagonal room to review explanatory placards showing diagrams of the priest hole and its construction.

With the kids busy, and Matthew available in the other room if they needed a parent, I decided to go into the priest hole myself. The kids had made it look easy, but as I lowered myself, I realized the entryway was a near-vertical combination of ladder, steps, and slide. It wasn't really safe; I was surprised the administrators of the house didn't restrict access to it.

Once I was in the room, I saw that the space was big enough for only two or three to stand. There was a bench. Niches in the far wall provided storage spaces for food or water or religious implements like crosses and chalices. Or for a chamber pot.

I sat on the bench. I shut my eyes and imagined what hiding here would have felt like. The unending darkness. The silence. The stench of the latrine and of the chamber pot. The cold, even on a warm day like this. I was within the very structure of the house, cut off from the world outside. Somewhere nearby, strangers were searching—searching for *me*, knocking on the walls and floorboards, listening for the telltale hollow sound of a hiding place. The searchers might be coming closer, but I couldn't hear them, because thick walls surrounded me.

From my reading, I'd learned that by the 1580s, Catholics in England were considered enemies of the state. They could be imprisoned. Tortured. Sometimes executed. Priests were labeled foreign spies plotting to overthrow the government, and they, too, were imprisoned, tortured, executed. The homes of Catholics were searched for rosaries, crucifixes, and the implements of the Mass, which were illegal. Their homes were also searched for secret chambers like this one. In 1581, a parliamentary act instituted a penalty of twenty pounds a month—a devastating sum in those days—for not attending Protestant church services. In the coming decades, the fines levied against Catholics became a convenient way to enrich the Crown, discouraging monarchs from moving toward tolerance.

But in the face of all that, some individuals, like the family here at Oxburgh Hall, still clung to their Catholic beliefs.

An image came to me of my grandparents going into hiding during the war . . . living in a concealed room behind a room, protected by friends. Now I had an inkling of what the term *hiding* truly represented. It wasn't like the children's game of hide-and-seek. Sitting in the dank priest hole, I visualized my grandparents here, trying to survive. If you hid in such a place, you wouldn't know whether it was day or night. If the sun was shining, or snow was falling. Depending on how the room was sealed, you might become weak as the oxygen ran low. If the people who took care of you abandoned you or were killed themselves, you'd die here. Your body might never be found.

As the dense silence pressed into me, I saw Isabella Cresham on her pallet, her body withering into bones, hundreds of years passing. I opened my eyes, and the walls were pushing against me. I had to get away. I rushed to the entryway and maneuvered myself up. When I reached the top, I couldn't lift myself out; I didn't have the strength.

"Mrs. Parker?" I called. "Matthew?" No response. I reached as far as I could, to grab hold of the trapdoor, and I was able to use the leverage to pull myself out. I collapsed against the bricks of the floor.

"Are you all right?" Matthew was with me, helping me up. He squeezed my shoulders, making sure I could stand. His closeness startled me—his solidity, the strength of his hands, after my waking nightmare in the hiding place. "I wanted to show you something rather fascinating, but I couldn't find you. Then there you were, on the floor."

I wished I could lean against him. Feel him wrap his arms around me and comfort me. A half inch was between my face and his shoulder.

Just do it, part of me said. *Take the half-inch step toward him.*

But I wouldn't betray my husband. I turned away. "I wanted to get a sense of the priest hole for myself." I couldn't look at him.

"I went down there once. It was tough going," he said. "Especially imagining what hiding there must have been like." He didn't trivialize or downplay it.

"I thought it was terrifying."

"They make it into a lark for children, but it's far from that," he said.

I felt light-headed. I gripped his arm to regain my balance, and he put his hand over mine, steadying me. His hand was warm. I needed that warmth, and I put my own hand on top of his, to press his warmth into me.

Realizing what I'd done, I pulled my hands away.

Covering the awkwardness, resuming his professorial tone, he said, "In the display case in the other room, there's a rosary that was found in the priest hole. It resembles the one that was with Isabella Cresham at Ashton Hall. Such things were smuggled into England illegally from the Catholic continent. It could provide a clue about who Isabella communicated with. I'm hoping we'll find more links between the two houses. In her era, rituals like saying the rosary if you were Catholic, or *not* saying the rosary because you were Protestant— these were believed to be matters of heaven and hell, eternal life or death. No wonder the sixteenth century was an era of religious martyrdom, when some people would sooner be killed than convert." He gave me an apologetic half smile. "Sorry. Possibly too much information. Can't help myself."

"No, I do appreciate it," I said.

"Feel free to protest, if ever . . ."

"You're okay so far."

He looked endearingly pleased. "I haven't studied everything in the cabinets yet," he said, an invitation.

"I want to hear the end of the tour. Then I'll join you."

I went back down to the octagonal room, and Matthew returned to the displays in the King's Room.

". . . It's possible that a clever man named Nicholas Owen designed our priest hole. He built many around the country," Mrs. Parker was saying. "No enemies ever found the priests who hid in shelters designed by Nicholas Owen."

She intentionally made this dismal history into an innocuous tale of long ago, part of the supposedly romantic panoply of the past, unconnected to our lives today.

"In conclusion," Mrs. Parker said, "you're entitled to special stickers, because you were brave and visited the priest hole." She peeled the stickers off a sheet and placed them lightly on the backs of the kids' hands.

"Thank you," they said again in unison.

"Are you brother and sister? Cousins?"

"We're *friends*," Nicky said, making it sound like the most wondrous relationship anyone could ever have. Which it was.

Janet looked surprised, as if only now realizing what the word meant. Her face took on an openhearted innocence that made her into . . . a child. "*Friends.*"

"I'm glad you enjoyed your visit," Mrs. Parker said.

Janet ran to Matthew. "Daddy, look at the sticker." Nicky followed.

"May I have a sticker?" I wanted to see what they looked like. "I was brave and visited the priest hole, too."

Mrs. Parker peeled it off the sheet and placed it on the back of my hand. "There you are."

"Thank you. And thank you for your kindness to the children."

"Seeing their excitement is gratifying," she said.

Another group, adults and children, entered the King's Room, their voices reaching us.

"Sorry. It's a busy day." She went to the entryway and called to the newcomers, "Would any of you children like to see the priest hole?" Three kids rushed to her.

I studied the sticker. It showed a boy and girl, about Nicky's and Janet's ages, grinning as they emerged from the priest hole, which the sticker called the *priest's hole*, as a possessive. I wished I didn't notice such trifling details, but I did.

I've been down the priest's hole at Oxburgh, the message read.

Four hundred years from now, was this how Anne Frank's attic would be viewed? After enough time had passed, and the trauma had faded, would the attic evolve into something fun for kids to see because it was gruesome in a shivery, Halloween sort of way, the horrifying truth rewritten to make the site more visitor-friendly? I prayed we'd never reach a day when kids could tour Anne Frank's hiding place and afterward receive smiley-face stickers for their shirts:

I visited Anne Frank's attic in Amsterdam!

Is that what the stickers would say?

Matthew drove down the row of lime trees, and we came into view of Ashton Hall. In the lowering sunlight, the house shimmered through the trees, the windows glittering, the bricks glowing orange-red. My love for this special place filled me.

Matthew pulled up near the pathway leading to our door, and Nicky and I got out.

Janet opened her window. "*When shall we two meet again?*"

I recognized the opening line of *Macbeth* and her adjustment of the number.

"*In thunder, lightning, or in rain?*"

"Or in sunshine," Nicky said.

The kids looked at me. "I'll discuss it with Matthew."

They turned to Matthew.

"The adults will confer," he said.

As we watched them drive away, Nicky held my hand, and when we could no longer see their car, we walked toward the house.

"I had fun testing the echo in the priest hole with Janet," he said. "I didn't like the priest hole, though. Not even for one second. I wanted to leave as soon as I got there. But Janet wanted to test the echo, so I stayed. Does Ashton Hall have a priest hole?"

"I don't think so. Mrs. Gardner hasn't mentioned one. I guess it could still be hidden somewhere."

"I don't want Ashton Hall to have a priest hole." He squeezed my hand. "Was Isabella's room like a priest hole?"

"We don't know yet."

He stared at the upper windows of the house, glistening with orange fire in the raking sunlight. "If it was, it's scary to think about."

I wouldn't lie to him. "You're right, it *is* scary."

"I don't want to go inside until I know. I won't go inside," he insisted. He stopped walking.

"There's still a lot of research to do, to figure things out. But our part of the house is safe. It's far away from where Isabella was."

"It's not far away!" he cried. "It's twenty-one minutes and thirty-two seconds from my bedroom door to Isabella's room."

"Twenty-one minutes and thirty-two seconds, plus over four centuries. No one's going to hurt you," I said.

"You have to find out what happened to her." He pulled down on my hand, fear filling his eyes. "You're my mom. I need you to. You *have* to."

"I'm trying, Nicky."

Trying for both of us. To stop the haunting that wouldn't leave me.

I woke in the night with silence pounding in my ears, as it had in the priest hole. My dreams had teemed with nightmares of sound: Dogs barking. Birds screeching. Conversations beneath my window—the gardeners were searching for something that was lost. What was it? I couldn't make out their words.

Isabella Cresham. The silence must have pounded in her ears, too. She lived in an era without electricity. I would have found it frightening. But she might have found our world equally frightening, with its constant light, music at the press of a button, blaring televisions, alarms to mark the proper duration to brush her teeth, social media—would she have felt obliged to post a daily photo of the view from her window?

I checked my phone, 3:42. About an hour remained before the sky would begin to lighten with the dawn.

If—*if*—her faith turned out to be the reason Isabella was in the room, she would have been thankful for the silence and the darkness. Silence and darkness meant another night of survival, no soldiers banging on the downstairs entryway with shouts and torches, searching for her because of what they considered her heretical beliefs.

How fervently you must believe, to endure this. My grandparents, in their hiding place, remained for the Nazis racially and genetically Jewish no matter what religion they professed. But if in fact Isabella had been imprisoned by her family because of her faith, achieving freedom would have been comparatively easy. She needed only to attend Protestant worship services.

She refused. Instead, she'd wake in her hidden room, feel her way in the dark for the prie-dieu, kneel, and recite her morning prayers.

Isabella Cresham, tell me who you are.

She was twenty-one minutes and thirty-two seconds away, the centuries vanished, our lives in tandem, in the darkness that surrounded us both.

CHAPTER 19

Seconde of Aprill, in 1562. *Ruffes for shirtes. Sylke for wastcotes.*

Joy flowed through me. The pure joy of research and discovery. *I can do this,* I thought; *I love doing this.* I felt utterly, truly alive, my mind focused and clear.

Baskett of figgs. Pomegranettes.

In the conservation center, I read the household-account ledgers that had been found in the muniment room. They were part of a daily record, spanning centuries, through many volumes, of the purchases made at Ashton Hall on behalf of the Cresham family. After Matthew's students had identified the relevant volumes for Isabella's era, Dr. Tinsley had asked me to review them. As I held the ledgers in my hands, their leather bindings soft against my skin, I'd felt a sense of reverence. I had decided on 1562, twenty years before the date of the coins in Isabella's keepsake box; that's where I would break into the river of the past. Depending on what I found, or didn't find, I could go further back in time. I'd arrived at the conservation center early this morning, giving up my own work for the day.

Vylvet for nightcaps. I imagined the family wearing their velvet nightcaps to ward off the cold in winter.

A mention of Isabella's name in the ledgers was too much to expect. Instead, the accounts would help to create a context for her life. I'd look for a pattern and a break in the pattern. In that break might be clues.

A *quyer of paper.* An *ynnke bottell.*

An accounting of my life would show patterns, too. A ream of paper for the computer printer. Not an ink bottle, but ballpoint pens. Groceries. Drugstore items. Cable, internet, phone, repeated every month. Nicky's and my therapists.

Oyle of roses. Crymson ribbon, to decorate a gown or wrap a gift.

The Tudor-era handwriting was both familiar and strange. Some letters were recognizable but oddly shaped. Others were decorated with flourishes. Still others were written with broad ascents or descents above or below the line. The spellings were variable, unstandardized. Initially the entries had been a mystery, illegible. *Sound out the words,* I'd told myself.

And so I'd voiced the letters, like a child learning to read by phonics, and slowly, haltingly, an entire way of life began to take shape.

Parfuming panne, to make a room smell sweet.

Grene cusshins, to soften a hard-backed chair.

Box of Cumfyttes. These must be comfits, a popular candy in the Elizabethan era.

Medecyns, obtained from an apothecary.

This was the minutiae of everyday life, each detail adding to my re-creation of the past. This *was* the past, brought to life.

Quinces.

Lynin clothe.

Drinking glasses.

A *spanniell,* and another.

Synamond. Cinnamon? I had trouble spelling *cinnamon,* too.

A tapestry of birds, and another of the hunt, *for the Grate Hall*, the pictures capturing Isabella's daydreams when she was young and taking her to other worlds.

Sylver damaske. Damask was a patterned cloth used for bed hangings and for high-status clothing.

Musique for the keybord. Possibly this was the music manuscript found on Isabella's virginal. She'd played for the family in the evening, when the room where she would die was still unimaginable.

A *Turkey carpet.*

I assumed a man held the job of account-keeper. He was a steward, or what today would be called a butler. A man who prided himself on being precise. An abstemious drinker. Accustomed to order and routine. A man who'd walk into the kitchen and the cooks and scullery maids would stop their banter.

A *payntyng of his lordship's greyhounds.*

Gascon wine.

Ginger, cardamom, pepper, raisins, dates, walnuts, almonds—the Cresham family had them all. The writer of these lines, joined by the cook and housekeeper, would visit the Stourbridge Fair during its season, in September. They'd make their purchases from merchants who'd traveled from far away. They'd hope, pray, that plague hadn't traveled with the merchants, too. At other times of the year, they'd go to the Market Square or arrange via correspondence for supplies to be sent from merchants in London. All of these purchases would be written down here, in the account ledgers.

Cloke of furr for milady. A *paire of gloves.*

Chak stik. Blak led stik. For Isabella, to make her sketches.

Waggs—wages—for a tutor.

Schoole fees for Piers of the village. Here was Lord Southbrooke, paying for a bright boy to be educated.

Candals, to keep the darkness at bay, the surrounding world both radiant and terrifying.

The brief pleasure from the visit of a *jogler* and a group of *musiciones.* A separate visit from a *harper.*

Strings for a lute. *Musique* for the lute.

The Cresham family walked in the garden, watched the dogs gambol across the lawns, felt the misty rain on their faces, as I did on mine. The staff worked in the weaving and sewing rooms upstairs and in the kitchens below.

The purchase of an apple roaster—I could smell those apples, taste them, soft and warm after roasting.

A chess table and a set of chessmen—there was the family, playing chess by the fire through the long winter evenings.

A necklace of pearls. I owned a pearl necklace, a gift from Kevin for our first anniversary. How cool it was against my skin when I put it on, cool even on a hot summer day.

Fees to the collar-maker.

A ring with emeralds, *for milady.*

A visit from a *phisiscian.*

The acquisition of books. *Waggs,* and gold leaf, for the bookbinder. *Waggs* for the keeper of the books.

Waggs to an embroiderer.

A silver thimble. Buttons of gold.

Compulsion drove me on, as I read each line on each page, gathering the evidence.

Saffron.

Sugar.

Cloves. When I was young, I'd stick cloves into oranges at holiday time, and the spicy smell would fill the apartment.

Soap.

Payments to the *shoomacker,* for *shoos.*

Waggs to the *mydwyfe* and to the nurse for *Lady Southbrooke's baby.* Payments for swaddling cloth for an infant. To the priest for a baptism. To the carpenter for a coffin. A payment for a shroud, and to the priest for a funeral.

Lady Southbrooke's baby, baptized. Lady Southbrooke's baby, dead. This repeated, again and again.

Lady Southbrooke's baby . . . Never a name for these babies. Their names must have been listed in the parish records after their baptisms, and after their funerals.

Lady Southbrooke . . . Never a name for the mother. Never a name in the eyes of the man creating the ledgers, as if whatever woman filled the role of Lady Southbrooke was only a vessel. Nor was there a first name for Lord Southbrooke. In the account ledgers, individual identity had been erased, creating a sense of eternity . . . of Lord and Lady Southbrooke living on this land through centuries, past, present, and future.

On July 28, 1593, the *phisiscian* visited. The next day, the priest was given a payment for a visit. The cost of a coffin was noted, without mention of whom it was for.

Then, nothing.

The remainder of the page was blank. The facing page was also blank, which must have been an inexcusable waste of paper in that era. I turned to the next page. There, on the top left-hand side, as if life had begun afresh, the records resumed on May 1, 1596:

Thre broomes.

Schoole fees for the younge lorde.

Lace for milady.

These records were written by a new account-keeper. This individual had difficulty keeping his writing straight across the page, and the lines tilted upward. Funny doodles filled the margins. Pigs, cows, humans—caricatures of people and animals he knew? Occasionally he became confused and had trouble matching his purchases with their cost; he had to cross out entries or use arrows to point to the correct amount. Was he tired and tipsy at the end of the day, as he wrote the records? He must have been capable enough, however, because he continued writing the accounts for years, I saw as I glanced ahead and into the next volume.

I returned to the empty pages. *My* account-keeper, the meticulous man I'd come to know—sober, responsible—was gone. Vanished.

Thus, the following months and years were skipped:

From August through December 1593: nothing.

1594: nothing.

1595: nothing.

January through April 1596: nothing.

What had happened in the household during those years of nothing?

I gazed at Dr. Tinsley, sitting at a workstation nearby and reading documents stained by age—her alabaster skin, the serenity of her expression, her steady focus, revealed by the high-intensity lamplight that illuminated her. As I watched her, I felt we two existed outside time, as if, despite the high-tech equipment, we were in a medieval scriptorium.

Dr. Tinsley glanced up. Not at me. At the analog clock on the wall—6:25.

"I should finish for today," she said.

I looked around. The graduate students had left. I hadn't registered their departure. The day had passed in an instant. Alice and Nicky must be waiting, dinner prepared.

"Will you return tomorrow, Ms. Larson?"

Yes, I wanted to say. *I'll be here tomorrow and the next day, all day, every day.* "I'll return in the afternoon. I have an online job, and I'm also trying to finish my dissertation."

"Are you at the long-slog stage?" she asked, sympathetic.

"That's exactly where I am. Pushing forward for the credential more than anything else, at this point."

"I understand. I hope you know you're welcome to work here whenever it's convenient for you." She'd already given me the code for the center's electronic lock.

"Thank you. And please, you must call me Hannah."

"Very well, then. You must call me Martha."

Such energy expended, to arrive at this restrained intimacy.

"If you have a moment . . . I found something." I took the ledger to her. "A break in the pattern." I showed her the years of nothing.

She paged through the records. Made notes on her laptop. "I'll compare the dates with other sources." She gave me a smile that felt like a bit of grace bestowed upon me. "In my experience, *nothing* always turns out to be something."

"In my experience, too. How has your work gone today?"

"I've met a man: the parish priest. His personality shines through these documents."

"So do the personalities of the men making the household accounts," I said.

"Curious, isn't it, what one can conclude from the way individuals make lists of everyday items and events. The priest is meticulous and unemotional. He writes down every expenditure for the upkeep of the church, no matter how small. He carefully records the marriages, baptisms, and deaths. Usually, but not always, he gives a cause of death. Simple *fever* is common, but in addition—look at these odd spellings." She turned the sheet toward me and pointed to the place. "*Fever of redde spots* and *fever with the Lord's own marque.*"

"He's describing a rash of some type?" I asked.

"I assume so. Smallpox, possibly? It's awful to think about. He reports many cases of the *bloody flux*, which means severe dysentery with bleeding. Several of his parishioners die of *burning ague*, which I think means malaria. He notes *pestilence*—what we call plague—again and again, in waves. What's most touching, though, is that he lists a surprising number of his parishioners as dying of *grief*."

"He uses that word to conceal suicide?"

"I don't think so, really. He also has a category he labels *made away themselves*, and he lists only a handful. Suicide was amongst the worst of sins. I checked the OED online, and there's a wide range of definitions for *grief*, dating back to the Middle Ages. Maybe these parishioners actually did die of grief, in the sense of mourning. During the worst plague years, in some places there weren't enough people alive to bury the dead. You never knew when plague would return, next year or tomorrow. How did you plan for the future, with that prospect staring at you?"

This is me. Blanche. The drawing of Blanche was now protected in an acid-free box in the storage area, but Martha had taken a photo of it with her phone, printed it, and tacked it on the wall near her work-station. The little girl stared at me with her quizzical, unfaltering gaze. Who was she? Did she die young of disease, making Isabella also die, of grief?

"In the midst of such upheaval," Martha said, "you could miss your spouse or child, or your mother or father or sibling, so much, miss them with such yearning and despair, that one day your heart stopped beating."

The pressure of my love for Nicky filled my chest. If anything ever happened to him . . . the records would list *grief* as the cause of death for me.

CHAPTER 20

On Saturday afternoon, July 25, I threw a stick to Duncan and contemplated adultery.

Apparently British dogs were more free to express enthusiasm than British people were, or, more likely, Duncan had been spending too much time with Americans for his own good, because he never flagged. Ten, fifteen, twenty tosses of the stick, and he remained exultant. He was well trained, bringing the stick back and leaving it at my feet. With a wiggle of his hips, he maneuvered backward to prepare for the next toss.

While playing throw-the-stick, I walked across the lawn, past the lake, toward the river. The air was damp, the breeze fresh. After several days of rain, the grass was a deep green. The clouds were breaking, and the late-afternoon sun spilled through, turning the landscape luminous.

Nicky and Alice were inside, and Nicky was packing: This evening he was having a sleepover with Janet and Rosie at their mother's house in Saffron Walden. His last attempted sleepover had been when he was six, and he'd been invited only because it was a party for all the boys in his class. At dinner he wouldn't, or couldn't, stop saying *fuck*. Before they'd reached dessert, I'd received a call to pick him up.

Duncan was accompanying Nicky on this sleepover, because Janet and Rosie had a dog, a Labrador retriever named Maisie. Theoretically the dogs would befriend each other. The purpose of the stick-throwing was to exhaust Duncan before the approximately half-hour drive to Saffron Walden. Knowing that Nicky would be with Janet and Rosie this evening, Matthew had asked me to dinner.

When I reached the end of the lawn, I sat on the bench beneath the giant copper beech tree, which was more than two hundred years old, according to the guidebook. The branches arched toward the grass, cocooning me. Through the leaves, I studied the lake and the house.

Duncan placed the stick, slobbery and slimy, on my lap. Ugh. Luckily, I hadn't yet changed for my evening out.

With the side of my hand, I pushed the stick to the ground.

"I'm resting, Duncan."

He pushed his muzzle against my hand, urging me to toss the stick again. He tilted his head sideways, waiting.

"Sorry, Duncan. My arm is tired."

With a heaving sigh, he lay down on my feet.

I knew what I was risking, in return for an evening to myself. Nicky's future. Our future with Kevin, as a family. Maybe instead I should be fighting to protect my relationship with Kevin, fighting to wrest him away from Tim and possess him solely. But I couldn't possess him. I didn't believe in possessing another person, didn't believe it was even possible. I wanted Kevin to choose, and to choose me. I couldn't force him to.

But the thought returned that he was in a position to force me to choose him. Because I was financially dependent on him, I'd become his possession, and he believed he was entitled to make the decisions on how both of us would live our lives.

Was I, then, entitled to the same freedoms he gave himself, within the framework of our marriage? In theory, yes, I was. But in practice, I wasn't sure.

Gradually, as the sun moved, the waters of the lake were filled with a reflection of the house. Isabella Cresham might have sat in this very spot, under the tree that preceded this one, her beloved dog at her feet, the late-afternoon breeze cooling her on a summer day, while she visualized the possibilities of her future. The landscape would have been different. The lake didn't exist; it was an eighteenth-century enhancement. The lawn was most likely planted with chamomile or thyme rather than grass.

Duncan sprang up and faced the house, his entire body poised, retriever that he was.

"What do you see?"

With his senses advanced far beyond human ones, he might have detected the spirits of the Cresham spaniels frolicking on the lawns and wanted to join them as they ran and played.

If only it could be.

But no. Nicky and Alice had emerged from the side door, *our* door, barely visible to me, obvious to him.

"Off you go." I gave Duncan a pat. He raced across the lawn.

I couldn't resolve any questions now, and I didn't need to. I'd wait for this one evening, at least, to unfold.

Nicky jumped up and down when the black SUV came into view. "There they are!"

As the car approached, I was suddenly anxious at the prospect of meeting Matthew's former spouse, a woman who worked in finance in London, while I . . . Well, my career could hardly be compared to hers.

When I opened the passenger door, Duncan leapt into the car, and Nicky climbed up and strapped in, talking nonstop. "Look, the Eiffel Tower is on my backpack." He held a pack printed with a nineteenth-century map of Paris, manufactured by one of my clients. Although Nicky had never visited Paris, he'd become enamored with the map, and he traced walking routes for himself throughout the city.

"I've been to Paris," Janet said.

"You've been to *Paris*? Paris is on the far side of the world."

"Not from England, it's not. The journey on the Eurostar train from St. Pancras station in London to the Gare du Nord station in Paris is on average between two hours and sixteen minutes and two hours and twenty-eight minutes. From Saffron Walden to St. Pancras station, the journey is on average . . ."

Nicky listened intently to her recitation.

As I walked to the driver's side to speak with Cecilia, I prepared for a version of the first wife in the novel *Rebecca:* sophisticated, with a fresh manicure and her hair professionally blown out. She'd hide her disdain toward Americans behind a veneer of extreme courtesy.

Cecilia opened the window. She was harried, unkempt, no makeup, pale-brown hair hanging loose. She looked exhausted. She reminded me of myself.

We introduced ourselves.

"You're kind to let Nicky stay with us," she said.

"You're kind to invite him."

"I promise to bring him home in one piece."

This sounded like a sincere promise, not a throwaway laugh line, unless her sense of humor was so dry it was beyond me. To my ear, she was truly pledging to return him in good health, without a chocolate-frosting-covered fork plunged into his back. I wished I could assure her that Janet and Rosie would likewise survive Nicky's visit unscathed, but I'd learned never to make such promises.

"Thank you," I said.

She stared at me, her brow pinched, as if she wanted to say more and longed for a connection with another woman who could understand her. She glanced at the children.

". . . Someday you'll go to Paris," Janet was saying. "I'll take you. I know everything about Paris."

Cecilia said, "Well, possibly someday they *will* go to Paris together."

"They already have. Metaphorically." Here I was, reassuring this woman I'd expected to be intimidated by.

"Can Duncan and Maisie come to Paris with us?" asked Nicky.

"Dogs go everywhere in Paris," Janet said. "Dogs eat dinner at restaurants in Paris. They sit on chairs at the table with the humans. I've seen it. That's how I know it's true. In Paris the dogs speak French."

"The dogs speak French? I don't know French." Nicky's enthusiasm collapsed. His school didn't teach foreign languages.

"I shall instruct you," Janet said.

I said to Cecilia, "Phone me if anything . . . if you need to discuss anything."

"It is to be hoped," she said as she focused on shifting the car into reverse, "that I can give you the rest of the weekend off."

Did she know or surmise that I had a dinner-plus-possibly-more appointment with her former husband in a few hours? Or was she simply projecting onto me her own wish to have a space to breathe?

"Right," she said. "See you tomorrow."

I stepped back as she turned the car around. "Bye, Nicky, have fun." I waved.

But he was absorbed by his conversation with Janet—she was saying, "Repeat after me: *Duncan est un chien. Nous sommes amis.*"—and he didn't hear me. I was glad for him.

CHAPTER 21

We were two adults in a restaurant filled with adults: Pint Shop, on Peas Hill, off Cambridge's town square. We sat at a table in the back room, away from the crowd by the bar. With its white clapboard walls, plank floor, wooden furniture, and chalkboard for the ever-updated beer menu, the space had a welcoming simplicity. Matthew wore his usual uniform of tweed jacket and button-down shirt without a tie, and also as usual he was relaxed yet formal, confident yet diffident.

After we ordered, I said, "I met Cecilia."

"How did she seem?" His tone was neutral, implying no judgment for or against her.

"Worn out."

"I'm not surprised. She's taken it upon herself to investigate other schools for Janet, should a change become necessary."

"What happened between you two?" I wasn't usually so direct, but Cecilia's distress had stayed with me. "A brief response will do."

"Janet happened," he said matter-of-factly. "Disagreements as we attempted to raise her. Crisscrossing condemnation. Lashing out at each other, because we couldn't lash out at her—only a child, after all. Indulgence in alternate methods of relieving stress. For both of us. Ignoring one's marriage vows. I'm not going to gloss over it. *He that is without sin,* et cetera. How have you and your husband carried on?"

"We're good at managing Nicky. We've experienced some challenges for different reasons." I wasn't certain if Matthew had a right to full knowledge of my circumstances. It was a secret that didn't belong to him, as Mrs. Gardner might say. I'd give a half confession: "Kevin turned out to be having a long-term relationship with someone else. Someone who was married and had children. Who *is* married and *has* children." With gender not mentioned, my dilemma sounded more stark. The default assumption would be that Kevin was involved with a woman. I'd never stay with him if it was a woman. "I found out right before Nicky and I came to the UK."

"I'm sorry."

"It was a shock. I'd thought we were close."

"I'm sure you were. Are. In the most important ways." I knew he was mistaken, but he'd said this to reassure me, and I appreciated the attempt. "You're in agreement about Nicky, after all."

"Kevin and I might not stay together," I blurted out, then regretted my candor. "Let's change the subject. I don't want to spend the evening discussing my husband." I'd intended this to sound light-hearted, but it didn't.

He paused, as if pondering whether or not he should let it go. "As you wish."

"How did you decide on a life in archaeology?" I landed on, as something easier to talk about.

"One day in geography class, when I was Nicky's age, I saw a map of Roman roads in Britain." My question seemed to have made him happy. "The roads went everywhere, connecting cities, towns, villages, and villas, a heretofore-unknown-to-me Britain which existed right along with the country I lived in every day. Just like that, I became obsessed with Roman roads."

That flirtatious smile of his, forever charming.

"I could, if I wished, relate more than you'd ever want to know about Roman road construction in Britain. You stand forewarned."

"That doesn't scare me."

"No, I'm sure not."

I wished I could trace his body with my fingertips.

"By the time I was eleven, I'd convinced my parents to take the family on a driving tour of the entire length of Hadrian's Wall, from east to west."

"How did it go?"

"Apart from my sisters proclaiming *it's just a stupid wall* every step of the way, the excursion was highly engrossing. I've often wondered why one person becomes obsessed with Roman roads and another with, say, the music of Johann Sebastian Bach." The server brought our food. "What are the origins of your obsessions?"

I told him: Margot and her experiment when I was young, teaching me Latin and arranging for me to learn ancient Greek. My job translating inscriptions at the Met. My conviction, walking the corridors filled with art from around the world, that I'd found a calling. Now that I knew him better, I could tell him about my dissertation, and he asked questions that showed curiosity and insight, without the condescension I was accustomed to hearing in the voices of (male) colleagues about the relevance of a topic centered on children.

The side of his knee happened to touch mine by accident under the table, and I kept my knee where it was, because truly, in the narrow surroundings, there was no room for a rearrangement of legs. When the couple next to us stood up to leave, awkwardly pushing past, I pressed my knee harder, to give them more room.

And so it went. As we began dessert, sharing a dense chocolate mousse topped with a thin layer of cream, I told him about my discovery of the years of nothing in the account ledger.

"Nothing is generally as important as something. In all walks of life," he said.

"I agree with that." Our spoons collided.

"You and your son are great discoverers."

"All I did was turn the pages of the ledger," I said.

"The ability to stay alert through every line, on every page, is more difficult than you might imagine, given that you're able to do it with such ease."

I wanted to caress him. That place at his right temple, where his hair shaded to gray.

"Ditto the ability to recognize that nothing may be something," he added. "Remember Sherlock Holmes and the mystery of the dog who didn't bark in the night?"

"I do remember that story. Is it significant, do you think, that *Isabella* is a Spanish name? Wasn't Spain the enemy? The Spanish Armada was defeated in, what, 1588?"

I wanted to press my hand against his face, feel the scratchiness of his beard on my palm.

"She might have been born during the reign of Queen Mary, who married Philip of Spain. Or she might have been named after a beloved grandmother or aunt who in turn had been named after Catherine of Aragon's mother, Isabella of Castile. Alliances shift; the name remains."

"What do you think might have happened to the family between August of 1593 and April of 1596? Not necessarily to Isabella—she might have been dead by then—but to the rest of them?"

"The first year of nothing, 1593, was the year when Catholics were required to have a license to travel more than five miles from their homes. It was also the year when a bill was introduced in Parliament calling for the removal of children from Catholic families so they could be raised in Protestant homes. The bill was withdrawn, but the point had been made, brutally. I remember how I felt when I learned about it, imagining myself taken away from my home and my parents."

He looked aside, the memory still powerful.

"However," he said, making an effort to bring himself back to me, "we've no indication that the whole of the Cresham family was Catholic. It's possible they suffered because of a kind of guilt by association—or feared they might. And I'm almost positive 1593 was a year of widespread plague. The terror and panic that gripped society would have been crushing."

He stopped, reflecting. "But the mid-1590s were also the years of Shakespeare's *A Midsummer Night's Dream* and *Romeo and Juliet*. This was the time of Elizabeth I—Gloriana, so-called. Her reign is referred to as the Golden Age, but it was a flowering of culture against a backdrop of religious suppression, torture, disease, and waves of starvation."

"How do you know so much about that era? How are you able to elucidate it so effortlessly?"

He became shy. "I'm not sure, really. From the time I was young—not much else to think about, in those days, beyond Roman roads and the rest of English history. I wasn't athletic, alas. Spent my time reading. Recovering the family's Anglo-Catholic heritage."

"That was me, too. Not the Catholic part. But alone, rather than lonely." I thought back, wistful and nostalgic, to the days when I'd lost myself in English history and literature, sitting in the window seat of the dormitory apartment where I was raised, overlooking the tree-lined street. "Filling the days with reading."

"So we have that in common." This seemed to make him melancholy.

"What are your plans for the rest of the summer?" I asked, to lift him out of his sadness.

"I'll be away most of August and part of September, for a dig at Chedworth Roman Villa. That's in Gloucestershire, not too far from the town of Cirencester. Janet and Rosie will be traveling with Cecilia, a sojourn in the south of France having been planned for their general edification and the perfection of their language skills."

"Lucky them."

"As with Scottish castles, I advise against being overly impressed. Going to France is not a major undertaking. It's next door. What about you?"

"My husband will visit at the beginning of September. The plan is for Nicky and me to return to New York with him, in time for Nicky to start school."

The Labor Day weekend felt abruptly close at hand. Too close, for ending the life Nicky and I had begun here and leaving the story of Isabella Cresham behind. Where would Christopher be, *how* would he be, in early September when we had to leave? I didn't want to return to New York and resume life where I'd left off, with the added knowledge that Kevin would be spending time with Tim, my acquiescence required. I felt shaky and also angry at the prospect.

Finishing the dessert, Matthew and I said nothing more.

The check arrived. I insisted on splitting it; I didn't want to be beholden to him. As I signed the receipt, I wondered what future historians of credit-card bills would deduce from this dinner on my record. One logical but incorrect conclusion would be that I was here on my own. How forlorn my life, they might conclude—dining out alone on a Saturday evening. On the other hand, if I'd let Matthew treat, there would have been no record at all of my presence here tonight. I would have been erased.

Leaving the restaurant, we entered a warm, lovely evening. The time was close to nine, and the light was pale but still bright.

"Let's take a walk," I said. I wanted to put off a little longer the decision about what would happen next.

We passed the Arts Theatre and turned left onto St. Edward's Passage, a narrow thoroughfare harking back to the Middle Ages. It was a lane that Isabella Cresham might have walked. On our right was a small medieval church. The churchyard smelled of pine trees. We passed secondhand bookshops, closed at this hour. A narrow café, also closed. Isabella might have known the precursors to these shops. Three teenage girls with multiple earrings and tattoos sat in the middle of the lane, drawing portraits of one another on large pads. We emerged onto King's Parade, busy with tourists and bicyclists. Behind the monumental gateway and arched barrier, King's College spread before us. The fanciful towers of the chapel held a warm sheen from the long sunset.

Matthew said, "The King's College Chapel is genuinely old, but much of what you see that appears to be Gothic is actually Gothic Revival, built during the nineteenth century. If you look carefully, though, you can still find hints and remnants of construction from earlier eras. Maybe it's a doorway. Or flagstones worn away by the steps of centuries of students. It might be old bricks and stonework. A staircase, or timbers in a hallway. That's my work: finding these hints."

I was content to let him speak on as he gave me a tour, from Senate House Passage to Trinity Lane, onto Garret Hostel Lane, leading to the river, the turrets, chimneys, and spires of the surrounding buildings creating a rhythm against the sky.

As we stood on an arched bridge across the Cam, we observed other visitors standing on other bridges, and they observed us. The stately college buildings lined the river, formal entryways leading to concealed courtyards. On the far side of the river, the lawns were meticulously clipped, the gardens lush, the trees silhouetted on the grass by the lowering sun. At the horizon, burgundy and mauve clouds filled the sky. I caught the sweet scent of lime trees. The people around us spoke Italian, French, Russian, Chinese.

Despite the late hour, punters made their way along the water. Matthew pointed to one punt in particular: In the stern, a stunning young woman wearing a black cocktail dress used a pole to propel the boat, while in the bow, a handsome young man, formally attired, studied his phone with unwavering attention.

Matthew and I retraced our steps, turning left on Trinity Street, a different roadway altogether from Trinity Lane. We stopped in front of Trinity College, Matthew's college, where he'd studied and where he now taught. The monumental gateway, with its statue of Henry VIII, was shut tight. Impenetrable.

THE COLLEGE IS CLOSED TO VISITORS, a sign read.

"I realize it looks unpromising from the outside," Matthew said, "but within you will find several grand interconnected courtyards. A private garden for the Fellows of Trinity College, a rarefied group to which I belong. A glorious dining hall. The Wren Library. A sixteenth-century chapel."

"Don't forget the statue of Isaac Newton."

"You've done your homework—isn't that what Americans call it?"

"I'm skilled at homework."

Night was upon us. The summer air enveloped me.

"The college isn't closed to us. I could show you my office."

"I'd like to see your office."

"Now?" he said, clearly regretting his too-quick invitation.

"Best to tour the college and see your office in the daylight."

"Agreed." He took my hand.

I felt desired. Desirable. Kevin had often made me feel desired and desirable, but Kevin might have been pretending, just as the buildings around me were façade upon façade.

Matthew left the decision to me, unspoken. Not pressuring me or trying to get me drunk. He was gracious. A gentleman. He wasn't making presumptions about me or my situation. I didn't have to be on my guard for fumbling approaches that might render future outings with the children impossible.

He let me be in charge. The choice was mine to make.

And I made it.

"So much history, waiting to be explored. For example, I'd like another opportunity to investigate the workings of a French drain."

"That can be arranged. Readily." I was taken aback by the high spirits that seemed to fill him, his shoulders relaxing as if, unbeknownst to me, he'd been wound tight, waiting for my decision. "I'm glad you share my fascination with it."

CHAPTER 22

When I awoke in the morning, I was alone, and I was cold. Coffee was being brewed downstairs, the aroma filling the cottage. This was followed by the blissful fragrance of frying bacon. A man's paisley dressing gown had been placed across the end of the bed.

The bedroom was sparsely furnished, no pictures on the walls. The beige carpet had seen better days. Because of the uneven floor, the wardrobe leaned to the right. The glass in the window embrasures on either side of the bed had been replaced by canvas, yet another mystery of England.

Our time together had been easy. Flowing. After I'd fallen in love with my husband, I'd assumed I'd never be with another man. Yet here I was, able to feel joy from another person's touch and from caressing him in turn. When I lay on top of him afterward, nestling my cheek against his shoulder, his arms around me, a layer of dampness formed where our skin touched, gliding between us, and an unexpected sense of peace had flowed through me.

Slipping out of bed, I put on the dressing gown, silky and soft. It came to my ankles and smelled of its owner in a most delightful way. I rolled up the sleeves. Drawn by the sunlight, I went to the front windows, which provided an oblique view of the river. The water was dazzling, reflecting the surrounding trees, the surface cut again and again by scullers. Water droplets poured off the oars and sparked in the light.

I made my way down the narrow, steep staircase and found Matthew in the kitchen. He wore a dressing gown that matched mine.

"Good morning," he said, his voice buoyant.

"Good morning." My burdens had dissolved.

He was creating a feast for us, the constituent parts spread out across the kitchen table. "Ready in ten minutes, I'm estimating."

"I'll take a quick shower."

The bathroom was under the stairs, and crazily designed, with the toilet on the left side, beneath the top of the stairway, and the bathtub with shower to the right, beneath the bottom of the stairway. The setup was weird, but presumably an architect, or plumber, had believed it made sense this way.

I climbed into the tub. The showerhead was installed at a good level for me, although I suspected the underside of the steps would graze Matthew's head when he stood here. The shower contraption itself included a box attached to the wall, whose function I couldn't ascertain. The shower hose could slip off its support to be handheld.

I turned on the bathtub tap, and when the water was hot, I switched the lever to the shower. After the initial burst of cold, the water was wonderfully warm against my face and chest. I closed my eyes and luxuriated in it. I turned. I loved the feeling of hot water on my shoulders and back.

I smelled smoke.

I opened my eyes. Black smoke was filling the room. It was coming from—the showerhead. Smoke, fire, water, electrocution, the house burning down.

I leapt out of the tub and turned off the water. Smoke continued to pour out of the showerhead until I could barely see. Until it was choking me.

The wages of sin. The punishment for adultery: dying in a shower fire. A surge of adrenaline told me to *get out now*.

Wrapping myself in a towel, I ran to the kitchen.

Matthew was whipping cream in a bowl.

"Black smoke is coming from the showerhead."

He looked up from his whipping project. A large bowl of strawberries, glistening, sat on the table. "Most likely a short circuit."

He flipped a switch on the kitchen wall, near the ceiling.

"There," he said placidly. "I turned off the electricity to the shower. I'll sort it later. You should take a bath instead. Much more soothing."

"You have to do something. The cottage could burn down."

"Don't worry. The cottage won't burn down." He resumed whipping the cream.

"How do you know? You can't know that."

"Sorry. You're concerned. Sorry." He put down the mixer. "I'll take a look."

I followed him. The bathroom was still filled with smoke. But no more poured from the showerhead.

"You see, it's fine."

"How can you be so nonchalant about it?" I asked in anger.

"I'm not," he said, confused.

"The room is filled with black smoke!"

"I'll open the front door to air the place out."

"*What?* You have to make sure there's no fire—in the wall, or in the pipes, if such a thing is possible."

"Shower fires happen all the time," he said.

"No, they don't! I've never heard of it."

"Granted, not *all* the time. But often enough. In this country, we use electric showers to raise the water pressure to acceptable levels.

The showers can short out, or the wires become frayed, or there can be any manner of problems that produce black smoke."

Then I understood: This wasn't something that had ever happened in a novel set in Britain (not one I'd read, that is), nor was it shown in movies or TV series set in Britain, and so I was unaware of it. I'd bumped against the fact that I actually knew very little about this culture I'd worshipped when I was growing up. I knew next to nothing about the day-to-day realities of living here or about the reactions and expectations of real-life British people—including the man who stood before me now, regarding me with what appeared to be sincere worry, not about the smoke but about me.

"Everything's going to be fine," he said, with a plaintive edge to his voice, as if hoping I wasn't offended. Hoping I wouldn't throw my clothes on, march out to the street, and phone for a taxi to take me home.

He pushed back my hair and rubbed my upper arms. "Sorry. You're very wet. You must be cold." He continued to rub his hands over me, warming me. "Do you actually need a bath, or may I dry you off?" He began to do just that, using the towel wrapped around me. I did begin to feel better. "Are you ready for breakfast?" he asked, then added with his usual glimmer, "Breakfast is just about ready for you."

I wasn't such an American literalist that I didn't realize he was talking about more than breakfast.

CHAPTER 23

Nicky and I sat at the dining table with paper, quill pens, and a glass of freshly squeezed orange juice spread out before us. I'd arranged several cork-backed placemats on the table to protect it.

"I bet Isabella did this," he said.

Keeping the discovery to himself, he'd told Janet that he was learning about the Tudors. She'd responded by explaining that Catholics during the Tudor era had used orange-juice ink to communicate with one another in secret. When it dries, orange-juice ink is invisible, and letters written with it appear to be blank pages. The words reappear when a candle flame, or other heat source, is put behind the paper. Janet had learned about this at school and practiced it at home. She'd given Nicky everything necessary for us to try, and he was eager to begin.

A worthy activity to fill our evening, after his successful sleepover.

"I'm going to write a thank-you note in orange-juice ink to Janet," he said.

"That's a good idea."

"What are you going to write?"

"I'm going to write a letter to Christopher, to tell him about your friendship with Janet."

This brought a smile.

"Maybe we should practice using the quills on scrap paper first," I said.

"I'm going to start right in. We'll *learn by doing*," he said, quoting his after-school tutor. He dipped the quill in the juice, and I did the same. He began to write, speaking aloud: "*Dear Janet, Thank you for inviting me . . .*"

The quill scratched against the paper.

I wrote, *Dear Christopher, I'm writing to you with orange-juice ink*.

The paper resisted the movement of the quill. Getting the juice down smoothly, without globs, wasn't easy.

"Too bad we don't have a strainer," I said. "It might make things easier. Fewer globs."

"Those olden-days people probably didn't have a strainer, either," Nicky said. "So this makes us more like them."

"That's true."

The angle and shape of the quill forced my hand to make unforeseen turns. No wonder the handwriting in the account ledgers had been difficult to decipher. The quill caused the letters to be shaped in specific ways, although actual ink would no doubt have been easier to use.

"I hope they write us back with orange-juice ink," Nicky said. "Then we can light a candle or just a lighter to make the words come out."

Again the memory assaulted me—the fire he'd started in his room with the lighter he'd found in Central Park. I struggled to keep my voice measured. He could hear me better that way, all his therapists agreed. "I hope they write back with orange-juice ink, too. But remember, you must never, ever, use a lighter or light candles on your own to read the letters. Always wait until a grown-up is with you."

"Do you think I'm stupid or something? Like a fucking baby?"

I didn't know whether to reprimand him for his swearing or praise him for understanding this critical rule, or both. I let it go, hoping I'd made the point.

"I wish Janet was here," he said.

"That would be nice."

"I miss her. We're going to see each other lots of times before she leaves on her holiday. She's my best friend. When you have a best friend, you miss the person when you're not with them. Rosie told me."

"She's right. Having a friend is worth it, though."

"I should write a thank-you note to Maisie, too," he said.

"Maybe you should write a pretend thank-you letter from Duncan to Maisie and sign it in Duncan's name, or make a drawing of his paw print."

Nicky smiled again. "That's what I'll do." Pushing aside the unfinished letter to Janet, he took a fresh sheet of paper. "*Dear Maisie,*" he read aloud. "*Thank you for the chew bone with peanut butter inside.*" He was relaxed. Content. "Maisie had the chew-bone treat waiting in the freezer for Duncan," he told me.

"She sounds like a wonderful dog."

"She is."

We returned to our writing. To the sound of the quills, scratching. This was the best part of a project: the chance to talk while doing something productive. This was what other moms and children did.

"My hand hurts," he said.

"Take a break."

He put down the quill and made a fist with his right hand, squeezing, then stretching his hand open. He repeated this a few times. "My fingers are achy. Using the quill is hard."

"It's hard for me, too. You're doing a great job, though," I said.

"I don't like that it's so hard."

"It must have been hard for Janet at first. Until she practiced and it became easier."

"It's too hard," he said.

"Isabella probably had a hard time with it at first, too."

He stared at me, his chin thrust forward, his shoulders tensed, his eyes alight with suspicion. "Aren't you listening to me?"

I stared at him, not understanding.

"I said, *it's too hard*."

With a sweep of his arm, he pushed the cup of juice, the quills, and the paper onto the floor. We both studied the juice as it was absorbed into the Persian carpet.

I couldn't move. Then, "You'll have to clean that up."

"*You* clean it up."

"I didn't make the mess."

"But you can fucking clean it up." His eyes widened in anger but also in fear, anguish, terror, a half dozen conflicting emotions mixed together, and like a trigger fired, he wailed, "I want Janet. I want Janet." He banged his hands, palms open, on the table—"*Janet, Janet*"—and then he began to smash his head against the table, hard, again and again, not noticing, or not caring, that he must be hurting himself.

I stood behind him and put my hands on his shoulders, to pull him away from the table. To stop him from bashing his head. He turned into my arms, rose from the chair, sliding it aside with his leg, and punched me in the abdomen. An onslaught followed, kicking, punching as hard as he could, my jaw, chest, neck, shoulders—and all I could think was, *My body is softer than the table. He won't get hurt punching me.* I struggled to gain a grip on his arms, to control him. He used his knees and feet instead, striking my shins. He wound one leg around my knee, to make me fall, but I made my muscles firm to resist.

I knew what to do, and although it was hard, I was still bigger than he was, still stronger. While taking his punches, I maneuvered our chairs one behind the other. Gripping his arms, pressing my body against him, I guided him into the front chair. I sat in the chair behind him and crossed his arms in a straitjacket hold as he kicked and squirmed and howled and cried.

"Quiet now, Nicky," I said softly, as his raging continued. "Shh. Quiet now." I breathed deeply, not raising my voice.

Kevin and I had often used this technique when Nicky was out of control, to protect him from hurting himself. To stop him from hurting us. A therapist had taught us. If chairs weren't available, we'd maneuver him onto our laps and cross his arms, with our arms around him, holding him tight. Other therapists disapproved of this method, said it was cruel and abusive to the child. But I couldn't let Nicky hurt himself. I couldn't let him continue to hurt me.

And, most basic, I didn't know what else to do.

Gradually he stopped kicking. Stopped squirming. His breathing came to match mine. Long inhale. Equally long exhale. I knew better than to let go of him too soon. Twice on other occasions, he'd pretended to be resting and turned on me after I'd released him.

Duncan came from beneath the table and pushed his body sideways against us, resting his chin on Nicky's lap, gazing up at his face. Still I couldn't risk letting go. I had to wait until Nicky dozed toward sleep. I needed to regard his rage as a type of seizure that gripped him and passed. It was a medical condition: That's how I had to view it.

He was always tired after an incident. That was what Kevin and I called it. An innocuous term, a code between us, and it stopped the truth from overwhelming us.

Nine years old, from a loving home, countless medical professionals having given their opinions, and, nonetheless, this.

What should I have done differently? He must have been overtired from his sleepover. We should have filled the evening by watching a movie on my laptop. I'd deluded myself into thinking we were doing something positive, and safe, with the orange-juice project. Nicky had suggested it, but I was the adult. I should have had the foresight to know better.

He seemed nearly asleep now. He'd become a sweet young boy falling asleep in a chair while a big cream-colored dog snuggled against him.

"Are you tired?" I asked.

He nodded.

Slowly, in small increments, I loosened my grip on him. What would happen when he was as tall as me? Then taller than me. As strong as me. Then stronger than me.

But now he needed sleep.

I stood and lifted Nicky beneath his arms.

"Time to get ready for bed," I said as if nothing were wrong.

As I led him down the hallway and up the stairs, Duncan following, my feet stumbled over themselves. I pressed my fingertips along the wall for balance. My jaw throbbed. My shins ached. When I tried to breathe, the pain in my chest hurt so much it frightened me. *Tiny breaths, tiny breaths,* I told myself, all the way up the stairs.

Nicky first. After he was settled, I could think about myself.

His bedroom, next door to mine, was unadorned. The blue-and-white-striped wallpaper was faded. The twin beds had simple metal headboards. The three Cresham sons killed in World War I looked out at us from the photograph on the bureau.

I helped him change into his pajamas, brush his teeth, use the bathroom. After tucking him into bed, I turned on his nightlight and switched off the table lamp. He rolled onto his side. I sat on the bed, and I rubbed his shoulder. His breathing slowed into the steadiness of sleep. I kissed him on the head and stood.

"Good night, Nicky," I said, as if this were any other night. It was seven twenty. Going to the door, I called Duncan to me. Our daily routines had to be observed, and Duncan needed a final walk. I'd set the coffee for the morning, so I'd only have to push a button to make it brew. As if everything were normal.

Raising a child: the most important calling of a woman's life. The rest of a woman's life was secondary to this, or so I'd been taught, absorbing the message from the society around me.

On an autumn afternoon when Nicky was three months old, Kevin and I had walked in Riverside Park, Kevin holding our baby against his chest in a carrier. We sat down on a bench in the sun, the leaves red and orange around us. Nicky weighed fourteen pounds. His small feet, in their knitted booties. His exquisite fingers. His bright eyes staring, following my voice. Such overpowering tenderness I'd felt for him. I'd put my index finger against his palm, and he'd squeezed my finger tight. I'd read that the most important thing parents could do for their children was to love them. And I did love him.

Like any parent, I'd had dreams for my child, imaginings of who he'd become. Simple-enough dreams. That he'd do well in school. Find a purpose in life, a profession he wanted to pursue. That someday he'd marry and have children.

But the love Kevin and I felt for him had never been enough to help him, and all my dreams for his future had come to this:

I went into my bedroom and from the bedside table retrieved the key to his room. The key had been in the lock when we arrived, and I'd put it away for safekeeping.

I locked Nicky's door. For the first time in his life, I locked him in.

I was afraid of him.

After I blotted the rug as best I could, hoping it wasn't a priceless antique—I'd ask Mrs. Gardner to recommend a carpet cleaner—I sat down at the dining table. I felt utterly alone. My jaw continued to throb. At least my breathing was easier.

I needed to talk to someone. I didn't know Lizzie well enough to call her. I could call Matthew. But at the thought of telling him what Nicky had done, about his violence toward me, shame overcame me. I barely knew Matthew. I didn't want him to dislike Nicky or to worry about me.

I could call Kevin. I wouldn't feel ashamed speaking to him. He'd instantly understand what had happened.

In New York, it was afternoon. Sunday afternoon. Kevin might be playing tennis. He might be with Tim. Or on a plane, returning to Chicago for the trial. I might not reach him for several hours.

But if I called Kevin, I'd be admitting that I couldn't survive without him. That I had no choice but to accept whatever terms he offered.

My phone vibrated. His name. I'd forgotten: the daily dinnertime phone call. Today Nicky was supposed to phone Kevin, because we didn't know exactly what time Nicky would return from his sleepover. Kevin must be worried.

"Hi. I'm sorry Nicky didn't call you. He's already in bed."

"How did things go?"

"Where are you?" I asked.

From the pause before his response, I knew he sensed something was wrong. He turned guarded. "In New York. Have been for a few days."

"Where are you exactly?" I wanted to have an image of him in my mind as I spoke to him and to delay the moment when I had to tell him. Dread grasped at me, certainty that I'd done wrong with Matthew, betraying my husband, risking Nicky's well-being.

"I'm in the study. Listening to the game while catching up on paperwork. I don't have to be in Chicago until Tuesday."

Baseball, and monthly bills. The stuff of daily life.

I could see him at his desk. Visualize his body. The tilt of his head. Kevin. How I loved him. All the love I'd been holding back, these many weeks, poured through me. I could pretend he was the person I'd known before that day in Central Park. I could slip back into my life beside him and not have to take care of Nicky on my own.

"The sleepover was good. But Nicky had an incident when he got back."

"Is he okay? Are you okay?"

"He's fine. Asleep. There's a bad bruise on my jaw. He's growing taller: He can reach my face. Other bruises, too."

"Oh, my God. What set him off?"

"Missing Janet. Being overtired. I should have put him to bed immediately after his snack. Or as soon as he got home."

"Don't blame yourself."

"Who should I blame?"

I could never blame Nicky. He was a child. Besides, I'd seen the fear on his face as he lost control, as if he knew that the wrong part of his brain was taking over and he was powerless to prevent it.

"You're not at fault." If Kevin had been with Nicky when this happened, I'd be comforting him the same way.

"I locked him in his room for the night. I didn't know what else to do."

"You did right. The dog will bark and wake you if Nicky's in any kind of trouble."

"This all seems hopeless. No matter what we do."

"The full-blown rages come less often now. What, four months since the last one?"

Four months—Easter. We'd been invited to an informal buffet dinner at the home of one of Kevin's senior law partners. A half dozen children would be there. Despite Nicky's unpredictability, Kevin and I felt we had to bring him to the gathering.

On that day, we'd walked along West 82nd Street toward Central Park West. Daffodils were blooming in the tree pits along the street. Nicky wouldn't walk properly, twisting and dragging his feet as we held his hands. He pulled away from us and sat down on the sidewalk. *I don't want to go to a goddamn party. You can't make me. You can't make me.* He began to bash his fists against the sidewalk. As Kevin tried to lift him, Nicky screamed, *fuck, shit, fuck, shit,* and he turned and punched his father in the stomach, over and over.

Another thirty-something man, pushing a stroller, moved around us, not believing what he was seeing—a man, like himself, being attacked by a child. Kevin turned Nicky and held Nicky's back against his chest, arms crossed in front of him, straitjacket style, Nicky still kicking and screaming, *fuck, shit.*

Passersby crossed the street to avoid us. I hoped no one would phone the police. In the support group I'd attended when Nicky was younger, a mom had related how a well-meaning but clueless stranger had in fact phoned the police—to report child abuse—when her young son was out of control on the street, her husband struggling to stop him from banging his soft head against the concrete sidewalk. No one had called the police on Kevin and me. Not yet.

Gradually Nicky had calmed, and he'd drifted into sleep.

We sat on the steps of a brownstone, Nicky between Kevin and me, his head on Kevin's knee as he dozed. Kevin and I exchanged a glance over Nicky's head, knowing each other's thoughts: What was the better punishment for Nicky, to go to the party or to go home? Kevin and I had wanted to attend the party, and in fact Kevin needed to attend.

So we went, and Nicky played quietly with the other kids, as if the incident had never happened. I spent the evening vigilant, never letting him out of my sight.

"Four months. That's progress," Kevin said.

"What do we do now?" I already knew the answer. There was nothing we could do, except prepare for the next time.

"We go on. Keep trying. In the fall, we'll have conferences with his doctors and reevaluate his treatment." This was the lawyer side of Kevin, logical and pragmatic. "We'll find a new solution. Maybe there's some new medication, one that won't put him into a daze. We'll always be finding new solutions as he grows older. I miss you," he said, cutting into his own words.

"I miss you, too," I said, because part of me did miss him—missed the person I thought I'd known.

"Have you . . . I mean, the future . . ." These brief, broken phrases, so unlike him and his usual precision, showed his pain. His suffering.

"No, I haven't." Surely I had more time before I had to decide. Suddenly I felt desperate. Going back to him, resuming where we'd left off, waiting for Nicky's next outburst—I couldn't. But I'd have to. I couldn't, but . . . The lack of choice roared through my thoughts.

A long silence opened between us.

Into the silence, Kevin said, "I went to see Christopher today. He's in the hospital again. He isn't doing very well. The doctors want him to stick it out for another few weeks, testing the medications. They still think they might find a combination of treatments that'll work for him. Or at least give them information to help others. After that, he wants to go home, for the end. Home to Ashton Hall. This will be soon. Within the next few weeks, as I say. While he has the strength to travel."

"That can't be true. I've spoken to Christopher or Rafe almost every day. Everything's been fine. Exhausting, but okay. Are you sure? Are the doctors certain?"

"Christopher didn't want to worry you."

He'd been keeping up appearances, as usual. I should have realized.

I didn't say my next thought, but Kevin said it for me: "You and Nicky might have to stay there longer than we expected."

Yes, we might have to stay, continuing the life we'd begun, giving me a reprieve, the decision made for me, at least for now, but not in any way I could be happy about or look forward to, waiting for Christopher to die.

After saying goodbye to Kevin, I let Duncan out. He did his business and returned promptly. I locked the outside door, turned out the lights, went upstairs. I opened Nicky's door. He was still asleep, in the same position. Duncan jumped onto the end of the bed, circled three times, and curled up by Nicky's feet. Nicky stirred but didn't wake. I left them, relocking the door behind me.

I went to my bedroom. I felt a weight inside me, pulling me down, urging me toward sleep. But it was only nine o'clock, and I was also over-alert and afraid to let go of consciousness. The bruise on my jaw was swelling, despite the ice pack I pressed against it.

Sitting at my desk, I felt a sudden ache in my side, below my ribs. I couldn't find a comfortable way to sit. Nonetheless, I put down the ice pack and opened my laptop. I wouldn't give in to pain and despair. I'd fill the hours before bed with work, to make me feel I had something worthwhile to show for the evening. I prepared a note to my thesis adviser, to let him know I was almost ready to show him my draft.

After so much time away, I checked his email address on the university website. He wasn't listed. I did a search on him. He was at Berkeley now. He could be an outside examiner for my thesis, but he could no longer be my adviser. I looked up several other professors I'd worked with closely. They weren't listed, either.

Fighting a sense of the floor slipping out from under me, I forged on, rewriting my note and addressing it to the department chair. I'd taken a class with her; I knew her. After saving the note to send tomorrow morning (I wouldn't bother her on a Sunday), I logged in to my work account. A slew of messages was waiting, clients catching up before the Monday rush. The images I'd gathered for the medieval-themed sneakers had received ardent approval from the marketing team. The company was expanding the line even before their first sales, planning to create a series of sneakers with these images for all ages and in all sizes. Okay, I could research that. No problem. The Tiepolo refrigerator magnets—excellent choices, the client said. Next was a note from Paul, my boss, congratulating me on the great job I was doing.

My phone pinged with a text. It was Matthew. *Lovely to see you.*

You, too, I wrote.

Cecilia texted me that everything went moderately well. That's an achievement for Janet.

I didn't know what he meant by *moderately well,* and Cecilia hadn't said this to me when she dropped Nicky off, but I played along: *For Nicky, too. He was exhausted, asleep around 7:30.*

If he's in bed, are you able to talk?

I didn't want to talk to him. I couldn't. I'd start crying if I spoke to him, this man who was so considerate toward me. He'd ask why I was crying, and I still didn't want to tell him what Nicky had done. Didn't want to admit to him that I couldn't control my beloved son, a nine-year-old child. Nor did I want to lie. Via text, I could pretend:

I was about to close my eyes. I'm exhausted, too.

Why disturb him, or upset his sleep or dreams?

I'm not surprised, he wrote.

Talking to you might wake me up.

Most probably it would.

Can we talk in the morning? I asked.

I've a conference tomorrow. I'll ring you at the end of the afternoon. Around five.

We texted our good-nights.

CHAPTER 24

At seven-thirty the next morning, I opened Nicky's door and watched him sleep. I followed his breathing, the gentle rise and fall of his back, as I'd done ever since he was a newborn, when he was a gift, a blessing from the universe, in the bassinet beside me.

Calling Duncan, I closed the door without locking it and returned the key to my bedside table. It was a new day, I was out of bed, and I no longer felt helpless. Duncan and I went outside and wandered the garden, which gleamed in the early light. The adrenaline surge of last night was gone, and I moved slowly. In addition to the now very visible bruise on my jaw, my chest and ribs continued to ache when I breathed deeply, and I'd found a painfully tender bruise on my right thigh and another on my left arm.

But as I roamed the gardens, lush in their colorful summer plentitude, I felt consoled. How lucky I was to be here, now, at this precise moment, nature surrounding me in the warm glow of morning.

When we returned to the apartment, Nicky was dressed and downstairs. He'd set the table for breakfast and was bringing out the cereal and milk. He was always more cooperative after an incident, the rage drained out of him.

When we were seated at the table, he said, "Why do you have a bruise on your face?"

"From where you punched me last night." I didn't say it in anger or bitterness, merely as a fact.

He stared at his cereal. "I'm sorry. I didn't mean it."

This was the first time he'd ever apologized.

"I know you didn't. You have to remember to slow down when you feel yourself losing your temper. Breathe deeply and count to ten, until you feel better."

This technique had never worked, but it was something to say, some advice to give. Again and again, Kevin and I had asked Nicky what he felt like inside before he began punching. *I don't punch people,* he'd always replied, even when confronted with evidence. Today, he wasn't denying it.

"You made a mess with the orange juice. I cleaned it up last night because we don't own the carpet or anything here. I wasn't able to wait until you could clean it up."

His tone and expression were oddly impassive as he said, "Can I still see Janet lots of times before she leaves on her holiday?"

A recognition of consequences, for the first time. What was the proper response to punching your mother? The incidents swept over him like a wave, and when they were gone, they were incomprehensible, to him as well as to me. He could barely remember what had happened. How could I punish him for something he didn't fully remember? Nonetheless, he had to be held accountable. I was at a loss, his new contrition as hard to deal with as his former denials.

And here was another problem: He had a friend—if in fact Janet was a beneficial friend for him. "What happened at the sleepover? Janet's mother said it went *moderately* well."

"Janet got mad because her mother wouldn't let us have our tea in the television room, and she called her mother a super bad name and wouldn't stop."

A verbal attack, rather than physical. "What happened after that?"

"Janet had to stay in her bedroom while I watched a movie with Rosie. Rosie likes movies about hero pets. Duncan and Maisie watched, too, and they barked at the dogs on the TV."

"That sounds like fun."

"It was, but it would have been funner with Janet."

"More fun." I couldn't help myself. "It would have been *more fun* with Janet."

"That's what I meant. Can I see her lots of times before her trip?"

He waited for my decision.

"You may see her once." This seemed fair. "I'll work out the details with her father."

Nicky didn't challenge me. Alice arrived, with a plan to bike with Nicky to a local farm that let customers pick their own vegetables. She proposed cooking a Moroccan vegetarian stew for our dinner.

As she stood before me, young, vivacious, bursting with good humor, I knew I should tell her. Warn her. Let her decide if she felt safe with Nicky. Or I should just pay her for the rest of the summer and take over his full-time care myself. He was my son and my responsibility.

But I had other things I needed to do and wanted to do, more than I could push into the hours before he woke up in the morning and after he went to bed at night. Selfish once again, I put myself first. Maybe I wasn't wired to be a mother.

"See you later, Nicky," I said. "Have fun."

They set off.

I kept Duncan with me. We went upstairs. In the bathroom, I tried to cover the bruise on my jaw with makeup, but it still showed, the greenish-blue color and the swelling both.

I returned to my desk. I sent my note to the department chair. I reviewed the sneaker specs for the various age groups, emailed to me overnight, and I began research. Duncan stretched out beneath the desk. I slipped off my sandals and rubbed my feet into the soft fur of his tummy, warm against my skin. He made rumbling sounds of contentment.

I touched my jaw. What should I say to anyone who asked about it?

I tripped on the stairs and hit the banister.

Nicky and I were roughhousing.

I was in Britain, however, surrounded by the British, and most likely no one would ask. Alice hadn't. The gardener I'd greeted on my walk hadn't. I'd reapply the makeup before I went to the conservation center this afternoon. Instead of a summer dress, I wore trousers and a long-sleeved shirt, concealing at least some of my bruises.

I never had to conceal my bruises from Kevin. He made me feel safe and comforted.

As I made my way through dozens of medieval representations of adorable animals suitable for sneakers in the infant-to-three-year-old category—a squirrel eating acorns, a lion playing the violin—my thoughts circled. Was Nicky's well-being alone a good enough reason to stay with Kevin?

Yes. No.

One thing I *was* certain about: I couldn't continue a relationship beyond friendship with Matthew. I hadn't resolved my marriage. I couldn't regard sex as nothing more than pleasure. A wife, a mother, simply enjoying herself outside her roles—the universe would never permit me this. Had never permitted women this.

CHAPTER 25

Caricatures: The cook, about to whack a spit boy with a pan. The shoemaker, long-faced, barefoot, the tools of his trade on a belt around his waist, holding a pair of boots upward in front of his crotch. Such drawings were called *marginalia*. They were common even in illuminated manuscripts, so no surprise to find them here, in the account ledgers. But I did wonder if anyone actually reviewed these records after they were prepared.

When I'd arrived at the conservation center after lunch, Martha, looking abashed, had touched her own jaw, as if my face were a mirror. I'd pretended all was well. She wore black tights and long sleeves every day, no matter the weather. She might simply have had an unvarying sense of style. Perhaps religious beliefs led her to modesty. Or maybe she, too, was hiding injuries.

A portrait of a baby, fat and screaming.

An entry reading *bokes for the lybrarye*, and, next to it, a picture of the keeper of the books collapsing under the weight of his charges, piled high in his arms.

The Second Hand, as Martha had dubbed him, had evolved from playful to nasty. The Second Hand made *milord's spaniels* look like dogs that would devour you—and there, on the next page, was a payment for a *henne* attacked by one of milord's spaniels, feathers flying in the Second Hand's cartoon of it.

I progressed through the era of King James, reading into the 1610s, past the time frame of the radiocarbon dating of Isabella's skeleton. Nothing broke the pattern. *Lady Southbrooke's baby baptized . . . Lady Southbrooke's baby buried . . .*

Which Lady Southbrooke was this? I wanted to see *her*, one specific individual. She was a mother, like me. I understood the pain she would have felt, giving birth. Her anguish when the baby died. The joy and worry as she watched her children grow—the children who survived. Mercifully, the Second Hand did no drawings of dead babies or suffering children.

"Good afternoon." Upon Mrs. Gardner's arrival, everyone rose, as if the conservation center were a military headquarters. "As you were," she said.

We sat down and resumed what we'd been doing. Mrs. Gardner went to the far side of the room, to the workstations of the four graduate students. She reviewed their progress. In addition to making an inventory of the documents from the muniment room, they were studying the fabrics, the virginal, and the other easily movable objects from Isabella's room.

When Mrs. Gardner circled back to me, she said, "Ah, Hannah." Had her surprise at my appearance caused her to use my first name? She stared at me as if debating whether to say more. Instead, she turned to Martha.

"Dr. Tinsley." Her tone was stern.

"Yes, Mrs. Gardner."

"Unfortunately, the county archivists will take possession of the parish records sooner than I'd hoped. They'll descend on us sometime this week. The official who telephoned refused to be more specific." Her voice dripped with annoyance. "Condemning us to the suspense, I suppose."

"This week?" Martha protested.

"Regarding other pending matters," Mrs. Gardner went on, allowing no time for complaints about the inevitable, "the folded letters from the keepsake box."

Martha gave a frustrated sigh. "I'll begin work on them after the archivists take the parish records. The letters will need six hours each in the humidification chamber, to allow me to unfold them. By the way," she added, "the proper word for what we're calling the keepsake box is a *coffret*."

"Noted," Mrs. Gardner said with forbearance. I smiled to myself. Martha was a research librarian and scholar from top to toe. "And the sketchbooks?"

"They're with one of our furloughed conservators."

"Good. And the books on Isabella Cresham's desk?"

"Ms. Larson has finished reviewing them."

"Anything noteworthy?"

"It was a surprising collection . . ." I didn't object to Martha speaking for me, going through the list, deflecting Mrs. Gardner's attention. "Also, we found a drawing of a little girl named Blanche." She gestured to the photograph of it on the wall. "We have no idea who she is."

"Hmm," Mrs. Gardner said, looking over at the drawing. She appeared unimpressed.

"And finally"—Martha paused with an emphasis that seemed designed to regain Mrs. Gardner's attention—"the books from Isabella's desk include an exceedingly rare and beautiful medieval illuminated psalter."

"Is that so," Mrs. Gardner said, noncommittal.

"It's in gorgeous condition."

"Upon initial review, would you say the volume is of such consequence that we should plan an official unveiling for it?"

"Definitely," Martha said with excitement, her eyes, her entire being, alight. "It's very similar to the Luttrell Psalter, though that book is larger. It's certainly on the level of the Macclesfield Psalter, which is roughly the same size and which sold at Sotheby's in 2004 for 1.7 million pounds. Not that we're going to sell our psalter, but for the sake of comparison. You can see the Macclesfield at the Fitzwilliam Museum in town."

Still inscrutable, Mrs. Gardner asked, "And where is our volume now?"

"Locked in the safe in my office."

"Excellent!" She was suddenly transformed. "We'll call it the Cresham Psalter. No, no"—she waved off this idea—"we'll call it the Ashton Hall Psalter, to bring attention to the house. Other stately homes have important books named after them; we will, too. The tourist income generated from one psalter might equal two conservators called back from furlough." She allowed herself a broad smile. "Well done, everyone."

Mrs. Gardner departed. Martha retreated into her usual state of serene timelessness as she continued to review the parish records, searching for even oblique references to Isabella Cresham. The others returned to their work, and so did I.

In the account ledger, *a pound of pynneapple compffets* was purchased. I'd never liked pineapple candy; it was too sugary. This was followed by *a pound of synnammonde compffets*—the eternal trial of spelling *cinnamon* as well as *comfits*.

A *saddell for milady.* There was Lady Southbrooke, riding along the river.

Malmsey, a type of wine. *I'll drown you in the malmsey-butt,* I remembered from Shakespeare's *Richard III*.

The purchase of a *hawke.* And another. Wages to a *fawlconner* and hoods for the *hawkes.*

In the margin, a hawk, fastidious and persnickety, picked up a terrified kitten by the scruff of the neck. Would a hawk eat a kitten? The Second Hand had an ugly imagination.

"Hannah," Martha said, startling me. I looked over at her. For the first time during our work together, she was squinting, her brows drawn together, her eyes narrowed, as if she had a pounding headache and could no longer clearly see the words on the page. "Would you look at this for me?"

I went to her. She pointed to an illegible entry in the parish register.

"The handwriting of our priest deteriorated rather badly as he grew older. Often, he wrote in a mixture of English and Latin. I'm now at the point where he provides the actual cause of death only when a person slips away peacefully of old age in his or her bed."

"Wishful thinking? Hoping the same will happen to him?"

"No doubt. His hand must have been shaking rather badly as he wrote this page. It's from 1552. I believe I've deciphered the relevant passage, but before I tell you, what do you think it says?"

I studied the passage she pointed to. It was a mess. Running my eyes over the entire page of spidery writing, inkblots, and thumbprints, I created an image in my mind of the elderly priest, half blind, his hand shaking, his legs wrapped in a blanket to ward off the chill that crept through him even during warm weather. I returned to the passage marked by her finger.

"Oh. I see." I matched her objective tone.

"It's the only example I've found so far of that name."

How restrained we were.

"We have to remember that families often used the same first names from generation to generation," she said, as if to raise any possible objections to the identification from the start. "And they often named later siblings after previous ones who'd died."

She'd done hours of work, studying the records entry by entry, page by page, and she'd found an answer—one answer, in the ever-flowing river of the past. Maybe Dr. Martha Tinsley was cheering inside herself. I was, on her behalf.

I summoned the elderly priest's wavering voice, mouthing the words he had written in 1552:

Twenty-seconde of June. Baptized this day, a daughter, of Lord Southbrooke and his wife, the Lady Southbrooke, called Isabella.

CHAPTER 26

Shortly before five, I sat on a bench in the walled garden. Beside me was a bed of rosemary, aromatic after basking in sunlight through the day. Beyond it were lettuce, zucchini, basil, cherry tomatoes. The throbbing sounds of nature surrounded me. Cirrus clouds serrated the sky. How deeply this place had touched me. I felt my heart expand to embrace it.

Having a few minutes before Matthew's call, I made the mistake of checking my email, promptly breaking the spell of the walled garden. A note from my department chair was waiting. As I read, the sentences turned into a blur of broken phrases:

I'm afraid I don't remember you . . . many years ago . . . bad timing . . . other candidates . . . will take a while . . . might as well send me a chapter or two, with the abstract . . . maybe I . . .

Another warning that I couldn't go back. My former dreams were fading. I'd send her the chapters and abstract, and fight, if I had to, to receive the degree, because I was so close and the credential could help me down the road. But my professional future—I had to build that anew.

The phone vibrated. Matthew, true to his word. I'd often heard from my single women friends about ghosting: Men not calling. Men never heard from again. Calling when he said he would was a low bar for responsible behavior, but I was glad Matthew had met it.

I answered.

"Good afternoon," he said.

I heard the happiness in his voice. I was sad for him, and for myself.

"How was your meeting?" I asked.

"You don't sound like yourself. Something wrong?"

"No."

"*No?*" he asked.

"Well, yes."

"Tell me," he said, concerned.

Having to say it was wrenching, but I knew I did have to say it. I owed him honesty. "Last night, Nicky . . . He did something troubling." I took refuge in Matthew's use of language, in which confession was also concealment.

"I'm sorry. What happened?"

"I don't want to recount every detail." From what little I'd said already, the scene pulsed through my mind like a horror movie. "The upshot is, I have a bruise on my jaw, my ribs are painful, and . . . more along those lines." Explaining, being honest, not concealing—I could feel some, at least, of my tension and anxiety melt away.

"Do you need to see a doctor?"

"I don't think so."

"I can recommend a doctor if you change your mind. I can drive you there. Do you feel safe?"

I didn't hear any judgment in his voice. Just worry. And support. "Safe enough, during the day. But I locked Nicky into his room last night, so I could sleep. I told Nicky that he could see Janet once before she leaves on holiday," I rushed on. "I'm trying to walk a line between discipline and the positive aspect of their friendship."

He waited for me to say more. I couldn't allow myself to say more.

"One visit sounds like a good compromise." When he spoke again, he seemed to be choosing his words with care. "I believe we have to keep offering them chances to try again. To do better. Giving up on them isn't an alternative."

Nicky was nine years old. He was a little boy. I'd never give up on him. "Would you arrange an outing for them?" I said. "For all of us?"

"Of course. In the meantime, I'd like to see you. Separately from the kids. No doubt Alice would be willing to babysit some evening, and—"

I broke in. "Matthew . . ." How drawn I was to him, with a different kind of attraction from what I felt for Kevin. Less desperate. More independent. But my independence couldn't be based on this: an affair. "I can't continue, from the other night. I have to resolve my marriage first. Figure things out. For Nicky's sake. For my sake."

"Has your husband shifted his behavior, do you think, whilst you're figuring things out? Or is he going along as he always has?" I heard his anger and also incredulity that I'd give in to the double standard.

"This isn't about him. It's about me."

It was about Matthew, too. I didn't want to have an affair that would run its course and end in boredom or recrimination and hostility. I needed a friend more than a lover. I didn't know if Matthew wanted or needed a friend, and I couldn't ask him without sounding pitiful.

"With all due respect, Hannah," he continued, "and I realize I've a vested interest here, but how would you react if I said I couldn't see you because of a difficulty Janet was having?"

"I'd think you were wrong. But that doesn't change what I feel about *me*."

"Did you get enough sleep last night?" he asked.

I didn't like admitting that my thoughts might be skewed. "No. What with everything, and the pain . . . only a few hours."

"You need to catch up with yourself."

Now Matthew would have to choose: whether anger would come between us, or whether the affection we'd developed over the past weeks would continue in some form.

He was silent for a good while. "Friends, then, I hope," he finally said, as if he'd heard my thoughts. "As before."

"Thank you for understanding." How much I wanted to embrace him and feel his arms around me.

"You don't need to thank me. You're traumatized."

Was I? No therapist had ever used that term about me. "I also found out that my uncle Christopher isn't doing well. He'll be returning to Ashton Hall soon. To die."

"That's terrible news. I'm so sorry."

"I'll stay here with him. I won't let him die alone."

"You're very compassionate. And an excellent mother, if I may say, under challenging circumstances."

"Not as challenging as most people have. I have enough money— well, at least I do now, from my husband. I live in a country at peace, with lots of food and drinkable water. I'm not about to be arrested or killed for being the person I was born as. I'm lucky in every way."

"I'm lucky, as well. Granted. You've faced some challenges, however, and I won't let you deny it."

I said nothing.

"What are you doing for the rest of the day?"

"Alice and Nicky will make dinner. Afterward, Nicky and I will probably watch a movie on my laptop." Our daily routines, flowing smoothly, and I reached for them. "Then I'll do some work, after Nicky is in bed. The project with medieval images on sneakers—the line is being expanded."

"What with the state of the world, a commitment to medieval

images on trainers has to be a positive step." I loved the wry humor in his voice.

"I agree."

"And tomorrow?" he said. "I want to imagine you filling your days."

"My own work in the morning, and in the afternoon I'll go to the conservation center to continue the research—I have to tell you something! Today Martha Tinsley discovered Isabella Cresham's baptismal record. We want to believe it's hers, at least. The date works. June twenty-second, 1552. I'm going to go back and review the account ledgers beginning at that date."

"That is good news. 1552 . . ." I could picture him figuring out the history, based on this date. Doing the math in his head. "That was during the reign of Edward the Sixth, so she was baptized a Protestant. Mary became queen in 1553, which means Isabella's earliest religious training would have been Catholic. Elizabeth succeeded in 1558, when Isabella was, what, six and a half."

"On an estate like this, isolated in many ways, would those changes in religion really have had an impact on a child?" I asked. "It seems unlikely to me."

"In the background of her life, I think. When she went to church with her family. In the discussions she might have overheard amongst the adults around her. The apprehension she might have sensed from them."

I saw Isabella when she was young, sitting on the floor by the fire in the great room with its tapestries, a spaniel resting its head on her lap, as the grown-ups discussed, debated, or whispered in fear about the changes in the country at large.

"Isabella was thirty in 1582, the date of the coins in the keepsake box," he determined. "She was forty-one in 1593, the beginning of the years of nothing, although we don't yet know how those years relate to her. But the evidence is accumulating. Right," he said, using the British signal that we were moving on.

I didn't want to move on. I wanted to stay here, sitting on a bench in a walled garden. I didn't want to confront what might have happened between Alice and Nicky today while I was indulging myself with my job and my passions, and with the pleasure of talking to Matthew.

It's not too late; say you'll have dinner with him.

"Thank you again for your understanding," I said.

"Hannah," he announced, as if to gain my full attention, although my attention hadn't wavered. "You never need to thank me."

CHAPTER 27

Josie Moran Zeitlin said, "Brilliant!"

Nicky and I stood in Lizzie's kitchen. We'd just opened the box of chocolate–almond croissants I'd bought at the bakery in the village.

"Well done, you," said Josie's brother, Ben.

They were two British children, using British vernacular and arch humor, seeming to perform in a play of their own lives. No one would guess their parents were American. Both kids looked like their mother, slender and blond, but with their father's brown eyes. Max Zeitlin, the person Lizzie had described as a cryptologist hero, turned out to be a stout middle-aged man who appeared older than his years and had a Santa Claus appearance and demeanor.

Josie sighed extravagantly. "We never have chocolate–almond croissants anymore," she said.

"Why not?" Nicky said.

"Our mother was *banished from the bakery*," Ben said with dramatic flair.

Lizzie said, "I chose to banish myself. I know when I'm not wanted." In contrast to her children, she spoke with straight-on sincerity.

Josie asked me, "How ever did you brave the queue?"

I was pleased by the stir I'd caused in the Moran Zeitlin household. "I was waiting when the shop opened. The woman at the cash register seemed suspicious of me, but what could she do? There I was."

"You're an exceptional guest," Josie said. "I hope you'll join us for dinner often."

"Okay, children, outside," Lizzie said. "Exhaust yourselves before we eat."

"I'm too old to be ordered to play outside," Josie said. As if to prove this, she tossed her head, bringing her long, flowing hair over one shoulder.

"You're correct. But out with you anyway. You can supervise the boys."

"How about some football? I mean, what you call soccer?" Ben asked Nicky as they left.

Lizzie's home was a small mansion surrounded by old trees. The interior looked as if years ago it had been decorated by a British designer who filled it with chintz, antiques, Persian carpets, and paintings of horses, and then, day by day, week by week, the house had deteriorated into an American just-throw-your-coat-and-shoes-anywhere type of home.

The dining room table was already set, and we three continued the preparations for dinner. Lizzie and Max clearly adored each other—Lizzie placing her fingers on Max's shoulder, Max dropping a hand onto her waist, neither making a big deal of this, not planning it, simply living with a daily intimacy that reminded me of Kevin and me in former years.

One wall of the dining room was stuffed with books in floor-to-ceiling shelves. I went to examine them.

"That's Lizzie's collection of English history books," Max said with pride.

"Yes, I admit it: I went through an obsessive phase," Lizzie said, as she put a vase of flowers on the sideboard. "That's why I'm so interested in your son's discovery. Don't worry," she said as I was about to explain again, "I'm not going to pressure you. The point is, I campaigned for this posting in the UK. A dream come true. Living in beautiful Cambridge. Raising our kids here. And it's been wonderful, but I can't say we've made any British friends, not even at the kids' schools," she said with disappointment. "For some reason, English people don't appreciate me lecturing them about their own history and cultural habits." Shaking her head, she managed a self-deprecating half smile.

"I always enjoy your lectures," Max said.

"That's because you're a darling." She touched his face with her fingertips. "Enough of that. Why don't you two join me in the kitchen while I do the finishing touches."

The kitchen overlooked the back garden, where the kids were involved in their soccer game. Since the incident, Nicky had continued to be kind and cooperative, and my fears about Alice's safety had eased. With Ben and Josie, he played the role of younger brother, doted on by the big kids. If nothing happened to frustrate Nicky, we'd get through the evening smoothly.

Projects I'd worked on filled the kitchen—botanical placemats, ancient Egyptian tomb paintings on pot holders, stained-glass windows on dishcloths. This was the largest collection of my research I'd ever seen out in the world.

"All right, my friend," Lizzie said, "now that the kids are busy, how are you?"

Did my distress show so plainly? I didn't want to discuss Nicky with them. "I just learned that Christopher, my honorary uncle, who lives at the hall, isn't responding to his medical treatment the way we'd hoped."

"Sorry to hear that," Max said.

Lizzie placed her hand on my shoulder. "I'm sorry."

"I might have to stay in the UK into the autumn to be with him."

"What about school for Nicky? What about visas?" Lizzie asked.

"I haven't thought about any of that yet."

"Good. Don't. Think about it, I mean. I'll look into it. That's part of my job."

Max said, "Lizzie's very good at getting things sorted, to use the local terminology. It's one of her specialties. Lizzie is a *fixer*."

"What's with the bruise on your jaw?" she said, ever blunt.

In fact, the bruise was better. But not better enough to escape Lizzie's attention. "I tripped on the stairs."

"You expect me to believe that?" she said, her eyes laser-focused on mine.

"It was an accident."

"Come on, Hannah, tell me the truth," she said, her anger rising.

"Lizzie always knows when her friends, family, and co-workers are trying to conceal something from her," Max told me.

"It was Nicky. He—he . . ." Haltingly, I explained my son to them. As I confessed to Lizzie and Max, I felt even more of my anxiety easing. With Matthew, and now with them, I was losing the necessity of keeping track of all the lies.

"Thank you," Lizzie said. "I appreciate you telling us." She gave me an evaluating stare, and she seemed to be pondering how best to help me and what advice to give. At this moment, I didn't want help or advice, beyond her supportive presence.

"These things are tough," Max said.

Lizzie turned and began mixing olive oil, mustard, and tarragon vinegar for the salad dressing.

"We feel for you," Max added. "And Nicky, too."

"We'll talk more another day, when children aren't waiting to be fed," Lizzie said. This sounded ever so slightly like a threat. Unlatching the window above the sink, she called to the kids, "Time for dinner. Wash your hands first."

After a few minutes, Josie and Ben were with us.

"Nicky's in the puzzle room," Ben said.

"What could we do?" Theatrically, Josie threw up her presumably clean hands. "You should keep that door closed, Daddy. Now he's stuck."

Maybe I should leave him there, working on puzzles for the rest of the evening, rather than risk an outburst if I insisted he join us.

Nicky ran into the kitchen. "Mom, they have an entire room with jigsaw puzzles. I finished the one on the table. It had a pet monkey."

"It wasn't your puzzle to finish," I said.

"My puzzles are available to everyone," Max said with a wave of his hand. "Open source."

"There'll be another puzzle on the table tomorrow," Josie said. "We've dozens of them."

"The one you finished was Seurat's *Sunday on La Grande Jatte*," Max said to Nicky as we sat down in the dining room. "In the art style called *pointillism*—riveting in a puzzle."

"I liked the part in the background, where it was shady in the trees," Nicky said.

"That *is* a gratifyingly difficult section," Max said, pleased.

"I want to do more jigsaw puzzles."

"Happy to loan you a few boxes. Very relaxing, I find," Max said.

"Me, too. I could work on them all day," Nicky said as if he was mimicking someone, I didn't know who. Could he really work on puzzles all day? I allowed myself to consider that maybe he'd come to an understanding of how to focus himself and keep his rage contained.

"That would remove some of the puzzles from our house, at least," Josie said.

"Josie has never opened her mind to the wonders of jigsaw puzzles," Max said.

"My sister doesn't have the patience, so naturally she hates them," Ben said. "I like them, though, and I'm glad you do, too." Ben regarded Nicky with a generous smile.

Nicky was aglow from Ben's acceptance. As we passed the platters of food, Nicky watched Ben and imitated how the older boy carefully served himself and held his fork with an outward motion of his elbow.

Beef Stroganoff was the main course. "This is terrific," I said.

"Lizzie is an excellent cook," Max said.

"Thank you, Mummy!" said Josie, in a better mood now that she was eating.

"Thank you for cooking dinner for us, Mrs. Zeitlin," Nicky said, taking the role of a perfect guest.

"You're welcome, Nicky." She revealed no hint of judgment against him for what he'd done to me.

When we finished, the kids cleared the table and brought out fresh plates for dessert.

"Everyone ready?" Lizzie called from the kitchen.

"Ready," Ben said.

She came out holding a crystal platter. Resting atop the platter was a cake covered with chocolate frosting, chopped nuts, and dollops of darker chocolate.

"Hazelnut dacquoise," she announced with a flourish. Her children applauded.

"We're big fans of the television show *The Great British Bake Off*. I'm baking my way through the recipes," she told Nicky and me.

She sliced the cake and passed around our portions. It was a scrumptious-appearing combination of meringue, coffee-flavored mousse, and chocolate, but the meringue was like glue, sticking to my teeth, and the overall flavor was cloyingly sweet.

"Well?" said Lizzie, waiting for our reactions, not eating the cake herself. "How do you like it?"

Josie took a bite and appeared to evaluate the taste expertly. "It's a bit dry."

"*Dry?*" Lizzie said. "How can it be dry? It's filled with cream."

Ben moved the cake around his mouth as if tasting wine but probably trying to detach the meringue from his teeth. "I would say it's quite good," Ben said.

"It's interesting," Josie said.

"Oh, no." Lizzie placed her head in her hands in mock despair. "You don't like it."

"It's not your best effort," Ben said. "I have to be honest, don't I? What's the point, if I'm not honest? The dollops of chocolate ganache on top are rather good, however." He licked his fork.

"Do you see what's going on here?" Max said to Nicky. "British English is rich with indirection."

"Not this again, Daddy," Josie said.

"In British English, if a cake—or anything else—is *rather* good, you're saying you love it. If you say it's *quite* good, you're saying it's mediocre. If you say it's *interesting*, you absolutely hate it."

"Nicky doesn't care about this," Josie insisted.

"I do care about it," Nicky said fervently.

"One of my goals is to create a program that will allow high-accuracy machine translation between American English and British English, with little or no post-editing required," Max said. "It could potentially be as useful as the improvements I'm making in machine translation from idiomatic Mandarin Chinese to idiomatic American English, and vice versa."

"No way is it ever going to be as useful as that," Josie said, not hearing his humor, which surprised me, given how adept she was with humor herself.

"I'll help," Nicky said.

"Very kind of you, indeed. Did you hear that? The uses of *indeed* in British English—"

"No," Ben said. "Not a lecture about *indeed*. We don't want to hear it!"

"I'd like to hear it," Nicky said. How I adored him.

"Forget the cake," Lizzie said, resigned to her failure. "Don't torture yourselves on my account. There's ice cream in the freezer."

"We're not torturing ourselves," Max said forthrightly. "Baking is a scientific experiment. How can you learn if you don't try?"

"That's very true," Nicky said.

"This experiment should go into the research bin," Josie said.

"Except for the ganache," Ben said, scooping another dollop off the top of the remaining portion of the cake, popping it into his mouth, and savoring it.

"Sorry, Mummy," Josie said.

"I'll tell you about *indeed* after dinner," Max said to Nicky. "When my incurious progeny are doing the cleanup. I plan to write a monograph about the uses of *indeed*. When I finish that, I'll begin a treatise on British usage of the word *right*. Then I'll move on to a learned disquisition about *actually*. When I'm in retirement, I'll take on the ultimate British English challenge: *sorry*."

"For the record, we're not incurious." Ben directed this to me. "But when you've heard something a thousand times . . ."

"A thousand million times," Josie said.

"It gets tired," Ben said.

Max leaned back in his chair, hands folded across his abdomen, a self-satisfied grin on his face, as if to say, *What a wonderful family, with well-adjusted teenagers, behaving as teenagers should.*

We left their home with three two-thousand-piece puzzles, Nicky clutching the boxes against his chest: a Monet view of the Thames; a Van Gogh picture of sunflowers; and a Rembrandt portrait of a young man against a dark background. The images were rough copies, probably not licensed. If Nicky really did enjoy doing jigsaw puzzles, I'd contact my Swedish puzzle-manufacturing client and order some that were properly vetted.

Tonight he'd been fine. He'd been wonderful. *"Hope" is the thing with feathers,* as Emily Dickinson wrote.

CHAPTER 28

As we left the new stable on Friday afternoon, Duncan realized how marvelous he looked. His fur was luxuriously fluffy, silky, and shiny. He smelled good. His ruff was impeccably styled. He trotted along the path with delighted confidence, his head at a jaunty angle, his fan-like tail raised high, its arc of fur catching the sunlight. Nicky put him on a leash so Duncan wouldn't race off and jump into the lake or roll around in the mud to celebrate how handsome he was. Nicky, Alice, and I were covered in his fur—fur that might, centuries hence, be found on our clothing and analyzed, revealing our love for this creature who spread happiness simply by existing.

In preparation for Christopher's return on Monday, we'd arranged for Duncan to have a special oatmeal bath, fur trim, and blow dry, more expensive than his usual biweekly grooming session. Nicky had pleaded that I join him and Alice in assisting Annabelle, the groomer. Because Nicky had been doing well—working in the evenings, with severe concentration, on the Rembrandt puzzle he'd set up on the dining table—and because my bruises were healing, I did join them. Life went on. Nicky and I continued forward, together.

When we turned the corner of the stable: "Dr. Tinsley, you're smoking!" Nicky said.

There she was, outfitted in a charcoal-gray pleated skirt and a pale-pink blouse with a scalloped collar, cigarette in hand.

"How did you find me?" Nonchalant, she took another puff, inhaling deeply, holding her breath for a few seconds, exhaling. "No one ever walks here."

"Alice and Duncan and I walk here every other week on the mornings when Duncan has his bath. Except today we had a special appointment, because my uncle Christopher is coming home."

"That explains it: I smoke only after lunch. You must warn me the next time you have an afternoon appointment, and I'll make certain you don't see me," she said, regarding Nicky with equanimity.

"But, Dr. Tinsley," Nicky insisted, "even if we don't see you, you'll still be smoking."

"I will, indeed," she said serenely.

"And smoking is bad for you."

I didn't want him preaching to adults, but I agreed with his judgment, and I didn't feel like reprimanding him.

"You're absolutely correct," she said, taking yet another deep puff, holding her breath, exhaling. "Smoking is bad for me."

"Please, Dr. Tinsley. You have to stop."

"I do appreciate your concern," she said. She tapped the line of ashes into a small metal container.

"Nicky," I said, "why don't you and Alice go on ahead with Duncan. Dr. Tinsley and I will talk for a while."

"Tell her how she shouldn't smoke."

As they left us, I caught Alice explaining to Nicky that he should have been more diplomatic in his anti-smoking campaign, Nicky protesting that Dr. Tinsley's life was at risk. . . . The breeze picked up, blowing through Duncan's fur. I hoped we could keep the dog clean long enough for Christopher to see him this way.

"Your family's dog is a wonder," Martha said.

"He is. Thank you for saying. We're lucky to have him."

"I find your son to be thoroughly charming."

What was the correct response to this? He *was* charming. Seeing him today, no one would suspect that sometimes he lost control and in his rage, attacked others. "Thank you," I said. Lizzie had texted me after our dinner, saying she wanted to talk in person. About Nicky, I assumed. I couldn't face her, although I'd texted my gratitude for the school and visa information she'd also sent.

Martha stubbed out the cigarette on the inside of the metal container, snapped it shut, and returned it to the handbag draped diagonally across her shoulder. "Mustn't leave a trace. Smoking in the gardens: Mrs. Gardner would *not* be pleased. The staff smoking area is behind the machinery-storage building, beside the bins. Highly unpleasant. For the record, I'm here only once a day."

"Unlike my son, I'm not passing judgment. Okay, I am, but I'm not mentioning it."

"Feel free to pass judgment," she said with a mild wave of her hand. "Once started, hard to stop."

"So I've heard."

"Have you never smoked?" she asked.

"I know this is going to sound strange, but I was afraid of lighters and matches when I was young. When my friends were beginning to smoke, I covered over my fear by announcing, *I'll never compromise my health by smoking.* I must have been insufferable."

She laughed. "Where did you grow up?"

"In a city in New York State called Buffalo."

"Near Niagara Falls, yes?"

"Exactly."

"What's the scenery like there?"

The ubiquitous English question, indicating that a friendship was

developing. Despite weeks of working beside her, I knew almost nothing about her. She didn't wear a wedding ring, so I'd assumed, perhaps incorrectly, that she wasn't married. She'd never referred to a
partner or to children. After telling her about the beauty of Buffalo, I
said, "What about you? What's the scenery like where you grew up?"

"Abysmal. Ghastly. Nightmare-inducing. I grew up in rural Wales.
Craggy hills. Shadowed valleys. The landscape was a shade of green
so dark and dismal it terrified me. That green is responsible for everything I've accomplished in life: I had to get away from it."

"It made you decide to become a librarian?"

"I assure you, it did," she said, clearly happy that I was playing
along with her. "Given the gruesome greenery everywhere I turned,
books were my escape. I'm the eldest of five." She gave me a roguish
smile. "I put my mother into such a bind. Whenever I thought she
might need me to help with the younger ones, I made sure I was reading, ostentatiously, in her presence. She loved to see her children read.
She was a Cambridge graduate, Girton College. She'd once had great
hopes for herself, hopes she transferred to her children. She was especially supportive of the ambitions of her two daughters, so she couldn't
very well say to me, *Get your head out of that damned book and change your
brother's stinky nappy.*"

Instead of laughing, she turned somber. "Actually, that's an awful
story. She was a servant to her children—to me—for years. I wish I'd
helped her. Relieved some of her burden."

"But she must have wanted to have her children."

"That would be some consolation." Martha said nothing more,
and I felt naïve to have said it, a spoiled New Yorker commenting on
the choices of a woman whose life was undoubtedly harder than mine.

"Sorry," Martha said. "Too much information. Would you walk
with me?"

We headed toward the topiary garden. Soon, rabbits shaped from
boxwood and yew guided our way from atop hedge plinths as high as
my shoulders. The air among the shrubs was densely humid, the sunlight almost weighty.

"This is one of my favorite places," she said, choosing our path amid swans, peacocks, and cats, all in a most welcoming shade of green. The figures were remarkably realistic, on a grand scale. This part of the garden dated from the nineteenth century.

Abruptly, she said, "The county archivists arrived this morning and seized the parish records. I'm rather shaken."

"I'm sorry. That must have been awful."

"It was. They were quite unnecessarily dramatic about it. Peremptory and patronizing. The entire experience upset me, and now I need another cigarette. I'm trying to discipline myself to one. Please tell me not to have another."

"Don't have another. You might want it, but you don't need it."

"Thank you. That was helpful." She breathed deeply, inhaling the humid air rather than smoke, and held her breath. She exhaled, long and slow, and repeated the process. "In one bit of good news, however, I worked late the past few evenings and found several references relevant to our inquiries."

"Fantastic!" Immediately, I regretted my American excitement.

Martha remained tranquil. "Isabella Cresham, it turns out, was one of seven children. I'm sure her mother *did* have help, but it didn't do much good, because five of the children died. The only one of Isabella's siblings to survive was her brother Hugh, four years younger."

The pleasure she took in her work was obvious from the warmth in her voice as she related even these sad facts.

"He inherited the estate when he was in his early twenties, after the death of their father. By now there was a new, presumably young priest, this one with tiny, precise, illegible handwriting instead of the medium-sized, shaky, illegible handwriting of the elderly priest I knew before."

I remembered the elderly priest's writing, from the baptismal record.

"In June of 1579, Hugh married a woman named Katherine. I couldn't decipher Katherine's family name, although I did make out that she was from Lincolnshire—home of the Luttrell Psalter. I'd love to prove a link between the Luttrell Psalter and ours. Maybe Katherine brought it with her. Have you found any references to her?"

"The account ledgers refer only to *Lady Southbrooke* and *Lord Southbrooke,* decade after decade, without first names."

"I've been after Mrs. Gardner to convince the vicar to open the church crypt for us. Katherine and Hugh might be—*must* be—buried there. She hasn't had any luck, though." Martha shook her head at the absurdity of this roadblock. "The vicar is a stubborn man."

"More stubborn than Mrs. Gardner?" I asked.

"The church is his personal fiefdom, so he has the advantage." A green topiary elephant seemed to greet us as we passed. "Let's walk to the tempietto." She pointed to the round, covered colonnade atop its hillock.

Two boxwood giraffes guarded the approach. We climbed the steps into the welcome shade. The view spread in every direction— the lake, the house, farmland, meadows. The river was a sparkling ribbon meandering through the landscape. In the distance, the spires of Cambridge caught the afternoon sun.

"The river looks placid and picturesque now," Martha mused, "but it was once a major trade and transportation route. When I stand here, I like to imagine Roman barges. Saxon warriors. Viking longships. The conquering Normans. The founders of the university in the thirteenth century. . . . All that history gathered together, generation to generation, century to century. I feel it washing over me."

I felt it, too. The past was as alive here as the present.

"I'm surprised you've not asked me to show you the Old Library," she said, all at once accusatory.

"I was waiting for you to offer," I replied, trying not to sound defensive.

"In my experience, Americans ask for what they want."

Why was she annoyed? "I was trying to be British."

"Cross-cultural confusion, then. I don't believe I ever told you the subject of my PhD dissertation." Even this sounded accusatory, her tone angry and impatient. Lack of a second cigarette must have made her jittery and tetchy.

"No, you haven't mentioned it," I said, purposely bland, trying to ease the tension.

"I wrote about what are called *borrowers' registers* at country-house libraries during the eighteenth and nineteenth centuries. Lists of who checked out books."

"I didn't know such registers existed!"

"They're not well known," she acknowledged. "The registers reveal a remarkable range of social history. They show not only who visited the houses and when but who was allowed to read the books, including, for example, boys from the local villages, as well as cooks and other servants. I hadn't expected to find servants and villagers using the libraries."

"I'd like to read your dissertation."

"That can be arranged." From her turned-away smile, I knew she was pleased. Nonetheless, I'd heard a hesitation in her voice.

"Has it been published?" I asked gently.

"No publisher was interested in it."

"What? I'm shocked."

"I was, too."

I understood her disappointment and sense of failure. The same could happen to me. "I'm so sorry to hear this. I—"

"Right." She shifted, as if we'd had enough intimacy for one day and she wasn't about to let me any closer to her inner being. "Here are the facts."

She sounded like Mrs. Gardner, preparing for battle.

"When I first came to Ashton Hall, with my remit to create an online catalog of the book collection, I was puttering around in the Old Library, attempting to gain an overview of my impossible task, when I made a somewhat staggering discovery. I found the borrowers' registers for the library of Ashton Hall going back to 1538, which was in the midst of Henry VIII's Dissolution of the Monasteries. The library is older than that, but there must have been an influx of books from the disbanded religious institutions."

"Purchased because the family remained secretly Catholic?" I asked. "Or the books were brought here for safekeeping by fugitive priests, for the same reason?"

"I don't know for certain, but my personal view is that the books were stolen. Or simply taken, or repossessed, to use less-incendiary words. In my opinion, the Dissolution of the Monasteries was nothing but a huge property grab by the aristocracy."

"I never thought of it that way."

"No, I don't suppose—" She seemed on the verge of saying something negative about educational standards in America, but instead she said, "In any event, the Lord Southbrooke of that era wanted to know who was reading his books, and he established the tradition of using registers. Which further means he must have approved of his books being read. Not always the case amongst collectors. According to my research, no one else has found borrowers' registers for country-house libraries going back this far."

"Did you tell Mrs. Gardner about them?"

"Yes, of course. I also published a note about them in a journal for librarians, to announce their existence and claim them for my future work." This was standard procedure in academia. "The note garnered zero reaction, although for me, the Ashton Hall registers were like an earthquake."

"All to the best, then. No competition."

"And I thought, here's my life's work: a social history of this house, based on who checked books out of the library. *Ashton Hall: Five Centuries of Reading.* Or is it six centuries? I've never excelled at arithmetic."

She turned silent.

Sensing there must be a reason for this detailed explanation, I asked, "Why are you telling me this, Martha?"

"Because I'm hoping you'll agree to read the registers and see what you can learn about Isabella Cresham and her immediate family. About Hugh, her brother, and Katherine, her sister-in-law."

"I'd love to read the registers. But why don't you read them yourself? They're part of the research for your book."

"I don't have time to do it now."

Slowly, I began to understand her uncharacteristic agitation. "Are you trying to say you'd like me to read the registers while remembering they belong to you?"

Sheepish, not meeting my eyes, she said, "Well, yes."

"Martha, I promise not to steal the registers for my own work. Besides, you already claimed them through your journal note."

"People don't always follow that, especially after a lot of time goes by. I've seen it happen to colleagues."

I'd seen this, too.

"And early in my career, I submitted an article to a refereed publication, and it was rejected—fine, it happens, but lo and behold, the following year, all my ideas appeared in an article by a senior scholar."

I'd heard about many instances of the work of young scholars, especially young women scholars, being stolen in this way. "Being careful is smart."

"After you finish your PhD dissertation, you'll be looking for another subject to write about."

"Martha," I said sternly, beginning to feel insulted, "no way I'm going to write a book called *Ashton Hall: Five or Six Centuries of Reading*. I'd love to *read* that book, but I won't write it. I've reached the end of the relevant passages in the account ledgers. I can start on the registers immediately. Where are they?"

"In a safe place." Martha stepped back, as if I'd crossed a boundary. Then she shrugged. "Oh, all right, I trust you. I hid them in the Old Library. Let's go retrieve them."

The Old Library smelled like autumn leaves. It was a series of large rooms, one leading into the next, enfilade-style, like other parts of the house. Light entered only from the windows at the far end. The ceiling was arched and wood-beamed, the floor made from wooden planks. Each room had a table and a few chairs. Martha and I entered through a jib door from the Long Gallery, and I waited in the sepia-colored shadows while she retrieved two flashlights from a nearby shelf.

"That's better," she said, when we turned them on.

Overflowing shelves lined the walls from floor to ceiling, as well as over the doorways. In this first room, some of the volumes had metal fittings at the corners and chains attached, for locking the books to the shelves or desks in medieval scriptoria and libraries. These chains now hung down in front of the books.

"There's no electricity," Martha said. "The staff examined the possibility of stringing electric lights in the 1950s, when the back cor-ridors were electrified, but it became too much to contemplate. The cleaners visit frequently, to try to keep control of the dust and check for pests."

I ran the light across the shelves. Gold leaf had been used for the lettering on some of the spines, and it glinted in our beams, bringing the books to life. They beckoned to me.

"Publication chronology has been the governing factor in the ar-rangement of the books, except for the final room, by the windows, where the librarians put books they didn't have room for anywhere else. You can more or less walk from the Middle Ages into the twenti-eth century. Or vice versa—there's another jib door on the far side. But I prefer to travel from the past into the present."

I preferred it, too. She began doing precisely that, and I followed, regretting how quickly she walked, how purposefully, ignoring the call of the books we passed.

"The Old Library is essentially uncataloged. There aren't even shelf marks," she said, glancing over her shoulder. "I suspect the li-brarians who were trying to organize these rooms over the centuries, especially without adequate lighting, must have become overwhelmed, exhausted, and defeated."

In the libraries I'd used over the years, I'd never considered how many people must have worked endless hours taking hundreds of books off the shelves in order to add more, fitting them into the pre-determined system, decade after decade—and they had the benefit of electricity.

She turned and waited for me to catch up with her. "I spend a good deal of time thinking about the customs for arranging books." She burst out laughing. "Really. I do. It's a compelling topic for me."

"It's an objectively important issue," I agreed, if a bit stiffly, but as we looked at each other, I felt the alliance between us restored.

We continued on, walking side by side. "Nowadays," she said, "some libraries are shifting to compressed storage, which means books are arranged by size, and a garden book ends up next to an astronomy book, a novel next to an introduction to physics, each bearing its crucial barcode, and browsing reveals only a hodgepodge."

And you lost forever the bliss of wandering the shelves, call slip in hand, and realizing that the book *next* to the one you were searching for was actually the one you needed, and you never would have found it if you hadn't been able to search for yourself.

"With compressed storage," she went on, even more passionate, "the stacks are so close together you have to push a button or turn a lever to make them move, in order to gain access. If there's an electrical failure, you can't use the computerized catalog to locate the books. You can't scan the barcodes. You can't make the push-button-controlled stacks move. You can't use the library. The architects and designers must have had absolute confidence in technology, or at least believed the advantages of this system outweighed the disadvantages. Or they thought people wouldn't need books during a power outage. But what if people need books *more* when there's no electricity?"

She gave me visions of a dystopian future: blackouts, pandemic disease, mass starvation . . . and the libraries, which are the storehouse of human knowledge, vital to rebuilding civilization, rendered inaccessible because of compressed storage.

We entered the final room, with its windows overlooking the lake. She stopped and pointed out a low shelf packed with large volumes.

"Here we have a row of medieval Gospels, acquired by the fourteenth Lord Southbrooke in the early 1900s. He had a reputation for profligacy—not as a gambler but as a bibliophile! As part of my research, I'll examine the twentieth-century account ledgers to learn if he was buying books instead of, for example, repairing a leaky roof."

Martha bent down and began taking the Gospels, heavy and unwieldy, off the shelf and transferring them to the nearby table. Purple and red jewels glowed from the cover of one. Another displayed a coat of arms enameled in shades of green and blue onto a silver panel.

"These Gospel volumes are rather valuable and should be transferred to the Long Gallery, but I don't have room for them there." A line of black dust clung to her skirt. "I've urged Mrs. Gardner to sell some of them, but she won't hear of it; she considers each one part of the history of the house. So here they sit. Nonetheless, they have their uses. I hid the borrowers' registers behind them, to keep them safe from the prying eyes of other researchers."

Ah, Martha. I didn't know what to say about that. Kneeling, shoulders hunched, her back turned to me, as if her entire body was protecting the registers, she examined the volumes in their hiding place. I couldn't see them.

"Here are the ones we need, for the Tudor and Stuart eras." She pulled them out. "We'll take them to the conservation center."

Standing, she gently, almost tenderly, handed two volumes to me. They were bound in soft brown leather and measured roughly twelve inches high and ten inches wide. In contrast to the Gospels, they were plain, almost nondescript. The plainness itself might be a sign of their value—they were designed *not* to call attention to themselves. If you spotted them on a table, you wouldn't automatically reach for them. You wouldn't be tempted to steal them.

"I don't exactly believe in God," Martha said, "but I hid the registers here because I thought, if there is a God, He or She will protect the Gospels and, due to geographic proximity, protect the borrowers' registers, as well."

I wanted to think Martha was being ironic, but really, I had no idea.

CHAPTER 29

In the conservation center, with my laptop beside me, I began my review of the registers with June of 1552, the month and year of Isabella Cresham's baptism.

On the second day of the month, *his lordship* borrowed *The Proprytees and Medycynes for Hors.* I hated to think an outbreak of disease among the estate's horses had prompted Lord Southbrooke to read about veterinary medicine.

Next, *Jon the gardener* borrowed *The Crafte of Graffynge and Plantynge of Trees.* Jon, as I visualized him, was dedicated to his work and trying to improve his skills.

The library of the house before this house . . . I imagined. A monumental space, the bookshelves topped with Gothic finials. Behind an imposing oak table sat the librarian, suspicious and protective, squinting from bad eyesight. *Find a book or go away,* he seemed to say to me. On the table before him was the register that I was reading now.

The library had been a busy place, judging from the number of borrowed books that were noted in the librarian's precise script. At the far right of each page, he'd created a column headed *Returned*. In this section of the register, every book had been returned. Nonetheless, I pictured the librarian greeting all visitors with mistrust, including *his lordship* himself, checking out *De Agriculturae,* committed as he must have been to making the estate's farmland more productive.

Often, the names in the register were followed by an identification: *guest of his lordship* or *Proffessor of the University.* A *Father Pierrepont* was listed, and given the frequency of his visits and the religious nature of his borrowings, he was most likely the parish priest.

Lord Southbrooke checked out a volume by Erasmus, *De Duplici Copia Verborum et Rerum.* This was essentially a textbook about rhetoric and writing, I learned from the internet. According to my imaginings, Isabella's father devoted himself to learning.

Cook borrowed *A Boke of Cookery, by A.W.* This cook, I decided, was young and innovative, a person who made it her, or his, business to learn recipes from a book rather than rely solely on family tradition, wanting to try something new and be part of the world beyond this estate.

The ability to read was more common than I'd assumed. Or perhaps Lord Southbrooke, with his commitment to education and to collecting books, wanted those around him to be able to use his library, and he'd arranged for them to be taught to read. I made a note to myself to check the account ledgers for the 1550s, to see if tutors were listed.

Richard of the village borrowed a volume by the philosopher Plutarch. At this entry, a phrase was added in the librarian's strict hand: *For to be red in the lybrarie only,* class divisions arising even here, the librarian asserting power over a local boy's studies. The mere presence of this phrase showed that other library users were allowed to take books away. *Richard of the village* returned his volume to the librarian, I was glad to see from the mark in the column on the right. I made another note, to see if school fees for *Richard of the village* were listed in the account ledgers, along with those I'd already read about for *Piers of the village.*

Lady Southbrooke checked out *The Boke of Keruynge of Wynkyn de Worde,* a book about feasting and other rituals of upper-class dining, the internet told me. I visualized the long table in the great hall, filled with family and friends, wine flowing, as each course was presented by servants in the candlelight.

Next, Lady Southbrooke borrowed *The Boke of the Cyte of Ladyes,* by Christine de Pizan. When I checked online, I learned that the odd title, *The Book of the City of Ladies,* was indeed correct. This was a collection of stories about accomplished and independent women. Christine de Pizan strongly advocated for the education of women. Was Lady Southbrooke already thinking about Isabella's education?

Months passed in the library, months and then years, filled with individuals and the books they read. Their lives, their thoughts and spirits, opened before me.

And one day in September of 1556, recorded in a large, exacting script, not quite straight across the page—this was the first entry not written by the librarian—*Isabella Cresham* borrowed *Historia Animalium, De Avium Natura. By Conrad Gessner.*

Could this be? I stared at the entry. In 1556, Isabella Cresham would have been four years old.

I felt a prickling on the back of my neck. Isabella's childhood handwriting brought her to life in my mind's eye. There she was— a little girl with reddish hair and a pert, round face. She was dressed as an adult, in a long gown over multiple layers, as was the custom of her time. Her governess or nurse had brought her to the library. She was a child who charmed those around her, rather like Rosie Varet, and the librarian allowed her to write her name in the register as a treat. Standing on tiptoe at the librarian's table, she held the quill pen and bit her lip in concentration, trying not to make a mistake, with the librarian watching her. Her father, who happened to be reading in the library that day, glanced up and smiled.

I did a Google search and learned that *Historia Animalium, De Avium*

Natura, by Conrad Gessner, was the third volume of a comprehensive work of natural history. It was known for its detailed, realistic illustrations, even of imaginary creatures. This volume focused on birds. It had been fully digitized by the British Library. And so, in a Jacobean-era stately home, I reviewed page by page on a computer screen a book published in the sixteenth century and read by a four-year-old child in September of 1556.

The woodcut illustrations were meticulously drawn and individualized. Here was an owl with a surprised expression on its face, eyebrows raised, wrinkles along its feathered forehead. On another page was a young eagle, noble but also silly, feathers puffed around its short legs. A chicken-like creature was portrayed in mid-squawk, one foot held up. Two pigeons appeared lost and befuddled, as if they'd wandered into this book by mistake.

September 1556 . . . On the late-summer day when young Isabella Cresham borrowed this book, the weather was glorious. The gardens were lush with shades of red, orange, and purple. The leaves were just beginning to turn. The little girl wrapped her arms around the book and carried it outside. Her *lord papa* allowed her to do this, because he trusted her to take good care of it. He also trusted that, even though she was small and the book was big, she was strong enough to carry it.

She sat in the shade of her favorite tree. The volume was heavy upon her lap. She paged through the illustrations. She knew if she was very quiet, and sat very still, one of the birds in the book might decide to visit her.

CHAPTER 30

Frowning, as if he couldn't believe what he was hearing, Matthew said, "You spent an entire term estimating the number of jelly beans in a jar?"

We sat at the table in the garden's riverside gazebo, surrounded by the still-blooming white hydrangeas. He'd landed on the perfect outing, fun but not too much fun: Sunday afternoon tea, followed by an hour of playtime for the kids. It was August 2, and tomorrow Matthew would depart for his archaeological dig. His children would leave for their vacation in France. Christopher would come home.

"We were allowed to eat three jelly beans each afterward," Nicky said, as if this both explained and justified the educational method.

Our plates were empty, scraped clean of any evidence of the vanilla cake with dark-chocolate frosting we'd devoured, courtesy of Rosie.

"Jelly beans," Matthew repeated. He wore a blue oxford shirt with

the sleeves rolled up and dark-blue trousers. I could almost feel my
fingertips caressing his muscles beneath his clothes.

"We estimated chocolate-covered malted milk balls, too," Nicky
said. "Those are bigger, so there aren't as many. Depending on the
size of the jar."

Matthew burst out laughing. "Sorry, Nicky. I know I shouldn't
laugh."

The girls were also laughing. Nicky looked close to tears, not necessarily because of their reaction. Due to the precision of his thought
patterns, Nicky had never understood the concept of estimating. Trying to help him, his teacher had encouraged him to take the smaller
jars home to work on. Several jars had been thrown across his room
that term, producing on one occasion the cheerless sight of multicolored jelly beans mixed with shards of broken glass. I knew his
school's free-ranging child-centered curriculum wasn't perfectly suited
to him, but his teachers cared so much and seemed so certain they
could help him. And, more basic, when it came to mainstream schools
in New York that would accept Nicky, I didn't have much choice.

"No more laughter. It's not Nicky's fault," Matthew said. "Things
are done differently in America."

"What about you two?" I asked Rosie and Janet, to cover Nicky's
feelings. "How are you learning math?"

Still basking in the triumph of her cake, her face alight, Rosie
said, "We call it *maths*."

"You don't need to understand maths," Janet said. "You only need
to know them. Six times six."

"Thirty-six," Rosie said. "Eighty-one divided by nine."

"Nine," Janet said.

"Wait," Nicky protested. "The calculator on my phone can do
maths. Faster, too. And never make a mistake."

"But this way, *our* way," Janet insisted, "you can trip up your classmates. You can win every maths contest. For example, *I* win every
maths contest. Seventy-two divided by six."

"Twelve," Rosie said.

Watching Nicky's face, I saw the satisfying implications of winning maths contests dawn on him. "I can learn to do that," he said.

"Of course you can," Janet said. "And after you do, you'll become a *proper* British boy going to a *proper* British school and you'll never estimate jelly beans in a jar again."

All this because Nicky had shared with them that we were staying on, waiting for Christopher to die.

"What I object to most about teaching maths by estimation," Matthew said, "is that learning maths then becomes a matter of *feelings* rather than facts. It seems a singularly American approach."

I bristled at his dismissal of an entire nation, *my* nation, because of one school's eccentric—to his way of thinking—curriculum.

"Maths are amongst the few things in this world that are provable," he continued. "You count the jelly beans, and you know how many there are."

"That's true for malted milk balls, too," Nicky noted.

"So it is. Well observed."

"We can teach you maths," Janet said. "We'll play a game. One plus one."

"That's too easy," Nicky said.

"You just wait, the game becomes difficult fast."

And so it did, the numbers flying by.

Matthew caught my eye and motioned toward the river, clearly wondering if I wanted to take a walk. I nodded, and we rose. Amid the onslaught of numbers, the kids didn't seem to notice our departure.

When we were out of their earshot, Matthew said, "Alone at last."

As we walked amid the plantings, lush in their midsummer profusion, I still felt rankled by Matthew's condemnation of Nicky's school and of America in general. Preemptively deflecting him from the personal, I said, "Martha Tinsley showed me Ashton Hall's library registers for the Tudor and Stuart periods."

"Library registers, going back that far?" he said, taken aback. "Such things actually exist?"

"I was surprised, too. I found the first book Isabella Cresham checked out of the library. She was only four years old."

"What was the book?"

"A natural history of birds. Filled with illustrations. I was able to read it online."

"What a world we live in, where we can call up sixteenth-century books in an instant and read them at our desks. It's astonishing."

"I know." My annoyance softened. I loved that he had the same sense of wonder I'd experienced as I paged through the book online. "It was so touching to imagine her as a child, holding that big book, studying the illustrations."

On the river, a group of eight scullers in one boat, obviously beginners, had panicked. As they struggled to stay afloat, pushing their oars in different directions, their scull wobbled wildly. Their instructor, on the opposite side of the river, shouted instructions as he tried to bring the group under control.

"Let's not watch," Matthew said. "I'd prefer *not* to see them fall in."

"Does that happen often?"

"I don't know, actually. I always look away."

We turned, heading past the flower beds in the general direction of his cottage.

"I've been meaning to tell you," he said. "My students have confirmed a link between Isabella's rosary and the one found at Oxburgh Hall. Both rosaries came from the same source, in France. This means she must have been in touch with an array of co-religionists, offering support to one another. I think we now have to accept the most straightforward explanation: She was imprisoned because she was Catholic, and she was allowed to starve to death."

He was raised Catholic, and he saw Catholicism everywhere in Isabella's story. But then again, I was raised without faith, and I didn't want to see it. We each continued to visualize her through the filters of our own preconceptions and concerns.

Even so, there had to be more than one reason for what had happened to her. Hundreds of strands of events, emotions, and beliefs must have come together to bring Isabella to her fate.

"Her story can't be that simple," I said. "Life isn't that simple."

"But sometimes things *are* simple," he replied. "There's a saying in medicine: *If you hear hoofbeats, think horses, not zebras.*"

"Doctors probably miss a lot of zebras, thinking that way. And the zebras would always be more interesting than the horses. Not that I have anything against horses."

"Granted." He smiled. "I hope you'll show me the library register when I return in September." He reached for my shoulder, as if to patch over our disagreement. "How are you?"

Christopher, Kevin, Nicky . . . My future confronted me like a wall.

"Well enough." I stepped just out of Matthew's reach. As we walked, I was alert to his every movement. If I were free to choose, would I choose to be with him? Easy enough to say yes when I wasn't actually free. Not being free allowed for all manner of fantasies and daydreams.

"I'm worried about Christopher," I said.

"Of course you are."

"I'm not certain I'll be able to keep up a cheery exterior after he returns."

"You'll do your best," he said.

"I also feel . . . I'll miss all of this"—I gestured to the big house and the gazebo, the garden, the river beyond, the centuries-old trees—"and you, while you're away."

"I'll miss all of this, as well. Plus you. I hope we'll stay in touch. My mobile will work even amidst the ruins of Roman Chedworth. You can ring me anytime."

"Thank you." Feeling awkward, I looked away.

As we approached the garden-facing side of his cottage, the exuberant flowers in the window boxes on the second floor caught my attention. And like the priest's handwriting in the parish register, becoming more distinct the longer I stared—the idea was outlandish, and yet . . . "Are those flowers painted onto the wall? Are the window boxes painted, too? Is the window itself painted on?"

"It is, as a matter of fact." From his tone, he seemed surprised that I'd remarked on it. "The pictures were touched up last week. That must be why you noticed. The fresh paint is a little garish for my taste, but the colors will settle in due course. A few weeks of rain, some air pollution, everything will be back to normal."

His bedroom was on the other side of that wall. I remembered the window embrasures covered with canvas. "Why have a painting of a window, on canvas, covering a window embrasure instead of an actual glazed window?"

"Because of the window tax." He said this with bewilderment, as if it was obvious.

"What window tax?"

"The one instituted in 1696 by William the Third. People bricked up or otherwise covered their windows so they wouldn't have to pay as much tax."

"Is there still a window tax?"

"No, no, of course not," he assured me.

"Then why hasn't the glass been put back?"

"Oh. I'm sure I don't know." Again, his bewilderment, his thoughtful, respectful confusion over questions he'd never asked himself. "It's not the way things are done."

"Not the way things are done," I repeated. In this country, in this culture, I'd forever be a foreigner, even though, in theory, I spoke the same language. Despite the many things that brought us together, Matthew and I would always, in some deep way, be foreigners to each other, unable to understand each other fully, using the same words but with different meanings, subtly condemning aspects of each other's opinions even while caring for each other.

"No, Hannah. Things aren't done that way." He was one second away from impatience as he attempted to comprehend why I couldn't understand or accept this.

The gap between us left me saddened. And yet we wouldn't see each other for weeks. I tried to smooth things over: "I was so cold after you went downstairs to make breakfast that morning. The canvas must not keep the wind out, the way glass would."

"You've not mentioned this before." He seemed relieved to shift away from our differences and toward what might bring us together. "Were you indeed so very cold, after I went downstairs?"

"I was."

"Good." His expression changed from puzzlement to pleasure. "You should let that be a lesson to you," he said, as desire filled me in spite of myself, "about what an excellent job I can do keeping you warm."

CHAPTER 31

Rafe retrieved the metal walker from the trunk of the Panther car and snapped it open.

Christopher waved it off. Instead, he relied on Nicky for support as he crossed the front drive, while Rafe organized the luggage. As Duncan leapt and barked around him in hysterical happiness, Christopher trudged half step by half step across the gravel, along the path beside the moat, across the bridge, and to his front door.

Once again, we gathered around the dining table in the early morning. Rafe had emailed me a list of foods that Christopher could tolerate. Strawberry ice cream had become his breakfast staple, and we joined him. I'd carefully covered the remnants of the bruise on my jaw with makeup, and I didn't think the discoloration was noticeable. I didn't want to have to explain the cause.

"How delightful. Ice cream before nine in the morning," Christopher said, licking his spoon. "We've certainly progressed as a family."

He gazed upon Nicky and me in benign approval. Despite his physical weakness, he looked and sounded much the same as when he left.

We talked—about Mrs. Gardner, the general, the proprietress of the village bakery, bringing him up to date on the local news, although he already knew the basics from our frequent phone calls and texts. We ate our ice cream, and filled the time with conversation, and never mentioned his condition. He was the one to address it if he wished. I was the one to give him a family, as far removed from the suffering and depression of illness as possible.

Christopher wanted to know the latest about Isabella Cresham, and Nicky obliged, with his usual flair. I'd review the details with Christopher later. I loved seeing the two of them like this, Christopher asking questions to bring out Nicky's experiences, Nicky voluble in his replies, his ease and confidence making my entire body relax.

"There's still a lot to learn," Nicky concluded. "For *me*, for *you*, for Duncan, *too*. It rhymes!"

"So it does," Christopher said, his voice low, his façade of coping gone. Suddenly I saw the pallor of his skin, the heaviness around his eyes. He put down his spoon. He stared at his empty bowl. "I'll freshen up now, Rafe."

Rafe brought the walker and helped him to stand. This time, Christopher didn't resist the contraption. Nicky went to assist.

Duncan appeared from under the table, placing himself near Christopher's legs with an absolute stillness, his concentration turning into a kind of trembling.

"Duncan's helping," Nicky said.

"Indeed he is," Christopher gasped.

They made their way down the hall to Christopher's bedroom. While I waited for Nicky to return, I checked my phone. Another text from Lizzie, this one more pointed. *I hope you're okay. We need to talk.* I replied that Christopher was here and I'd be in touch when I could.

Nicky came back. "Duncan decided to stay with Uncle Christopher, because Uncle Christopher needs his help. Duncan knows when people need his help."

"He's a very special dog," I said.

"I think so, too."

Nicky went to the opposite end of the table, to the Rembrandt portrait puzzle. He studied the hundreds of pieces remaining to be placed. He picked one up and tried it here, there, and in a third place, where it fit. An aura of tranquility enveloped him. Sunlight began to pour into the window behind him, and I could no longer see his face.

When Alice arrived, they decided to go to the Market Square to buy strawberries to make fresh ice cream for Christopher, using the ice-cream maker in Mrs. Gardner's flat.

Handmade strawberry ice cream, sweet and tangy, evocative of summer gatherings on the lawn. Something to stay alive for.

After Isabella borrowed the *Historia Animalium, De Avium Natura,* its return duly noted, she took out a volume she called *abcdarium*. She was learning the alphabet, and I wanted to think she was also learning how to draw by copying the illustrations. Next, she read *Aesop's Fables*—or a governess read it to her. She borrowed many more books, and by the time she was seven, she'd become the most frequent user of the library.

Others in the household borrowed books, too. Among them, Lady Southbrooke, Isabella's mother, read *Banckes' Herball,* by Richard Banckes. Herbs were considered medicinal in her era, and the female head of a household was expected to practice medicine informally for the family and household staff, as well as for the local villagers. Several months later, she borrowed *The Myrrour or Glasse of Helth,* by Thomas Moulton.

Lord Southbrooke read Baldassare Castiglione's *Book of the Court-ier,* a philosophical treatise and guide to proper aristocratic behavior.

Beginning in 1560, when she was eight, Isabella began borrowing books in Latin and Greek:

Virgil's *Aeneid.*

Homer's *Odyssey.*

Works by Plato and by Livy. She was learning the classical languages, as I had.

In 1562, when Isabella was ten and Hugh was six, she took out *Le Morte d'Arthur,* and she noted, in the handwriting I now knew well, *To read aloud to Hugh.*

She borrowed *The Mastering of the Game of Chess* and explained in the register, *For learning chess with Hugh.* I imagined her having fun with these notations. I saw her self-possession and the brightness of her smile as she glanced at her younger brother beside her and then at the librarian, whose vigilance and rectitude relaxed only for her, among all in the household.

In 1563, she borrowed *The Boke Named the Governour* and wrote, *To plan the education of Hugh,* as if he were completely under her control and care.

When Isabella was fifteen, she again checked out *Historia Animalium, De Avium Natura.* Was she developing an interest in science and natural history?

Hugh borrowed *A Treatyse of Fysshynge wyth an Angle.* This was the first time he'd written in the register himself. Isabella must have secured permission for him—or more likely, as the heir, he felt himself entitled to take whatever freedoms he wanted. Next he read *Toxophilus,* by Roger Ascham, a treatise on archery. He fished in the river. He practiced archery on the lawn.

The siblings must have enjoyed chess, because together they borrowed *The Game and Playe of the Chesse, by Jacobus de Cessolis,* with Hugh writing *For Isabella and Hugh* in the entry.

Then Hugh's borrowings paused. He might have been sent away to school. I double-checked the account ledgers: *School fees for the young lord* were duly listed around that time. I also found, looking back, *School fees for Richard of the village* and *Waggs for the tutor of reeding for the household.* So Lord Southbrooke had indeed arranged for his staff to be taught to read.

By December of 1570, Isabella's handwriting was graceful and elegant, the letters like musical notes, as she checked out a volume on astronomy. There she was—outside on clear winter nights, identifying the constellations.

She borrowed an atlas of the British Isles—she was undertaking a journey, if only in her daydreams.

Months, years, passed in the register, as I divined their lives, entry by entry.

Isabella read *The Consolation of Philosophy*, by Boethius. She borrowed a collection of the plays of Sophocles, in ancient Greek, the stark world of Greek tragedy opening before her, as it had for me.

Hugh returned to Ashton Hall and borrowed books about agriculture and the care of horses, as his father had done. He borrowed *The Boke of Hawking and Hunting*. He rode across the estate, a hawk or falcon on his fist.

In 1579, Isabella was twenty-seven. Hugh was twenty-three, and he no longer borrowed books. According to the parish records reviewed by Martha, his father had died. Hugh was Lord Southbrooke now.

And in the library register, I met Katherine, who married him.

My phone pinged. I was back in the present. It was a text from Rafe. Christopher wanted to see me.

CHAPTER 32

I found him in his study. Showered, face washed, clothes changed, he looked shiny and renewed. He sat at his desk going through a stack of mail.

"Ah, Hannah, thank you for joining me. Feeling a bit more human now. Surprisingly alert, too. It's dawn in New York, that must be the reason. I'd like to discuss a few things with you. Can't guarantee I'll be *compos mentis* tomorrow." He didn't wait for my opinion on this. "Rafe is preparing tea."

I'd never been in his study. The door had been closed while he was away, and I'd had no reason to open it. The room shared the simplicity and elegance of the rest of the apartment. Waist-high bookshelves lined the room, and two dozen or so paintings, arranged salon-style, filled the upper wall space. The antique desk was placed to face into the room, with the sitter's back to the windows, which overlooked the croquet court and the lake beyond.

While we waited for tea, I examined the paintings. Near the doorway was a Winslow Homer, a woman reaching up to place laundry on a line while apple blossoms blew around her on the breeze and a toddler, dressed in white, gripped at her skirt. On the far wall was a William Merritt Chase view of Venice, the canal churned by a storm, a palazzo in the distance. Next to this, a Childe Hassam, of a field of wildflowers on the coast of Maine. And more, each one exquisite. My work at the museum, my calling, poured back and filled me with yearning.

"Christopher, these paintings are astonishing. I had no idea that you had these."

Studying his mail, he suppressed a smile. "I've been fortunate in my work."

I knew he'd been successful, but even so. "Seeing these in a private home, living with them from day to day . . ."

"They've kept me going through the rough patches, I must say. Take a look at that one, why don't you."

He motioned to a smaller picture on the wall behind the desk, out of the light from the windows and covered by a navy-blue velvet curtain on a rod. It was probably a watercolor, covered to prevent fading. I pulled the fabric aside.

A female figure wearing a voluminous gown reclined on a gondola on a Venetian canal, a parasol shading her face.

Could it be? Intuition, an electrified tingling in my fingertips, said it was: a watercolor by John Singer Sargent. It wasn't signed, but a signature didn't prove anything; a signature could be easily forged. The fluid brushwork, the billowing dress rendered in a dozen shades of color that magically created an impression of white—this artistry identified the painter, as did the portrayal of the young woman in the gondola. She was Sargent's niece, Rose-Marie Ormond. He painted and drew her again and again, dressed in flowing gowns or Turkish costumes, as she reclined in mountain meadows or upon luxurious sofas or lounged on benches beside garden walls in the dappling sunlight. Most often she was laughing, or, more touching, Sargent portrayed her on the cusp of laughter, her eyes sparkling, as here.

"Sargent's niece looks rather like you," Christopher said.

"Hardly." He'd assumed I would recognize her, and that made me happy. "The watercolor is gorgeous. The energy and verve."

"That's what I love about it, too."

I joined him at the desk. Looking over his shoulder, I spotted three photographs in silver frames. The first was a snapshot of me at the Met, standing in front of a statue of Diana, goddess of the hunt. Christopher had taken the photo when I was still an undergraduate at Barnard, working part-time with the inscription fragments in my basement cubicle. We'd had lunch at the museum, and I'd given him a tour of the Greek and Roman collection.

The second showed four people, appearing to be in their late twenties, Constance and Christopher at the center. He stood behind her, with his arms around her. She leaned against his chest, sinking into his embrace. Christopher wore a boutonniere on his suit jacket. Constance wore a silk evening suit and held a bouquet. Their wedding. A man, dark haired, taller than Christopher, also wearing a boutonniere, his expression open and boyish, stood next to Christopher. His best man. An outdoorsy-looking woman, smiling broadly, hair short and curly, wearing a corsage, stood next to Constance. Her maid, or matron, of honor.

The third photo had been taken in Venice, in the rain, at St. Mark's Square. These same four people stood under two umbrellas: Constance and Christopher, their hair touched by gray. The other man and woman, older but still recognizable. All four were . . . *distinguished* in their maturity. Prosperous. Confident. Some, at least, of the goals and dreams of their lives fulfilled. Who were these two, Constance and Christopher's friends through decades?

"Tea at last," Rafe said, bringing in the tray and setting up the tea service on the round table in the corner.

After Rafe departed and we'd established ourselves at the table,

Christopher said with satisfaction, "Well, well, here we are, preparing for the end."

"You don't know that."

"I do know it. We don't need to discuss it every day, but we need to acknowledge it, if only as a kind of background music. We need to tell Nicky."

I felt tears welling. "I don't want you to be gone." All at once I was a child. . . . I'd wave a wand and grant Christopher survival.

Instead of responding, he sipped his tea and slowly consumed an oat biscuit, breaking it into ever-smaller segments. Light and shadows moved in shifting patterns across the walls, as sunlight filtered through the shrubbery that grew along the moat.

When he finished the biscuit, he said, "I'm grateful to end my days here, in this idyllic place. I'd like to live through the autumn. England in September and October is a bit of heaven. I'd also like to learn the full story of Isabella Cresham before I go. She's our contribution to the history of the house, after all."

"It's an entire world behind this one, and it feels so close," I said, "as if I could step into it and inhabit it. I've been going through the library registers, and—"

"Kevin confided in me about the source of the tension between you," he said, cutting me off as if he sensed himself running out of time.

The abrupt shift left me reeling. "He had no right to do that. Not on his own."

"Obviously, I heard only one side. But balancing the one-sidedness was that my first sympathies were with you. And always are." He patted the armrest of his chair as if he were actually patting my hand. "Fortunately, I was familiar with his predicament. The situations are different, although in some ways similar. Kevin had realized my familiarity, long ago. That's why he confided in me."

I didn't know what Christopher meant, but my anger flared at the thought that he and Kevin shared a connection that excluded me.

"I'm glad to have this excuse to tell you," he continued, not noticing my discomfort. "I wish I'd told you years ago. The fact is, Constance and I were simply—miraculously—friends."

I still didn't understand. "I'm glad you were friends. Married people should be friends."

"It was a miracle that we found each other and were able to create lives of such compelling friendship."

I felt as if we were speaking two different languages that used the same words but all the definitions were shifted. "What are you talking about?"

"A *lavender marriage* was what we had. How I love that phrase. It immediately transports one to the milieu of John Singer Sargent." He motioned toward the watercolor, its crystalline brilliance hidden once more behind the velvet curtain.

And, like seeing the jib door concealed within the wallpaper world in the Chinese Bedroom, I knew. "The photos on your desk."

"Constance and me, Jill and Rick. Rather a neat trick, I must say. I met them when I was in law school. Constance and Rick were fellow students, and Constance and Jill had known each other since their Bryn Mawr days. We built our lives around one another. Rick became an attorney who put together international business deals. Jill was a chemist, a professor at NYU—with tenure, I'll have you know. During an era when few women had professional lives as scientists. Jill tried to encourage your mother, to provide moral support, when Margot dreamed of becoming a chemist, but the opposition was too fierce for Margot."

I knew my mother had been a great fighter, but nonetheless she'd been defeated. I wanted to believe she hadn't considered her life a waste. She'd certainly been a powerful influence on her students at Macaulay.

I said, "But why did you—"

"If Constance or Jill had been known as being . . . *deviant* was the term then used, what would have happened? We were the four of us *deviants*. I must say, I enjoyed life as a *deviant*. Not that I had much choice in the matter, the equivalent of brown hair or blue eyes. But I embraced the term, the way young people embrace the formerly derogatory term *queer*. Thank you for allowing me to speak frankly."

He sipped his tea. I tried to catch up with him. I'd known him since I was young, but I hadn't comprehended his true essence until now.

"We made certain decisions, in order to maintain our careers. In order to help keep us safe. Safe from arrest and for Constance and Rick, safe from being disbarred from law practice as a result of exposure and its consequences. Not a foolproof method. Far from it. But it was something. Constance and I were ideal daily companions. We shared everything except sex. We used to laugh, as close as we were, as *loving* as we were, that neither of us found the other sexually attractive in the least. Privately, Constance and Jill were *partners,* I believe is the appropriate modern term. As Rick was mine. The idea of marriage began when we four happened to be talking on campus a few days after a police raid on a certain local establishment and the attendant arrests."

I had to reimagine my image and memories of him—exactly as I'd had to do with Kevin after I'd learned the truth of his life.

"In the beginning, we had fantasies of living next door to one another in the same apartment building in Manhattan, but professional achievement was important for Constance and Jill, and Connie's work took her to London. Jill would have been hard-pressed to find an academic position here in England equal to the one she'd secured at NYU. As the years passed, Constance and I were with our true partners only infrequently, alas. Whenever Jill's academic schedule allowed. Rick traveled constantly for his work, and he and I were able to see each other more often."

The photo of the four of them in St. Mark's Square: "And you all went to Venice together."

"Yes, we had our divine weeks in Venice every July. Those days together . . . two couples, renting a palace on a canal. Only we knew the sleeping arrangements. Most likely the servants knew, too, but they were paid to be blind. As if we were all characters in a Henry James novel."

He'd played the role of a heterosexual man out of necessity, not choice. I'd never seen the truth right in front of me.

"Then the world changed," Christopher said. "Not for everyone, tragically. Not even for most. But for many. The younger generation might find our story inconceivable. How quickly history is forgotten. I'm amazed by how open the young have become. Amazed and thrilled—although with such openness, they've lost the secret codes that once defined our lives and created a special bond. You would have liked Jill and Rick. All gone now. And me, too, soon enough."

His eyes turned rheumy, his voice hoarse.

"Do you ever wish you'd found a way to stand up to the judgments of society and live with Rick openly?"

He coughed, clearing his throat. "A fine dream, and easy to visualize now, but it was impossible then." Sadness filled his voice. "I know that's hard to understand. The blind prejudice. The fear and hatred. The law against us, as it still is in many places around the world. We did the best we could. Constance and I were the closest of friends. I wouldn't have wanted to miss that. And Rick and I, well, the forced separations kept things . . . *fresh*. Never having to worry about mowing the metaphorical lawn. Impromptu afternoons at out-of-the-way hotels in foreign cities. I wouldn't have given that up, either."

He stared into the distance, then breathed sharply, as if pushing away his sorrow. When he turned to me, his gaze was pointed and fixed.

"Now here's the crux of the matter. Although Rick and I considered ourselves a couple, and Constance and Jill considered themselves one as well, none of us demanded sexual fidelity. What is true fidelity, after all? Emotional allegiance. Being available for each other during times of need. We took private vows of that, even though society wouldn't allow us to be together openly. We discussed our lives forthrightly."

I saw the links, and the differences, between his life and mine. Was I being intolerant not to let Kevin have his freedom, the way Christopher had given Rick the freedom not to be monogamous? But Christopher and Rick had *both* had this freedom, and they'd talked about how they would live. "It's something Kevin and I never discussed."

"I know. I had strong words with Kevin when he told me that you didn't know the truth of his life until recently. That you weren't given a chance to love him in full, for who he really is. And I've no doubt you would have done, that he's worthy of you. I can't comprehend such concealment between people who so clearly love each other as you two do."

My and Kevin's love for each other had always existed alongside Kevin's betrayal; I felt the stab of it.

"I hope you'll find a way to stay together."

"For Nicky's sake," I said automatically.

"No, for *your* sake. For *your* happiness."

"My happiness?" I said, surprised to hear the idea applied as a possibility for me. "I don't see how that could be. Kevin living the life he wants, and me having to go along with it. I can't support myself." I was losing control as I voiced my fears. "He's the one setting the rules. Right now I don't see what options . . . I don't see how—" Then I did break down, the anxieties of the past weeks overwhelming me. I couldn't look at him. Ashamed, I turned my body away, to hide. He was silent as I cried.

Finally he said quietly, "There are always options. Always choices to be made, questions to be asked, consequences to be faced. I'm sure you'd get some settlement in a divorce."

I wasn't about to tell him about the prenup I'd stupidly signed.

"But let's not talk about that yet," he said. "Let's put financial considerations aside. I want you to think about what you would need from Kevin apart from his financial support, so that you wouldn't feel dictated to or that he set the rules and you just had to follow along."

I looked up at Christopher. He regarded me with a frank sincerity that I seldom saw, this side of him usually kept well hidden.

"Ask yourself, what would make it possible?" he said. "No need to tell me. Just something for *you* to mull over."

As we sat together in an amiable silence, drank our tea, and ate our biscuits, I studied the paintings all around him. They took me to Venice, and to the coast of Maine, and to the peaceful countryside of my far-off homeland, and gradually I realized what I needed in order to stay with my husband.

CHAPTER 33

Lizzie said, "I'm worried about you."

About a week after Christopher's return, we walked along the Cam, on a path through the Grantchester Meadows. Children and dogs waded in the river. Punts glided by, and canoes and kayaks.

"That bruise really wasn't good," she added.

"Nicky loses control sometimes. Less frequently than he used to."

"The *less frequently* is made up for by his growing bigger and stronger."

A giant Bernese mountain dog raced along the bank and, directly beside me, leapt into the river. Water splattered onto my face and sunglasses.

I knew she was right. "I don't want to talk about it again."

"You *have* to talk about it," she said.

I'd told her enough at dinner. I didn't want her questions and advice bombarding me, making me regret my previous honesty and jeopardizing the bond I'd felt with her and Max.

"Are you seeing a therapist here?" she went on. "Is Nicky seeing one? If not, I can get some names for you."

"It's the summer," I said. "We're on vacation. Every day of our lives doesn't have to be ruled by therapists."

As if she hadn't even heard me, she said harshly, "I don't want you to be phoning me someday from Addenbrooke's. Although it's fine if you do. In fact, you have to. If you're at Addenbrooke's, you should call me. I'll come right over. Have you ever had a diagnosis for Nicky?"

This I could answer: It was objective. Scientific. "He's been evaluated for pretty much everything relevant. Autism spectrum, attention-deficit hyperactivity disorder, oppositional defiant disorder, Tourette's. He doesn't have an official diagnosis, which is fine with me. Labels can be liberating, but they can also be limiting, putting an always-developing child into a box."

"Is he on medication? If he isn't, maybe he should be."

"He's been on all kinds of medications, tried and rejected. They made him into a passive shell of himself. I couldn't stand seeing him that way. He's been to lots of therapists, each with a different plan. Nicky's young enough to adapt." I had to believe this. I had to cling to it. "He's *himself,* not a diagnosis, and he's learning how to manage life and society in his own way."

"You may be right," Lizzie assured me. "But the thing is, from what I see, from doing HR, some kids grow out of it, some don't. We all look for hope in the narrative, for a positive trajectory, but sometimes there isn't hope, it's more of the same for decades, and parents have to adjust. Not just take things day by day, with everything unpredictable. Hoping against hope that their kid will become the child of their dreams, instead of reconciling themselves to the person their child actually is. Parents have to find a way to stop the roller coaster of hope and disappointment, hope and disappointment."

Her voice was gentle and supportive as she said these words that were hard to hear. I had a sense she'd been professionally trained to speak this way, first agreeing and showing sympathy, then presenting an evaluation closer to what she believed was the truth, couched in general terms that the listener—me—might be more able to hear. But her truth wasn't mine, and she didn't know Nicky in all his complexity.

"You have an outdated view of these issues," I said. "Kids can have challenges in one area and excel in another." I knew I sounded defensive, but I wasn't going to accept her arguments. "The trick as a parent, any parent, is to help kids find the places where they can be successful and help build their confidence."

"Granted. But have you ever talked to other people experiencing things like this?"

In the river, a swan family, two adults and six gray cygnets, took refuge among the rushes.

"I went to a support group when Nicky was younger." I thought back on it. "All those parents trying to do the right thing, giving everything, in time and money, whatever they could do, trying every suggestion, following up on every idea."

"I'm in awe of parents like you."

"I'm not entitled to complain. Nicky is extraordinary in so many ways."

"To repeat, I'm in awe of parents like you, downplaying their challenges, hardly ever sharing their doubts or stress, doing what needs to be done, putting aside their own lives. Everybody focuses on helping the kids, but I wish experts would try to figure out how to make things easier for parents."

I agreed with her on this. "The negative judgments from well-meaning—or just know-it-all—acquaintances and even strangers on the street who understand absolutely nothing about you or your child . . . that can be—"

"Terrible, is what it is," Lizzie said.

"And then there's the online shaming," I said. "*Your kid is spoiled. You're a bad mother. You're too weak; you have to be tougher. You're too tough; you have to be more understanding.* God, I wish that would stop."

I couldn't go on about this. I had to find something else to talk about. Up ahead, six cows reclined on the path. "Why are there cows everywhere? Why can't you take a walk around here without constantly watching out for cow patties"—I stepped around one, foul-smelling and covered with flies—"and worrying about a cattle stampede?"

She gave me a questioning glance. "All right. I've said my piece about Nicky. For now. As to the cows, I've gotten used to them. They don't bother anybody. Unless someone bothers them."

"Doesn't lying down on the path constitute bothering us?"

"In Oxford the cows are paddocked. That's the biggest difference between Oxford and Cambridge, as far as I can tell."

"Paddocked cows: There's an innovation."

"Why do you dislike them so much?"

"It's not that I dislike them, not personally," I said, trying to reach for a bit of humor. "Getting to know them has certainly made me think twice about eating red meat but . . . well, I live in New York City. I grew up in a city. I'm not accustomed to so much nature."

The path forked, one side going up a rise across the meadows. With the cows still relaxing on the footpath that continued along the river, I said, "Let's go up, see the view."

We turned onto the new path. Around us, breezes shaped the un-mown grasses into ever-changing patterns. When we reached the top, the landscape opened.

And there was Ashton Hall, on the other side of the river. When I saw it this way, from above—the Flemish gables, the multiple chimneys and turrets, the brickwork warm and glowing in the sunlight—the house filled me with wonder.

"Wow, Ashton Hall is incredible from here," Lizzie said.

Where in the house had Isabella Cresham been imprisoned? She'd gone from being a four-year-old proudly paging through a book about birds to dying on a pallet in a prison room. The image of her skeleton assailed me—her skull, her teeth, almost blinding me, like a sudden glare in the sunlight.

"Lizzie," I said, too loudly, trying to pull myself back to the present.

"What?" She grabbed my arm. "Are you okay?"

"Yes, yes." I swayed as she held me up. I made myself breathe. "Okay, I'm okay now. I felt a little light-headed for a second."

Letting go of my arm, she appraised me.

I had to talk to her about Isabella, to escape the horror. To calm my quickened heartbeat. Mrs. Gardner didn't have the right to maintain secrecy about Nicky's discovery indefinitely. Besides, so many people knew already. "Lizzie, I need your opinion on what Nicky found. But then you'll be part of the secret." At least I'd try to follow Mrs. Gardner's wishes. "Would you mind promising not to share it, until the news is official?"

She placed her hand across her heart, an unexpected gesture from her. "I promise."

As we walked along the ridge, the hall beckoning in the distance, I slowly told her the details she hadn't learned through village gossip. Gradually my breathing returned to normal, and I could be objective and rational once more. When I reached the end of the story, I said, "One thing I can't understand is why the room was so well organized. It's as if Isabella Cresham chose everything herself and arranged it just the way she liked. But she couldn't possibly have done that."

"Why not?" Lizzie asked.

"Created her own prison? Walked into it willingly?" My insides rebelled against the notion. "That's crazy. I mean, only a disturbed person would do that. And the room seems to belong to someone who's completely sane."

"It's not crazy. Maybe she *did* choose to imprison herself. She might have been an anchoress type. I once read about those women— in those books you saw in my dining room. Anchoresses chose to be walled up in a room next to a church so they could contemplate God. Usually they had an opening that faced the street, and sometimes they taught kids and gave advice."

"What?" This sounded absurd. "What kind of advice could they possibly give, from a locked-up room and with no experience of the world?"

Up ahead, a bird emerged from the grasses, its wings flashing in the sun.

"Advice inspired by God. Like they had a direct link to Him, because they gave up their everyday lives and comforts."

"But they couldn't go anywhere?" I asked, disbelieving. "Not ever?"

"No. That was the whole point. When they went in, a priest recited the prayers for the dead. They were supposed to be dead to the world. Sometimes there was a separate room where a servant lived, and the servant pushed food through an opening and did everything that needed doing, like emptying the chamber pot, all through that opening. I suppose the walls could be knocked down, if the woman needed to get out, but that would have been considered a terrible sin, to want to get out after you'd already made the commitment."

"Did a lot of women live that way?" As the breezes grew stronger, the meadow grasses seemed to toss like the sea. I tried to imagine myself, asking to be locked up. . . . I couldn't imagine it.

"Apparently, England had more anchoresses than any other country. Never a huge number, but enough. In the hundreds. I even read that usually the anchoresses were from the upper classes. They were educated and had money. After all, they had to pay for their servants and their food. Although sometimes they got paid for their advice. Being an anchoress gave them authority in the community. It was a way for women to serve God *and* find personal fulfillment."

"In a locked-up room?" I felt sickened. I couldn't bring myself to look at Lizzie, as if by not looking, I could keep this possibility away from Isabella. In the far distance, cumulus clouds were rolling in from the Fens and the North Sea beyond them.

"Who are we to judge?" Lizzie insisted. "When old churches are dug up and renovated, sometimes they find the skeletons of anchoresses still in their rooms, right where they died. That sounds similar, doesn't it, even though this room wasn't attached to a church?"

"Okay, Isabella had religious books and objects in her room. But there were other things, too, for playing music and doing embroidery. For sketching. She read other types of books, too. There can't be just one reason for anything. What sort of woman would choose to lock herself up?"

Even as I said this, I knew that one of the biggest roadblocks to understanding history was the false notion that the individuals of the past were more or less like us, thought like us, and would do only things we would do. I realized that I'd been thinking about Isabella this way all along. I had to stop seeing her only through the filter of myself.

Lizzie said, "When I was first learning about the Middle Ages—this was back in high school—I thought, if I was alive then, I would have become a nun."

"*You?*"

"I know—weird but great, right?" Now I did look at her. She nodded enthusiastically and seemed pleased with herself. "We went to church, Episcopal, but I was never religious. Anyway, I was reading about the Middle Ages, and it seemed like there were basically three choices for most women in those days, apart from becoming something radical like an anchoress: You could be a wife and mother, and anything you had of your own—property, whatever—automatically belonged to your husband, and you were basically his servant for life, but you probably wouldn't have a long life, because a lot of women died giving birth."

The hillside grasses turned from green to silver to gold as the breeze continued to toss them.

"*Or* you could be a maiden-aunt type and serve as a permanent babysitter or governess for the children of your siblings."

I spotted a hawk, soaring.

"*Or* you could become a nun and spend your time doing good deeds and rise up through the ranks to be an abbess in charge of dozens or hundreds of people and supervising vast tracts of land.

Even then, the abbess concept was totally *me*," she said with satisfaction.

"Isabella Cresham lived after the English Reformation," I said, trying to bring us back to this one woman and her plausible choices. "There weren't any more anchoresses, and Englishwomen who wanted to become nuns had to go to the Continent to do it."

Trees dotted the meadow. Sheep grazed in a far pasture.

"Isabella couldn't do it the old-fashioned way, so she found a new way. A way to make the new rules work for her."

"But there was faith to reckon with. You had to have faith."

"Did you? You could announce you were completely into faith when what you really wanted was a little freedom to accomplish something that was important to you or to escape the nonstop pregnancies and daily drudgery. Maybe that's what Isabella Cresham wanted. She could stay in that room and read her books and do her embroidery, and play her music, and pray or pretend to pray a few times a day, and who was going to challenge her? Everybody left her alone or even admired her, for her devotion and courage, and sought her out for the good advice she gave, inspired by God Himself."

"But she was wealthy," I said. "For her, daily life wouldn't have been drudgery."

"I'm not sure about that. Like I said, usually the anchoresses were from the upper class. What does that say about the lives of women? I think upper-class women actually had fewer choices. Their only job and their primary purpose in life was to have sex with their husbands and give birth to sons."

Women as broodmares—a dismal thought.

"If for some reason they didn't get married, they were still completely dependent on their families. At least women in the equivalent of the middle or lower classes could work in a family business, or on a family farm, or become artisans of one kind or another," Lizzie went on. "And nuns could nurse the sick, educate the young, or copy and illustrate books in a scriptorium, and do farming, too."

I didn't know what to say to counter her certainty. Up ahead on the path, a little girl of about three, wearing a long dress and pink rubber boots, picked the grass, making a bouquet in her fist. Her father stood beside her.

"Think about Anne Boleyn. She was married to Henry the Eighth for roughly three and a half years, and during that time she had four pregnancies. Her first child, born nine months into the marriage, grew up to be Elizabeth the First. After Elizabeth's birth, Anne had three miscarriages or stillbirths. Therefore, Anne must have been pregnant or recovering from pregnancy basically all through her marriage—she'd have spent all her time suffering from morning sickness, or trying to recover after giving birth, or bleeding from a miscarriage, or living in confinement, the way they isolated pregnant women before and after birth in those days, and mourning her dead children."

I'd had a miscarriage before becoming pregnant with Nicky. It was early on, but I still remembered: Waking in the night to find blood pouring from me. Climbing into the bathtub as a place to contain the red deluge. Feeling terror, that I might bleed to death, and heartbreak, for my lost baby.

"When Anne couldn't produce a living son," Lizzie continued, "she was accused of adultery with seven guys, including her *brother*. Five of the guys ended up being executed. I don't know about you, but I'd be reluctant to have sex with, say, my brother, while I was nauseated from morning sickness or bleeding from a miscarriage. And hers was the life of a wealthy and prominent woman."

This turned my thoughts away from my dead baby. "No wonder her daughter never married."

"Exactly. Elizabeth Tudor was too smart and had seen too much to opt for the life of a *normal* woman. Maybe Isabella Cresham couldn't make herself be *normal*, either."

"Being walled up in a room was her answer?" I said.

"It's all about the context. Maybe that *was* normal. For her. She didn't have many options. Who gets to decide what's *normal*, anyway?" Lizzie asked.

"The great conundrum," I said.

Our path sloped down toward the river, and we lost sight of Ashton Hall.

CHAPTER 34

When I arrived at the conservation center the next afternoon, Martha was staring at a collection of papers protected in transparent Mylar sleeves and arrayed on the table before her.

"I'm glad you're finally here," she said, turning to me. She looked drained, her shoulders slumped, her pleated skirt twisted to one side.

"You okay?" I asked.

"Yes, of course. Fine." But I could tell she wasn't. "I just finished reading the letters from Isabella's keepsake box."

"And?"

"They're not what I anticipated."

I sat down in the chair beside her. She pulled her own chair away infinitesimally, even though there was plenty of space between us. This seemed to represent how Martha always reacted: We could be close, but not too close. "What did you anticipate?"

"I'd allowed myself to assume the letters would unlock Isabella's secrets. I was counting on it, actually. Always a mistake." She gave me a resigned smile. "I thought the letters would answer all our questions. But they don't."

"Who are they from?"

"The letters are from Hugh."

"Hugh, her younger brother?" I asked.

"Yes. From when he was away at school. Eton, naturally. Take a look."

I went through the letters, each one in its own sleeve, allowing me to examine the front and back. The paper was yellowed, but otherwise the letters were in good condition. Hugh's handwriting was neat and clear, and he wasted no space, turning the paper sideways to write in the margins when he reached the bottom of a page. I imagined Isabella's happiness when she received each of these letters, delivered by a messenger. She'd find an isolated place to read it, maybe sitting on her favorite bench under a tree in the garden. She'd want to keep the letter to herself at first, not sharing Hugh's news with the rest of the family until she'd had time to savor it.

"He reports on his Latin and Greek lessons," Martha said. "His history lessons. He wins a chess competition. Tells her about his favorite meals. Thanks her for a gift she sent him—although unfortunately for us, he doesn't say what the gift was."

"Judging from the entries in the library register, they were close," I said. "She must have been like a mother to him. Keeping an eye on him when he was young. Missing him when he went away to school. Terribly lonely without him."

"In one letter he says he's filled with *melancholie* to hear about the death of Ned and says he'd been looking forward to teaching Ned how to play chess. He remembers how silly Ned could be, playing games like running backwards as fast as he could. Ned was amongst the five of his siblings I found in the parish records who died young."

"It's so sad," I said. "She must have been terrified that Hugh would die young, too."

"I think about my own family," Martha said. "The five of us. What if only two grew to adulthood? And which two?" Her pearl-drop earrings shook as she turned her head away in sorrow. "It's impossible to comprehend. I remember bickering with them constantly. I also remember relying on them one hundred percent in school to come to my rescue if I needed them, just as I went to their rescue."

It was an experience I'd never had. "I've always wished I had a sibling. Maybe that's why I feel so touched by the relationship between Hugh and Isabella."

"I can't imagine my life without my siblings."

How reflective we were. The silence in the center seemed even deeper than usual; the graduate students weren't here today. Martha was such a contrast to Lizzie, who was always operating at high speed, thinking fast, making her arguments, convinced of her point of view, and eager to convince others.

"What else does Hugh write?" I asked.

"One of his longest letters is about the death of Jasper—about how awful Hugh feels that he wasn't with Jasper during his final days. How much he misses him. At first I thought Jasper must be another sibling, but when he wrote about Jasper chasing sticks and jumping in the river, I realized Jasper was a dog."

"A type of sibling."

"And then there are these." She indicated several letters she'd placed aside. "In these letters, Hugh begs Isabella not to leave him. *Don't go. I need you. You can't, you mustn't.*" She imitated the voice of a whining adolescent, and she didn't inject any humor into her performance. "*It's too far; it isn't safe. I'll never see you again.* He doesn't mention, alas, where she was considering going. Did she want to go to France to become a Catholic nun? Were her parents trying to arrange a marriage for her, somewhere far away? You read nothing in the account ledgers about money or household goods set aside for her marriage—dowry, bed linen?"

"Nothing," I said.

"That's surprising."

"Yes, it is, now that I think about it." The primary goal of an upper-class girl's life, apparently never considered for this particular girl.

"I don't understand why her parents allowed this petulant boy's wishes to take priority over what should have been a normal, for want of a better word, life for her," Martha said.

"We don't know if it was Hugh's decision, in the end. Maybe Lord and Lady Southbrooke wanted Isabella to stay home, too. They wanted their one surviving daughter to be with them, to keep them company in their old age."

She considered this, and I had a sense that she, too, was imagining herself in Isabella's shoes. "It's possible. The fate of many an unmarried daughter throughout history. It could have happened to me. Easily. Could still. I'm the only one of us not married or attached." This was the first time she'd mentioned that she didn't have a spouse or partner. "I'm *free,* as the others would put it, to abandon my work and assume the duty of caring for our parents, if necessary. And I would. Of course I would," she assured me, even as she shook her head *no.* "In one letter, Hugh writes, *You're my sister. I won't allow you to go away.* Although I don't know how he thought he was going to stop her."

"The lord-of-the-manor-to-be, asserting his authority."

"It's as if he assumed he owned her. Believed she was a possession of his," Martha said.

She might have been an anchoress type. I heard Lizzie's voice. She hadn't convinced me. But I hadn't *wanted* to be convinced. Hadn't allowed myself to be.

"Martha, do you think there's a chance Isabella might have *chosen* to be imprisoned? That she was an anchoress, or her own best version of it?"

"An anchoress?" she said doubtfully. "I've always thought those women must have been slightly insane. To do something so extreme,

from religious devotion. Insane is one thing Isabella has never seemed
to me."

"Not to me, either. But it could explain some things, some mysteries that are hard to understand otherwise," I said, playing devil's ad-
vocate.

"I refuse to let that be the answer," Martha said.

"I agree with you. And yet . . ."

"Here's what I've come to believe," Martha said, suddenly as
strong and confident as Lizzie had been. "Someone put her in that
room to keep her safe—*his* definition of safe, which wasn't safe for her
at all. In that room, she was under his complete control. We hear hid-
eous stories like that nowadays, about girls, women, kept imprisoned
for years."

"But he couldn't access her. Not her body," I protested. "Not the
way the room was set up."

"Maybe the separation was part of his plan."

I felt ill at the prospect. "But let's be practical: Who would have
done that? Hugh? Who else was there?"

"People are capable of all kinds of things," Martha said, an
oblique reference to her own life, I felt certain. "Things you'd never
even dream of."

I stared at her. She said nothing more. "Let's just go one step at a
time," I said. "These letters. The actual evidence we have before us
now. The letters do reveal one crucial truth about her life: that her
relationship with Hugh was the most important she ever had. She
kept his letters with her until the end and stored them with her other
special things. She must have cared for him deeply."

"She could have kept the letters because she hated him and the
letters reminded her of her anger," Martha said with uncharacteristic
force.

Feeling a need to soothe her with a half measure of agreement, I
said, "Her love for him might have evolved from one into the other."

"As with so many relationships," Martha said softly, glancing away.

I studied her—the pageboy haircut, her sharp chin, her dark eyes and pale skin. She bit her lip. She looked about to cry. I wished I could find a way to draw her out. If I were more like Lizzie, I'd simply demand to know what she was talking about. I'd justify myself by saying that confession would do Martha good. Instead, I joined in her British restraint. I'd have to wait for her to tell me.

CHAPTER 35

In the front vestibule, Nicky stopped before the mirror to admire himself in his school uniform: diagonally striped gray-and-teal tie over a white shirt, gray jacket with teal-green piping, knee-length gray trousers, horizontally striped gray-and-teal socks, and black leather shoes. For his school in New York, Nicky had usually thrown on whatever clothes were at hand, along with sneakers. This uniform gave him a role to play, and he was eager to play it.

From the bridge over the moat, I watched him through the open door. It was the first day of classes, seven forty-five on a cloudy morning in early September, the week before Labor Day. I'd found a place for Nicky at the Paston School, which Ben Moran Zeitlin attended. True to her word, Lizzie had guided me through the admissions process and the visa issues.

Kevin would arrive on Friday. *No,* I ordered myself. No thinking about that now, at this landmark moment for Nicky. Mrs. Gardner had joined Christopher, Rafe, Duncan, and me on the bridge. Alice was nearby, holding her and Nicky's bikes. Wearing a cowboy hat with his running clothes, the general arrived, greeting us with a rousing "Howdy."

Mrs. Gardner said, "Where precisely did you find—"

"Now, there's an intriguing question," the general said with a grin, pushing down the hat more firmly on his head.

"Come along, Nicky," Alice called. She was taking one cookery class this term, entitled Soups, Stocks, and Sauces, along with a lab called Knife Skills. Her schedule would allow her to bike with Nicky to school in the morning and pick him up in the afternoon, earning money for her following term.

Nicky ran outside, put on his backpack and helmet, and climbed onto his bike. He'd established that the trip took fourteen and a half minutes, on average, from the beginning of the asphalt drive. Yesterday they'd done several trial runs, Nicky using the stopwatch on his phone. They were leaving early, in case of unforeseen delays.

"Bye, Nicky," I said. "Love you."

"Love you, too. Bye, everybody," he called over his shoulder.

These past weeks, he'd seemed stable enough, on good behavior for Christopher, and I was no longer locking him in his room at night. Paston was a mainstream school, and Nicky had done well at his interview and on the admissions test, especially the maths section. Nonetheless, I'd told the school headmistress about his challenges. She was an older woman, buttoned-up in a navy-blue skirt suit, and she'd surprised me by replying, with a sparkle in her eyes, as if pleased that Nicky was out of the ordinary, *You needn't worry; we delight in all manner of student.*

Perhaps, finally, I'd found a school where Nicky could thrive. We watched them until they were far along the drive, and I sent my love to surround and protect him.

"Right," Mrs. Gardner said. "Kitchen inspection." She strode toward the café.

"I intend to circumnavigate the lake," the general said, and he jogged off at a moderate pace.

Christopher gazed around at the landscape as the cloud cover broke and sunlight reflected off the still-damp plantings. "How marvelous, to be at ease whilst others are busy. I should think that tea is called for. With oat biscuits. In the sitting room, if you please, Rafe."

"Yes, sir."

"Must ward off our feeling of emptiness."

His voice broke. Nicky and Christopher had been spending hours together each day. Nicky had pushed Christopher, who used a wheelchair over the greater distances, along the paths. As they went, they threw tennis balls for Duncan. Henceforth, our lives would be regimented by the school schedule.

"No choice but onward," Christopher said as he made his way inside, his cane sufficient.

The sitting room, despite the architectural stateliness of its high ceilings and decorative moldings, was a comfortable mess. Duncan's bed boasted a quarter-inch-thick mat of fur spread about on top. Books, magazines, and newspapers were placed haphazardly upon the end tables. The old-fashioned lamps, with their bell-shaped shades and silk fringes, gave off barely enough light to read by. The photographs displayed on the mantel showed Christopher and Constance, Jill and Rick. He'd brought out these pictures after our conversation, adding them to the photos of Nicky and me, bringing his closest companions into our daily lives.

Displayed on a card table was an antique chess set that Christopher had asked Rafe to retrieve from a closet after I'd told him and Nicky that Isabella and Hugh had played chess. The intricately carved wooden set was from the early nineteenth century, made in China, bought in Macau, according to a handwritten note the original owner had placed inside the box. Each piece incorporated the image of a phoenix rising from ashes. Under Christopher's instruction, Nicky had come to adore chess.

Studying the set, his companion in games off at school for the day, Christopher said, "Ah, Hannah, not so marvelous after all, is it, to be at ease and leisure. What to do with the hours of the day? I used to be working, working, working. Meetings with clients, exhibitions, publications, auctions, luncheons at one club, before-dinner drinks at another. After I retired here, long walks, visiting, and generally making a nuisance of myself with friends and acquaintances alike. But today we have—what?"

I didn't know how to comfort him.

"Must find something to fill the time." He gazed at the overflowing bookshelves on either side of the fireplace. "I fancy I'd like to fill the void by reading a novel. We've had a bit too much reality recently, studying the fate of poor Isabella Cresham." He examined the shelves more closely. "Hmm . . . An entire section for Charles Dickens. Maybe *Great Expectations.* Loved that, once upon a time. Nicky should read Dickens. Magnificent novels. Here's Jane Austen. Constance adored Jane Austen."

These novels, the English classics, had been at the center of my education. Austen, Dickens, Eliot, the Brontës . . . They were the authors who'd shaped my imagination. Maybe this was why so many Americans were Anglophiles, because of the English novels they'd read when they were young. Parents with children older than Nicky told me these books were seldom taught anymore in high school or college. Perhaps Anglophilia would fade away in America without such inspiration. The stories held within these books would be replaced by others, from cultures around the world, along with the stories of Americans whose histories had been silenced.

"*Jane Eyre* was Jill's favorite novel. Look, Trollope. Rick loved Trollope, especially the political novels. So many volumes, though, continuing the plots from book to book. I'd be dead long before we finished."

He touched the novels lightly with his index finger as his gaze traveled down the shelves, as if he could connect with Rick, Constance, and Jill through the book spines.

"Here's *Middlemarch*. I recall hearing somewhere that Tolstoy said it was the only English novel written for adults. I'm an adult, shocking though it may be to think of myself as such. Perhaps the time has come. *Middlemarch*. I remember Constance, Jill, and Rick in the London house one summer. We were about to leave for Venice, and all of us remarked that we'd never read it, despite wanting to. We'll read it now." He stared at the photos on the mantel. "I'll read it for the four of us."

He took *Middlemarch* from the shelf and opened it. Turned to the first page of text. Adjusted the book to catch the light from the window. Pulled the book closer. Looked up at me, squinting. "Eyes aren't what they used to be. Can't make out the small print."

"Would you like me to set up audio streaming?"

"Audio streaming?" he said, affronted. "Oh, no. I don't believe that's for me. Dealing with the technology. Rafe," he asked, as Rafe entered the room with the tea tray, "do we want to deal with the technology to *stream*, as Hannah has called it, audiobooks?"

"Whatever you like, sir. Simple enough to arrange."

"I don't know, I don't know."

"Or you could use a tablet to read an ebook," Rafe said. "Make the print size as big or small as you like it."

"You *are* thoughtful, Rafe. But I don't think so. Too late for all that. Old dog, new tricks—forgive me, Duncan, please don't take it personally." Duncan was curled on his bed, evidently asleep, but he flicked his tail at the mention of his name.

"I'm sure we can find a large-print edition," I said. "Whatever you prefer is fine."

"Is it?" He brightened. "In that case, how about you read it aloud to me, Hannah? You'll inhabit the story along with me. Cruel of me, isn't it? Putting you through your paces, instead of pressing a button and letting the disembodied voice of a stranger sound forth in our midst. Or going off to my room alone with my—what did you call it, Rafe?—my *tablet*. Or using a large-print edition—most unattractive. Excellent; we've decided."

We've decided? He'd decided. I'd planned for a morning of work on my paying job before returning to the library register. My newest client was an umbrella manufacturer who wanted weather scenes, and I was putting together a selection of Japanese woodblock prints by Hiroshige, evocative images of snowstorms and rain showers. Yes, my job could be wonderful. But it could wait.

Christopher gave me the book. We sat down, me taking the chair beside the lamp that gave off the highest-intensity wattage, such as it was. Rafe poured the tea and passed the cups and biscuits, then sat down, too.

"Ready," Christopher said with a smug smile.

This was a woman's life: caring for the young and for the old. Her work and her desires took second place to the needs of others. I'd fulfill the role that family, and society, and I myself, expected of me. I *wanted* to see Nicky off to school. I *wanted* to spend time with Christopher and help to make his final days better in whatever small way I could. I was grateful to have the financial stability to do it. Nonetheless, I knew that Kevin would have excused himself at this point and gone back to work. Instead of condemning him as selfish and self-serving, everyone would have praised him for his work ethic and ambition.

I began at the Prelude and continued into Chapter One: "*Miss Brooke had that kind of beauty which seems to be thrown into relief by poor dress . . .*"

Reading aloud from a long, dense text with small print turned out to be more difficult than I'd expected. Much more difficult than my previous read-aloud efforts with such preschool classics as *Goodnight Moon* and *Franklin Fibs*. My voice gave out at the bottom of the second page of the first chapter, in the middle of the paragraph beginning, *It was hardly a year since they had come to live at Tipton Grange . . .*

My throat felt scorched. I couldn't force my voice to make any more sound. I stopped. My companions waited for me to resume. I shook my head and motioned to my throat. My vocal cords weren't responding to the orders from my brain.

"You'll get better at it," Christopher said jauntily. "I say, I enjoyed that. Now it's time for a nap." Despite his fixed smile, he needed Rafe's support as he made his way to his room.

CHAPTER 36

Once again, Kevin and I walked along a woodland path. After these many weeks away from each other, he was like a stranger to me. I needed to remind myself of him: His lithe torso. Dark hair, silky like Nicky's. Brown eyes, framed by tortoiseshell glasses. But I had trouble even looking at him.

". . . and then," Kevin was saying, "we stopped for food, and I heard a full recitation of the multiplication and division tables, up to eighteen times eighteen—going higher every day, Nicky bragged—and I heard all this while we ate incredibly delicious chocolate bread-and-butter pudding at Stickybeaks. It was surprisingly restful. I didn't need to say a word. Luckily, the couple next to us took it in stride."

"If they were British, they're accustomed to hearing what they call maths recited in odd locations."

Once again, a passing shower had left beads of rain on the ferns,

luxuriant beneath the trees, the raindrops sparkling where the sunlight filtered through. Nicky was off somewhere with Alice. Christopher was in his study, catching up with correspondence.

"I was glad to revisit eight times eight and nine times nine. I'd
forgotten those."

"Sixty-four and eighty-one, respectively."

"I'm impressed."

"Nicky's been practicing with me."

"He also told me the latest details about Isabella Cresham, the
books she read, that she played chess with her brother, that he's learning chess in her honor. Amazing—both what you've found and Nicky's
passion for the whole thing."

"I feel passionate about it, too."

"I've been thinking, if Nicky does well at this new school, we could
stay here for the rest of the school year, even after Christopher . . ." I
was glad he didn't complete the sentence. "The tuition is paid for the
entire year. I could work out of the firm's London office. I haven't
mentioned this to anyone at work, but it's an idea. I mean, if you'd like
to do it . . ."

I thought about this. Living here, Kevin commuting by train to
London each day, as many people did. Arranging private assignations
after working hours.

"Kevin, I want to talk to you about something." I knew I needed
to make my request—my requirement—sound logical and nonthreat-
ening. "How would you feel if I had permission"—immediately I
regretted my use of the word *permission*, which granted him control
when I was trying to find equality, but I couldn't take it back—"within
our marriage to have a lover?"

"What do you mean?" He didn't seem to take it in.

"It's a hypothetical, mirroring your life. I want the same freedom
you have."

I had no compulsion to confess to him. I'd deleted Matthew's
texts. My connection to Matthew, the guilt I'd felt afterward—Kevin

didn't need to know this. The freedom I asked for *was* theoretical. I believed in monogamy, and it was the way I wanted to live. I needed to make a point, however, for myself as much as for Kevin, the point that equality in a marriage meant equal rules. Equal choices. I couldn't live with an arrangement that was one-sided.

"If it was a woman, I'd understand. I'd be fine with that."

We walked amid cooling, dappled shadows, the trees a sun-filled canopy above us.

"As I said before, I'm not interested in women. Not sexually."

"So you're talking about a man?"

"Yes," I said.

He was silent for a long time. The path opened into a clearing, and a small pond was before us, its surface covered with full-blooming white water lilies. He stopped, studying them. "To be honest," he said, grief in his voice, "I wouldn't want that. It hurts just thinking about it. Why would you do that? I thought we loved each other."

"We do," I said to reassure him, even though I wasn't certain of it anymore.

"Not like that," he said with confusion. "Not with you seeing other men."

"I only want to have the same choices you have," I said. "The person's gender shouldn't matter."

"But it *does* matter." He looked at me with eyes alert like a fox's. "I'd never betray you by taking up with another woman."

"My first choice would be mutual monogamy," I said, still trying to sound reasonable. "But you say it isn't possible for you. I understand that you're bisexual, and that's fine and it's who you are. But we never discussed it before we got married. We never agreed that you would see other people. You let me assume we'd be monogamous. Now that I know the truth, there has to be a balance."

"How would you like it if I started having sex with other women?" He spat out the words, his face pinched and suddenly ugly. He began walking away from me, faster than I could keep up. "Maybe

I should try it," he called over his shoulder. "We'll see how you feel then."

I knew his fast pace was meant to make me feel weak and inferior, and so I tried all the more to catch up with him. When I reached him, I managed to keep my voice steady. "I wouldn't like it. But I'm not suggesting I'd have sex with other men to punish you."

He seemed not to hear this. He turned onto a new path, where the foliage was thicker and the air itself appeared to take on a greenish hue. "Plenty of women have approached me over the years. Don't think they haven't."

"I'm sure they have." I hadn't been so naïve as to think women ignored him because of his wedding ring. I'd trusted him to be faithful.

"I've never responded," he said. "When it comes to women, you're enough for me. And I don't want to hurt you, because I love you. I want you to know, though, that there are plenty of women who would jump at the—" He broke this off, but I knew where he'd been going.

"Instead, let's say there are plenty of *people*, men and women both, who'd accept whatever you propose in return for your love, if not your sexual fidelity, along with an apartment on Riverside Drive. Is that the type of partner you want?"

He said nothing. We both had to slow down and step carefully, because of fallen branches and protruding roots on the path.

"Were you seeing Tim this summer?"

"You know that. I'm not going to lie about it anymore."

"I don't understand how you can give yourself a permission you won't give me. Maybe you need to shift *your* perspective and try to see this from my point of view."

"I don't need to shift my perspective." In the afternoon warmth, his shirt clung to his shoulders from sweat. This could have been attractive, virile even. Today it wasn't. "We won't have an open marriage. After you get back to New York, we'll start seeing a marriage counselor. Then you'll understand."

"What makes you certain a therapist would agree with you?"

"Because it's obvious." No humor in this. No glimmer, even, of recognition that I might have a valid point. I couldn't conceive of a therapist concluding that Kevin's proposal was a good arrangement, especially when I didn't want it.

"I'm not going to a marriage counselor," I said.

The path turned, and the view opened. We were near the river and Ashton Hall's wide lawns.

We stopped walking. I turned to him. A lock of his hair had fallen onto his forehead and was plastered there from sweat. In former days, I would have pushed it back into place and pressed my palm against his head in a touch of love.

"Just to be clear, here's my requirement," I said, trying to be patient as I explained again. What was the point of raising my voice, crying, screaming, raging? No point. "If we stay together, I want the same freedom you have. Most probably I'll never use it. I want to know I could. Otherwise, I feel as though I'm just one of your possessions, like a car or a TV. Not an independent person in my own right."

"You're not a possession." His entire being softened, his face relaxed, his shoulders dropped, as if he thought, *Oh, now I understand.* He brushed his hand down my arm. "You're my wife. I love you. I respect you. What more do we need?"

"I told you what I need."

He pulled away. "You aren't giving me much choice."

"No, I'm not. You haven't given me much choice, either. As I said, I understand and accept who you are. I *respect* who you are. I just want us to be equal."

"My friendship with Tim has nothing to do with my feelings for you. I've told you that. Compromise is what creates a family."

"Compromise on both sides," I said.

"You could get pregnant, and we wouldn't know who the father was. I'm not going to get involved with some other guy's kid."

These words could have been said as easily to Katherine Cresham or Isabella Cresham. It was the excuse used throughout history to keep women separated from the world. "I'd have the responsibility to make certain that didn't happen."

"Your answer's not good enough. Have you thought about how much you'll lose if we divorce?"

There it was—the threat of money, into the open, and it was staggering to hear.

"I do realize," I said. But all my fears of the past weeks slammed me in the face. Should I have consulted an attorney before this conversation?

"You won't get much spousal support," he said quietly, his voice focused, mean-spirited. "Not from that prenup you signed. You'll lose the apartment for sure."

If that was the worst of it, he didn't scare me. I'd grown up in a school residence hall. I could create a new home for Nicky and me, someplace simple. My real estate needs weren't great.

"*I* built our life," he said.

I became attuned to every sound of the woods around us, the background hum of insects, every scent of the rich, fertile earth.

"*I* did everything. My money paid for our apartment. You contributed essentially nothing."

I gasped. "Raising Nicky counts as nothing?" I swayed. I needed to hold on to something, but in this place where we'd stopped, there wasn't anything to reach for, and I breathed deeply, fighting against revealing my weakness to him.

"In a divorce, you could lose custody of Nicky. You haven't been very successful with him, have you? You can't control him. You have to lock him up at night." Kevin's eyes were bright and menacing, and he loomed over me, using his size to scare me. I forced myself not to step back. "What have you done to him that he has such hatred toward you? For your own safety, he'll have to live with me, especially now that you want to have affairs."

He could make it look like that, to an outsider. To the judge deter-

mining our futures. I felt as though I was falling, tumbling over a prec-
ipice, even while keeping myself perfectly still.

"You'll be allowed to visit him for an hour a few times a week, under
court supervision. Court-appointed experts will interview him to determine what went on at home while I was at the office working twelve or
fifteen hours a day to support the lifestyle you demanded." His entire
body had tensed, like a string pulled tight; even the muscles of his neck
were visible. "Have you already invited your lovers to the apartment?"

"You're the one who's been having an affair, Kevin. For years."

"That's different."

"Is it?"

"And never at the apartment. I'm just telling you what my attorney would say in court."

"What your attorney would say with your permission. With your
approval, even though you know it's not true."

"How can you fight back?" he asked softly and slowly, as if time
had stopped. His hands were fisted at his sides, ready to lash out. "You
can't. It's a convincing argument. The facts are against you."

I'd claw his face, I'd kill him if I needed to, to keep my son. I kept
myself frozen in place.

"You can avoid this by compromising. You aren't seeing things
properly right now. You're stressed because of Christopher's illness."
His voice turned into unctuous reassurance. "You're waiting for someone to die. It's easy to get muddled. You're projecting your anxiety
onto our marriage. It's only natural."

After the threats of just seconds earlier, the extreme sympathy left
me floundering.

"Once Christopher— Down the road, this will seem absurd.
When you and Nicky are home, where you should be. This isn't real
life, here at Ashton Hall. You're just living out a fantasy. Afterward,
everything will slip back into place, the way it was before."

He gave me a long smile—not cruel, not sly, but affectionate.

"We'll put all this on hold," he said tenderly, holding out his arms,
inviting me into a hug.

I began to see him from afar, as if through the reverse side of binoculars.

"I won't let you make the worst mistake of your life because you're stressed. You take care of Christopher, and I'll take care of you and Nicky. I'll keep you safe."

I didn't want his definition of *safe*.

CHAPTER 37

The first book Katherine checked out of the library after her marriage to Hugh in 1579 was *Le Roman de la Rose*. The second book she borrowed was *Blanchardyn and Eglantyne*. The internet told me these were entertainments. Diversions. I saw her in my mind. . . . Each sunny afternoon, Katherine sat on a bench in the garden, reading.

After walking away from Kevin on the woodland path, I'd retrieved my laptop from my bedroom and come here, to the conservation center. The center was deserted on this Saturday afternoon, although Martha's tote bag was on the chair in her glassed-in office.

I built our life. I did everything. My money paid for our apartment. You contributed essentially nothing. All the nights I'd stayed up with Nicky when he ran a fever. The times I did the shopping, cooked our meals, organized the apartment, took Kevin's clothes to the dry cleaner, had sex with him—all that, considered worthless, because none of it earned money.

Next Katherine read William Turner's *A New Herball*, in three volumes. Then she borrowed *A Nievve Herball, or Historie of Plantes*, by Rembert Dodoens. She was educating herself, in the tradition of her mother-in-law and most likely her own mother, fulfilling her role as lady of the manor.

In a divorce, you could lose custody of Nicky. You haven't been very successful with him, have you? How hard I'd tried—we'd both tried—to help our son.

As the months passed, Katherine's interests expanded to books directly about medicine, and she borrowed Galen's *Methodus Medendi* and Avicenna's *Canon of Medicine*. She now wrote in the library register herself. Her handwriting was bold, impatient.

You can't control him. Rage began to take hold inside me. My hands shook with it as I read the register.

I skimmed over the many entries—the boys from the village, the household staff, the professors and the vicar, family members during their visits—and focused only on Katherine and Isabella. Katherine read *A Most Excellent Homish Apothecarye*, by Von Braunschweig.

You have to lock him up at night. What have you done to him that he has such hatred toward you? Hatred? He defined Nicky's struggles as *hatred*?

Isabella, with her elegant handwriting, checked out a breviary and other religious works, including what she described as *Vaux, Catechism*. These were books of Catholic devotion, and I knew from my research that they were illegal. Yet here they were, available in the family's library.

For your own safety, he'll have to live with me, especially now that you want to have affairs. He was deliberately misunderstanding everything I'd said.

Isabella read *First Booke of the Christian Exercise, Appertayning to Resolution*, by Robert Persons, the edition printed in Rouen in 1582, the year of the coins found in her keepsake box. Robert Persons was a Jesuit, although the internet explained that this particular book was popular not only with Catholics but also, in an adaptation, with Protestants. Unless I found their actual copy of the book in the Old

Library, I had no way of knowing which version the Cresham family owned.

You'll be allowed to visit him for an hour a few times a week, under court supervision. So Kevin would wake Nicky and help him to get dressed and organized every morning and pick him up at school in the afternoon and stay at home with him every night?

In 1583, Isabella checked out *A Very Proper Treatise, Wherein Is Breefely Sett Forth the Arte of Limming.* This work concerned the art of painting portrait miniatures, which were tremendously popular in Elizabethan England. Was she teaching herself to paint miniatures? As of now I had no evidence that she was.

Katherine read Thomas Elyot's *The Castel of Helth.*

From the storage cupboard, I retrieved the account ledgers, taking them out of their protective gray box. I brought them to my workstation and found the volume I needed. I compared the dates in the ledger with Katherine's borrowings.

Court-appointed experts will interview him . . .

Katherine was the *Lady Southbrooke* of these years—the woman who gave birth to many babies, half of whom died, I realized as I skimmed through the recurring payments for coffins and for funerals for *his lordship's child, her ladyship's baby.*

She'd obsessively studied herbs and medicine to try to save her own children, their small bodies filling the crypt at the church by the gates—just as I'd once read book after book, desperately, in the early morning, before Nicky woke up, trying to find ways to help him.

. . . to determine what went on at home while I was at the office . . .

Isabella began borrowing books that she and Hugh had read as children, and she added in her entries, *For the education of Margaret.* And *For teaching Latin to Bess.*

Edmund Pettitt, tutor to his young lordship Hugh and Arthur his brother, borrowed Ovid's *Metamorphoses.*

I struggled to keep my focus on the research in front of me: These youngsters must have been among the surviving children of Katherine and Hugh, the boys instructed by a male tutor, a recent graduate of the university perhaps, while the girls were taught by Isabella, their aunt who'd never married.

. . . working twelve or fifteen hours a day to support the lifestyle you demanded. I'd never wanted a *lifestyle,* whatever he meant by that. I'd wanted a home for our child. I wasn't the venal and selfish person he was portraying.

Katherine borrowed Walter Bailey's *A Short Discourse of the Three Kindes of Peppers in Common Use.* A book about cooking? No. An internet search showed the full title: *A Short Discourse of the Three Kindes of Peppers in Common Use and Certaine Special Medicines Made of the Same, Tending to the Preservation of Health.*

In 1588, Isabella borrowed *De Imitatione Christi, Thomas à Kempis.* There was no check on the right side of the register to indicate that she'd returned it. Was this the same edition that was on her desk when she died?

How can you fight back? You can't. He was wrong. I could fight back. I would.

Little Margaret was now permitted, or decided to take permission, to write in the register herself. *Virgil,* she noted, without giving a title.

In 1589, Margaret: *Virgil again, to read with my aunt Isabella. Aeneid.* Proof that Isabella was still alive.

In 1590, *CHESS for BESS,* another niece wrote in large letters, taking up half the page. Was there no longer a librarian employed to monitor these entries? Or had he given up, this new generation running wild, beyond his control and comprehension? At least Isabella added the title, *The Mastering of the Game of Chess.*

In 1591, *Aesop's Fables,* Isabella wrote. *To rede to me, Blanche,* the child added in her broad, open script. I stared at the entry, the first appearance of Blanche in the library register. With my fingertip held just above the paper, I traced her words. I saw aunt and niece sitting together, side by side, in the library, Blanche following the printed words as Isabella read aloud. I felt the love between them.

Also in 1591, *Abcdarium for me, Blanche.* I noted the idiosyncratic spelling of the title; she spelled it the same way Isabella had, years earlier.

In 1592, Isabella borrowed Robert Southwell's *Marie Magdalens Funeral Teares*. Like Persons, Southwell was a Jesuit, and he believed in martyrdom as a type of religious devotion. This book was also popular with both Catholics and Protestants, and it went through many editions.

In February of 1593, Margaret wrote, *Oh, no, Cicero*. As usual, personality shone through, even in the simplest list. Isabella borrowed the *Thesaurus Ciceronianus*, by Marius Nizolius. Margaret must have gulped at the sight of its thousand pages. Isabella was still alive.

In mid-July 1593, Katherine borrowed *The Poor Man's Jewel, That Is to Say a Treatise of the Pestilence*, by Thomas Brasbridge.

It was a plague year.

The facts are against you. I knew the facts. I resolved to write them down—the truth of our lives, ready to show the attorney I would hire.

And here the listings in the register ceased, even though a blank page remained within the volume.

I opened the next volume. In May of 1596, the borrowers' register resumed. The financial accounts had also resumed in May of 1596.

For her first entry in the new register, in her own handwriting—on the same day the account-keeper noted the purchase of *thre broomes*—Katherine Cresham, Lady Southbrooke, borrowed Timothie Bright's *A Treatise of Melancholie, Containing the Causes Thereof*. Was she the one suffering from *melancholie*?

Next she borrowed *The First and Chief Groundes of Architecture*, by John Shute. Her thoughts must have turned to the renovation of the hall.

You're just living out a fantasy. Ashton Hall was far from a fantasy.

I knew I'd never go back to him. Not because of who he was, but because of what he'd said to try to convince me to stay.

Isabella Cresham never checked out another book.

CHAPTER 38

As the weeks passed, Christopher, instead of dying, appeared to stabilize.

"It's the tea," he said one morning at the beginning of October.

He liked PG Tips, a strong, so-called *builder's tea*, meant for everyday consumption.

"This tea, combined with the wholesome milk from the local cows, plus Scottish oat biscuits and homemade ice cream—and look at me now."

He was weak, but he didn't become weaker. He developed a hankering for the café's crumpets, with honey. He requested peaches in his ice cream, then plums. He continued to enjoy being pushed along the paths in his wheelchair by Rafe, Nicky, or me. We basked in the radiant days, even as the air became cooler, the leaves turned red and orange, and the yellowing light waned.

"Heaven, as forecast," Christopher said.

Day after day Nicky did his revision, as homework was called here, willingly, not even needing a reminder. He got out of bed in the morning without a fight. Dressed himself in his uniform, tying his school tie. Ate breakfast. Was ready to leave on time. The British educational approach of rote memorization suited him. The rules were stringent. Little in the course of a day was fun. Self-expression and self-discovery weren't encouraged, and Nicky didn't miss them. His oddities became eccentricities. He was liked, by teachers and schoolmates both. He was invited to join the maths and the history teams, because he could memorize anything and his reactions were quick. There wasn't much parental involvement, so I didn't have to worry about being snubbed.

Every day around dinnertime, Nicky spoke with Kevin on the phone.

Unbeknownst to Kevin, I'd emailed a friend in New York to get the name of her divorce lawyer. I'd gone into London, to an American bank, and set up an account in my own name. I'd arranged for my salary checks from the art-licensing company to be deposited there rather than into the joint checking account I shared with Kevin. I began taking out more cash than I needed from the joint account. Not so much cash that Kevin would notice it was missing, but enough to create a small stockpile, part of me feeling I was stealing from him, the other part knowing it was my money, too, the salary I'd earned for doing *essentially nothing* to contribute to our lives.

Kevin seemed to think his decision to put everything on hold had resolved our differences. This suited me, giving me time to prepare, in whatever small ways I could, for the coming separation. I restricted my communications with him to text messages about Nicky.

Toward the end of October, at the British half-term school holiday, Kevin took Nicky to London for a week. On the morning Kevin arrived to pick Nicky up, I arranged to be doing research all day at the university library.

With Nicky away, Christopher gave Alice a week of paid vacation. Rafe took vacation days, too, and his temporary replacement, sent from an agency, was efficient but kept his distance.

And so Christopher and I were even more isolated than before, living in our own world. I wasn't in touch with Lizzie or with Matthew. I secured permission from Martha to take the library register to the apartment, to share it with Christopher. In the evenings, when he was too tired to focus on *Middlemarch*, I read aloud from the register, and we watched Hugh and Katherine's surviving children grow up.

"In April of 1598," I said, "Margaret Cresham borrowed Richard Hakluyt's *Divers Voyages Touching the Discoverie of America*."

"Planning a vacation to the New World, was she?" Christopher asked.

"I'm certain of it. She was a feisty one. I wonder what became of her." Marriage, children . . . early death?

"Maybe we'll find out," Christopher said.

"I hope so. In 1598, young Arthur Cresham read George Chapman's translation of the *Iliad*."

"A boy reading Homer. He reminds me of myself," Christopher said.

"I'd love to see a photo of you when you were young. Do you have any?"

"Mercifully not," he said, deflecting with a wave of his hand any questions about his childhood in Arkansas. "Do continue."

"All right. I won't push you on it," I said. We exchanged smiles. "Let's see . . . Toward the end of 1598, Katherine Cresham borrowed John Gerard's *The Herball or Generall Historie of Plantes*."

"Where would we find John Gerard's *Herball* or any of the herbals Lady Southbrooke read, if we wished to consult them? To find out if they have anything to offer *me*?" He glanced away, grimacing, all at once revealing the pain he suffered.

"In the Long Gallery or, if they're not there, the Old Library," I said quietly.

"The Old Library, indeed," he harrumphed, quickly returning to his usual wry tone. "I've never been there. I've never been *permitted* to go there. Mrs. Gardner thinks it amusing to forbid me. *The Old Library is absolutely* not *open to the public, Mr. Eckersley,* she says. She claims. For some time I've suspected that the Old Library doesn't exist. It's part of an elaborate joke they're perpetrating on curious outsiders."

"The Old Library very much exists. I've been there."

"Have you, then." He frowned, suspicious. I knew him well enough to realize he was playacting at being perturbed, covering over the confession of his pain. "And when was this, precisely?"

"While you were in New York," I said.

"And why, pray tell, did you have occasion to go there?"

"I went with Martha Tinsley. To retrieve the library registers."

"Was Nicky with you?" he asked, as if this would be the final insult.

"No, he was not."

"At least I haven't been outdone by the entire family. What's it like, the Old Library?"

"Disorganized. Dusty. Dark. No electricity."

"Why don't we go there together?" Brows raised, he appeared very happy with himself at the prospect, as if he were a boy contemplating a prank. "Have an excursion. You can arrange it with Dr. Tinsley. We needn't tell Mrs. Gardner until afterward. Oh, I want to see the expression on her face when I surprise her with the news. And who knows what we might learn." He rubbed his hands together in his enthusiasm for our adventure. "Maybe we'll find a diary written by Isabella Cresham that explains everything. Or love poems exchanged between Isabella and Katherine. One big happy family, eh? How about eleven o'clock tomorrow morning? When the end is nigh, one wants to indulge one's whims."

Martha placed five large flashlights, two upright and three facing sideways, on the table in the sixteenth-century section of the Old Library. "Is this enough light for you?"

It wasn't, not nearly, but with the help of the flashlight on my phone and the morning light seeping in from the windows at the end of the enfilade, we'd manage. I didn't want to take more of her time. "It's perfect, Martha. Thank you."

"I'll work on the online catalog at the table just outside, in case the books become unruly and you require assistance."

"I'd enjoy a confrontation with unruly books," Christopher said, pressing one hand onto the table to support his weight and, with the other hand, waving his cane at the shelves.

"I'm glad I can count on you to maintain discipline," Martha said. "These uncataloged books are sorely in need of regulation. I'll leave you to it, then." Martha departed.

Christopher gazed at the shelves. I picked up one of the large flashlights and ran it across the volumes. The spines with gold tooling glimmered, but most appeared to be unmarked, the book titles faded or possibly never even added to the spines. One section of shelves held what looked like portfolios, placed horizontally and suitable for storing maps or architectural plans.

Christopher said, "This is not what I expected, for a site of such high repute."

"No. But still."

"That's the spirit: *but still*. We're here; let's make a go of it. I see that judging a book by its cover will be impossible."

"Why don't you sit down? You can use your cane to point to the books you want to look at, and I'll bring them over."

"An excellent plan." He pulled out a chair. His hand shook from the effort. To save him from embarrassment, I didn't assist him. He sat down heavily, almost collapsing, exhausted after the walk up the stairs and through the Long Gallery.

"How will we recognize the herbals?" he asked.

"I'm guessing the herbals must be large and shabby-looking."

"Based on what do you make these assumptions?"

"Herbals weren't purchased to sit on a shelf, although they could be beautiful. They were meant to be used. The owners made medi-

cines from the recipes included in the books. The volumes would become stained and begin to fall apart. Plus, when I noticed how many
Katherine Cresham checked out, I looked up pictures of the oldest
editions I could find on the internet, and that's what they were like."

"As solid a proof as any." He pointed with the cane. "There's a
rather large and well-used volume over there, on the bottom shelf,
third from the right. Let's try that one."

I pulled it out and turned to the title page. "*The First and Chief
Groundes of Architecture*, by John Shute, from 1563."

"Interesting, I'm sure, but not for us."

"Wait. Katherine Cresham read this." I brought the volume to
the table, into the light, and paged through it, looking for notes and
markings. I found nothing. Reviewing books at random was such a
long-shot proposition. A sense of futility seized me as I returned the
volume to its place. I'd follow through, however, to make Christopher
happy.

"Try over there, third from the right."

"*Learned Tico Brahe, His Astronomicall Conjectur of the New and Much
Admired Star Which Appeared in the Year 1572*. This looks fascinating. Isabella was interested in astronomy and checked out a book about it. I
can't remember which one. Not this one. We should go stargazing
some evening."

"So we should. Let's move on. No time to get distracted."

Not with the end looming, as he himself might say.

"What about that one—no, there, there."

"It's by Flavius Josephus. *Opera*. His collected works. In English
translation."

"Back it goes."

We went through about a dozen and a half. I sneezed, and sneezed
again, from the dust.

"Bless you! Let's try the opposite wall. Faded brown binding,
about a foot tall, second shelf from the top."

"*The Elements of Geometrie of the Most Auncient Philosopher Euclide of
Megara*. London, 1570."

"Back it goes. On the bottom shelf, by the wall. No, no, farther to the right. The dirty-looking one."

I dragged it out. It was about six inches thick and too heavy for me to hold and open simultaneously. I heaved it over to the table.

Christopher opened it. "Well, well."

He turned the book to show me the title page, illustrated with a picture that included a Tudor garden and a cascade of flowers.

And as if for this one instant my life had turned enchanted, the title page read, *The Herball or Generall Historie of Plantes Gathered by John Gerard of London . . . Imprinted at London by John Norton 1597.*

"Am I not just the cat's pajamas?" Christopher said with a long, self-satisfied grin.

"Yes, you are."

Arranging the herbal in the book cradle Martha had left us, I sat down next to Christopher. I moved the flashlights to give us the best possible lighting, and we paged through the volume together. The paper was thinner than I would have expected, the pages rippling in small waves, darkened at the edges, scratchy against my skin. Images bled through each page from the other side. The printing itself was clear and easy to read. The numerous illustrations were vivid and precise. The volume was a work of art.

And stuffed into the middle of the book, making it misshapen, was a collection of papers bound together by a piece of yarn.

Christopher and I stared at the papers in silence. Then I picked them up. I read aloud, "*Recipe to cure deepe wounds: mix in a bole, oyle of roses, oyle of St. Johns-worte, leaves of tobacco . . .* and more steps I can't decipher. The next one is, *For the eyes, betony.*"

"It's a listing of medical treatments?" he asked.

"So it seems. I guess we shouldn't be surprised." Nonetheless, I was surprised. Who had written these notes? I brought one of the flashlights closer. "*For gripe in the stomak, boil mint and tyme of equel mesure for to make a soothing drink.*"

"As it happens, I've rather a gripe in, and a gripe with, my stomach," Christopher said.

"Mint and thyme grow in the walled garden. We can try this. I'll make a tea for you."

"Thank you," he said, abandoning his usual witty tone.

Through a blot of ink, I made out the next entry. "*A garland of Pennie Royall cures the swimming of the head.*"

"*Swimming of the head*—dizziness and nausea, I assume. My head swims," he said. "More often than I care to admit, my dear Hannah. Do people use pennyroyal today?"

I looked it up on my phone. "It can help with colds and pneumonia. And it's a flea repellent for dogs and cats. But there's a warning about serious safety issues."

"All right, we'll skip that one," Christopher said. "I don't care to consume, or wear a garland of, what is otherwise a flea repellent."

"I'd also prefer that you don't," I said.

"I'd hazard a guess, though, that if it's a flea repellent for dogs and cats, it's a flea repellent for humans, too. It could have helped our sixteenth-century friends, if only they'd known that flea bites transmit plague."

If only they'd known. The great regret across the centuries. If only my grandparents had known early enough what the future would bring and had escaped from Germany, when escape was still possible. If only . . .

"What's next?" Christopher said.

"*For fever, broth of hen boiled many hours, with mace, borage, violet leaves, pepper, parsley, dill, juice of lemon, to create a broth to sip of.* That sounds like a traditional chicken soup, the kind my mother made when I had a cold. I can make it for you, if you like. Her recipe, without the violet leaves."

"I *would* like it. Very kind of you. And next?"

The writing was smudged at this entry. I maneuvered the paper even closer to the light. "*Infusion of roses, for the bloody flux.*"

"Happily, I've never had the bloody flux. I don't know what it is, but it doesn't sound like something one would ever wish to have."

"Absolutely not; you would never ever wish to have it," I said. "It was a common cause of death in Tudor England. I don't know if roses helped."

"It's nice to think they did. Roses, stopping a deadly disease. I do love roses," he added wistfully.

"Me, too." These notes were disturbing me, deeply, and I tried to figure out why. "There's a desperation in these records. People trying to find something, anything, to save the lives of their children. Their spouses. Their parents. Nicky's life could have depended on an infusion of roses."

"So could the life of one's honorary uncle."

Christopher and I were as desperate as they had been.

Paging ahead, I found a second part of the notes, the application of the recipes . . . the name of an individual, the ailment he or she suffered from, the date of the treatment, the results, filling dozens of pages.

And gradually I realized, recognizing it from the borrowers' registers: "This is the handwriting of Katherine Cresham. These must be her medical records, for the treatments she gave her patients."

She might have been sitting at the table with us: Katherine Cresham. She'd married in 1579, so when she checked out this book, in 1598, she was probably in her early forties. She was stately in her full maturity, very much in command, or skilled at putting on the trappings of command. She projected calm control, and her movements were studied, her body slender despite her many children. Katherine reviewed her case notes, writing down the treatments she'd used, questioning what she'd done wrong when they hadn't worked, carefully recording when they had, for use next time.

"I'd better ask Martha to come in here to take a look," I said.

"Then we'll go home," he said, his voice sounding strangled. He used his hands to turn himself away from me, then crossed his arms over his abdomen.

"When you're settled downstairs," I said gently, to his back, "I'll go to the walled garden and pick mint and thyme to make you tea."

While I was there, I'd also pick rosemary, although I didn't read this passage aloud to him:

For grief, take Rosemary and make powder therof and bynde it to the ryght arme in a lynen clothe, and it shall make thee lyght and mery.

CHAPTER 39

On a cold gray morning in early November, after Isabella Cresham's memorial service, Christopher and I waited in the churchyard. Today he was using his wheelchair. Nowadays he generally did. A green plaid blanket was wrapped tightly around his legs. He was always cold.

During the service, Nicky had explained—with zeal and self-confidence, not at all nervous about speaking in front of a crowd—how he'd discovered Isabella. Matthew had presented the research to date. And the Anglican vicar had led us in prayers and hymns.

For the interment of Isabella's body, the vicar had relented and allowed the stairs to be inspected and reinforced. After the service, Nicky had gone to the crypt with Matthew and Mrs. Gardner, along with the vicar and sexton. Due to the restricted space, they were the only ones allowed. Nicky was planning to search for Isabella's family and take photographs on his phone of any plaques, markers, or tombs for them.

Glancing at the nearby rows of gravestones, Christopher said, "When the time arrives—*after* we've finished reading *Middlemarch*—I'd like to be buried here. Surely a path can be forged through the overgrown bracken and nettles to a suitable spot."

This would take some doing; the churchyard looked as if it had been abandoned decades ago.

"Beneath the sheltering arms of the ancient yew tree—that's where I'd like to be."

He spoke with strained joie de vivre, as he often did these days, producing a forced smile whenever he caught me looking at him. When he didn't realize I was looking, his face was grim. The mint and thyme tea I made for him each morning seemed to help, as far as his gripe with his stomach was concerned, but I had to accept that he was growing weaker.

"Let's speak with the vicar to see if it can be arranged. Possibly with the promise of a nice donation to the church, eh?"

Kevin, who'd arrived early that morning, at Nicky's invitation, stood apart, reading something on his phone. The others were milling about or heading to the café, where Mrs. Gardner had arranged an informal lunch. A few days ago, she'd contacted local news outlets, and a half dozen or so journalists had attended the service. Finally the story would be public.

"And I'd like to be buried with Constance's ashes. They're in my desk drawer, lower left side. Would you take care of that for me?" he asked, his mask of good humor gone. "I'd once thought to scatter her ashes on the lake—surreptitiously, as I doubt Mrs. G. would permit it—but I was never ready to say goodbye."

"Yes, of course, I—"

"I found them!" Nicky was with us. He looked exceedingly good in a bespoke suit, made for this occasion by a shop in town, at Christopher's insistence, and he wore his school tie. As usual, he didn't wear an overcoat; he was always moving too fast to be bothered. "The Lord Southbrooke named Hugh, and his parents, and his brothers and sisters who died young, who were also Isabella's brothers and sisters. And I found the Lady Southbrooke named Katherine, who was married to Hugh, and Hugh and Katherine's four children who died when they were kids, who would have been the nieces and nephews of Isabella, and their names were Eleanor, Blanche, Lettice, and Walter."

"Blanche?" I started at the name.

"Blanche, born 1586, died 1592," Nicky recited, pulling from his memory.

So feisty Margaret had survived, but Blanche was gone. The girl with round, dark, staring eyes, cradling her doll to her chest. Practicing her writing. Listening to *Aesop's Fables* read aloud by her aunt. Gone before I'd had a chance to watch her grow or to learn about the person she might have become as the years unraveled before her.

"Matthew says the kids who *didn't* die when they were young probably would be buried somewhere else, except for the next Lord Southbrooke, and we found him, and his name was Hugh, *t-o-o.*"

Nicky was almost dancing.

"And he had children who died when they were young, but *his* family also included Hugh *three.* It's kind of confusing, with lots of the same names and different *generations,* but I'm going to make a chart of *genealogy.*" He said the big words with precision, lifting his chin, proud of himself for knowing them. "Katherine Cresham lived until 1634. She was born in 1557, so she was seventy-seven years old when she died. She was super old, for those days. But the Hugh who was her husband died in 1593. That means 1593 was a really important year for Ashton Hall."

Was it also the year Isabella was imprisoned and died?

"I took pictures of everything, and I'll send them to you. Now I'll start over at the beginning, so you know every single detail. First, the workmen used a kind of a slide to take the coffin down the stairs. Then the rest of us climbed down, one by one. The stairs were steep but not as steep as the priest-hole steps at Oxburgh Hall, and don't worry, Mom, I held the railing really tight . . ."

As Nicky continued his narration, Kevin joined us. Nicky, still talking, began to push Christopher's wheelchair toward the café. I held back. Nicky didn't notice. Others filed in—Matthew's students, officials from the trust—forming a line. Matthew walked with Mrs. Gardner and the general.

Spotting Martha, I went to join her. With her usual sense of style, she wore a royal-blue cloth coat, a velvet cloche hat, and three scarves of different colors braided together and circled around her neck. Her cheeks were rosy from the chill.

"Did you hear what they found in the crypt?" I said.

"I was about to ask you."

I briefed her. "Nicky rattled off the names of the children without any understanding of the heartbreak those names represented. Blanche died in 1592—six years old forever." My voice caught. "I know this is going to sound strange, but I felt attached to her. The sensitivity and insight of the drawing made me think, somehow . . . well, that I actually knew her." *This is me. Blanche.*

"I understand," Martha said.

We were silent for a time, as if in tribute to her. Then Martha said, "The conservator has returned about half of Isabella's sketchbooks. I wonder, might you have time to review them, now that you're essentially finished with the library registers?"

"I'd love to! Thanks for asking." The research continued, the work carrying me forward.

"I'll put them at your workstation in the center."

"I'll start on them later today if I can. I hope today." If Christopher and Nicky were content and settled.

"The conservator told me that Isabella numbered each volume and put her signature on the flyleaf. That was good of her. Didn't date them, though. The rest should be ready in a month or so. Look!" Martha said, transformed by excitement and pointing to the sky. A rectangular sliver of blue peeked through the clouds. "One streak of blue sky, and I'm outside for it! Usually I glance out the window, see a bit of blue, rush to put my coat on, run through the corridors and down the stairs and through the door—and the blue is gone. What luck," she said, delighted, "to be outside already when it appears. I'm a blue-sky worshipper."

I understood how she felt. At the end of October, we'd turned the clocks back an hour, and night was upon us by four fifteen or so. The cloud cover seldom broke. BBC Radio Cambridgeshire used an array of cloud descriptions the likes of which I'd never heard before. *Dark bright, gray bright, gray white,* among others. Today's *white* clouds had also been called *bright,* that is, *white bright,* giving a hint that somewhere behind them, the sun still, possibly, lurked.

These were features of living in Britain that the guidebooks didn't mention. In New York, the sun shone almost every day, and we complained on the days of rain. In Cambridge, *the rain it raineth every day,* to quote Nicky quoting *Twelfth Night,* Act V, Scene 1—he was reading and performing Shakespeare in school—and the sun felt precious, not a second of it to be missed. The summer made up for it, with the early sunrise and long dusk and the overflowing gardens.

"I'm afraid I need a cigarette," Martha said. "The never-ceasing plight of smokers: We have to smoke. Boring. Also rude, smoking at a funeral. Or a memorial service. Would you mind taking a circuitous route with me to the café, so I can smoke without being seen by either Mrs. G. or Nicky?"

"I'd be honored," I said, with a touch of irony that made her smile, as we acknowledged that I'd be keeping her company while she did something I disapproved of.

We left the path and wandered toward the formal garden, sunk into November decay, the tendrils of recent life dried, curled. The wind picked up, and I wrapped my scarf more tightly around my neck. As expected, clouds covered the sliver of blue. A light rain began falling. We took umbrellas from our handbags. These days, I carried an umbrella with me whenever I went outside.

"I've received an email about Katherine Cresham's medical papers from the expert I sent them to. The email teems with enthusiasm," Martha said with ever-so-slight reproach. "Subject to further study and official authentication, these records would constitute a rather significant discovery. The expert is absolutely thrilled. He assures me that only a limited number of collections of medical treatments prepared by women in England in the early modern period—or any period, actually—have survived. Lady Grace Mildmay created one almost contemporaneously. You're good at this work."

"As I'm sure you remember, I didn't really do anything to find the herbal or the medical notes. Christopher used his walking stick to point to particular books, and I took them off the shelves and examined them."

"As you wish. You had nothing to do with it."

I laughed. "That's better."

Rain rippled across the surface of the lake.

"By the way, I thought Nicky spoke beautifully at the memorial."

"I was proud of him. He loved doing it."

"I do enjoy your son," she said.

"Thank you. You're kind to say it." I wished I could discuss with her the complex challenges the world gave Nicky, but I still felt a barrier between us. Once again, I wanted to ask her directly about her personal life, boyfriends, girlfriends, both. But I couldn't.

And yet . . . we'd just attended a memorial service. I knew more about Isabella Cresham, a woman of the past, than I did about Martha, whom I saw almost every day. I didn't want to go on this way. It didn't make sense.

"Martha," I began tentatively, "I remember you told me that you're not married or attached. . . . Have you ever thought about getting married? Of having children, whether you're married or not? My mother chose to have a child without being married—she had *me*," I added with humor.

"I've thought about it." Martha didn't sound upset by my question. She put her arm through mine as we walked, although she didn't look at me. "The fact is . . . I was raped while I was at uni." Her voice was as calm as ever. "It could have happened anywhere, though. He was my best friend, from when we were little. We'd never been romantic. We grew up next door to each other."

"I'm so sorry. That is so, so awful." Now that she'd said it, I wasn't surprised . . . the way she kept her body covered, even on the hottest days, and took natural British reticence further than most people I'd met here. I thought back to the day in the conservation center when she'd talked about love turning to hatred. Friendship was a kind of love, and it could also turn to hatred.

"I never did anything to encourage him." She glanced at me now, her face twisted with anguish, warding off an accusation she must have heard at the time.

"Don't blame yourself," I said. "It's not your fault. He's the one responsible."

Turning away, she studied the surface of the lake. "When it happened, the four people I told said I must have done something to provoke him."

"You didn't do anything to provoke him."

"You can't know that, Hannah," she said angrily, facing me, her eyes intent, wild—she seemed angry at *me,* because I wouldn't join in her self-condemnation.

"I know *you,* don't I?" I said, feeling as if I had to defend myself. "I know the kind of person you are. So I know you didn't provoke or encourage him."

"Thank you," she said softly. She squeezed my hand. "Thank you," she repeated, sounding more sure of herself.

"And anyway, what kind of an explanation is that?" I asked. "I can't believe we're even discussing whether you're to blame. He's the one who did it!"

"I've gone over it a million times. I just can't seem to shake it from my memory. Things can go wrong so fast. In an instant. It's made me careful. And as to children—" Abruptly, she gave me a playful look. She'd allowed me into her inmost thoughts for a moment, then closed the door again. "After growing up with four siblings, two parents, and limited household plumbing, I don't like sharing. I love my work, seeing my friends, occasionally having men friends—thoroughly vetted beforehand, with letters of recommendation, and only in a public place for the first year or so—but I enjoy being alone in my own flat, with the door locked and no nappies to change, at the end of the day."

How could I respond? "I'm just so sorry."

"Don't be. All to the best. I've an ideal life, really. Work, work, work. Always learning. Always discovering." She let go of my arm. "I don't think I'll go to the luncheon. I don't enjoy parties. Too many people." And the impossibility of predicting what any one of them might do. "Work has a way of calling me. Did I mention I love my work?" She smiled as she said this, as if she was mildly teasing herself.

"I've noticed that about you," I said, laughing.

"I feel completely safe when I'm working," she added more seriously.

"We have that in common," I said, remembering the day I'd found refuge in the book register after Kevin and I had argued.

"Ah, your husband approaches."

I glanced in the direction she indicated. Kevin was heading toward us across the lawn.

"Coming to collect you for lunch, I suppose." She must have sensed my awkwardness, because instead of waiting to greet him, she said goodbye and went off toward the staff entry, on the opposite side of the house.

When he reached me, Kevin said, "I've been looking for you." With a flirtatious look and tone, he added, "We should make up for our time away from each other while Nicky is busy and before we're exhausted."

Was he actually suggesting that we go upstairs and have sex? The idea was absurd. But not so long ago I would have taken his hand in response, and we would have done exactly that, sneaking away as if we'd only just met, and I would have felt lucky, so very lucky.

"No, Kevin. I've arranged for you to sleep in the other twin bed in

Nicky's room. I told Nicky it's a treat. Like going camping. He's counting on it."

"What are you talking about?" he asked, sounding genuinely confused.

"Things are over between us, Kevin." I made my voice emotion-
less, without apology or anger. "I want to separate. Divorce. I'm prepared to fight you on the custody issue."

"Oh, Hannah—don't be ridiculous." Dismissive, he waved my
words away with a sweep of his hand. "You're carrying things too
far."

"I disagree."

"This isn't the time for you to be making important decisions."

"This is exactly the time to make important decisions."

"You should make a list of the reasons you think you want this and
tell them to me." He didn't sound hurt, or perplexed, or enraged. He
sounded . . . sympathetic, as if I were an adorable, misguided child.
"When you say the reasons out loud, you'll hear how silly they sound."

"I have reviewed the reasons. Countless times. Why would I want
to be with you after the threats you made, trying to terrify me into
staying? And how would you feel, knowing I was with you only out of
fear?"

"Okay, I admit I shouldn't have said some of the things I did say
the last time we discussed this. I lost my temper." He shrugged at the
recognition and gave me a half smile. "None of what I said meant
anything."

"None of it *meant* anything? None of the threats you made about
taking Nicky?"

"As I say, I lost my temper. I panicked. You should have realized.
You take things too seriously." He shook his head while smiling at me.

"Condescension isn't a good tactic," I said.

"I'm not being condescending. People always say things they don't
mean," he explained in a schoolmasterish tone, giving me the guidance he thought I needed. "For example, I don't take what you're
saying right now seriously."

"Kevin, if I can't take what you say seriously, and you don't take what I say seriously, then how do we talk to each other? How can I rely on anything you say? Love could sweep you up as easily as rage, with neither one reliable. I forgive Nicky when he loses his temper and acts out. He's a child and can't help it. I'm not going to accept the same behavior from my husband."

"It's the nature of life," he said, exasperated. "For everyone." He seemed bewildered that I couldn't grasp this basic, to him, fact of life.

"Not for me. Really, not for me."

"The fact remains, and admittedly I shouldn't have expressed it the way I did, but I'll make certain you never get custody."

"You keep saying you'll fight me, Kevin. But I'll fight you, too." I made my best effort at bravado. I realized there'd come a day—soon, most likely—when I'd go to the local ATM and find that our joint account had no money in it, or had been closed, and that my credit card, linked to that account, wasn't working.

"Don't think for a second I'll allow Nicky to stay in the UK," he said.

"Even though he's doing so well at school here? Having academic and social success for the first time in his life? You'd take that away from him?"

Kevin was silent. He looked into the distance, preoccupied. I knew he loved Nicky and wanted the best for him. And so he had no answer to this argument. Saying nothing more, he headed back to the café.

I turned and studied the house—the broad windows, turrets at each corner, the multitude of chimneys, Flemish gables curving upward, the gargoyles of sheep, cows, and pigs, hearkening to the estate's long history as a farm. I stood where Romans had walked, and Anglo-Saxons, Vikings, Normans, and all the rest. They'd left traces on the land and, beginning with the Normans, shaped the earliest iterations of the house, each building campaign encircling the previous one, integrating and concealing the past, circle upon circle, layer upon layer.

Generations of women had made their home here, women with

dreams, visions, intellect; women who'd struggled to find their way, to be taken seriously by the men around them, and who'd tried to achieve something, anything, and found themselves stymied. Their stories and their limited range of choices weren't as distant as they sometimes seemed. We were living the same stories today.

Isabella's and Katherine's lives were one moment in the flow of time. I imagined myself into their era, and gradually, as if my senses had become a thousand times more attuned and past and present truly were simultaneous, I saw . . . The garden laid out in the intricate knot patterns the Elizabethans favored. The moat filled with water. The house castle-like and crenellated, designed for defense, with few windows. Part of the second floor half-timbered.

A little girl played with a spaniel, ruddy brown with a white chest and a white stripe on its muzzle and head. Girl and dog raced across the lawns, chasing each other . . . a little girl whose dark hair spilled from her bonnet and glowed with a reddish sheen in the sunlight. Blue eyes, freckles. Tall for her age. She wore a dress with a heavy woolen skirt and what looked like layers of tops. Despite the weight of her clothing, she ran and jumped with glee. She rolled, over and over, on the lawn, fragrance released as she went, the scent of herbs filling the air.

At a call from an older woman watching from the doorway, the girl stood up. She smoothed her skirt. She ran into the house, her dog following.

Time shifted. The girl—Isabella—had become a woman. Her clothes were dark, simple, utilitarian, although finely made. She held a sketchbook, which resembled a commonplace book, and a pencil. As she worked, she pressed the sketchbook against her waist to balance and support it. Concentrating on her chosen task, she was simultaneously intent, passionate, and tightly contained. She drew a child who toddled across the lawn, helped by his mother—Katherine.

I knew it was Katherine, and not a nurse or nanny, because of the look on her face of fierce love and equally fierce possession. Although heavily pregnant, she was also regal. Her clothes were complex, multilayered, embroidered. Seed pearls had been sewn into her head covering. Wrapped around her right upper arm was a folded linen band—filled with powdered rosemary, to make her *lyght and mery.*

Katherine was protective of the child, making certain he wouldn't fall. The toddler was chubby-faced. His hair was a shade of yellow that was almost white. Giggling with each step, he took delight in everything around him. A dog slept in the sunlight. On the bench under a tree, someone had placed a basket of pickings from the garden. Two other children, both girls, played nearby, spinning hoops across the lawn. Was one of them named Blanche?

With an absolute focus, Isabella gazed from mother and child to her sketchbook, over and over, her attention never wavering. She frowned, catching herself in a mistake, shaking her head sharply in frustration. She studied the mother and child even more intently as she reworked one particular section of her drawing.

Baptism for milady's baby. A coffin for his lordship's child. Would the pregnant woman's unborn baby survive? The same question, for all of them: The toddler throbbing with life. The girls spinning hoops across the lawn. Would the pregnant woman find medications to rescue at least a few of her loved ones?

As for the woman holding the sketchbook: Would she decide to barricade herself behind the wall of a hidden room, and would her family agree that she belonged there?

As if the two women had heard my questions, they turned and stared at me, challenging me to find out.

CHAPTER 40

A cup. This was the first drawing made by young Isabella Cresham in her sketchbooks. It was an approximation of a cup, resting on a table. How difficult, to draw a cup, to capture the perspective across to the opposite side. She practiced this cup over and over, filling pages. She couldn't master it. At least not yet.

Next, an apple. She tried again and again to achieve the curving arc of the sides. She moved on to a ring. A book. A loaf of bread. A flight of stairs.

Over time, she improved. In the second volume, she tried a cup again, and it *was* a cup, with shading and proportion. She'd learned to create three-dimensionality and perspective. She returned to the apple, and it *was* an apple, the perfection of the curve from the stem to the base miraculous. The roses in the garden became almost a photograph of roses, heavy with raindrops.

She copied other drawings, to learn from them, as art students have always done. Here were the lost and befuddled pigeons from the *Historia Animalium, De Avium Natura,* and the young eagle. She was fifteen when she checked this book out of the library for the second time; therefore, she must have been fifteen when she made these drawings.

She began to focus on portraiture. Her first attempts were cartoon-like. She made an oval and filled it in with eyebrows, eyes, nose, mouth, over and over. And finally . . . here was an older woman. The woman's head covering and clothing were plain, unadorned. Her cheeks were sagging, her eyelids drooping, yet her eyes were alight with laughter. She pressed her thin lips tightly together to pretend she wasn't smiling, because Isabella had told her to be serious. *Lucie Howell, mistress of myself,* Isabella wrote beneath the drawing, indicating, to me at least, that the woman was Isabella's nanny or governess. This was the first identification Isabella had written, and I felt in the words and portrait the affection between them.

Hands became Isabella's next focus. Hands of all ages and shapes, as if she'd corralled the entire household into sitting for her. She especially loved the curve of the thumb toward the index finger and the graceful angle made by the wrist. I could visualize her rearranging her subjects until they were just so, accentuating these characteristics. She became an expert in skin: Old, wrinkled, mottled. Youthful, sleek, tight.

Here was Lucie Howell once more, sitting at a spinning wheel, fuzzy wool in her hands. *In celebration on her most special day,* Isabella had written.

A series of portraits followed, men and women of the household and estate. These included *Geoffrey Bannister, master of our librarie.* He was older than I'd expected, his beard white, wrinkles around his eyes, a velvet cap covering what I sensed, from Isabella's skill, was his bald head. He must have served the family for decades. She'd posed him at his desk in the library, and despite her best efforts to make him relax, he sat stiffly straight. Books were on the shelves behind him. The library register was on his desk, open, his hand and forearm resting upon it possessively. His expression combined resigned disapproval for the time that was being wasted on a portrait with the shy, grand-fatherly affection he reserved for Isabella alone among the household.

The family dogs were here, too, playing together, collapsing ex-hausted in a patch of sunlight. In one drawing, a spaniel turned its head over its shoulder as it ran, looking for approval, as Duncan did when he ran ahead. *Jasper*, she wrote beneath this picture. I remem-bered the carving of a spaniel that Isabella had placed in her keepsake box and the touching letter that Hugh had written about Jasper's death.

The next volume was dedicated to drawings of the plantings in the walled garden—the fruits, vegetables, and medicinal herbs, her images executed with ever-greater precision, in a botanical, scientific style. She labeled them: *Pennyroyal. Betony. Thyme, rosemary, borage*, and more.

She sketched the landscape around Ashton Hall, the lawns, river, woods, and farmland. *Wet spring*, she wrote under a picture showing the river above its banks. *Late summer*, the branches of the apple trees weighted with fruit. *Full moon*, the trees ghostly.

She drew a boy. He played chess. Stretched out on the lawn, hands behind his head. Threw a stick to a dog. Years passed, and he grew up in the pages of the sketchbooks, among dozens of other images. Now he was about seventeen, eighteen. Lean, muscular. A lock of hair fell across his forehead. His beard was still sparse but well shaped. He leaned against the flank of a horse. Isabella caught the young man's diffident demeanor, staring at her sidelong, and I felt her tenderness toward him. When a portrait particularly pleased her, she wrote his name beneath it, adding decorative curving lines above and below the name, flourishes whose only purpose was to increase the beauty of the calligraphy. *Hugh*.

Filling both the right and left pages of her sketchbook, she created a formal portrait of her parents. They sat side by side in the great hall. Her mother's face was long, cheeks angular, nose pointed, and she glanced aside, not showing her eyes, her spirit burdened with sadness for all the tragedy she'd seen. She wore a necklace that held minia-tures of her children. Seven miniatures, although only two of her seven had lived to grow up. On the table beside her were large, weathered volumes—the herbals.

From my reading, I knew that Tudor portraits often incorporated objects and symbols important to the lives of their subjects.

On the table beside Isabella's father, multiple volumes of various sizes were stacked, meant to show his broad-ranging interests. With an expression of merriment, his dark eyes wide, brows raised, his beard pointed and full, brushed with gray, his entire being a contrast to his wife's somber bearing, he gazed directly at the artist. At his one surviving daughter. *Lord and Lady Southbrooke,* Isabella wrote with many flourishes beneath this portrait.

And again, always, Hugh. He swam in the river. His wet shirt clung to his torso. He reclined on the ground at the riverbank, leaning against a tree. His feet were bare, and she drew them from the side, the arch, the heel, the curve upward to the ankle. Then she drew the side of his neck, the sweep from collarbone to ear. Drew his body, in its glory, the muscles hardened and trained by hawking and hunting and archery.

Near the end of this set of volumes was a portrait of a woman standing in front of a mirror, although she didn't draw the mirror—the viewer took the place of the mirror. The artist gripped her sketchbook with her left hand so tightly that her knuckles protruded. In her right hand, the pencil was poised above the paper. She had an oval face, with no softness to her cheeks, and bold eyebrows. Her hair, uncovered and pulled back, appeared dark; in this pencil rendering, I couldn't determine if it was actually red. A high, intricate, lacy collar rose around her neck, concealing her ears. She was skilled enough to make the viewer sense the crispness of the lace and the silky sheen of the fabric of her dress. She wore no jewelry. Her expression was severe. She drew her eyes as if staring into her own, intense and inescapable in their reflection. Staring into *my* eyes. Arresting. Accosting.

Isabella dated this portrait: *22 June, 1579.*

The month and year that Hugh and Katherine married.

June 22 was also her birthday. In the drawing, Isabella Cresham was twenty-seven years old.

CHAPTER 41

The door to Christopher's study was ajar. "Is that you, Hannah?" he called as I walked by.

I opened the door.

"Come in, if you would." He was sitting at his desk. "Please, shut the door behind you." He was uncharacteristically solemn.

"Is everything okay?" I asked.

"I must discuss something with you."

"All right." I was still in Isabella's world, in the Ashton Hall of her drawings.

"At the luncheon, Nicky made reference to his father *camping* in his room, and I had to accept that the break between you and Kevin is irrevocable."

All at once I was thrust back into my daily struggles. But I didn't want to worry or upset Christopher with the details. I said simply, "We couldn't work things out."

"I have my responsibilities to fulfill."

I didn't know what he meant.

"There must be things you need," he said, regarding me astutely.

Money. That's what I needed. He'd give it to me, I felt certain. But I wouldn't ask him for it. Not after everything he'd given me in the past. I couldn't bear to ask him to finance my future, too, as if I were helpless.

He stood, drew himself straight, and inhaled deeply, preparing to make a declaration. "The time has come, Hannah, to discuss the work of John Singer Sargent."

"*Now* is the time to discuss the work of John Singer Sargent?"

"Precisely." Using his walker, he made his way across the room and lowered himself into a chair by the tea table. "Please, join me."

I did as he asked.

"Often I think of John Singer Sargent's beloved niece. She who looks like you."

Rose-Marie Ormond.

"She inspired so much of his work," he said.

I knew all about them. But because Christopher loved telling stories and had only limited time left to tell them, I let him explain to me John Singer Sargent's fatherly love for his niece. Christopher told me of their travels with friends and other family members, most famously in the Alps, where Sargent painted Rose-Marie again and again.

Rose-Marie Ormond died in March 1918, the final year of World War I, when the church in Paris where she was attending Good Friday services was hit by a German shell. She was twenty-four years old.

"Her death must have shattered him," Christopher said, his own face contorted. "I know the death of a beloved niece would have destroyed me."

He shifted, gripping the armrests of his chair, trying to find a position without pain.

"The fact is, I earned a good living in my day, doing what I loved, and Constance—she was a genius at what she did: the Law of the Sea. Constance earned rather impressive amounts of money, and she was charitable. I'm charitable, as well. All but one of the paintings and watercolors in this room are earmarked for the trust that owns this house, to sell as they see fit. My way of thanking them for taking me in, after Constance died."

"That seems right," I said. The inheritance of his art collection wasn't anything I'd considered.

"Mrs. G. and I have discussed some of her plans for the money. Bring back the furloughed employees. Hire junior librarians, subject to Dr. Tinsley's guidance, to organize and catalog the Old Library at last. She'll use some of the profits to make Ashton Hall more accessible to the surrounding communities, with more free-admission days. I do very much approve of that. Only Mrs. Gardner knows of my bequest. Can't have the entire staff looking forward to my demise." He smiled gently.

I didn't know how to react, and when I didn't respond, he continued, "I must say, Constance and I enjoyed our lives and our occasional extravagances. For example, Constance always wore exceedingly costly shoes. In recent years, I've been rather more charitable than I would have been, had I known about the change in your circumstances. I'd assumed you'd be taken care of by Kevin."

I bristled at this, though he hadn't been wrong to assume it. I'd let myself become dependent in order to raise a child, and in the process I'd sabotaged my ability to give my child what he needed if ever our situation changed.

"The point being, when I'm gone, you'll have my John Singer Sargent watercolor. It's a symbol of who you are to me. You already know it's ravishing. The sunlight fluttering on the water. Rose-Marie, reclining in a gondola, her gown puffing up to fill the boat."

I was floored. What could I say? *Thank you* was insufficient. He was rescuing me. I had no choice but to accept being rescued, going from being dependent on Kevin to dependent on Christopher, from one man to the next. At least, though, I'd safeguard my son.

"Constance gave me the watercolor decades ago. She found it in an antiques shop in a village in Scotland during a brief holiday, and she paid the twenty-six pounds the shopkeeper was asking. He didn't know what he had. I knew the instant I saw it. It has the spark that Sargent conjured like a sorcerer. It must have been part of the collection of a big house up there. The heirs didn't know what they had, either. In other words, there's no official record of this work. The receipt from the shop is attached to the back. I want you to take the watercolor off the wall today—we'll find something else to take its place—and put it away in your bedroom. Your suitcase would be an amusing place for it. When I die, the taxman will come calling, but he won't find it."

Despite my gratitude, something began to disturb me. Although I didn't know anything about tax issues surrounding works of art, Christopher's scheme certainly didn't sound proper. "Isn't this against the law?"

"Is it?" He took on a playacting expression of confusion and surprise. "I shouldn't have thought so. I never authenticated the watercolor. Why would I? Twenty-six pounds in a village antiques shop; a pretty little watercolor most probably painted by the daughter of a wealthy household. It's a mere trifle. The twenty-six pounds was the value of the modestly elegant frame, I'd suspect, and so would you."

He paused, waiting for this to sink in.

"The watercolor is your insurance policy," he resumed. "When the dust settles after I'm gone, you'll return it to its place here on the wall, because pulling away the curtain and studying it will make you happy. Doing so will also, I hope, remind you of me."

He saw me at Ashton Hall indefinitely. How I wished this could be true.

"Someday, should you ever need assistance, you'll have it authenticated by experts. The truth won't be difficult to determine; I did it in a few hours. You'll sell it for the fortune it's worth, you'll pay the taxes then, and you'll keep the rest. It's in superb condition. Works like this have sold at auction for several hundred thousand dollars."

The coming legal fight over the divorce; Nicky's future school fees, if Kevin refused to pay them; our food, clothing, housing—I could manage now. "Christopher . . . ," I began.

"Come, come, let's not get emotional. I'm not doing it for *you*. I'm doing it for *me*. To free me from worry. To allow me to depart this world in peace. Dreadfully selfish of me. Let's have tea and biscuits to celebrate how selfish I am. Go tell Rafe, would you? I believe he mentioned ginger biscuits acquired during a recent excursion he made to Waitrose. Those would be most welcome."

I started to stand, but he grasped my hands, making me stay in place.

"Hannah, before you—" Anguish constricted his face. "Constance never wanted children," he blurted out. "Not that she disliked children," he said, rushing on. "She liked *you*. I was the one who wanted children."

I felt myself enter another realm of understanding. The long journeys he took to visit me. The letters he wrote. The books he sent me, whenever I expressed an interest in a particular subject. I heard Margot's voice: *After three tries over eight months, I was pregnant with you . . .* arrangements made, long ago.

His eyes were pleading.

Did I look like him? Not the way he looked today, ravaged by disease, but in the photos when he was younger. Did Nicky look like him? I'd never expected to see a resemblance, and I'd never searched for one.

Ask him, part of me thought.

But as he regarded me, begging for acceptance, I couldn't bring myself to. I didn't want to risk finding out that the answer was no.

Get a DNA test.

I couldn't. He'd played the role of father to me, and he was wonderful. Not from day to day, not at a micro level, but at a macro level. Not the trees, but the forest. He'd encouraged me. His very presence in my life was like a beacon of the wider world. He'd transformed my future. Therefore, the answer was *yes*, always *yes*, from the beginning.

If I didn't ask, if I didn't demand a DNA test, I'd have the power of that *yes* forever.

"What I'm trying to say is," he said, gathering his strength, "I've always loved you, Hannah."

His hands were trembling, as he answered my unspoken question with *yes* and *no* simultaneously. I wrapped my hands around his. His skin was puffy. If I held his hands too tightly, his bones might break. I felt the link that bound us together, regardless of answers.

"I've always loved you, too," I said.

"Such a gift, your love has been to me," he said. "I'm so grateful."

CHAPTER 42

As the days became ever shorter, we never saw the sun. The clouds remained gray and impenetrable. The cold damp persisted in Christopher's flat, unaffected by the central so-called heating. The radiators provided a warmth that spread no more than four inches, highlighting another facet of Englishness: the preference to feel smug about quietly tolerating things that don't work instead of figuring out how to fix them. We didn't set up a portable heater, because Christopher and I worried it would be a danger to Duncan, with his fan-like tail.

By the third week of November, Christopher preferred, as he described it, to stay in his room. Rafe ordered a hospital-style bed, set up by two workmen at dusk, which was three-thirty in the afternoon. From then on, Christopher rarely left the bed. At Rafe's instigation, three nurses worked in rotation, covering all twenty-four hours of the day, seven days a week. Each was equally hardworking and equally dour.

The bedroom's Persian carpet was frayed, and patches of paint peeled near the ceiling. The wardrobe doors were warped, and Rafe had tied a shoelace around the handles to stop them from swinging open.

After school, Nicky did his revision at the antique writing desk, its legs wobbly. The card table was set up in the bedroom, and in the evenings after dinner, Nicky and Christopher played chess, Christopher calling out his moves, and Nicky adjusting the pieces accordingly.

"You're using the Semi-Slav Defense!" Nicky exclaimed one day as he realized what Christopher had done. In the bookshop, the general had found an advanced study guide to the game, and Nicky had memorized the moves.

"Next time, I'll aim for Alekhine's gun," Christopher replied.

As I looked from one to the other, searching for a physical resemblance, I saw a link that transcended the physical. A connection of love.

"I'm going to get you in zugzwang!" Nicky said, dissolving into gales of laughter.

While Nicky was at school, I read aloud to Christopher from *Middlemarch*. Only eighty pages remained, and I read slowly, as if I could ward off his death by never finishing. I stayed close to him, and I didn't go to the conservation center. I dealt with my part-time job in the evening, while Christopher and Nicky played chess. Even Isabella Cresham seemed far away.

One afternoon, as I reached the end of a sad chapter about the lack of understanding between Dr. Lydgate and his wife, I stopped. Christopher's hands clutched at his bedsheet. His knuckles were white. His eyes were squeezed shut, his brows pushed together in a frown that was terrible. He was in pain—biting, consuming pain. I saw how thin he'd become, thinner than I would have thought possible for a person who was still alive. He took up almost no space. With his spirit so full, I hadn't noticed. His body was disintegrating.

I was about to ask him whether he needed more medication. Suddenly I understood he wouldn't want me to ask. I'd grant him that: I wouldn't break his façade. I'd give him the right to be who he wanted to be while surrounded (as he might describe it) by the indignities of his demise.

I asked Rafe instead, when we met in the hallway, me on a break, Rafe returning from a break. "Are the nurses dealing with his pain?"

"Please, don't be concerned," Rafe said, the tone of his voice a comfort. "Mr. Eckersley confides in me, and I speak with the nurses. He doesn't want to receive so much medication"—by this Rafe meant morphine—"that he isn't alert for his daily read-aloud and for his evening chess."

As the days passed, Rafe and I conspired, helping Christopher to continue pursuing the amusements he loved. According to these particular amusements, the nurses were hidebound, prudish, and un-reasonable, disturbing Christopher's peace and quiet to no end with their insistence on adjusting his position (to avoid bedsores), changing his bed linens entirely too frequently, and—unforgivably—refusing to allow Duncan to sleep on the bed.

This last battle Duncan himself won, by sheer determination and a tendency to howl if he was put out of the room, the door closed in his face.

"In any battle between nurse and dog," Christopher told me one morning in triumph, while his nurse was in the kitchen making her-self tea, "dog will be the victor." Duncan had stretched out full-length along Christopher's legs, warming his master in the ever-chilly room. The dog looked over his shoulder at me, his expression placid, his desires satisfied. Christopher rubbed the thick fur where the back of Duncan's head met his neck, and Duncan made a sound that resem-bled purring.

That day after school, while Nicky was having a snack in the kitchen before going to Christopher's room to begin his revision, I said, "Uncle Christopher's losing strength. He doesn't have much time left."

"I know," Nicky said, gulping down a glass of milk. "That's why he needs me to finish my revision as soon as I can and tell him the kings and queens. All the kids can tell the kings and queens except for me. Starting with the Norman ones. I have to learn them right away. Christopher and I are going to practice. We planned it yesterday. Learning something new will make him feel better. William the Conqueror to Elizabeth the Second and back again." Nicky put his glass in the sink, grabbed his backpack, and raced down the hallway. "Uncle Christopher," he called as he went. "William the Conqueror, William Rufus, Henry the First . . ."

The next morning, I woke Nicky in the dark and helped him to get organized. I gave him breakfast and said goodbye to him and Alice before their bike ride to school in the dawn light.

"Please say, *Good morning, Uncle Christopher,* from me," Nicky said.

"I will."

"Remind him that William the Fourth is after George the Fourth. *Then* Queen Victoria. He should try not to forget."

"I'll tell him."

After Nicky and Alice left, I poured another cup of coffee and went down the hall to Christopher's room.

Rafe stood at the door, waiting for me. His hands, ordinarily busy holding several things at once as he pursued a half dozen chores simultaneously, rested at his sides. Duncan lay at Rafe's feet, his body spread flat, his paws forward, his eyes staring fixedly at the baseboard.

CHAPTER 43

That afternoon, the vestibule door opened, and Nicky's and Alice's voices reached me.

"Hi, Mom, I'm home," Nicky called.

"I'm in the dining room." I'd spent the morning in a daze of arrangements, Rafe and Mrs. Gardner helping and advising while offering me endless cups of tea.

"Hey," Nicky said.

There they were, at the dining room entryway. Alice met my eyes with a look of sympathy. I'd texted her earlier, asking her not to tell Nicky the news.

"If you don't need me, I'll be off," Alice said to me.

"Thank you, Alice."

"See you tomorrow, Nicky," she said.

"Bye." He was already distracted, his mind rushing toward the next step of his day. "I have to say hi to Christopher. He's waiting for me."

"I need to show you something."

"I'll look later."

"I need to show you now."

"Okay." Scuffing his feet, he came into the room.

I stood at the far end of the table, where I'd been organizing Christmas and Hanukkah gifts for family and friends. This afternoon, I'd pushed aside the wrapping paper, tape, scissors, and ribbons to make space to set up a jigsaw puzzle I'd been planning to give to Nicky as one of his gifts. I'd laid out the puzzle and placed several of the framing pieces. I wanted Nicky to be occupied when I told him the news.

Trying to draw his attention, I said, "I found a puzzle with a map of Britain in 1583, when Isabella was alive."

He joined me. He examined the picture on the box. "Did Uncle Christopher see this?" he asked, looking up at me eagerly.

"No. It's a surprise for you."

"Thanks!" He studied the box more carefully. "Only a thousand pieces, though," he said with mild disappointment.

"But the map is filled with details. Look, tiny castles, groupings of trees to show forests, and imaginary sea creatures in the oceans."

"Wow. I'll start it now." He took off his uniform jacket and tie, draping them across a chair. He began to work on the puzzle, separating the pieces with straight sides to continue the frame. "I'll do sixteen pieces, and then I'll tell Uncle Christopher about it."

"Why sixteen?"

"It's my new favorite number. Four times four. Eight times two. Two times eight. Thirty-two divided by two. And lots more. Each of the ways to get there makes a separate picture in my head, but every picture means *sixteen*."

"That's a terrific observation." The workings of his mind left me astounded. "Most people would never think of that."

"It's just the truth," he said, shrugging. He became absorbed in the puzzle. I had to begin.

"Uncle Christopher left us this morning." I couldn't bring myself to use the real, actual word. The word that would choke me.

"Where did he go?" Nicky stayed focused on the puzzle. "Did he go to Waitrose?"

"No," I said.

"Did he go to the hospital in New York?"

Now I did have to use the real word, blunt and cutting.

"He died this morning."

Nicky stopped work on the puzzle and stared at me. "When will he be back?" he asked, confused.

"He died. He won't be coming back," I said as tenderly as I could.

"Not ever?"

"No, not ever."

"That's not true," he said, tossing his head to dismiss the possibility.

"Remember when I told you he didn't have much time left and he was becoming weak?"

"That didn't mean he was going to *die*," Nicky insisted. "You didn't say, *Uncle Christopher is going to die.*"

No, I hadn't.

"I didn't tell him goodbye," Nicky said.

"He wouldn't have wanted to say goodbye. It would have been too sad for him."

"But he was my friend." Nicky's eyes widened, his expression doubting and fearful. "How could he do that to me? Why would he?"

"He didn't want to upset you."

"He shouldn't have left me without saying goodbye." Nicky banged his right fist onto the table.

"People can't pick the time they die," I said.

"But he should have told me. Why didn't he tell me? Why didn't *you* tell me?" Nicky demanded.

Then I realized: Christopher had always remained himself, his distinctive personality intact, and that's why Nicky hadn't registered the end point, and I hadn't forced him to. I should have.

"No one told me," he screamed. He banged his fist again and again. "Rafe didn't, and you didn't, and *he* didn't." His eyes were glazed and shining. "Fucking puzzle—" He pushed the puzzle pieces across the table, scattering them. "He should have told me."

And like a movie unspooling in slow motion, Nicky reached for the scissors amid the wrapping paper and ribbons. The scissors were big, old-fashioned, heavy steel, with a black handle, the scissors from the kitchen drawer.

"I hate him." Nicky opened the scissors and gripped the open blade in his fist, not noticing that it cut into his skin. "I hate him, I hate him, I hate him." Blood began to seep around his fingers. He raised his hand, ready to bring down the blade—

I caught his wrist before he could strike himself or the table. He kneed me in the gut. The force of it made me let go of his wrist. He held on to the scissors, bringing the blade down onto the outer side of my forearm, slicing through my sweater and turtleneck and into my skin.

Was that my voice screaming *help*? I felt myself enter another plane of sight, and from there I watched Nicky . . . heard his voice shouting, *I hate him, I hate him*. From my distant place, I thought, *Poor Nicky*. A film of red covered his fingers.

He lifted his arm and brought the blade down into my arm again, slashing, cutting through to the skin. Burning, burning, more and more . . . My skin was burning up with pain. *I hate him, I hate him*. Nicky raised his arm, preparing to strike again.

Duncan was with us, wrapping his mouth around Nicky's ankle in a soft hold, the way a retriever is trained to pick up a dead bird, never hurting it but never letting go. Duncan pulled on Nicky's ankle, and Nicky lost his balance and reached for the side of the table to give himself support as again he lifted the scissors—

Rafe was with us. He took hold of Nicky's arm. Put himself between Nicky and me. "All right, then, Nicky," he said gently. "It's all right."

Nicky couldn't move within the circle Rafe created. Rafe pried the scissors from Nicky's fist and pushed them to the other side of the table. They left a trail of blood.

I felt myself sink back into reality. Nicky's hand was covered in blood. His shirt, too. And his face, smeared with blood.

Seeing the blood, I felt faint. I sat down on one of the dining room chairs. I put my head between my legs. Rafe was repeating, "It's all right then, Nicky, let's see," his voice soothing, as he took Nicky to a chair, sat him down. Nicky began to whimper as the seizure drained away from him.

When I could, I raised my head. Duncan had pushed his muzzle into Nicky's hand and was licking the blood from his wound. I'd once read that during World War I, the overwhelmed doctors brought dogs into the hospital tents to lick the soldiers' wounds, to clean them.

Rafe looked from Nicky to me. "Shall I ring 999?"

An ambulance would arrive. The police might be called. An attack, an assault. The hospital staff might be required to report suspected domestic abuse to the authorities. Nicky might be taken away from me. Our visas wouldn't be renewed or might be revoked altogether, and we'd have to leave the country. This incident would be on my, our, record. It would be evidence for Kevin's claim that I couldn't handle my son.

"I'll begin with the first-aid kit," Rafe said, as if he'd intuited everything I was thinking.

"Thank you. Maybe that's all we need."

"It's in Christopher's bathroom." Unspoken, he asked, *Will you be all right while I go to get it? I'll take the scissors with me.*

"We'll be fine now," I said.

Nicky continued to whimper.

"Hold your arms up," Rafe ordered. My forearm was still bleeding, losing a lot more blood than Nicky's palm. "Both of you. Arms up."

When Rafe left the room, Duncan positioned himself between Nicky and me. He seemed to puff himself larger, becoming a big, big dog, a lion of a dog, with a thick, thick ruff, filling the space.

After Nicky's hand was washed at the kitchen sink and disinfected, his injury didn't look as bad as I'd feared. The bleeding had almost stopped. Rafe bandaged the wound professionally. "I've paramedic training," he replied to my unspoken question, not looking up from his work. "You're going to be fine, Nicky," he said.

My injury was more difficult. Two slashes on the outer part of my forearm. I felt sickened, seeing the wounds when Rafe cut away my sweater and the sleeve of my shirt. He expertly examined my arm. After the washing and disinfecting, and the application of surgical tape to keep the slashes closed, one wound still oozed blood.

"Press this against it. Keep your arm up," Rafe said, giving me a thick piece of gauze. "You may need stitches. I don't have that equipment. You don't want a scar. I'd feel more comfortable if . . . You're both up to date on your tetanus jabs?"

"Yes."

"I'll go with you to Addenbrooke's," Rafe said. "We'll ring a car service. Alice will stay with Nicky."

Or I could phone a friend with a car. Lizzie. Matthew. Either would take me. Arriving by car would be less dramatic than by ambulance. I might not be required to explain every detail. I'd have to tell the staff something, though. Something besides the truth: *My son attacked me. My precious, beloved boy whom I love so much. If someone else hadn't been in the flat . . .*

"If it becomes infected, I'll go to the hospital," I said.

"We don't want to wait that long. Let's say, if it's still oozing blood at suppertime," Rafe said.

Nicky stood close by, listening.

I nodded in acceptance. "I'm feeling light-headed again."

"To be expected. Why don't you two sit in the dining room. I'll bring you your tea."

Less than an hour had passed. Nicky hadn't had his after-school snack. His revision was waiting to be done. "Thank you, Rafe." I realized he may have saved my life. "Thank you."

"No need," he said.

Nicky and I went to the dining room. Nicky gathered the puzzle pieces from across the table and the floor and put them into the box.

I sat down in my usual place, with its panoramic view, except outside all was dark.

You have to get help. You aren't safe. He needs medication, something, anything, part of me insisted. *How can you take care of him if he kills you?*

I'd lock his door at bedtime. Rafe would be here, although his bedroom was downstairs, near Christopher's. I could ask Matthew to stay with me. Although I'd seen him at Isabella's memorial service, I'd barely spoken to him, not since the summer. But I knew he'd respond, to protect me. With Matthew here, I wouldn't be afraid of my child in the next room.

But who would protect me tomorrow night, and the night after, if I didn't find a way to protect myself?

You mustn't do this. Don't hide that you're abused.

Of course I had to hide it. I wouldn't let my son be taken away.

A consoling memory came to me: a morning when Nicky was ten or eleven months old. I'd gone into his room, responding to his call of *Mama,* and there he was, standing in his crib, smiling at me, reaching out his arms to me. My love for him had flooded through me, and I'd picked him up and hugged him close, his hair soft against my cheek, smelling like powder. My faith in the future—his, mine, ours—had suffused me.

"I'm tired," Nicky said. "I want to go to bed."

"I know. But it's too early. After your snack, you need to do your revision. Then we'll have dinner. We'll practice the kings and queens."

He sat down at the table. "I didn't mean to hurt your arm. I'm sorry it happened."

"Thank you for saying that."

"I don't really hate Uncle Christopher."

"I know you don't."

"I just said it. I just felt it. For a second. I didn't *mean* it. I love Uncle Christopher. I miss him."

"I know. I love him, too. I miss him, too. We'll remember him forever."

"I'm going to do that." Nicky stared at the empty place at the head of the table, as if envisioning Christopher there. "I'm going to put a picture of him inside my brain and remember him forever."

A nineteenth-century woman in a long gray dress, surrounded by apple blossoms blowing on the breeze, placed laundry on a line as a child reached for her skirts—the tranquility of Winslow Homer's scene enveloped me.

Nicky was asleep. I'd locked his door, keeping Duncan with me, and I'd gone to Christopher's study. I felt close to him here. My arm ached, and I felt another wave of burning in my skin. I checked the bandages. No seepage of blood.

Waiting for the pain to ebb, I sat at the tea table in the corner. Adjusting my position, I regarded the several file folders of documents neatly arranged on Christopher's desk. I didn't have the energy to walk over and open them. Earlier in the day, I'd retrieved the box holding Constance's ashes from the desk drawer and given it to the undertaker, to be placed in Christopher's coffin. The box had been surprisingly heavy, although admittedly I didn't have any previous experience with human ashes.

Christopher had visualized Nicky and me living here, but practical questions needed answering. I didn't know the details of his lease. We might have to move. I might have to sell the Sargent watercolor as soon as Christopher's estate was settled, to rent a place where Nicky and I could live.

I needed to talk to someone. Not Lizzie, with her practical, take-charge attitude. She'd drive over, read the documents, and begin organizing.

Did I dare phone Matthew at this late hour? It felt like three in the morning. I checked the time. It was only eight-thirty.

"When your name came up . . . Is everything okay?" he asked.

"No." I couldn't continue.

He said, "Christopher?"

"This morning."

"I'm sorry. That must have been hard. Must *be* hard."

"I'd been preparing myself. Trying to prepare myself. But it's still hard. Then Nicky . . . Nicky had a tough time when I told him the news after school."

He paused. "A tough time how?"

"He . . . attacked me. With a pair of scissors."

"Are you all right?" he asked with quick concern.

"Rafe bandaged my arm. I'm well enough. It wasn't as bad as it might have been."

"Hannah, shouldn't you go to A and E at Addenbrooke's?" He said this with forced restraint, as if holding himself back from ordering me to go.

"Rafe has paramedic training," I said, trying to convince myself that I didn't need to do anything more. The prospect of the police or social services becoming involved continued to be more than I could face.

"Shall I join you? I'd feel better if you weren't alone. Alone with Nicky, I mean."

"Rafe's here. Nicky's asleep. We're okay. Okay until the next time . . . I feel as though you and I are repeating a conversation we had months ago."

He paused again, as if debating whether to drop the question of going to Addenbrooke's. I was relieved when he said, "Children like Nicky and Janet require many nearly identical conversations over the years. Cecilia and I have had more than a few."

"I don't know what to do for him next."

"I'm not only worried about him. I'm worried about *you*. There has to be a way to help *you*."

"He matters more."

An even longer pause. I sensed Matthew didn't like this answer. But what mother wouldn't say the same?

"I can give you the name of the therapist Janet sees. It might help both of you, seeing a professional here. If you're planning to stay."

"We'll stay through the end of the school year. If we can. I hope we can."

"Will you be able to live there, in Christopher's flat?"

"I don't know. I have to find out. The day's been, well, it's been—" I was beginning to lose control.

"Things will work themselves out," he said gently. "One step at a time."

"I'll make an appointment with Janet's therapist. Thank you."

"Maybe there's a medication. Something new. Or something old used in a new way. To help control these episodes of rage."

"I don't want Nicky to be on a medication every day for incidents that happen . . . not all that often." Talking to Matthew about these issues was easier than discussing them with Lizzie. He understood firsthand, and I didn't feel as if he were berating me. "And I won't have him so medicated that he walks through life in a stupor. I've seen him that way, and I've seen other kids like that, sleeping on the floors of their classrooms."

"I've seen it, too."

"I won't send him to an institution or a group home," I said, anger filling me even though Matthew hadn't suggested it.

"No one says you should," he said.

I didn't mention the therapist who'd told me to prepare myself for it.

"But right now," he said quietly, "it's as if you're living with a volcano always on the verge of erupting."

"What's the alternative?" I asked, sounding harsh, taking out my anger and despair on him.

"I don't know. Truly, I don't. For myself, I try to take comfort in small changes that make life easier from day to day."

And I realized: "Nicky's grown so much this year. He adores school. He even loves doing his homework. He was wonderful with Christopher."

"I try to guide Janet toward independence and help her to make a positive contribution to her family and friends," Matthew said. "Nicky already makes many positive contributions to those around him. He's made a positive contribution to *my* life."

"How do you mean?"

"He found Isabella Cresham, and he found the muniment room. Although he violated every rule in the process. But he did make a substantial discovery, without which you and I never would have met."

"I like the *without which* part," I managed to say.

"I rather like it myself. When things settle down . . ." He hesitated. "If ever you want to have dinner. Together, I mean. The two of us. Fine if not, though."

Eventually, life could, would, begin again, and the possibility of this dinner, so small in itself, made my spirit soar. "I'd enjoy that. Let's do it." I found myself smiling for the first time all day.

We said good night. Duncan followed me to the front vestibule, where I put on my coat, hat, and gloves, gingerly maneuvering my injured arm. We went outside, into the cold, pure, bracing air. Duncan ran, and I walked, across the lawn. Inexplicably, the sky was clear—boundless, expanding to eternity. The winter stars were dense, and close. Bright enough to guide our way.

CHAPTER 44

Wounds heal. Rafe cleaned and bandaged Nicky's hand each morning and did the same for my arm. Our injuries didn't become infected. Nicky's mood was considerate and calm, as always after an incident. But I knew I had to begin planning for the next incident, and the one after that. I made an appointment with Janet's therapist, who wanted to speak with me alone before meeting Nicky.

Nicky asked to go to school the day after Christopher's death, and I allowed it. To explain the bandage on his hand, he told his friends, and told Kevin, too, that he'd had an accident. He'd settled on this explanation by himself. I didn't insist on anything else, because it was true, in its way. The community at large didn't need to know the more exact truth and judge him for it.

Regarding my own injuries, they were covered by long-sleeved sweaters, and I hadn't needed to tell lies to anyone. With his usual foresight, Christopher had arranged for Rafe to stay on for a few weeks, paying him in advance. We worked together to organize Christopher's personal effects, and, more generally, Rafe took care of Nicky and me. His presence was reassuring.

The Monday after Christopher's death, we held his funeral in the church by the gates. In preparation, Mrs. Gardner placed an announcement in a London newspaper, and a group of Christopher's professional colleagues arrived for the service. A contingent from his club also arrived, elderly gentlemen enjoying themselves on an outing. They reminded me of Christopher. Kevin flew in from New York, and I made certain we were never alone together. Nicky wore his bespoke suit, not yet outgrown. Rafe, Matthew, Martha, Lizzie, Max—they passed in a blur before me.

Nicky asked if he could speak at the service, and he did, about the man who'd taught him chess and helped him memorize the kings and queens. I'd asked both Mrs. Gardner and the general to speak, and I opened the service to anyone who wished to share memories. Some of the older gentlemen gave eulogies—humorous, English-type speeches—and I cannot remember one single detail of any of them. I chose not to speak; I knew I wouldn't be able to without crying.

At the end of the funeral service, at my request, the organist played the Ralph Vaughan Williams organ prelude "Rhosymedre," my favorite, for its joy and sorrow intermingled.

The vicar had agreed to a burial in the churchyard, and at the graveside he recited the 23rd Psalm, *The Lord is my shepherd; I shall not want . . .*

The staff from the café prepared a feast for the reception: miniature sandwiches, along with petit fours, brownies, shortbread, gingerbread cake, and they hadn't forgotten dog biscuits for Duncan. Alice had coordinated this.

"Mr. Eckersley told me what he wanted," Alice said. "He was rather specific."

I didn't know when this conversation had taken place.

"He wanted to surprise you with your favorites. And Nicky's. Also *his* favorites."

The elderly gentlemen enjoyed themselves extravagantly at the reception, taking advantage of the open bar. One in particular, an impeccably dressed, roundish man who used a walking stick with a silver handle, approached me as if he'd been appointed their spokesperson. His black silk pocket square was folded with precision. The others gathered close to listen to our conversation while pretending they weren't, facing sideways or with their backs to us.

"You must forgive this bold and rather rude intrusion," said the man. "Nigel Summers, longtime friend of Eckersley's from the art world."

He shot out his hand, and I shook it.

"And you must be his . . . *niece.*" The way he said the word gave it a freighted meaning. "You do look very much like him, around the eyes and the cheekbones."

So, he had suspicions. I nodded my thanks, but I silently disagreed. I'd studied the photos of Christopher in the flat, trying to find a resemblance, but I didn't see one. Maybe I was too close to him to be able to see it.

"As he was in his younger days, that is. Oh, dear—please don't misunderstand; most definitely *not* as he looked in his older days!"

The others laughed, proving they had been listening all along.

"Once upon a time, he was handsome as a god. A veritable Adonis. Brilliant in his work, too. He adored you, I don't mind saying. Spoke about you continually. Could be quite a bore on the subject of *you* and that son of yours." His voice became strained. "How the years have flown by. . . . Are those smoked-salmon sandwiches?" he asked a passing waiter. "Marvelous." Distracting himself, he took three from the proffered platter and merged back into his circle of friends.

The gentlemen threw surreptitious glances at me throughout the afternoon.

While everyone was occupied, laughing over shared memories, Mrs. Gardner took me aside, to a quiet corner near the French doors leading to the terrace, windswept in the rain.

"I didn't want to mention this earlier, but I do need to make certain you're aware," she said. "The rent for the flat is prepaid through the next two years. This would include the general's spare rooms. You'd be welcome to renegotiate after that, should you wish," she added brusquely, and of course I understood that her brusqueness was a way of masking her solicitude. "Knowing Mr. Eckersley's penchant for surprises, I would imagine he chose not to share this with you."

No, he hadn't shared this with me. A whole world of anxieties collapsed. I wouldn't have to move. With no rent to pay and the salary from my part-time job, I could get by. I wouldn't have to sell the watercolor, at least not yet; not until I began paying legal fees.

Christopher . . . I yearned for him. I was only beginning to get to know him, beyond his fatherly role in my life. I'd only just met, through his reminiscing, the people who were most important to him, including Constance, whom I'd seen many times when I was young without ever comprehending the truth of her life.

Tears filled my eyes. "Thank you for telling me, Mrs. Gardner."

"I know I speak for everyone on the estate when I say that we'll miss Mr. Eckersley," she said. "But we're pleased indeed that you and your son will be staying on."

CHAPTER 45

It was left to me to say farewell to Rafe, who'd been our close companion and my rescuer. To write a letter of recommendation for him, for his next assignment, and to give him the letter of recommendation written by Christopher himself, along with Christopher's parting gift, commensurate with his deep-felt appreciation. I'd found these in the folders on his desk, along with his will, financial statements, and contact information for his attorney and accountant.

To whom it may concern, Christopher's letter began. *If you're reading this, I've met my demise and gone to my maker. I wish to recommend for your consideration Rafe Connors, who has been my daily nursing assistant, performing his many duties with extraordinary . . .* and so it went.

It was left to me to read to the end of *Middlemarch.* I read silently, for myself alone, in Christopher's bedroom, the rented hospital bed gone, the original bed returned. I also read in Christopher's bedroom because Duncan insisted on spending the day there, curled in mourning. Sick with grief. Poor, poor dog. He brightened only when Nicky returned from school, following him everywhere and sleeping on his bed through the night.

On page 797, two pages from the end of the book, I read:

Dorothea could have liked nothing better, since wrongs existed, than that her husband should be in the thick of a struggle against them, and that she should give him wifely help. Many who knew her, thought it a pity that so substantive and rare a creature should have been absorbed into the life of another, and be only known in a certain circle as a wife and mother. But no one stated exactly what else that was in her power she ought rather to have done.

In a later era, Dorothea might have been a pioneering politician or social reformer. A scientist. A physician. With so many doors closed to her, she'd found purpose where she could.

Women's lives, interweaving . . . Isabella, too, had tried to find a way to do more. Katherine, as well. The talents possessed by women had been overlooked, denigrated, dismissed, and suppressed for centuries. The diseases they might have cured. The technological advances they might have made, the wrongs righted, works of art created, buildings designed—all denied. The tragedy and failure of it affected not only individuals but communities and societies. The women who'd found meaning by devoting themselves to their families had also been silenced by history, erased, the importance of their household labors unrecognized.

The injustice filled me with anger and sorrow. I'd attended a girls' high school and a women's college. My education had instilled in me the notion that I could do anything, achieve anything, if I worked hard enough. Then reality had caught up with me.

When I was in college, my mother told me that in her generation, she and her friends were raised with the notion that marriage was the ultimate objective of a woman's life—that everything in a girl's upbringing was aimed not at independence, not at a career, or a career and marriage combined, not even toward children and the satisfactions of raising them, but at marriage alone. Once that goal was achieved, their lives were essentially over, wrapped in a ribbon and put on a shelf, preferably by age twenty-two or twenty-three.

Then the years would go by, and most women had to learn, often through bitter disappointment and hardship, that what had seemed like an all-encompassing, governing goal leading to long-term fulfillment was only a point on a continuum.

Maybe this was the reason Margot claimed she'd never found someone she loved enough to marry: She'd never allowed herself to find such a someone. She'd pursued a career so she could support herself, and she'd raised the child she'd carefully planned for. But she'd never wanted to tie the ribbon and say, *The primary objective of my life is accomplished*, the decades ahead rendered insignificant in comparison.

I reached the final page of the book. When I finished, I closed it with more force than I'd intended. Duncan, startled by the sound, lifted his head and stared at me, frowning, his grief disturbed. The injury on my arm twinged, and I rubbed my palm against it.

As I held the book within my hands, I realized that I, too, didn't want my life to be wrapped in a ribbon and put on a shelf. I wanted each moment to feel like a beginning. To *be* a beginning. I would divorce Kevin. I would have dinner, and maybe many dinners, with Matthew. But I wouldn't make myself dependent again. I wanted to be able to start over again and again and again, possibilities not closing in around me but spooling out before me.

If Nicky . . . if the challenges the world gave him allowed it. Our lives were bound together, intertwined in uncertainty and hope forever.

CHAPTER 46

Isabella awaited me.

The final set of sketchbooks had been returned from the conservator, and I opened the next volume, taking up where I'd left off.

A young woman sat on a bench under a tree, a book on her lap. Her back was straight, and she leaned slightly forward, her head held high. But her expression as she gazed toward the artist was somehow doubting, almost beseeching, begging for acceptance. *Katherine,* Isabella wrote beneath the portrait.

Turning the page, I found a series of kitchen scenes: The cook, beads of sweat on her forehead, preparing pie crust. A teenage girl, her arm muscles well defined, almost rippling, as she kneaded bread. A boy of about twelve, his face a mass of freckles, stirring soup over the kitchen fire.

After that, Isabella became obsessed with landscapes and daily life on the farm, the passage of time reflected in the changing weather and activities across the drawings: Snow piled atop the gravestones in the churchyard. Mud so thick it trapped a cart on the roadway. The shearing of the sheep. Bees doing their rounds amid the overgrown gardens of summer. The dappled beauty of a country lane. The grain harvest. The collection of honey.

The next volume began with a baby nestled in the arms of Lucie Howell, who looked elderly now and frail. *Eleanor*, Isabella noted. The baby grew into a toddler, and other babies followed. As the years passed, from volume to volume, children ran across the lawns.

In the sketches, the children's mother, Katherine, no longer needed Isabella's acceptance. She'd matured into her role, and she was confident and self-assured, the household swirling around her. Most often Isabella portrayed her sister-in-law half-reclining, half-sitting, on a chair, cradling her pregnant belly with her hand, trying to find a comfortable position, studies that were compassionate, touching.

Highly adept botanical drawings, much more skilled than those she'd done when she was younger, took up an entire volume and part of another. Notes about colors and textures filled the margins. Isabella might have used these sketches as inspiration for watercolors or oil paintings, works that hadn't survived, unless . . . I remembered the portfolios lying horizontal on the shelves in the Old Library. I'd assumed they held maps or architectural drawings. I hadn't opened them, because they weren't what we were looking for. So much research was shaped and limited by one's preconceptions. I would return to the Old Library, to learn whether those portfolios held Isabella's unframed botanical paintings.

I made a note to myself to reread the account ledgers, to look for entries that might refer to oil paints or to vellum for watercolors— although Isabella could have purchased these herself, with money of her own, at the market at the town square or from merchants who approached Ashton Hall with their wares. Or she might have gone each year—accompanied by the steward, because going alone wouldn't have been appropriate for a woman of her station—to Stourbridge Fair, where she would have had a wider choice of art supplies, some sold by vendors who'd traveled to the fair from France, Italy, Germany.

The next volume: a baby lying in a cradle, embroidered mittens warming her hands. Although I couldn't prove my hunch, these mittens looked like the ones Isabella had placed in her keepsake box. Over time, across many pages and volumes, this baby grew up and became a focus of Isabella's attention. With the abecedarium on the table before her, she stared at the artist, a hesitant smile transforming her face. Later, she held out a treat for her spaniel, who sat waiting obediently. On a summer afternoon, she slept on her side on a bench under a tree, her small body not filling the space, her hands crossed over her chest, the tenderness of Isabella's feelings palpable. For this portrait, the artist had written an identification: *Blanche.* Farther along, I saw that a page had been torn out of the sketchbook—perhaps Isabella had given a drawing to Blanche, the one she'd later placed in the back of her psalter.

Isabella's growing faith was also reflected in the drawings: In the sunlight flowing through stained glass at the family church, no matter that it was now officially a Protestant church. Later, at the center of what looked like a barn, a robed priest lifted up a chalice, and four people, strangers to me, were kneeling to pray. I'd read that Catholics often held secret, illegal Masses in barns or other private places.

A competent amateur, Martha had called her. *Family pets. Informal family portraits. The flowers in the garden.*

Male art critics often denigrated women artists for portraying domestic scenes. All too often, these were the only subjects women were allowed. A circular problem: Women artists were limited to domestic subjects, then condemned for portraying them. Isabella had the additional challenge of being from the upper class, so she was more *protected*—to use a euphemism for what was in effect an imprisonment—than other women. She wasn't allowed to pursue art or anything else as a profession, unlike, for example, the renowned Tudor court painters Susanna Horenbout and Levina Teerlinc, both of whom were trained at family workshops in Flanders.

How quick Martha, Mrs. Gardner, and I had been to dismiss Isabella's talent, without fully examining her work. I'd studied art history and knew the struggles of women artists, yet I'd been disappointed to learn that her commonplace books were filled with sketches, not words.

Isabella Cresham wasn't a competent amateur. She was a gifted artist.

The next volume: Hugh—now in his thirties?—riding, hawking, hunting, fishing. Isabella must have accompanied him. Where was Katherine during these outings? Here were drawings of Katherine in the herb garden. Katherine in the still room, making medicines. Katherine, always pregnant, or shown in exhaustion, holding an infant, recovering from pregnancy. Katherine, mourning her children who had died. In these drawings, Katherine no longer looked at the artist, and I felt Katherine's anger in the turn of her shoulders, in the angle of her back, as she shut herself off from conversation with Isabella. They were two women living in one household, but Katherine and Isabella, I saw, were no longer friends—if they ever had been.

Isabella must have been Hugh's daily companion. *Don't leave me,* he'd written to her when he was a boy, and she never did. He was possessive of her—but she was possessive of him, too. Observing him. Taking care of him, as she'd done when they were young. Helping with his children. Could it be jealousy that I saw in Katherine's hardened bearing?

And then Blanche died. Here she was, lying in her coffin, her small arms crossed over her chest. Katherine sat beside her, one hand gripping the box's edge, the other shielding her face, her entire body transfixed by grief as she kept vigil for her daughter. I felt Isabella's own grief, in the portrayal of her sister-in-law. Flowers had been placed around the child's head.

I tried to imagine daily life at Ashton Hall, as revealed to me through the sketchbooks. Katherine had married into this family. She might not even have met Hugh before their wedding day. She came here, and she discovered a sibling bond she couldn't sever. Katherine could never compete with Isabella. Could never come between the two siblings, their bond strengthened by the deaths of *their* siblings when they were young. Katherine received the sexual favors, if they could be called that, and the pregnancies and children, and the deaths of children, that followed. Isabella received the emotional favors, whether she wanted them or not. In fact, she didn't want them. She wanted to escape. But Hugh had triumphed over her many years before. *Don't leave me.*

And what of Hugh? He may not have been cruel. He may simply have been fulfilling, as best he could, the role that was given him.

Until—I turned the page—he died. Isabella portrayed him on his deathbed. She dated this picture *29 July, 1593.* Coins rested on his eyelids, to keep them closed. These must be the two silver coins she'd later retrieved and placed in her keepsake box.

So, no, Hugh couldn't have been the one who'd walled her into a room to keep her safe.

Following Hugh's death, Isabella made dozens of drawings of the ferns in the parkland, the rainwater gathering in droplets on the fronds. Nothing else. No children. No dogs. No portraits of beloved servants or of her sister-in-law.

Her brother and her beloved niece had left her. These were the two who'd bound her most closely to Ashton Hall. Now she was free. What would she choose to do with her freedom?

As I prepared to turn each of the final pages in this, the final volume, I knew that here, at last, her secrets would be revealed.

The next page was blank. The remaining few pages . . . all blank.

CHAPTER 47

Isabella was twenty-one minutes and thirty-two seconds, plus four centuries, away, as Nicky and I had once said.

Holding a large flashlight, I made the journey to Isabella's room. Martha and I, Nicky, Matthew and the graduate students—we must have missed something. I wouldn't allow Isabella Cresham's story to end with nothing.

I sat at her desk. Closing my eyes, I tried to conjure her presence. To hear, touch, smell, taste. Even to see. To understand. I visualized Isabella's self-portrait, seared into my mind.

But I heard only silence. Smelled only the room's dankness.

I opened my eyes. Gazing around, I studied each item that remained. These were the larger, heavier items, which couldn't easily be moved—desk, chairs, table. The trunk that had held her blankets and extra clothing. The prie-dieu, where she knelt to pray.

Faith was where she and I were most different. Maybe this was the reason I couldn't sense or understand her presence here.

Rising from the desk, I went to the prie-dieu. I knelt on it, even though doing so felt disrespectful toward the God I didn't believe in. The prie-dieu was a comfortable-enough size for me, the slanted top providing a good placement for my arms, if I wanted to read, for example, the Ashton Hall Psalter. The wooden kneeling board was painful against my knees. I hoped she'd had a cushion.

Beneath the slanted top was a shelf. I hadn't noticed this before. Most likely Nicky and the team had examined it. I reached into it, just in case a book had been overlooked in the back shadows. I did this the way I might put my hand into a long mailbox, searching for one last letter not seen at first but there nonetheless, waiting.

Nothing.

It was no use. I was wasting my time here. I'd go to the Old Library next and examine the portfolios, to see if they contained botanical paintings.

Trying to stand from my awkward kneeling position, I positioned my hands at the corners of the prie-dieu, where the slanted surface met the shelf. My thumbs hit something inside. I looked, but the shadows were too dark to make anything out. Using my phone's flashlight, I leaned over to examine the shelf more carefully. What I'd felt was a second, recessed shelf. An upper shelf. Not secret, not designed to be hidden. Hiding in plain sight.

Putting down my phone, I slipped my hands into this upper shelf. I felt leather. A binding. Paper. Whatever it was, I slid it forward and out.

It was brown leather, the same size and shape as all of Isabella's sketchbooks.

Grasping the volume gently in my hands, I took it to the desk. I retrieved my phone and sat down, each of my movements slow and considered, as if I were observing myself from a distance. I opened the volume. Positioning the large flashlight and my phone, I had just enough light to examine what was within.

The volume began with a series of scenes of this very room, as if Isabella had started a new book to mark her new life. She drew the objects exactly as Nicky had found them. The candelabra. Her plate and cup. The virginal. The view from her high windows, which hadn't yet been bricked over.

There was no indication that she'd been misled or dragged here. The drawings revealed, rather, the patience and serenity she must have experienced, allowing her to appreciate and value every detail she saw, no matter how small.

Confined to this room, she no longer felt the heat of the sun on her face in summer. No longer walked in the garden and smelled its fragrance in the rain. Or watched the light rippling through the leaves in the woods.

But judging from these pictures, she hadn't considered this a loss.

She wrote beneath the pictures. Not precisely a diary. A noting of events, and brief reflections. I imagined myself transcribing the entries and modernizing the spellings as I went.

The first dawn. Birds. I give thanks to Thee for the sound of them.

Her handwriting was as clear and confident as it had been in the library register.

I am imprisoned and yet more free than ever I thought to be. Alone but not alone, for Thou art with me.

These were the words of an anchoress finding fulfillment. Lizzie's supposition had been correct. Nonetheless, a constellation of causes must have brought her here, made her decide on this as her destiny.

Second dawn, birdsong, the sacred marking of the day.

A drawing of Katherine, outside in the vestibule, staring into the opening in the middle of the wall. Months before, Nicky had measured the opening: eleven inches high, sixteen across, sufficient to show Katherine's head but not her shoulders. This was the first drawing Isabella had done of her sister-in-law's face in months. No, in years. Katherine's face was stiffened and severe. Judgmental. But she was here.

Katherine, Isabella wrote beneath it. She added,

> *She came to say farewell. They will go north to her family, to try to save themselves. The pestilence sweeps the land. She gave me her psalter, her family's most precious possession. For sustenance, she said. I had never tried to be her friend. She was Hugh's wife. The children's mother. A subject for my drawings. But in selfless generosity, she gave me this sacred book. Forgive me, Lord, for I have sinned. I should have let her be my friend.*
>
> *She brought me food and water, too. Thomas the spit boy, she told me, will care for me. Bring my food and water and candles tomorrow and from now on. He cannot leave with the rest of the household. His mother needs him.*

Isabella made a drawing of the book, open upon the prie-dieu.

> *I read the psalter, its exquisite beauty reflecting God's own creation.*
> *Dawn. The calling of the birds. Thomas does not come to me.*
> *Dawn. The calling of the birds. I have finished the food and water. The candles have burned down.*

She drew the candelabra.

> *Thomas does not come to me.*
> *I look from the window. No one. Shall I shout? I do shout. I call out to the world, but only silence returns to me. Have they all died, all of them, of the pestilence, and only I remain? Lord, I shall find my way to Thee.*

I remembered what Martha had said, that in some villages during the plague years, there was no one alive to bury the dead.

Another dawn. Another night. Thomas does not come.

What had Nicky told me? A person can survive for three weeks without food but only four to seven days without water.

I might have been allowed to go to France to become a nun. To practice my art, created for Thee alone. Why was I kept here? For what purpose?

She wrote out a prayer: *Adveniat regnum tuum, fiat voluntas tua, sicut in caelo et in terra.*

Then she continued:

The church bells, tolling. So not all dead. Not every single one. Someone alive to ring the bells. Unless I hear them when they do not truly ring, and I hear them only in my mind, a comfort sent from Thee. Yes, the bells are a comfort sent from Thee. Birdsong, a comfort sent from . . . and her words stopped, her strength failing, and she couldn't remember or formulate what she wanted to say. Later, her writing weak, small, as if she had traveled far distant from herself:

Gloria Patri, et Filio, et Spiritui Sancto: Sicut erat in principio, et nunc, et semper, et in saecula saeculorum. Amen.

After this, she stopped writing and only drew. Paging through these final sketches, I recognized something I never would have anticipated: her joy, expressed through the light that bathed each scene, even in these drawings of her prison, cell, anchor-hold, or whatever the correct word for it was. I'd assumed her faith was like a darkness upon her soul; that her faith was superstition, self-flagellation; that it had led her here with the threat of never-ending judgment and punishment.

Instead, her faith brought her joy, and her joy was her faith. I couldn't understand it or accept it for myself, but I could see the reality of it for her. For her, even as she faced death, or especially as she did, the beauty of the world reflected the beauty of God. Sunlight streamed through her window and made patterns on the floor. The Virgin and Child statue behind the prie-dieu basked in the light.

The lines became messy, imprecise. As she grew weaker, she switched to the colored chalk from the bowl on her desk and drew clouds, capturing the light surrounding them. In an affirmation of her faith, comforting herself and easing her fear, her final picture showed the clouds parting, making way for the light of God.

Below this picture, she wrote, *Soli Deo gloria*. To God alone the glory.

I saw her close the sketchbook and place it on its special shelf in the prie-dieu.

She returned the chalk to its proper place. She was tidy, to the end.

She lay down on the pallet with its straw and blanket. She prayed to God to forgive her sins and to forgive those who had sinned against her, as there was no priest to administer last rites.

She said the rosary, and she waited for God to receive her.

CHAPTER 48

At dawn a week before Christmas, Nicky and I left Ashton Hall for our flight to New York. I locked the door behind us. The cold air woke me up. It carried the damp chill of Cambridge, brought by the wind from the North Sea and across the broad, flat fields of the Fens.

"Goodbye, castle," Nicky said. "See you in three hours plus sixteen days. Two times eight, eight times two. *A bientot, château.*" Nicky was doing well in his French class and his Latin class. We'd discovered that he had a gift for languages, not surprising given how easy memorization was for him. "*Vale, mi canis.*" Mrs. Gardner and Alice were taking care of Duncan during the weeks we'd be away. "Don't be sad, *mon chien.* Before you know it, we'll be back."

Nicky grabbed the larger of our two suitcases. Nicky, helpful. Confident. Nicky, a wonder and a mystery. A boy who received good

grades in school. Who had friends. Who tried to avoid time-out because he had places he wanted to be, things he wanted to do.

In New York, we'd stay with friends, and I'd tell Nicky about the
change coming to his life. These same friends would take Nicky to our
apartment to see Kevin, and Nicky would go to Albany with Kevin to
spend the holidays with his grandparents. I'd meet with my department chair and my attorney. And after the New Year, Nicky and I
would return here.

Seeing Nicky content, I couldn't imagine the other side of him,
the side of *seizures* and *incidents*. But my perspective was shifting, and in
January, I would tell Alice about his violence toward me. She would
decide if she still felt comfortable taking care of him.

My most recent wounds had healed. I might suffer such wounds
from him again, and they'd heal again, the cycle repeating. I'd find
new therapists, for Nicky and me both, new strategies. Maybe I'd even
find a medication that could help him without suppressing the best
parts of him. I wouldn't give up on him. He was my son. I loved him.
I'd guide him toward the things he could accomplish *because* of who he
was, not in spite of it. And as he grew older, he would learn better
ways of coping. Hope filled me, for his future.

The sky over the garden brightened into shades of pink. The light
touched the frost on the grass, making it shimmer.

As I stared at the landscape, I experienced an eerie sensation of a
door opening in my mind and beckoning me through: I would write a
book about Isabella Cresham. A novel. I'd weave in the present, too,
Nicky's story, and how he'd discovered her. In telling Isabella's story,
I'd also need to tell the story of her family. I'd need to describe her
relationship with her brother and discern the role that her sister-in-
law had played in her life—and perhaps in her death.

Suddenly, the certainty of this goal focused me and gave me courage and confidence to face the unknowns of the future.

"The car is here," Nicky called. He led the way as we walked
down the path toward the front drive, where a Panther stealthily
waited to take us to the Cambridge railway station. We'd board the

train to King's Cross, London. There we'd catch the Underground to Heathrow. Nicky was eager to make notes on the timings of the multiple connections, for himself and to share with Janet.

As Nicky hurried forward, I saw him in full—my son, an explorer who'd found Isabella Cresham and transformed our lives.

Ashton Hall

A novel by

Hannah Larson

Katherine's
Chapter

atherine Cresham stood beside the moat and observed her children playing tag across the lawn. Was Isabella studying them, too, from her window? Listening to their laughter?

Just now, Katherine had bid her sister-in-law farewell. As soon as the preparations were complete, the household would depart, taking only minimal supplies. The pestilence was upon the land, and they would flee to the home of Katherine's parents in Lincolnshire.

Thomas will care for you, she had told Isabella.

This was a lie. Thomas was dead.

In a modest attempt to assuage her guilt, Katherine had given Isabella her prayer book, a psalter. Isabella had interpreted this as a token of friendship—now, at last, when it was too late for friendship. The sweetness of her thanks, the innocence and trust, as if Isabella, in her new dwelling place, had truly been spiritually reborn . . . all this almost made Katherine doubt herself. Almost.

But no. Resolute, she'd come outside to watch her children. . . .

Young Hugh, as they called him, sturdy and determined. Eleven years old. The eldest now. Lean yet strong, already like his father.

Arthur, small for his age, but toughened from running to catch up.

Bess, quiet, off to the side, observing. Always the responsible one.

Margaret, tossing her head, throwing herself into everything she did with exuberance, filling the days with her high spirits.

Katherine allowed herself to picture the dead, too, at play amongst the living:

Eleanor, her firstborn, who died at three from a morbid sore throat, drowning at the end, screaming—silently, because she couldn't breathe—and pointing to her throat, begging her mother to help her.

Blanche, dead at six, from a winter fever. Blanche had been Isabella's favorite. Katherine had been ill for months after Blanche was born, and Isabella had supervised Blanche's nurse and mothered the girl, too.

Lettice, born too soon . . . Her exquisite face and body. Her dusting of pale hair.

Walter, her youngest. Such a big name for a little boy, eighteen months old forever. Dead from the bloody flux. Her Walter. He'd always be her infant boy with a grown-up name.

Katherine had given birth to eight children in fourteen years of marriage. A week ago, the pestilence had caught her children's father. As she nursed him and watched him die, there was nothing she could do, despite her herbs and treatments, despite her tireless study of medical texts.

Enough. Katherine didn't have time to mourn the dead. She had to attend to the living. Not simply her family but also those who worked in the household, farmed the land, lived in the village. She was responsible for them, until Young Hugh reached twenty-one. He was Lord Southbrooke now. She herself would buy his wardship with funds from her father, so the estate wouldn't be decimated whilst they waited for him to grow up.

It was a year of drought and crop failure. The pestilence had quickly taken dozens in the village and on the estate. These included the family's faithful steward and also their elderly librarian, the last members of the staff who had served Hugh's parents, too. The pestilence swept like a scythe across the land.

Several days ago, the parish priest had asked to see her. He harbored radical Puritan sympathies, Katherine knew. She was on her guard. *God is punishing us*, the priest had said. *The Lord will not abide offense against His glory.*

The cause of this divine punishment? Katherine had inquired of him.

Isabella Cresham. The heretic amongst us. Hardship is upon the land. Your husband has died. Four of your children have died. The steward, he is no more. The librarian, no more. Many in the village. God will not be mocked. Do you wish each of your remaining four children to perish because of your sin?

Judging from his tone, Katherine thought the priest would have been happy to drag Isabella to the village common that instant and burn her at the stake, to appease his angry God.

Isabella Cresham, heretic. Cause of pestilence, drought, crop failure. Murderer of her family.

There's more, the priest said. Isabella had come to the attention of the authorities because she would not participate in Protestant worship and because of her links to other known heretics. She was being watched by the defenders of the true faith.

I trust my sister-in-law is watched always by God, Katherine said. And with that, she'd dismissed the priest. But she'd pondered his words.

Catholic, Protestant—each side envisaged a future in hell for those who adhered to the other, erring faith.

In Katherine's view, once you began proclaiming *what God wants*, once you avowed knowledge of God's sacred will, human existence made less sense, not more. Had a Catholic God arranged Walter's death as punishment for his Protestant upbringing? Or had a Protestant God yearned to bring faultless Walter home, into His heavenly presence for eternity?

After Hugh's death, Isabella had come to Katherine and pleaded for permission to go to France to become a nun. She'd longed to do this years earlier, to use the gifts of her drawing and painting to serve God. Hugh, and their parents before him, had forbidden it. Had such a thing become known, the entire family would have fallen under suspicion and likely persecution.

Let me have my freedom, Isabella had begged of Katherine. *Or let me live a life of faith here, in the old ways. Alone.*

Was it for Katherine to forbid, or grant, her sister-in-law's dearest wish? To heed, or ignore, the warnings of the priest?

Yes, it was. Katherine was the head of the family until Young Hugh came of age.

Isabella herself had provided Katherine, as she now saw, with the means to grant her sister-in-law's sacred desire while also acceding to the demands of the priest. Acceding, also, to the demands of Katherine's own darkest thoughts.

Hugh had wanted Isabella always by him. He'd relied on her. Looked to her, not to his wife, for advice and companionship. Isabella had taken care of him when he was young. There was nothing immoral or untoward between them, but their bond was closed to others. The laughter they shared. The banter, enduring from childhood, even as Isabella's ever-deepening faith wove through and around their daily lives. All this whilst she, Katherine, Lady Southbrooke, repeatedly suffered the illnesses of pregnancy and birth, and the deaths of her children. But Hugh and Isabella scarcely took notice.

So Katherine had made her decision. She would allow Isabella to become an anchoress. Indeed, in Katherine's own family there had been such a woman, her grandfather's aunt Philippa. This was in the time before the new religion. Philippa was still remembered within the family for the holy choice she'd made. The bishop himself had recited the traditional Catholic prayers for the dead. All knew that for an anchoress to abandon her anchor-hold was to be condemned to hell.

Yesterday, two workmen began their labors on the space where

Isabella would be voluntarily confined. The Protestant priest, endorsing Katherine's plan, had secretly brought the men here. They undoubtedly shared his radical beliefs and most likely had done much worse than this to suppress those they called Papists. Already inside the room, Isabella had prayed as the men worked, and she'd blessed them when they finished.

As it was in the beginning, is nowe, and ever shal be: worlde without ende. Amen. The words from the Book of Common Prayer reverberated in Katherine's mind.

How long would it take for Isabella to die? Days? Weeks? After the household departed for Lincolnshire, only a few caretakers would remain here. They knew nothing of Isabella's fate and would assume that she'd left with the rest of the family, as would the estate manager and his assistants, continuing to supervise the lands as they always did.

And if the children asked after their aunt? Their beloved aunt, who'd made such wonderful portraits of them, played games with them, and taught them Latin and Greek and the astronomy of the heavens? Katherine had often admired (with jealousy) the affection between the children and their aunt. In her position, with her many household responsibilities, and with the exhaustion of her pregnancies, Katherine had few opportunities to spend time with her children. It galled her that Isabella had the leisure to spend hour upon hour with them. That she enjoyed the rewards of motherhood without any of the costs.

Aunt Isabella died in the pestilence, Katherine would tell her children. They wouldn't inquire further. Their siblings, their father, now their aunt—how much death could they confront or question? Her children were well acquainted with grief.

And Isabella *wanted* to be walled into an anchor-hold. It was her most ardent wish. As pangs of doubt clutched again at her chest, Katherine held to her certainty of this.

When the family returned to Ashton Hall, whenever that would be—a year, maybe more, if she even survived—Katherine would undertake a project to redesign the house. She'd often considered rebuilding, to make Ashton Hall more like Burghley House or Longleat. Amassing the required funds would be difficult and would most likely take years, but Katherine would see it through, and in so doing conceal forever the remains of her husband's sister and all trace of her earthly existence.

Watching her children, Katherine couldn't help but smile: Margaret, as was typical of her, had turned a simple game of tag into a complex undertaking governed by her own decrees. Bickering was surely about to ensue.

Isabella was like a child. She wouldn't compromise. She wouldn't honor the well-being of her family and go along with the rules. She had never married, never had children. Never watched her children die.

Now Isabella must bear the burden of her choices.

Will she haunt me? Katherine wondered. Most likely.

But if God desired to save Isabella, He could, and would, Katherine consoled herself. *Thy kyngdome come. Thy wyll be done, on earth, as it is in heaven.*

And if at the end Isabella began to scream as she suffered . . . the walls were thick, the village was far, and there would be not a soul nearby to hear.

No one would ever know.

AUTHOR'S NOTE

Re-creating the Past in *Ashton Hall*

When I was in my early twenties, I was invited to stay at Blickling Hall, a National Trust historic mansion in Norfolk. Blickling was constructed in the early 1600s, on the site of homes dating back to the eleventh century. Legend holds that Anne Boleyn, the second wife of King Henry VIII, was born in a medieval manor on the site and that she haunts the estate each year on the anniversary of her execution.

Remarkably, an acquaintance of mine was renting an apartment at Blickling Hall, and I was thrilled by the invitation. English history had long fascinated me, and I'd nurtured a dream that someday I would live in England. During my stay at Blickling, I toured the gorgeous gardens, complete with a drained moat, and the magnificent rooms open to the public. I also explored the private areas, the back hallways and attics, accessible to me after visiting hours. As I made my way through the rambling, shadowed corridors and the old nurseries and storage rooms, walking deeper and deeper into the mysteries of the past, the plot of the novel that eventually became *Ashton Hall* began to take shape. I jotted down some notes and a rough outline of the story, but I didn't begin writing. Other projects were demanding my attention, including life itself, because I stayed at Blickling before I was married and before I became a mother.

Years later, after I'd published two novels and was completing a third, and my son was grown up, my husband was invited to spend an academic term at an institute affiliated with Cambridge University in England. The institute provided us with accommodation in a drafty, ramshackle seventeenth-century cottage, with what the English call a French drain: an open cesspool in the outside alleyway that received much of the water used in the house (though not from the toilet!) and that required stirring every day. I was advised to pour a kettle of boiling water into the cesspool each morning that the temperature fell below freezing.

During my months in Cambridge, I learned that my youthful dream of living in England was far different from the actual experience. In some ways, it was even more wonderful than I'd ever imagined, because of the beauty, the layered history, and the surprising warmth of the people we met. In other ways, it was quite comically worse, with shops closing at weirdly early hours or perversely not stocking the items that were most in demand, and electric showers that short-circuited, giving off black smoke. Despite the so-called central heating in our cottage, my husband and I were forced to dress for dinner: We put on our hats, coats, scarves, and gloves with the fingers partially cut off before we sat down at the dining table, so that we wouldn't be frozen by the end of the meal. I confronted the fact that British and American cultures are vastly different, even though the two nations share, to all appearances, the same language.

One day as I wandered the narrow streets of Cambridge, half in a dream as I tried to land on an idea for my next novel, I suddenly realized: I could move Blickling Hall from Norfolk to the outskirts of Cambridge, rename the house, fictionalize other details along the way, develop my characters . . . and I'd be ready to begin work. Now, at last, many years after I'd first visited Blickling and planned to set a novel there, I embarked on the project in earnest.

I decided to place the central mystery of *Ashton Hall* in the Tudor period because I wanted to explore the religious conflicts of that era. I'm embarrassed to confess that during my initial studies of English history, my eyes glazed over whenever I tried to read about the religious clashes. As I grew older, however, questions of faith had become more pressing to me. I knew I didn't want to portray the lives of royalty or of royal courtiers, even though such real-life people are indeed fascinating. Instead, I would write about small communities far from the royal panoply. And so I created the fictional Cresham family, living in the fictional Ashton Hall, and while outlining the novel, I found myself particularly focusing on Isabella Cresham, a devout Catholic in an officially Protestant, anti-Catholic country, a woman who, in many ways, never fit into the box labeled *normal* for her era.

Whenever I design the plot of a novel, I realize anew, with a combination of awe and anxiety, that the narrative could go in a dozen, a hundred, a thousand different directions. How to choose one over the others? Most of these decisions are intuitive; they simply *feel* right and can't be explained rationally. Once I heard a fellow writer say he knows he's onto something worthwhile when the material is *playing his song*, and that idea resonates with me.

After I sketch an outline, I put it away in a drawer, and only then do I begin writing. Inevitably the story evolves while it's being written, as the characters take on lives of their own. By putting away the outline, I feel as if I'm giving my characters their freedom. During the course of writing *Ashton Hall*, I learned that Nicky was passionate about what the British call maths and that Hannah loved ancient Greek art. Isabella became an increasingly skilled artist, and in response, I investigated artistic methods of the late sixteenth century. I found out, for example, that graphite pencils wrapped in string were used during her lifetime, following the discovery of graphite deposits in Borrowdale, England, in 1564. This highlighted something I love about delving into the past to write historical fiction: The process leads you to a good deal of offbeat information, in this case the history of the pencil.

During my years of researching and writing the novel, I visited the magical Blickling Hall again and I toured the National Trust's Oxburgh Hall, home to a family that has remained Catholic throughout the centuries. I returned to Cambridge several times as I tried to capture the ambience of that storied and lovely town, free-roaming cows in its public greens and all. When my husband attended academic conferences at Cambridge University's Madingley Hall, a stately home dating from the 1540s and surrounded by evocative gardens, I was grateful for the opportunity to accompany him.

Although the plot of *Ashton Hall* unravels a secret from the past, I chose to set the novel in the present. I wanted to examine how historians go about gathering evidence—concerning not battlefields and political debates but rather the daily lives of individuals. When I stumbled on surviving account ledgers from the Tudor era, I was mesmerized. I'd never before read account ledgers. As I wended my way through such items as velvet nightcaps and woolen blankets purchased for Robert Dudley, Earl of Leicester, I considered what a financial accounting of my own life—my credit-card bills, checking-account statements, charitable donations, and tax returns—would and wouldn't show about what I valued and how I lived from day to day. This prompted me to write account ledgers for the fictional Cresham family as a way to reveal the details of their lives.

Similarly, when I learned that library borrowers' registers exist going back centuries, I was amazed. These registers opened another door into the past for me. Since childhood, I've been an avid reader, frequently visiting my local libraries. I realized that a comprehensive listing of the books I've borrowed since I first possessed a library card would disclose a great deal about me. Such a listing would do exactly the same for my novel's characters.

Determined to fill Ashton Hall's fictional library with real volumes, I did extensive research into medieval and early-modern books in England. I figured out what each member of the Cresham house-hold would read—or, more correctly, the characters informed me of the books they wanted to read. Although I haven't found library reg-isters going back quite as far as Isabella Cresham's era, I feel certain such registers did exist. . . . Perhaps they're in dusty, as-yet-uncataloged book collections, waiting to be discovered.

Because of my abiding interest in the history of medicine, I felt drawn to explore Tudor medical practice. I learned, for example, that upper-class women often served their families and communi-ties as informal physicians and that they made remedies from herbs. To portray Katherine Cresham as a female medical practi-tioner, I immersed myself in books on herbal medicine, and I pieced together evidence about women of that period who had done such work.

I did much of my research into Tudor medicine during the worst months of the Covid-19 pandemic. Reading about high percentages of sixteenth-century urban populations dying from plague, which was then called *pestilence*, and about rural villages abandoned altogether when most of the residents died from the disease—and always bear-ing in mind that these stark facts and statistics represented parents, children, and grandchildren; brothers, sisters, and friends—well, in-vestigating all this while coping with the pandemic of today was a powerful and often heartrending experience.

And so, step by step, I mapped the lives of Isabella Cresham and her family. For me, the past became as compelling and vivid as the present, even though none of the novel's narrative is actually set in the past. In fact, *Ashton Hall* is the first of my published novels to take place entirely in the present. After becoming so accustomed to writ-ing about the past, I found portraying the details of my own era to be surprisingly daunting. As I worked, I discovered that past and present have more in common than I'd anticipated, and I tried to show that individual memory, too, is always in motion, weaving through our thoughts and feelings, affecting and shaping us from day to day.

One crucial aspect of creating the present-day narrative involved the children in the novel. To portray Nicky and Janet, I relied on personal experiences that included, over many years, consultations with therapists, conferences with educational specialists, and discussions with parents and young people. I also read countless books and articles. Given their exceptional ways of thinking, children like Nicky and Janet often grow up to change the world, or at least their part of the world. Each is an individual with a distinctive story. I'm grateful to live in an era when the term *neurodiversity*, with its broad reach, has come into use. I'm also grateful to live in an era when neurodiverse children are celebrated for who they are rather than condemned and punished for the ways they differ from society's definition of *normal*, as they so often were in the past.

I consider Nicky the hero of *Ashton Hall*, and I look forward to a day when all neurodiverse children can discover and fulfill their innate talents.

Here, arranged by subject, are several of the many books and articles that were helpful to me in my research. For a complete bibliography and information on resources relating to neurodiversity, please visit my website, LaurenBelfer.com, where you'll also find more information about the novel, including photographs of the places that inspired me.

Everyday life in Tudor England, with a focus on the lives of Tudor women

Burton, Elizabeth, with illustrations by Felix Kelly. *The Elizabethans at Home.* London: Secker & Warburg, 1958.

James, Susan E. *The Feminine Dynamic in English Art, 1485–1603: Women as Consumers, Patrons and Painters.* New York: Routledge, 2016.

James, Susan E. *Women's Voices in Tudor Wills, 1485–1603: Authority, Influence and Material Culture.* Farnham, UK: Ashgate, 2015.

Mortimer, Ian. *The Time Traveller's Guide to Elizabethan England*. London: Vintage, 2013.

Norton, Elizabeth. *The Hidden Lives of Tudor Women: A Social History*. New York: Pegasus Books, 2017.

Catholicism in Britain during the Reformation

Childs, Jessie. *God's Traitors: Terror & Faith in Elizabethan England*. New York: Oxford University Press, 2014.

Duffy, Eamon. *The Voices of Morebath: Reformation & Rebellion in an English Village*. New Haven and London: Yale University Press, 2001.

McClain, Lisa. *Lest We Be Damned: Practical Innovation & Lived Experience Among Catholics in Protestant England, 1559–1642*. New York: Routledge, 2004.

Walsham, Alexandra. *Church Papists: Catholicism, Conformity and Confessional Polemic in Early Modern England*. Woodbridge, UK: Boydell & Brewer, 1999.

Account ledgers

Adams, Simon, ed. *Household Accounts and Disbursement Books of Robert Dudley, Earl of Leicester, 1558–1561, 1584–1586*. Cambridge, UK: Cambridge University Press, 1995.

Alcock, N. W. *Warwickshire Grazier and London Skinner 1532–1555: The Account Book of Peter Temple and Thomas Heritage*. London: Oxford University Press, 1981.

Libraries, library registers, and medieval and Tudor books

Barnard, John, and D. F. McKenzie, eds. *The Cambridge History of the Book in Britain, Volume 4, 1557–1695*. Cambridge, UK: Cambridge University Press, 2002.

Brayman Hackel, Heidi. *Reading Material in Early Modern England: Print, Gender, and Literacy*. Cambridge, UK: Cambridge University Press, 2005.

Gessner, Conrad. *Historia Animalium, De Avium Natura.* Zurich: 1555.

Leedham-Green, Elisabeth, and Teresa Webber, eds. *The Cambridge History of Libraries in Britain and Ireland, Volume 1, to 1640.* Cambridge, UK: Cambridge University Press, 2006.

Purcell, Mark. *The Country House Library.* New Haven and London: Yale University Press, 2017.

Wellesley, Mary. *The Gilded Page: The Secret Lives of Medieval Manuscripts.* New York: Basic Books, 2021.

Archaeology and forensic anthropology

Bruwelheide, Kari, and Douglas Owsley. "Written in Bone: Reading the Remains of the 17th Century." *AnthroNotes,* vol. 28, no. 1 (Spring 2007): 1–7.

Haglund, William D. "Archaeology and Forensic Death Investigations." *Historical Archaeology,* vol. 35, no. 1 (2001): 26–34.

Pitts, Mike. *Digging for Richard III: The Search for the Lost King.* Revised and expanded edition. London: Thames & Hudson, 2015.

Pitts, Mike. *Digging Up Britain: Ten Discoveries, a Million Years of History.* London: Thames & Hudson, 2019.

Tudor medicine, with a focus on women practitioners

Gerard, John. *The Herball, or, Generall Historie of Plantes.* London: 1597.

Hellwarth, Jennifer Wynne. *"Be unto Me as a Precious Ointment:* Lady Grace Mildmay, Sixteenth-Century Female Practitioner." *Dynamis,* vol. 19 (1999): 95–117.

Laroche, Rebecca. *Medical Authority and Englishwomen's Herbal Texts, 1550–1650.* London and New York: Routledge, 2016.

Pollock, Linda. *With Faith and Physic: The Life of a Tudor Gentlewoman, Lady Grace Mildmay, 1552–1620.* London: Collins & Brown, 1993.

Webster, Charles, ed. *Health, Medicine and Mortality in the Sixteenth Century.* Cambridge, UK: Cambridge University Press, 1979.

Histories of the Tudor era

Brigden, Susan. *New Worlds, Lost Worlds: The Rule of the Tudors, 1485–1603*. New York: Penguin, 2000.

Guy, John. *Elizabeth: The Later Years*. New York: Penguin, 2016.

Hubbard, Kate. *Devices and Desires: Bess of Hardwick and the Building of Elizabethan England*. New York: HarperCollins, 2019.

Whitelock, Anna. *The Queen's Bed: An Intimate History of Elizabeth's Court*. New York: Picador, 2013.

ACKNOWLEDGMENTS

I will be forever grateful to Susanna Porter, my brilliant, perceptive, and altogether extraordinary editor. Susanna's revelatory insights brought clarity, nuance, texture, and vivid immediacy to every sentence. Her dedication to this project has been remarkable.

My agents, the marvelous and wise Emma Sweeney and her successor, the equally marvelous and wise Margaret Sutherland Brown at Folio Literary Management, read many early drafts and offered carefully considered reflections. I thank them for believing in the potential of this book, and I especially thank Margaret for her tenacious spirit.

I've been supported by a phenomenal team at Ballantine. Publisher Kara Welsh, deputy publisher Kim Hovey, and editor in chief Jennifer Hershey, as well as Allyson Pearl, director of sales, have moved and humbled me with their commitment to *Ashton Hall*. With their astonishing attention to detail, production editor Loren Noveck and copy editor Kathy Lord rescued me from many mistakes large and small, and I send them special gratitude. Editorial assistant Sydney Shiffman answered my questions and soothed my nerves time and again, always with a generosity and understanding that made me thankful for her presence. I'm grateful to Allison Schuster and Emma Thomasch in marketing for their creativity and excitement as they took the novel out into the world. Karen Fink and her colleague Katie Horn were ideal publicists, deeply involved in the novel and filled with terrific ideas, amazing me again and again with their skill. And I thank Susan Corcoran for her encouragement and support over decades.

Carlos Beltrán created the evocative cover, which still makes me gasp every time I see it, both because it's so beautiful and because it perfectly captures the mood of *Ashton Hall.* I thank Tom Hallman for the gorgeous jacket art. And once again, I thank Sigrid Estrada for a stunning photo. I'm likewise grateful for the artistry of Susan Turner, who designed the captivating interior of the book and worked her special magic on the contrasting layout of the final chapter.

Alexandra Stephens helped immeasurably by advising me on issues of forensic anthropology and archaeology. Dr. Theodore Feder gave generously of his time to discuss his art-licensing company, Art Resource. I send special thanks to Thayer Tolles, a Marica F. Vilcek curator at the Metropolitan Museum of Art, for conversations about art history and museum work.

I'm grateful to Ludmilla Jordanova and Howard Nelson for their friendship and support, with special gratitude to Howard, formerly a curator at the British Library, for his advice and for sharing his knowledge of such arcane topics as orange-juice ink.

I thank Edward Kessler, founder of the Woolf Institute in Cambridge, England. By sponsoring my husband's residency there as a visiting fellow, the institute allowed me to fulfill a lifelong dream of living in England. I thank both Ed and his spouse, Dr. Trisha Kessler, for their warm welcome in Cambridge and their enduring friendship.

For their hospitality and friendship in Cambridge and London— and Buffalo!—I thank Molly Andrews, Charlotte Andrews-Briscoe, and Peter Andrews-Briscoe, and I also thank Peter for sharing his personal knowledge of school life in Britain.

In Cambridge, Sue and Don Mackay gave their warm hospitality, and Don generously shared his immense knowledge of local history. I'm grateful to them both.

The staffs of Blickling Hall, Oxburgh Hall, and Madingley Hall were ever helpful, maintaining these glorious historic houses and their surrounding landscapes. Their work helped me to create the atmosphere of my fictional Ashton Hall.

Carolyn Waters, head librarian at the New York Society Library, generously allowed me to review the library's copy of the 1633 edition of John Gerard's *Herball*. I send thanks to her and to Peri Pignetti, Barbara Bieck, and Christina Amato, as well as the entire staff of the library, for providing access to their astonishing collection and creating a haven of tranquility for writing and reading.

My life has been touched by many close friends (you know who you are!) who've inspired and supported me with their wise counsel and warm encouragement, particularly during the most difficult months of the Covid-19 pandemic. Without them, I never would have been able to write this novel or any other novel or even, on certain days, walk out my front door. I send them my deepest gratitude.

For her inspiration as an artist and a professional woman, I thank my mother, Nancy Belfer.

For being themselves, I thank Tristan Church, Lisa S. Church, and Lucas, Kaleigh, and Carson.

And I remember Jasper, our magnificent, noble, affectionate, and absurdly cheerful golden retriever, who lives on as Duncan of Ashton Hall.

Once again, above all I thank Michael Marissen. Once again, he knows the reasons why.

ASHTON HALL

—

Lauren Belfer

A Book Club Guide

A CONVERSATION WITH LAUREN BELFER

Random House Book Club: Did you know how *Ashton Hall* would end when you began writing it?

Lauren Belfer: I always knew that Hannah and Nicky's story would end with them traveling to New York City for the December holidays. The circular structure felt right to me: the novel opens with them standing at the side door of Ashton Hall at the beginning of the summer, and it ends with Hannah locking that same door as she and Nicky temporarily depart, their lives transformed.

I also knew how Isabella and Katherine's story would end, but originally "Katherine's Chapter" was at the beginning of the novel. Katherine's voice was the first I heard in my mind, and her chapter was the first part of the book that I wrote. I imagined that *Ashton Hall* would unfold like one of those detective stories in which the

reader sees who committed the crime in the first scene and the suspense involves watching the investigators solve the mystery.

When I finished my initial draft, however, I wondered if "Katherine's Chapter" would be more effective at the end, and so I moved
it. Over the course of the writing process, I went back and forth
several times before resolving to keep it at the end. My hope is that
the reader will be drawn ever more closely into Hannah's search,
re-creating the Ashton Hall of the past just as she does, clue by clue,
until the meaning of each detail is revealed in the final chapter.

Nonetheless, to this day I find myself pondering at random moments, when I'm at the supermarket or taking a walk in the park,
What if the novel had begun with "Katherine's Chapter"? Would
the brooding sense of mystery have been heightened?

RHBC: How did you learn about anchoresses?

LB: My answer to this question is linked to how I became fascinated with English history. When I was growing up, my mother
often took me to our local branch of the Buffalo, New York, public
library. One day when I was eleven or twelve, she pulled out from
the fiction stacks a copy of the historical novel *Katherine*, by Anya
Seton, and gave it to me. *Katherine* is a very long book (the most recent edition has 593 pages), and I've teased my mother that she
must have been hoping it would keep me busy for a few weeks at
least.

Katherine did keep me busy—for the rest of my life! From the
moment I read it, I was hooked on English history and, soon, all
things British. *Katherine* is about a remarkable woman named Katherine Swynford who lived in the fourteenth century and defied the
conventions of her day. The novel taught me that historical fiction
can bring the past to life with vivid immediacy, and do so by realis-
tically portraying individuals.

One section of *Katherine* focuses on Julian of Norwich, a real-life
mystic and anchoress who lived in an anchorhold beside a church

in the city of Norwich during the late fourteenth and early fifteenth centuries. Reading about Julian of Norwich had a powerful impact on me, and I was prompted to learn more about her and women like her. I was intrigued, moved, and also disturbed by the choice that anchoresses made as a way to pursue their religious faith and also achieve a paradoxical kind of independence—deciding their own destinies, governing their own fates, within the limited confines of their anchorholds. In college, I majored in medieval studies and art history, and so I continued to learn about anchoresses, as well as other women of the Middle Ages.

RHBC: Did you know about priest holes before you began to write *Ashton Hall*?

LB: Not until I began researching the novel. When I visited Oxburgh Hall and lowered myself into its narrow priest hole, I was terrified, and I re-created my experiences through Hannah's eyes. Like Hannah, I thought about the members of my own family who were murdered in Europe during the Holocaust. Because I couldn't put out of my mind that the priest hole is a remnant of a horrifying moment of religious intolerance, I was troubled by the way it was presented as a fun tourist adventure for today's children—even though I realize that exploring such upsetting, complex issues with children isn't appropriate.

RHBC: Ashton Hall is like a living character in the novel. How did you go about creating the fictional house?

LB: Ashton Hall was inspired by Blickling Hall in Norfolk, where I stayed when I was in my twenties, but when I began writing the novel, I knew immediately that I'd need to change Blickling and create a fictional house that would serve the story I wanted to tell. To do this, I visited and studied several Tudor and Jacobean homes and wove together the features that resonated with me, taking the windows from one, a moat from another, a chimney from a third. From Madingley Hall, which is now a conference center near Cambridge, I took the double row of lime trees on the front drive, as well as the parish church, parts of which date back to the thirteenth century. From Audley End, not too far from Cambridge, I took some of the monumentality and the rambling layout. From Baddesley Clinton, I borrowed the half-timbered second story, which I describe during Hannah's vision of Isabella and Katherine on the grounds of Ashton Hall.

The landscape at Ashton Hall, with its artificial lake, croquet court, garden, and woodland, is closely aligned to the landscape at Blickling, which lives in my memory from the time I stayed there—except for Ashton Hall's extravagant topiary garden, which I mapped out entirely in my imagination.

RHBC: You write about the illuminated manuscripts of the Middle Ages, with their whimsical figures and beautiful images. Were these manuscripts intended for children?

LB: In the Middle Ages, books for adults, particularly highly valued religious works, were often illuminated. This was done for several possible reasons, including to show the wealth of the patron who had commissioned the book and for the joy and religious devotion evoked by the images. Some of the pictures reflected sophisticated philosophical and theological beliefs expressed through fanciful, colorful imagery. The illustrations in some of these manuscripts provide insights into the daily lives of people at the time the books were created, insights we might never have otherwise. While I was researching *Ashton Hall*, I was astonished when I saw images of the remarkable Luttrell Psalter online. The illustrations were so magnificent that I knew I had to include the Luttrell Psalter in the novel, and it inspired me as I created the fictional Ashton Hall Psalter.

RHBC: Are you ever surprised by ideas that come into your mind, seemingly out of nowhere, when you're writing?

LB: I'm constantly surprised, and this is one of the most fulfilling aspects of the writing process. For example, Lizzie Moran wasn't in the rough outline I made before I began work on *Ashton Hall*. But one day Hannah went to the bakery in the village and found another shopper there, a bossy American. Though Hannah was put off by Lizzie at first, gradually they became friends. Once Lizzie came into my mind—once I found her, just as Hannah found her, at the bakery—I had fun developing her character and her unique perspective on life, and I think she added an important element to the book, one I could never have predicted when I began.

RHBC: Do you finish the research for your novels before you begin writing?

LB: For all my books, I do a great deal of research first, focusing on the setting and the history involved in my story. Once I begin writing, the research not only continues but intensifies. As the characters take on lives of their own, they develop their own interests, which I then need to describe convincingly. In *Ashton Hall*, to give one small example, Nicky becomes obsessed with chess. I knew next to nothing about chess when I began work on the novel, but I needed to respond to his interest, and so I researched it. I've learned over the years always to follow my characters' interests, wherever they may lead, because these details bring their personalities to life on the page.

My father was a history teacher, and maybe because of this, I feel an extra measure of responsibility to make certain that every fact I include is correct. I take the "historical" part of the phrase "historical fiction" very seriously. This is the reason I worked hard to make certain that all the books in Ashton Hall's library—with the single exception of the Ashton Hall Psalter—are real books that the family might have owned. Collecting information about these books was time-consuming, and most readers might not notice this detail or, truthfully, care about it, but for me, it was crucial. Toward the end of my work on *Ashton Hall,* I was lucky enough to spend time with a centuries-old copy of John Gerard's *Herball* in a New York City library. Watching how lovingly the librarians arranged the volume in the book cradle, then touching the book with my own hands, turning the pages, reading the medical remedies it offers . . . I could imagine myself in Katherine Cresham's place. Yes, the Cresham family is fictional, but the books they read are real, and for me, this brings a solidity and a sense of reality to their lives.

RHBC: What novels inspired you as you became a writer?

LB: I keep a group of novels on a shelf near my desk and when I glance at them, their stories pour back into my mind. I think of this as my writing shelf, and the novels there seem somehow magical. They are all books that have touched my heart, and they include novels by George Eliot, Charlotte Brontë, Emily Brontë, and Edith Wharton. From these extraordinary writers, I learned how fiction can reveal inner lives, portray entire societies, and create evocative settings.

Among the dozen or so novels on my writing shelf:

Middlemarch, by George Eliot. *Middlemarch,* of course, plays an important role in *Ashton Hall.*

Jane Eyre, by Charlotte Brontë. I reread *Jane Eyre* every five years or so. Each time, I'm surprised all over again by how contemporary it feels in terms of the issues that it examines regarding women's lives.

Possession, by A. S. Byatt. I'm in awe of the way this novel creates two complete worlds, past and present, along with two fictional poets and their poetry.

Flush: A Biography, by Virginia Woolf. This delightful book is the ultimate example of how to write about dogs in fiction.

Arcadia, by Tom Stoppard. This is a play, not a novel, and I've reread it many times. By interweaving past and present scene by scene until the two finally merge on the stage, *Arcadia* reveals the limits of what we can ever know about the past—yet it also shows how certain aspects of the past can in fact be uncovered. One pivotal question in the present-day plot is solved by evidence discovered in a so-called game book, a list, spanning generations, of who shot animals on the estate where the play is set. The discovery in the game book shows that the smallest details of daily life can be clues to the re-creation of an entire moment in time. The game book in *Arcadia* is rather like the account ledgers and library registers in *Ashton Hall*.

RHBC: How did you go about creating the fictional John Singer Sargent watercolor that figures in the novel?

LB: I love the work of John Singer Sargent, and I use Sargent notecards, coasters, trivets, scarves, bookmarks, and refrigerator magnets—the results of Hannah's professional work figure in my life, too—so his artistry is present in my mind on a daily basis. To create the fictional Sargent watercolor that Christopher gives to Hannah, I brought together a gondola from one watercolor, a Venetian canal scene from another, and, most of all, the images of Rose-Marie Ormond, Sargent's niece, whom he portrayed so sensitively in his work.

RHBC: Your novels seem very visual and are filled with detailed descriptions, so that the reader can really see the scenes unfolding. How do you create this effect?

LB: I don't consciously set out to create highly visual scenes, but this is the result of how the writing process unfolds for me. When I'm writing—that is, when the writing is going well and flowing smoothly—I have the sense that I'm watching the scenes pass before me in my mind like a movie, and I often feel as if I'm simply describing what I see and hear.

RHBC: Are Nicky and Janet based on children you know? What do the words *neurodivergent, neurodiverse,* and *neurodiversity* mean?

LB: I created Janet and Nicky from the many neurodiverse young people I've come to know over the years, including children in my own family. Many families experience neurodiversity, and I've tried to show the challenges as well as the rewards and joys of raising neurodiverse children.

Neurodivergent, neurodiverse, and *neurodiversity* are relatively recent terms, and as I've talked about *Ashton Hall* with book clubs and at bookstore events around the country, I've discovered that many people aren't familiar with these words. I think of them as all-encompassing, non-judgmental terms to describe people whose brains work differently from the majority. The words draw together, under an inclusive umbrella, a range of more specific diagnoses, such as ADHD, autism spectrum, and others. I prefer the broader terms because no child is simply a narrow label. Every child is an individual with a wide range of abilities and interests.

In *Ashton Hall,* I tried to portray Nicky and Janet as first and foremost *themselves,* filled with their own, often passionate interests, like all young people—like all human beings, for that matter.

RHBC: One of the most important characters in *Ashton Hall* is a golden retriever named Duncan. How did you develop his character?

LB: Duncan is closely based—okay, entirely based—on my own golden retriever, Jasper. I changed his name to Duncan, though, to protect Jasper's privacy.

QUESTIONS AND TOPICS FOR DISCUSSION

1. This book's themes include marriage, motherhood, family, sexuality, neurodivergence, and the dependence and independence of women. Which resonated the most with you? Are there other themes or ideas that you see as crucial to this novel?

2. The novel's characters are distinctive and diverse. Did you have a favorite character throughout, or a storyline that spoke to you the most?

3. Neurodivergence plays a large role in the story through Nicky's character. How did this character impact you? Why do you think the author decided to create Janet as a second neurodivergent character?

4. Discuss Hannah's relationship with Nicky. Did you learn anything from it? Do you identify with their relationship in any way?

5. What are some of the parallels between Hannah and Isabella Cresham, the woman locked away in Ashton Hall? How do Hannah's time there and her investigation into Isabella's life help her to process her life changes?

6. In chapter 3, Mrs. Gardner asks: "How many lives can you imagine yourself living?" This question sticks in Hannah's head throughout the rest of the book, prompting reflections on an "alternate" life that could have been hers. Do you ever reflect on the other ways your life could have gone? Do you find that compelling or stress-inducing?

7. Discuss the role of money, privilege, and class in *Ashton Hall*.

8. What do you think of Hannah's often humorous observations of British behavior? If you've spent time in the U.K., do you think her observations have the ring of truth?

9. What do you think of the storyline focused on Hannah's marriage? Do you agree with how Hannah handled Kevin's infidelity? And what about her relationship with Matthew? Would you have handled either of those situations differently?

10. *Ashton Hall* is a contemporary novel, but it deeply explores a historical era through Hannah's investigation into Isabella's life. What do you think of this dual timeline structure? Do you wish either side of the story had been further developed?

11. How has each of the main characters changed by the end of the novel?

12. What do you think of the ending? Were you surprised by how events unfolded? What do you think of the final chapter, written by Hannah herself? What would you imagine came next for the characters?

PHOTO © SIGRID ESTRADA

LAUREN BELFER is the *New York Times* bestselling author of *And After the Fire*, winner of the National Jewish Book Award; *A Fierce Radiance*, a *Washington Post* Best Novel and NPR Best Mystery of the Year; and *City of Light*, a *New York Times* Notable Book, a *Library Journal* Best Book, a Main Selection of the Book-of-the-Month Club, and an international bestseller. Belfer attended Swarthmore College and has an MFA from Columbia University. She lives in New York City.

LaurenBelfer.com
Facebook.com/AuthorLaurenBelfer
Instagram: @LaurenBelfer1